A SPOT OF BOTHER

A Spot of Bother

Mark Haddon

THORNDIKE
WINDSOR
PARAGON

This Large Print edition is published by Thorndike Press, Waterville, Maine USA and by BBC Audiobooks Ltd, Bath, England.

Thorndike Press is an imprint of Thomson Gale, a part of The Thomson Corporation.

Thorndike is a trademark and used herein under license.

The text of this Large Print edition is unabridged.

Other aspects of the book may vary from the original edition.

Set in 16 pt. Plantin.

LIBRARY OF CONGRESS CATALOGING-IN-PUBLICATION DATA

Haddon, Mark.
    A spot of bother / by Mark Haddon.
        p. cm. — (Thorndike Press large print core)
    ISBN 0-7862-9123-0 (alk. paper)
    1. Middle-aged men — Fiction. 2. Mortality — Fiction. 3. Large type books. 4. Psychological fiction. I. Title.
PR6058.A26S66 2006a
813'.54—dc22   2006028201

BRITISH LIBRARY CATALOGUING-IN-PUBLICATION DATA AVAILABLE

Published in 2006 in the U.S. by arrangement with Doubleday,
a division of Random House, Inc.
Published in 2007 in the U.K. by arrangement with
The Random House Group Limited.

U.S. Hardcover: ISBN 13: 978-0-7862-9123-6; ISBN 10: 0-7862-9123-0
U.K. Hardcover: 978 1 405 61694 2 (Windsor Large Print)
U.K. Softcover: 978 1 405 61695 9 (Paragon Large Print)

Printed in the United States of America on permanent paper
10 9 8 7 6 5 4 3 2 1

To My Continuity Girl

With thanks to Sos Eltis,
Clare Alexander, Dan Franklin,
and Bill Thomas

1

It began when George was trying on a black suit in Allders the week before Bob Green's funeral.

It was not the prospect of the funeral that had unsettled him. Nor Bob dying. To be honest he had always found Bob's locker-room bonhomie slightly tiring and he was secretly relieved that they would not be playing squash again. Moreover, the manner in which Bob had died (a heart attack while watching the Boat Race on television) was oddly reassuring. Susan had come back from her sister's and found him lying on his back in the center of the room with one hand over his eyes, looking so peaceful she thought initially that he was taking a nap.

It would have been painful, obviously. But one could cope with pain. And the endorphins would have kicked in soon enough, followed by that sensation of one's life rushing before one's eyes which George himself had experienced several years ago when he had fallen from a stepladder, broken his elbow on the rockery and passed out, a sensation which he remembered as being not unpleasant (a view from the Tamar Bridge in Plymouth had figured prominently for some reason). The same probably went for that tunnel of bright light as the eyes died, given the number of people who heard the angels calling them home and woke to find a junior doctor standing over them with a defibrillator.

Then . . . nothing. It would have been over.

It was too early, of course. Bob was sixty-one. And it was going to be hard for Susan and the boys, even if Susan did blossom now that she was able to finish her own sentences. But all in all it seemed a good way to go.

No, it was the lesion which had thrown him.

He had removed his trousers and was putting on the bottom half of the suit when he noticed a small oval of puffed flesh on his hip, darker than the surrounding skin and flaking slightly. His stomach rose and he was forced to swallow a small amount of vomit which appeared at the back of his mouth.

Cancer.

He had not felt like this since John Zinewski's Fireball had capsized several years ago and he had found himself trapped underwater with his ankle knotted in a loop of rope. But that had lasted for three or four seconds at most. And this time there was no one to help him right the boat.

He would have to kill himself.

It was not a comforting thought but it was something he could do, and this made him feel a little more in control of the situation.

The only question was how.

Jumping from a tall building was a terrifying idea, easing your center of gravity out over the edge of the parapet, the possibility that you might change your mind halfway down. And the last thing he needed at this point was more fear.

Hanging needed equipment and he possessed no gun.

If he drank enough whiskey he might be able to summon the courage to crash the car. There was a big stone gateway on the A16 this side of Stamford. He could hit it doing 90 mph with no difficulty whatsoever.

But what if his nerve failed? What if he were too drunk to control the car? What if someone pulled out of the drive? What if he killed them, paralyzed himself and died of cancer in a wheelchair in prison?

11

"Sir . . . ? Would you mind accompanying me back into the store?"

A young man of eighteen or thereabouts was staring down at George. He had ginger sideburns and a navy blue uniform several sizes too large for him.

George realized that he was crouching on the tiled threshold outside the shop.

"Sir . . . ?"

George got to his feet. "I'm terribly sorry."

"Would you mind accompanying me . . . ?"

George looked down and saw that he was still wearing the suit trousers with the fly undone. He buttoned it rapidly. "Of course."

He walked back through the doors then made his way between the handbags and the perfumes toward the menswear department with the security guard at his shoulder. "I appear to have had some kind of turn."

"You'll have to discuss that with the manager, I'm afraid, sir."

The black thoughts which had filled his mind only seconds before seemed to have occurred a very long time ago. True, he was a little unsure on his feet, the way you were after slicing your thumb with a chisel, for example, but he felt surprisingly good given the circumstances.

The manager of the menswear department was standing beside a rack of slippers with his hands crossed over his groin. "Thank you, John."

The security guard gave him a deferential little nod, turned on his heels and walked away.

"Now, Mr. . . ."

"Hall. George Hall. My apologies. I . . ."

"Perhaps we should have a word in my office," said the manager.

A woman appeared carrying George's trousers. "He left these in the changing room. His wallet's in the pocket."

George pressed on. "I think I had some kind of blackout. I really didn't mean to cause any trouble."

How good it was to be talking to other people. Them saying something. Him saying something in return. The steady tick-tock of conversation. He could have carried on like this all afternoon.

"Are you all right, sir?"

The woman cupped a hand beneath his elbow and he slid downward and sideways onto a chair which felt more solid, more comfortable and more supportive than he remembered any chair ever feeling.

Things became slightly vague for a few minutes.

Then a cup of tea was placed into his hands.

"Thank you." He sipped. It was not good tea but it was hot, it was in a proper china mug and holding it was a comfort.

"Perhaps we should call you a taxi."

It was probably best, he thought, to head back to the village and buy the suit another day.

2

He decided not to mention the incident to Jean. She would only want to talk about it and this was not an appealing proposition.

Talking was, in George's opinion, over-rated. You could not turn the television on these days without seeing someone discussing their adoption or explaining why they had stabbed their husband. Not that he was averse to talking. Talking was one of life's pleasures. And everyone needed to sound off now and then over a pint of Ruddles about colleagues who did not shower frequently enough, or teenage sons who had returned home drunk in the small hours and thrown up in the dog's basket. But it did not change anything.

The secret of contentment, George felt,

lay in ignoring many things completely. How anyone could work in the same office for ten years or bring up children without putting certain thoughts permanently to the back of their mind was beyond him. And as for that last grim lap when you had a catheter and no teeth, memory loss seemed like a godsend.

He told Jean that he had found nothing in Allders and would drive back into town on Monday when he did not have to share Peterborough with forty thousand other people. Then he went upstairs to the bathroom and stuck a large plaster over the lesion so that it could no longer be seen.

He slept soundly for most of the night and woke only when Ronald Burrows, his long-dead geography teacher, pressed a strip of duct tape over his mouth and hammered a hole through the wall of George's chest with a long metal spike. Oddly, it was the smell which upset him most, a smell like the smell of a poorly cleaned public toilet which has recently been used by a very ill person, heady and curried, a smell, worst of all, which seemed to be coming from the wound in his own body.

He fixed his eyes on the lampshade above his head and waited for his heart to slow down, like a man pulled from a burning building, still not quite able to believe that he is safe.

Six o'clock.

He slid out of bed and went downstairs. He put two slices of bread into the toaster and took down the espresso maker Jamie had given them for Christmas. It was a ridiculous gadget which they kept on show for diplomatic reasons. But it felt good now, filling the reservoir with water, pouring coffee into the funnel, slotting the rubber seal into place and screwing the aluminum sections together. Oddly reminiscent of Gareth's steam engine which George had been allowed to play with during the infamous visit to Poole in 1953. And a good deal better than sitting watching the trees at the far end of the garden swaying like sea monsters while a kettle boiled.

The blue flame sighed under the metal base of the coffeemaker. Indoor camping. A bit of an adventure.

The toast pinged up.

That was the weekend, of course, when Gareth burned the frog. How strange, looking back, that the course of an entire life should be spelled out so clearly in five minutes during one August afternoon.

He spread butter and marmalade on the toast while the coffee gargled through. He poured the coffee into a mug and took a sip. It was hair-raisingly strong. He added milk till it became the color of dark chocolate then sat down and picked up the *RIBA Journal* which Jamie had left on his last visit.

The Azman Owen house.

Timber shuttering, sliding glass doors, Bauhaus dining chairs, the single vase of white lilies on the table. Dear God. Sometimes he longed to see a pair of discarded Y-fronts in an architectural photograph.

"High-frequency constant-amplitude electric internal vibrators were specified for the compaction, to minimize blowholes and to produce a uniform compaction effort . . ."

The house looked like a bunker. What was it about concrete? In five hundred years were people going to stand under bridges on the M6 admiring the stains?

He put the magazine down and started the *Telegraph* crossword.

Nanosecond. Byzantium. Quiff.

Jean appeared at seven thirty wearing her purple bathrobe. "Trouble sleeping?"

"Woke up at six. Couldn't quite manage to drift off again."

"I see you used Jamie's whatsit."

"It's rather good, actually," George replied, though, in truth, the caffeine had given him a hand tremor and the unpleas-

17

ant sensation you had when you were waiting for bad news.

"Can I get you anything? Or are you fully toasted?"

"Some apple juice would be good. Thank you."

Some mornings he would look at her and be mildly repulsed by this plump, aging woman with the witch hair and the wattles. Then, on mornings like this . . . "Love" was perhaps the wrong word, though a couple of months back they had surprised themselves by waking up simultaneously in that hotel in Blakeney and having intercourse without even brushing their teeth.

He put his arm around her hips and she idly stroked his head in the way one might stroke a dog.

There were days when being a dog seemed an enviable thing.

"I forgot to say." She peeled away. "Katie rang last night. They're coming for lunch."

"They?"

"She and Jacob and Ray. Katie thought it would be nice to get out of London for the day."

Bloody hell. That was all he needed.

Jean bent into the fridge. "Just try to be civil."

3

Jean rinsed the stripy mugs and put them onto the rack.

A few minutes later George reappeared in his work clothes and headed down the garden to lay bricks in the drizzle.

Secretly she was rather proud of him. Pauline's husband started to go downhill as soon as they handed him the engraved decanter. Eight weeks later he was in the middle of the lawn at 3:00 a.m. with a bottle of Scotch inside him, barking like a dog.

When George showed her the plans for the studio it reminded her of Jamie's plans for that machine to catch Santa Claus. But there it was, at the far end of the lawn, foundations laid, five rows of bricks, window frames stacked under blue plastic sheeting.

Seven or fifty-seven, they needed their projects. Bringing something dead back to the cave. Setting up the Wellingborough franchise. A solid lunch, twenty minutes of playtime and gold stars to show that someone was taking notice.

She unscrewed the espresso maker and a pat of sodden grounds slumped onto the draining board and disintegrated. "Shit."

She got a disposable cloth wipe from the cupboard.

You'd think they were coming back from Vietnam the way some of them talked about retirement. Not a thought for the wives. It didn't matter how much you loved someone. Thirty-five years of the house to yourself, then you had to share it with . . . not a stranger exactly . . .

She would still be able to see David. With her mornings at the primary school and her part-time job at Ottakar's bookshop in town, it was simple enough to spend a few extra hours out of the house without George noticing. But it had seemed less of a deception when he was working. Now he was having lunch at home seven days a week and some things were far too close to one another.

Luckily he enjoyed having the place to himself, and had precious little interest in what she did when she was elsewhere. Which made it easier. The guilt. Or the lack of it.

She rinsed the grit off the cloth wipe, wrung it out and hung it over the tap.

She was being unkind. The prospect of Katie coming to lunch probably. Him and Ray being polite when they wanted to lock horns and grapple.

George was a decent man. Never got drunk. Never hit her, never hit the children. Hardly ever raised his voice. Only last week she'd seen him drop a monkey wrench on his foot. He just closed his eyes, straightened his back and concentrated, like he was trying to hear someone calling from a very long way away. And only one speeding ticket.

Maybe that was the problem.

She remembered being jealous of Katie when she got together with Graham. Their being friends. Their being equals. George's face that suppertime when they were talking about the birth. Graham using the word *clitoris* and George with this forkful of gammon hovering in front of his open mouth.

But that was the trouble with being friends. Graham walks out one day, leaving her to look after Jacob. Which a man like George would never do.

He was right about Ray, though. She wasn't looking forward to lunch any more than him. Thank God Jamie wasn't coming. One of these days he was going to call Ray "Mr. Potato-Head" in Katie's hearing. Or Ray's. And she was going to be driving someone to hospital.

Half Katie's IQ and Ray still called her "a wonderful little woman." Though he did mend the Flymo that time. Which didn't endear him to George. He was solid, at least. Which was what Katie needed right now. Someone who knew she was special. Someone with a good salary and a thick skin.

Just so long as Katie didn't marry him.

4

George poured mortar onto the square of hardboard and checked it for lumps with the blade of the trowel.

It was like the fear of flying.

He picked up a brick, mortared the underside, laid it and shifted it gently sideways so that it sat snug against the upright spirit level.

It had not bothered him in the beginning, those bumpy rides on prop planes to Palma and Lisbon. His main memories were of sweaty prepackaged cheese and that roar as the toilet bowl opened into the stratosphere. Then the plane back from Lyon in 1979 had to be de-iced three times. At first he had noticed only that everyone in the departure lounge was driving him to distraction (Katie practicing handstands, Jean going to the duty-free shop after their gate number had been called, the young man opposite stroking his excessively long hair as if it were some kind of tame creature . . .). And when they boarded, something in the cloistered, chemical air of the cabin itself had made his chest feel tight. But only when they were taxiing to the runway did he realize that the plane was going to suffer some catastrophic mechanical failure mid-flight and that he was going to cartwheel earthward for several minutes inside a large steel tube with two hundred strangers who were crying and soiling themselves, then die in a tangerine fireball of twisted steel.

He remembered Katie saying, "Mum, I think there's something wrong with Dad," but she seemed to be calling faintly from a tiny disk of sunlight at the top of a very deep well into which he had fallen.

He stared doggedly at the seat back in front of him trying desperately to pretend that he was sitting in the living room at home. But every few minutes he would hear a sinister chime and see a little red light flashing in the bulkhead to his right, secretly informing the cabin crew that the pilot was wrestling with some fatal malfunction in the cockpit.

It was not that he could not speak, more that speaking was something which happened in another world of which he had only the vaguest memory.

At some point Jamie looked out of the window and said, "I think the wing's coming off." Jean hissed, "For God's sake, grow up," and George actually felt the rivets blowing and the fuselage dropping like a ton of hardcore.

For several weeks afterward he was unable to see a plane overhead without feeling angry.

It was a natural reaction. Human beings were not meant to be sealed into tins and fired through the sky by fan-assisted rockets.

He laid a brick at the opposite corner then stretched a line between the tops of the two bricks to keep the course straight.

Of course he felt appalling. That was what anxiety did, persuaded you to get out of dangerous situations fast. Leopards, big spiders, strange men coming across the river with spears. If anything it was other people who had the problem, sitting there reading the *Daily Express* and sucking boiled sweets as if they were on a large bus.

But Jean liked sun. And driving to the south of France would wreck a holiday before it had begun. So he needed a strategy to prevent the horror taking hold in May and spiraling toward some kind of seizure at Heathrow in July. Squash, long walks, cinema, Tony Bennett at full volume, the first glass of red wine at six, a new *Flashman* novel.

He heard voices and looked up. Jean, Katie and Ray were standing on the patio like dignitaries waiting for him to dock at some foreign quay.

"George . . . ?"

"Coming." He removed the excess mortar from around the newly laid brick, scraped the remainder back into the bucket and replaced the lid. He stood up and walked down the lawn, cleaning his hands on a rag.

"Katie has some news," said Jean, in the voice she used when she was ignoring the arthritis in her knee. "But she didn't want to tell me until you were here."

"Ray and I are getting married," said Katie.

George had a brief out-of-body experience. He was looking down from fifteen feet above the patio, watching himself as he kissed Katie and shook Ray's hand. It was like falling off that stepladder. The way time slowed down. The way your body knew instinctively how to protect your head with your arms.

"I'll put some champagne into the freezer," Jean said, trotting back into the house.

George reentered his body.

"End of September," said Ray. "Thought we'd keep it simple. Not put you folks to too much trouble."

"Right," said George. "Right."

He would have to make a speech at the reception, a speech that said nice things about Ray. Jamie would refuse to come to the wedding. Jean would refuse to allow Jamie to refuse to come to the wedding. Ray was going to be a member of the family. They would see him all the time. Until they died. Or emigrated.

What was Katie doing? You could not control children, he knew that. Making them eat vegetables was hard enough. But marrying Ray? She had a 2:1 in philosophy. And that chap who had climbed into her car in Leeds. She had given the police a part of his ear.

Jacob appeared in the doorway wielding a bread knife. "I'm an effelant and I'm going to catch the train and . . . and . . . and . . . and this is my tusks."

Katie raised her eyebrows. "I'm not sure that's an entirely good idea."

Jacob ran back into the kitchen squealing with joy. Katie stepped into the doorway after him. "Come here, monkey biscuits."

And George was alone with Ray.

Ray's brother was in jail.

Ray worked for an engineering company which made high-spec camshaft milling machines. George had absolutely no idea what these were.

"Well."

"Well."

Ray crossed his arms. "So, how's the studio going?"

"Hasn't fallen down yet." George crossed his arms, realized that he was copying Ray and uncrossed them. "Not that there's enough of it to fall down."

They were silent for a very long time indeed. Ray rearranged three small pebbles on the flagstones with the toe of his right shoe. George's stomach made an audible noise.

Ray said, "I know what you're thinking."

For a short, horrified moment George thought Ray might be telling the truth.

"My being divorced and everything." He pursed his lips and nodded slowly. "I'm a lucky guy, George. I know that. I'll look after your daughter. You don't need to worry on that score."

"Good," said George.

"We'd like to foot the bill," said Ray, "unless you have any objections. I mean, you've already had to do it once."

"No. You shouldn't have to pay," said George, glad to be able to pull rank a little. "Katie's our daughter. We should make sure she's sent off in style." *Sent off?* It made Katie sound like a ship.

"Fair play to you," said Ray.

It wasn't simply that Ray was working class, or that he spoke with a rather strong northern accent. George was not a snob, and whatever his background, Ray had certainly made good, judging by the size of his car and Katie's descriptions of their house.

The main problem, George felt, was Ray's size. He looked like an ordinary person who had been magnified. He moved more slowly than other people, the way the larger animals in zoos did. Giraffes. Buffalo. He lowered his head to go through doorways and had what Jamie unkindly but accurately described as "strangler's hands."

During thirty-five years on the fringes of the manufacturing industry George had worked with manly men of all stripes. Big men, men who could open beer bottles with their teeth, men who had killed people during active military service, men who, in Ted Monk's charming phrase, would shag anything that stood still for long enough. And though he had never felt entirely at home in their company, he had rarely felt cowed. But when Ray visited, he was reminded of being with his older brother's friends when he was fourteen, the suspicion that there was a secret code of manhood to which he was not privy.

"Honeymoon?" asked George.

"Barcelona," said Ray.

"Nice," said George, who was briefly unable to remember which country Barcelona was in. "Very nice."

"Hope so," said Ray. "Should be a bit cooler that time of year."

George asked how Ray's work was going and Ray said they'd taken over a firm in Cardiff which made horizontal machining centers.

And it was all right. George could do the bluff repartee about cars and sport if pressed. But it was like being a sheep in the Nativity play. No amount of applause was going to make the job seem dignified or stop him wanting to run home to a book about fossils.

"They've got big clients in Germany. The company were trying to get me to shuttle back and forth to Munich. Knocked that one on the head. For obvious reasons."

The first time Katie had brought him home, Ray had run his finger along the rack of CDs above the television and said, "So you're a jazz fan, Mr. Hall," and George had felt as if Ray had unearthed a stack of pornographic magazines.

Jean appeared at the door. "Are you going to get cleaned and changed before lunch?"

George turned to Ray. "I'll catch you later." And he was away, through the kitchen, up the stairs and into the tiled quiet of the lockable bathroom.

5

They hated the idea. As predicted. Katie could tell.

Well, they could live with it. Time was she'd have gone off the deep end. In fact, there was a part of her which missed being the person who went off the deep end. Like her standards were slipping. But you reached a stage where you realized it was a waste of energy trying to change your parents' minds about anything, ever.

Ray wasn't an intellectual. He wasn't the most beautiful man she'd ever met. But the most beautiful man she'd ever met had shat on her from a great height. And when Ray put his arms around her she felt safer than she'd felt for a long time.

She remembered the grim lunch at Lucy's. The toxic goulash Barry had made. His drunken friend groping her arse in the kitchen and Lucy having that asthma attack. Looking out the window and seeing Ray with Jacob on his shoulders, playing horses, running round the lawn, jumping over the upturned wheelbarrow. And weeping at the thought of going back to her tiny flat with the dead animal smell.

Then he turned up at her door with a bunch of carnations, which freaked her out a bit. He didn't want to come in. But she insisted. Out of embarrassment, mostly. Not wanting to take the flowers and shut the door in his face. She made him a coffee and he said he wasn't good at chatting and she asked if he wanted to skip straight to the sex. But it sounded funnier inside her head than out. And in truth, if he'd said, "OK," she might have accepted just because it was flattering to be wanted, in spite of the bags under her eyes and the Cotswold Wildlife Park T-shirt with the banana stains. But he meant it, about the chatting. He was good at mending the cassette player and cooking fried breakfasts and organizing expeditions to railway museums, and he preferred all of them to small talk.

He had a temper. He'd put his hand

through a door toward the end of his first marriage and severed two tendons in his wrist. But he was one of the gentlest men she knew.

A month later he took them up to Hartlepool to visit his father and stepmother. They lived in a bungalow with a garden which Jacob thought was heaven on account of the three gnomes around the ornamental pond and the gazebo thing you could hide in.

Alan and Barbara treated her like the squire's daughter, which was unnerving till she realized they probably treated all strangers the same way. Alan had worked in a sweet factory for most of his life. When Ray's mother died of cancer, he started going to the church he'd gone to as a boy and met Barbara who'd divorced her husband when he became an alcoholic ("took to drink" was the phrase she used, which made it sound like Morris Dancing or hedge laying).

They seemed more like grandparents to Katie (though neither of her own grandfathers had tattoos). They belonged to an older world of deference and duty. They'd covered the wall of their living room with photos of Ray and Martin, the same number of each despite the unholy mess Martin had made of his life. There was a small cabinet of china figurines in the dining room and a fluffy U-shaped carpet around the base of the loo.

Barbara cooked a stew, then grilled some fish fingers for Jacob when he complained about the "lumpy bits." They asked what she did in London and she explained how she helped run an arts festival, and it sounded fey and crapulous. So she told the story of the drunken newsreader they'd booked the previous year, and remembered, just a little bit too late, the reason for Barbara's divorce and didn't even manage a graceful change of subject, just ground to an embarrassed halt. So Barbara changed the subject by asking what her parents did and Katie said Dad had recently retired from managing a small company. She was going to leave it there but Jacob said, "Grandpa makes swings," so she had to explain that Shepherds built equipment for children's playgrounds, which sounded better than running an arts festival, though not quite as solid as she wished.

And maybe a couple of years ago she'd have felt uncomfortable and wanted to get back to London as fast as possible, but many of her childless London friends were beginning to seem a little fey and crapulous themselves, and it was good to spend time with people who'd brought up children of their own, and listened more than they talked, and thought gardening was more important than getting your hair cut.

And maybe they were old-fashioned. Maybe Ray was old-fashioned. Maybe he didn't like vacuuming. Maybe he always put the tampon box back into the bathroom cupboard. But Graham did tai chi and turned out to be a wanker.

She didn't give a toss what her parents thought. Besides, Mum was shagging one of Dad's old colleagues, and Dad was pretending the silk scarves and the twinkle were all down to her having a new job after thirty years of motherhood and housework. So they weren't in a position to lecture anyone when it came to relationships.

Jesus, she didn't even want to think about it.

All she wanted was to get through lunch without too much friction and avoid some grisly woman-to-woman chat over the washing up.

6

Lunch went rather well, right up until dessert.

There was a minor hiccup when George was changing out of his work clothes. He was about to remove his shirt and trousers when he remembered what they were hiding, and felt that horror-film lurch you got when the mirrored door of the wardrobe swung shut to reveal the zombie with the scythe standing behind the hero.

He turned off the lights, pulled down the blinds and showered in darkness singing "Jerusalem."

As a result he walked downstairs feeling not only clean but proud of having taken such rapid and effective action. When he reached the dining room there was wine and conversation and Jacob pretending to be a helicopter and George was finally able to loosen his grip a little.

His fear that Jean, being Jean, would make some well-meant but inappropriate comment, that Katie, being Katie, would rise to the bait and that the two of them would proceed to fight like cats proved unfounded. Katie talked about Barcelona (it was in Spain, of course, he remembered now), Ray was complimentary about the food ("Cracking soup, Mrs. Hall") and Jacob made a runway out of cutlery so his bus could take off and got quite heated when George said that buses did not fly.

They were halfway through the blackberry crumble, however, when the lesion began to itch like athlete's foot. The word *tumor* came to mind and it was an ugly word which he did not want to be entertaining, but he was unable to remove it from his head.

He could feel it growing as he sat at the table, too slowly perhaps for the naked eye to see, but growing nevertheless, like the bread mold he once kept in a jam jar on the windowsill in his bedroom as a boy.

They were discussing wedding arrangements: caterers, photographers, invitations . . . This part of the conversation George understood. Then they began discussing whether to book a hotel (Katie and Ray's preferred option) or hire a tent for the garden (the preferred option for Jacob who was very excited by the whole tent concept). At this point George began to lose focus.

Katie turned to him and said something like, "When will the studio be finished?" but she could have been speaking Hungarian. He could see her mouth moving but was unable to process the noise coming out of it.

The accelerator was being pressed to the floor inside his head. The engine was screaming, the wheels were spinning and smoke was pouring off the tires, but he was going nowhere.

He was unsure what happened next, but it was not elegant, it involved damage to crockery and ended up with him exiting rapidly through the back door.

7

There was a clatter of plates and Jean turned to find that George had vanished.

After about five seconds of stunned silence Jacob looked up from his bus and said, "Where's Grandpa?"

"In the garden," said Ray.

"Right," said Katie, her jaw hardening.

Jean tried to head her off. "Katie . . ."

But it was too late. Katie stood and marched out of the room to hunt her father down. There was a second short silence.

"Is Mummy in the garden as well?" asked Jacob.

Jean looked at Ray. "I'm sorry about this."

Ray looked at Jacob. "Bit of a fiery lady, your old mum."

"What's *fiery?*" asked Jacob.

"Gets cross, doesn't she," said Ray.

Jacob thought for a few moments. "Can we get the submarine out?"

"Come on, then, Captain."

When Ray and Jacob reached the landing Jean went into the kitchen and stood by the fridge, from where she could see Katie without being seen.

"And water sprays out of the sprayer," shouted Jacob from upstairs.

"I don't care what you think, Dad." Katie was marching up and down the patio waving her arms around like a mad person in a film. "It's my life. I'm going to marry Ray whether you like it or not."

Precisely where George was, or what he was doing, it was hard to tell.

"You have no idea. No idea. Ray is kind. Ray is sweet. And you're entitled to your own opinions. But if you try and stop this we'll just do it ourselves, OK?"

She seemed to be staring at the ground. Surely George wasn't lying down?

When he ran out of the room, Jean assumed he'd spilled custard on his trousers or smelt gas and Katie had simply jumped to conclusions. Which was par for the course. But clearly something more serious was happening, and it worried her.

"Well?" asked Katie from the far side of the glass.

There was no answer that Jean could hear. "Jesus. I give in."

Katie vanished from the window and there

were footsteps down the side of the house. Jean whipped open the fridge door and grabbed a carton of milk. Katie burst through the door, hissed, "What is wrong with that man?" and strode down the hallway.

Jean replaced the milk and waited for George to reappear. When he didn't, she put the kettle on and went outside.

He was sitting on the patio with his back against the wall and his fingers pressed to his eyes, looking for all the world like that Scottish man who drank cider and slept on the grass outside the magistrates court.

"George?" She bent down in front of him.

He took his hands away from his face. "Oh, it's you."

"Is something wrong?" asked Jean.

"I just . . . I was finding it hard to talk," said George. "And Katie was shouting a lot."

"Are you OK?"

"I don't feel terribly well, to be honest," said George.

"In what way?" She wondered if he had been crying but this seemed ridiculous.

"Having a bit of trouble breathing. Had to get myself some fresh air. Sorry."

"This wasn't about Ray, then?"

"Ray?" asked George.

He seemed to have forgotten who Ray was, and this was worrying, too.

"No," said George. "It wasn't about Ray."

She touched his knee. It felt odd. George didn't like sympathy. He liked Lemsip and a blanket and the room to himself. "How are you feeling now?"

"A little better. Talking to you."

"We'll ring the doctor and get you an appointment tomorrow," said Jean.

"No, not the doctor," said George, rather insistently.

"Don't be silly, George."

She held out her hand. He took it and slowly got to his feet. He was shaking. "Let's get you inside."

She felt uneasy. They had reached the age when things went wrong and didn't always get better. Bob Green's heart attack. Moira Palmer's kidney. But at least George was letting her look after him, which made a change. She couldn't remember the last time they'd walked arm in arm like this.

They stepped through the door and found Katie standing in the middle of the kitchen eating crumble from a bowl.

Jean said, "Your father's not feeling very well."

Katie's eyes narrowed.

Jean continued: "This has nothing to do

with you getting married to Ray."

Katie looked at George and spoke through a mouthful of crumble. "Well, why didn't you bloody say?"

Jean ushered George into the hallway.

He let go of her hand. "I'll go and lie down upstairs, I think."

The two women stood waiting for the dull click of the bedroom door above their heads. Then Katie dumped her empty bowl in the sink. "Thanks for letting me make a complete prat of myself."

"I don't think you need any help from me on that score."

8

Being alone in a darkened room was not as comforting as George had hoped. He lay on the bed and watched a fly turn randomly in the speckled gray air. To his surprise he missed being shouted at by Katie. Ideally he would like to have done some shouting himself. It seemed like a therapeutic thing to do. But he had never been very good at shouting. Being on the receiving end was probably as close as he was going to get.

The fly came to rest on the tassels of the lampshade.

It was going to be all right. Jean was not going to make him go to the doctor. No one could make him do anything.

He only had to say the word *doctor* inside his head and he could smell rubber tubing and see that ghost-glow from X-rays on light boxes, the dark mass, doctors in beige side-rooms holding clipboards on their knees and being diplomatic.

He had to distract himself.

The eight American states beginning with the letter *M*.

Maine. Missouri. Maryland. That was the one everyone forgot. Montana. Mississippi. Or was that just a river?

The door opened.

"Can I come into your cave, Grandpa?"

Without waiting for a reply Jacob raced across the room, climbed onto the bed and stuck his legs under the duvet. "Then the big . . . the big . . . the big yellow monster-eating monster can't get us."

"I think you're safe," said George. "We don't get many yellow monsters round this way."

"It's the yellow *monster-eating* monster," said Jacob firmly.

"The yellow monster-eating monster," said George.

"What's a Heffalump?" asked Jacob.

"Well, a Heffalump doesn't actually exist."

"Is it furry?" asked Jacob.

"It doesn't exist so . . . no, it isn't furry."

"Does it have wings?"

George had always felt uncomfortable around small children. He knew they were not very clever. That was the point. That was why they went to school. But they could smell fear. They looked you in the eye and asked you to be a bus conductor and it was hard to shake the suspicion that you were being asked to pass some fiendish test.

It did not matter when Jamie and Katie were young. Fathers were not meant to play peepbo or put their hands up a sock and be Mr. Snakey-Snake (Jacob and Jean were inordinately fond of Mr. Snakey-Snake). You built a tree house, administered justice and took control of the kite in strong winds. And that was it.

"Does it have a jet engine or a peller?" asked Jacob.

"Does what have a jet engine or a propeller?" asked George.

"Does this plane have a jet engine or a peller?"

"Well, I think you're going to have to tell me."

"What do you think?" asked Jacob.

"I think it probably has a propeller."

"No. It has a jet engine."

They lay on their backs, side by side, looking at the ceiling. The fly had gone. There was a faint whiff of wet nappy. Somewhere between chicken soup and boiled milk.

"Are we going to do sleeping now?" asked Jacob.

"To be honest, Jacob, I think I'd prefer to keep talking."

"Do you like talking, Grandpa?"

"Sometimes," said George. "A lot of the time I like just being quiet. But at this precise moment I think I prefer talking."

"What's 'this price moment'?"

"This precise moment is now. Just after lunch. In the afternoon. On a Sunday."

"Are you funny?" asked Jacob.

"I think the general opinion would be that I'm not funny."

The door opened again and Ray's head appeared.

"Sorry, George. The nipper slipped the leash."

"That's OK. We were talking, weren't we, Jacob."

It felt good squaring up to his prospective son-in-law in one of Ray's acknowledged areas of expertise.

But then it was not so good because Ray

came into the room and sat on the end of the bed. On his and Jean's bed.

"Seems like you blokes have got the right idea. Keeping your heads down."

Ray lay on the bed.

And this was where the children problem overlapped with the Ray problem. You got the impression, sometimes, that parts of his brain were actually missing, that he could quite easily wander into the bathroom looking for a towel while you were on the toilet and have no clue as to why this might be inappropriate.

Jacob scrambled to his feet. "Let's play ring-a-roses."

And here it was. The test. You started a benign conversation about Heffalumps and before you knew it you had been shoehorned into some mortifying charade.

"OK," said Ray getting onto his knees.

Sweet mother of God, thought George. Surely this wasn't going to involve him?

"George?"

It was.

He got up onto his knees. Jacob took hold of his left hand and Ray took hold of his right. He hoped sincerely that Jean or Katie did not come into the room whilst this was taking place.

Jacob began bouncing up and down.

"Ring-a-ring-a-roses . . ."

Ray joined in. "A pocket full of noses."

George moved his shoulders up and down in time with the song.

"A-tishoo, a-tishoo, we all fall down."

Jacob leapt into the air and fell shrieking onto the duvet with Ray. George, having given up hope of escaping with any dignity, slumped backward onto his pillow.

Jacob was laughing. Ray was laughing. And it occurred to George that if he could find the handle he might be able to open up the secret door and slide down that long chute all the way back to childhood and someone would take care of him and he would be safe.

"Again," shouted Jacob, clambering to his feet. "Again, again, again, again, again . . ."

9

Jamie dunked his jacket onto the back of the chair, loosened his tie and, because no one was watching, did a little pirouette across the floor of the kitchen, ending up in front of the fridge. "Oh yes."

He took out a bottle of Corona, closed the fridge, removed the Silk Cut from the drawer under the toaster, went through the

French windows, sat on the bench and lit up.

It had been a good day. Contracts exchanged on the Miller house. And the Owens were going to bite. You could see it in their eyes. Well, you could see it in hers. And she quite clearly wore the trousers. Plus, Carl was still off work on account of his broken ankle, so Jamie had been dealing with the Cohens and very publicly not screwing it up. Unlike Carl.

The garden was looking great. No cat shit for starters. Maybe the lion dung pellets were working. It'd rained on the way home so the big pebbles were clean and dark and shiny. The chunky railway sleepers round the raised beds. Forsythia, bay, hosta. God knows why people planted grass. Wasn't the point of having a garden to sit in it and do nothing?

He could hear the faint strains of reggae from a few gardens away. Loud enough for that lazy summer feeling. Not so loud you wanted them to turn it down.

He took a swig of lager.

A weird orange blister appeared on the gable of the house opposite. It turned slowly into a hot-air balloon and floated westward behind the branches of the cherry. A second balloon appeared, red this time, in the shape of a giant fire extinguisher. One by one the sky filled with balloons.

He blew out a little cloud of cigarette smoke and watched it drift sideways, keeping its shape until it spilled over the top of the barbecue.

Life was pretty much perfect. He had the house. He had the garden. Elderly lady in rude health to the left. Christians to the right (you could say what you liked about Christians, but they didn't yodel during sex like the Germans who'd lived there before). Gym on Tuesdays and Thursdays. Tony round three nights a week.

He took another drag on the cigarette.

There was birdsong, too, along with the reggae. He'd have recognized the species at ten. He had no idea now. Not that it mattered. It was a good noise. Natural. Soothing.

Tony would be here in half an hour. They'd go down to the Carpenters' for something to eat. Pick up a DVD from Blockbuster on the way back. If Tony wasn't too knackered, he might get a shag.

In a nearby garden a child kicked a football against a wall. *Doink. Doink. Doink.*

Everything seemed suspended in some kind of balance. Obviously someone would come along and fuck it up, because that's what other people did. But for now . . .

He felt a little peckish and wondered whether there were any Pringles left. He stood up and went inside.

10

Katie sometimes wondered whether Mum chose her opinions just to wind her up.

Clearly she'd rather the wedding didn't go ahead. But if it did she wanted it to be a grand and public celebration. Katie pointed out that it was a second wedding. Mum said they didn't want to seem cheap. Katie said that some restaurants were very expensive indeed. Her mother suggested a church blessing. Katie asked why. Her mother said it would be nice. Katie pointed out that nice was not the point of religion. Her mother said she should arrange to have a dress made. Katie said she didn't do frocks. Her mother told her not to be ridiculous. And Katie began to realize they should have tied the knot in Las Vegas and told everyone afterward.

The following day Katie was watching *Brookside* on telly while Ray and Jacob made some kind of rudimentary shelter out of two dining chairs and the picnic blanket. She asked what they were doing and Jacob said they were making a tent. "For the wedding." And Katie thought, "Sod it." She was getting married to Ray. Her parents were going to have a party. They were simply going to do these things simultaneously.

She rang her mother and suggested a compromise. Her mother got the marquee and the flowers and the cake. Katie got the civil ceremony, no blessing and a dress off-the-peg.

The following Saturday Ray and Jacob went to get a new exhaust fitted while Katie met Mona in town to buy an outfit before Mum changed her mind.

She bought herself a long silk strapless dress in sky blue from Whistles. You couldn't run in it (Katie made a point of never buying anything you couldn't run in) but if the register office caught fire she reckoned Ray could sling her over his shoulder. She bought a pair of suede shoes in a slightly darker blue with a bit of heel from a place on Oxford Street, and it was quite fun being girly for a few hours with Mona, who could do girly till the cows came home.

When she got home she did a twirl for the boys and Jacob said, "You look like a lady," which was weird, but sweet.

She bent down and kissed him (bending down wasn't particularly easy either). "We should get you a sailor suit to match."

"Don't be hard on the little chap," said Ray.

Jacob gave her a serious look. "I want to wear my Bob the Builder T-shirt."

"I'm not sure what Granny is going to think about that," said Katie.

"But I want to wear my Bob the Builder T-shirt," said Jacob.

They'd cross that bridge when they came to it.

11

George sat in the car outside the surgery, gripping the steering wheel like a man driving down a mountainside.

The lesion felt like a manhole cover of rotted meat under his shirt.

He could see the doctor, or he could drive away. He felt a little calmer just putting it like that. Option A or Option B.

If he saw the doctor he would be told the truth. He did not want to be told the truth, but the truth might not be as bad as he feared. The lesion might be benign or of a treatable size. Dr. Barghoutian, however, was only a GP. George might be referred to a specialist and have to live with the prospect of that meeting for a week, two weeks, a month (it was entirely possible that after seven days without eating or sleeping one went completely insane, in which case matters would be taken out of his hands).

If he drove away, Jean would ask him where he had been. The surgery would ring home to ask why he had missed the appointment. He might not get to the phone first. He would die of cancer. Jean would find out that he had not been to the doctor and be livid that he was dying of cancer and had done nothing about it.

Alternatively, if the lesion was benign or of a treatable size and he drove away, it might subsequently mutate into a malignant and untreatably large cancer and he might be told this and have to live, for however brief a time, with the knowledge that he was dying as a direct result of his own cowardice.

When he finally got out of the car it was because he could no longer bear his own company in such a confined space.

The presence of other people in the surgery calmed him a little. He checked in and found himself a seat.

What could he say about Ray in his speech at the wedding reception? Now there was a puzzle he could get his teeth into.

Ray was good with children. Well, good

with Jacob at any rate. He could fix things. Or thought he could. The mower had died a week after he tinkered with it. Either way it was not a sufficient recommendation for marriage. He had money. A sufficient recommendation, certainly, but one which you could add only as an amusing aside once you'd established that you liked the chap.

This was filling his head.

Ray was in love with Katie, and Katie was in love with him.

Was she? His daughter's mind had always been a mystery to him. Not that she had any qualms about sharing her opinions. About the wallpaper in her bedroom. About men with hairy backs. But her opinions were so violent (could wallpaper matter that much?), so changeable and so clearly not part of a coherent worldview that he wondered, sometimes, during her teens especially, if there were something medically wrong.

No. He had got everything back to front. It was not the job of the bride's father to like his prospective son-in-law (he could feel sanity returning even as he formed the thought). That was the job of the best man. In which respect, if Ray's best man improved on the buffoon at her last wedding George's relief might outweigh his misgiving about the marriage itself ("So I rang all Graham's previous girlfriends to find out what Katie was in for. And this is what they said . . .").

He looked up and saw a poster on the far wall. It consisted of two large photographs. The photograph on the left showed a patch of tanned skin and bore the words HOW DO YOU LIKE MY TAN? The picture on the right bore the words HOW DO YOU LIKE MY SKIN CANCER? and showed what looked like a large boil packed with cigarette ash.

He came very close to being sick and realized that he had steadied himself by gripping the shoulder of a tiny Indian woman to his right.

"Sorry." He got to his feet.

What in the name of God were they doing putting up a poster like that, in here of all places? He aimed himself at the exit.

"Mr. Hall?"

He was halfway to the door when he heard the receptionist saying it again, more sternly this time. He turned round.

"Dr. Barghoutian can see you now."

He was too weak to disobey and found himself walking down the corridor to where Dr. Barghoutian stood beside his open door, beaming.

"George," said Dr. Barghoutian.

They shook hands.

Dr. Barghoutian ushered George inside, closed the door behind him, sat down and reclined with the stub of a pencil jammed like a cigar between the first and second fingers of his right hand.

"So, what can I do for you today?"

There was a cheap plastic model of the Eiffel Tower on a shelf behind Dr. Barghoutian's head and a framed photograph of his daughter on a swing.

This was it.

"I had a turn," said George.

"And what kind of turn are we talking about?"

"At lunch. I was finding it very difficult to breathe. I knocked some things over. Rushing to get outside."

A turn. That was all it was. Why had he got himself so worked up?

"Chest pain?" asked Dr. Barghoutian.

"No."

"Fall over?"

"No."

Dr. Barghoutian stared at him and nodded sagely. George did not feel good. It was like that scene near the end of the film, after the Russian assassin and the unexplained office fire and the member of Parliament with the penchant for prostitutes. And it all came down to this, some old Etonian in the library of a London club, who knew everything and could have people wiped out with a single phone call.

"What was it that you were trying to get away from?" asked Dr. Barghoutian.

George could think of no conceivable answer to this.

"Were you frightened of something?"

George nodded. He felt like a five-year-old boy.

"And what were you frightened of?" asked Dr. Barghoutian.

It was all right. It was good to be a five-year-old boy. Five-year-old boys were looked after. Dr. Barghoutian would look after him. All he had to do was hold back the tears.

George lifted his shirt and unzipped his trousers.

With infinite slowness Dr. Barghoutian retrieved his spectacles from the desk, put them on and leaned close to the lesion. "Very interesting."

Interesting? Jesus. He was going to die of cancer surrounded by medical students and visiting professors of dermatology.

A year seemed to pass.

Dr. Barghoutian removed his spectacles and leant back in his chair. "Discoid eczema, unless I'm very much mistaken. A week of steroid cream should sort that out." He paused and tapped some imaginary ash from his pencil onto the carpet. "You can tuck yourself back in now."

George tucked his shirt back in and did up his trousers.

"I'll print you out a prescription."

Crossing the reception area he passed through a column of sunlight falling from a high window onto the flecked green carpet. A mother was breast-feeding a small baby. Beside her an elderly man with ruddy cheeks and Wellington boots leant on a walking stick and seemed to gaze, past the baby buggies and the dog-eared magazines, to the rolling fields where he had doubtless spent the greater part of his working life. A phone rang like church bells.

He pushed open the glass double doors and reentered the day.

There was birdsong. Actually, there was no birdsong but it seemed like a morning which deserved birdsong. Above his head, a jet was opening a white zip down the middle of a blue sky, ferrying men and women to Chicago and Sydney, to conferences and colleges, to family reunions and hotel rooms with plump towels and a view of the ocean.

He paused on the step and breathed in

the good smells of bonfire smoke and recent rain.

Fifteen yards away, on the far side of a neatly trimmed, waist-high privet hedge, the Volkswagen Polo was waiting for him like a faithful dog.

He was going home.

12

Jamie ate a seventh Pringle, put the tube back in the cupboard, went into the living room, slumped onto the sofa and pressed the button on the answerphone.

"Jamie. Hello. It's Mum. I thought I might catch you in. Oh well, never mind. I'm sure you've heard the news already, but Katie and Ray were round on Sunday and they're getting married. Which was a bit of a surprise, as you can imagine. Your father's still recovering. Anyway. Third weekend in September. We're having the reception here. In the garden. Katie said you should bring someone. But we'll be sending out proper invitations nearer the time. Anyway, it would be lovely to talk to you when you get the chance. Lots of love."

Married? Jamie felt a little wobbly. He replayed the message in case he'd heard it wrong. He hadn't.

God, his sister had done some stupid things in her time but this took the biscuit. Ray was meant to be a stage. Katie spoke French. Ray read biographies of sports personalities. Buy him a few pints and he'd probably start sounding off about *"our colored brethren."*

They'd been living together for what . . . ? six months?

He listened to the message for a third time, then went into the kitchen and got a choc-ice from the freezer.

It shouldn't have pissed him off. He hardly saw Katie these days. And when he did she had Ray in tow. What difference did it make if they were married? A bit of paper, that was all.

So why did he feel churned up about it?

There was a bloody cat in the garden. He picked up a piece of gravel from the step, took aim and missed.

Fuck. There was ice cream on his shirt from the recoil.

He dabbed it off with a wet sponge.

Hearing the news secondhand. That's what pissed him off. Katie hadn't dared tell him. She knew what he'd say. Or what he'd think. So she'd given the job to Mum.

It was the other-people thing in a nutshell.

Coming along and fucking things up. You were driving through Streatham minding your own business and they plowed into your passenger door while talking on their mobile. You went away to Edinburgh for a long weekend and they nicked your laptop and shat on the sofa.

He looked outside. The bloody cat was back. He put the choc-ice down and threw another piece of gravel, harder this time. It glanced off one of the sleepers, flew over the end wall into the adjoining garden and hit some invisible object with a loud *crack.*

He shut the French windows, picked up the choc-ice and stepped out of sight.

Two years ago Katie wouldn't have given Ray the time of day.

She was exhausted. That was the problem. She wasn't thinking straight. Looking after Jacob on six hours sleep a night in that crap-hole of a flat for two years. Then Ray pitches up with the money and the big house and the flash car.

He had to call her. He put the choc-ice on the windowsill.

Perhaps it was Ray who'd told their parents. That was a definite possibility. And very Ray. Marching in with his size fourteen boots. Then getting shit from Katie on the way home for stealing her thunder.

He dialed. The phone rang at the far end.

The phone was picked up, Jamie realized it might be Ray and very nearly dropped the receiver. "Shit."

"Hullo?" It was Katie.

"Thank God," said Jamie. "Sorry. I didn't mean that. I mean, it's Jamie."

"Jamie, hi."

"Mum just told me the news." He tried to sound breezy and unconcerned, but he was still jumpy on account of the Ray panic.

"Yeh, we only decided to announce it on the way to Peterborough. Then we got back and Jacob was being rather high maintenance. I was going to ring you tonight."

"So . . . congratulations."

"Thanks," said Katie.

Then there was an uncomfortable pause. He wanted Katie to say *Help me, Jamie, I'm making a terrible mistake,* which she obviously wasn't going to do. And he wanted to say *What the fuck are you doing?* But if he did that she'd never speak to him again.

He asked how Jacob was doing and Katie talked about him drawing a rhinoceros at nursery and doing a poo in the bath, so he changed the subject and said, "Tony's getting an invite, then?"

"Of course."

And it suddenly sank in. The joint invitation. No bloody way was he taking Tony to Peterborough.

After putting the phone down he picked up the choc-ice, wiped the brown dribble off the windowsill and walked back into the kitchen to make some tea.

Tony in Peterborough. Jesus. He wasn't sure which was worse. Mum and Dad pretending Tony was one of Jamie's colleagues in case the neighbors found out. Or their being painfully groovy about it.

The most likely combination, of course, was Mum being painfully groovy and Dad pretending Tony was one of Jamie's colleagues. And Mum being angry with Dad for pretending Tony was one of Jamie's colleagues. And Dad being angry with Mum for being painfully groovy.

He didn't even want to think about Ray's friends. He'd known enough Rays in college. Eight pints and they were that close to lynching the nearest homosexual for sport. Apart from the closet case. There was always a closet case. And sooner or later they got paralytic and sidled up to you in the bar and told you everything, then got shirty when you wouldn't take them up to your room and give them a hand job.

He wondered what Jeff Weller was doing these days. A sexless marriage in Saffron

Walden, probably, with some back copies of *Zipper* hidden behind the hot water tank.

Jamie had spent a great deal of time and energy arranging his life precisely as he wanted. Work. Home. Family. Friends. Tony. Exercise. Relaxation. Some compartments you could mix. Katie and Tony. Friends and exercise. But the compartments were there for a reason. It was like a zoo. You could mix chimpanzees and parrots. But take the cages away altogether and you had a blood-bath on your hands.

He wouldn't tell Tony about the invitation. That was the answer. It was simple.

He looked down at the stub of choc-ice. What was he doing? He'd bought them to console himself after the binoculars argument. He should have chucked them the next day.

He pushed the choc-ice into the bin, retrieved the other four from the freezer and shoved them in afterward.

He stuck *Born to Run* on the CD player and made a pot of tea. He washed up and cleaned the draining board. He poured a mug of tea, added some semi-skimmed milk and wrote a check for the gas bill.

Bruce Springsteen was sounding particularly smug this evening. Jamie ejected him and read the *Telegraph.*

Just after eight, Tony turned up in a jovial mood, loped into the hall, bit the back of Jamie's neck, threw himself lengthways on the sofa and began rolling a cigarette.

Jamie wondered, sometimes, if Tony had been a dog in a previous life and not quite made the transition properly. The appetite. The energy. The lack of social graces. The obsession with smells (Tony would put his nose into Jamie's hair and inhale and say, "Ooh, where have you been?").

Jamie slid an ashtray down to Tony's end of the coffee table and sat down. He lifted Tony's legs into his lap and began unlacing his boots.

He wanted to strangle Tony sometimes. The poor house-training mostly. Then he'd catch sight of him across a room and see those long legs and that brawny, farm-boy amble and feel exactly what he felt that first time. Something in the pit of his stomach, almost painful, the need to be held by this man. And no one else made him feel like that.

"Nice day at the office?" asked Tony.

"It was, actually."

"So why the Mr. Glum vibes?"

"What Mr. Glum vibes?" asked Jamie.

"The fish mouth, the crinkly forehead."

Jamie slumped backward into the sofa and

closed his eyes. "You remember Ray . . ."

"Ray . . . ?"

"Katie's boyfriend, Ray."

"Yu-huh."

"She's marrying him."

"OK." Tony lit his cigarette. A little strand of burning tobacco fell onto his jeans and went out. "We bundle her into a car and take her to a safe house somewhere in Gloucestershire —"

"Tony . . ." said Jamie.

"What?"

"Let's try it again, all right?"

Tony held his hands up in mock-surrender. "Sorry."

"Katie is marrying Ray," said Jamie.

"Which is not good."

"No."

"So you're going to try and stop her," said Tony.

"She's not in love with him," said Jamie. "She just wants someone with a steady job and a big house who can help look after Jacob."

"There are worse reasons for marrying someone."

"You'd hate him," said Jamie.

"So?" asked Tony.

"She's my sister."

"And you're going to . . . what?" asked Tony.

"God knows."

"This is her life, Jamie. You can't fight off Anne Bancroft with a crucifix and drag her onto the nearest bus."

"I'm not trying to stop her." Jamie was starting to regret this topic of conversation. Tony didn't know Katie. He'd never met Ray. In truth, Jamie just wanted him to say, *You're absolutely right.* But Tony had never said that, to anyone, about anything. Not even when drunk. Especially not when drunk. "It's her business. Obviously. It's just —"

"She's an adult," said Tony. "She has the right to screw things up."

Neither of them said anything for a few moments.

"So, am I invited?" Tony blew a little plume of smoke toward the ceiling.

Jamie paused a fraction of a second too long before answering, and Tony did that suspicious thing with his eyebrows. So Jamie had to change tactics on the hoof. "I'm sincerely hoping it's not going to happen."

"But if it does?"

There was no point fighting over this. Not now. When Jehovah's Witnesses knocked on the door Tony invited them in for tea. Jamie took a deep breath. "Mum did mention bringing someone."

"Someone?" said Tony. "Charming."

"You don't actually want to come, do you?"

"Why not?" asked Tony.

"Ray's engineering colleagues, my mother fussing over you —"

"You're not listening to what I'm saying, are you." Tony took hold of Jamie's chin and squished it, the way aunts did when you were a kid. "I would like. To come. To your sister's wedding. With you."

A police car tore past the end of the cul-de-sac with its siren going. Tony was still holding Jamie's chin. Jamie said, "Let's talk about it later, OK?"

Tony tightened his grip, pulled Jamie toward him and sniffed. "What have you been eating?"

"Choc-ice."

"God. This thing really has depressed you, hasn't it."

"I threw the rest away," said Jamie.

Tony stubbed out his cigarette. "Go and get me one. I haven't had a choc-ice since . . . God, Brighton in about 1987."

Jamie went into the kitchen, retrieved one of the choc-ices from the bin, rinsed the ketchup from the wrapper and took it back through to the living room.

If his luck was in, Katie would throw a toaster at Ray before September and there wouldn't be a wedding.

13

George spread a generous helping of steroid cream onto the eczema, changed into his building clothes, then went downstairs where he bumped into Jean returning laden from Sainsbury's.

"How was the doctor?"

"Fine."

"So . . . ?" asked Jean.

George decided that it was simpler to lie. "Heat stroke, probably. Dehydration. Working out there in the sun without a hat. Not drinking enough water."

"Well, that's a relief."

"Indeed," said George.

"I rang Jamie."

"And?"

"Wasn't in," said Jean. "I left a message. Said we'd be sending him an invite. I told him he could bring someone if he wanted."

"Excellent."

Jean paused. "Are you all right, George?"

"I am, actually." He kissed her and headed

off to the garden.

He scraped the contents of the bucket into the miniskip, hosed it out, made some fresh mortar and began laying bricks. Another couple of courses and he could think about cementing the door frame into place.

He didn't have a problem with homosexuality per se. Men having sex with men. One could imagine, if one was in the business of imagining such things, that there were situations where it might happen, situations in which chaps were denied the normal outlets. Military camps. Long sea voyages. One didn't want to dwell on the plumbing but one could almost see it as a sporting activity. Letting off steam. High spirits. Handshake and a hot shower afterward.

It was the thought of men purchasing furniture together which disturbed him. Men snuggling. More disconcerting, somehow, than shenanigans in public toilets. It gave him the unpleasant feeling that there was a weakness in the very fabric of the world. Like seeing a man hit a woman in the street. Or suddenly not being able to remember the bedroom you had as a child.

Still, things changed. Mobile phones. Thai restaurants. You had to remain elastic or you turned into an angry fossil railing at litter. Besides, Jamie was a sensible young man and if he brought someone along he was bound to be another very sensible young man.

What Ray would make of it Lord only knew.

Interesting. That was what it would be.

He laid another brick.

"Unless I'm very much mistaken," Dr. Barghoutian had said.

Just covering himself, no doubt.

14

Jean undressed while David was showering and slipped into the dressing gown he'd left out for her. She wandered over to the bay window and sat on the arm of the chair.

It made her feel attractive. Just being in this room. The cream walls. The wooden floor. The big fish print in the metal frame. It was like one of those rooms you saw in magazines which made you think about living a different life.

She gazed onto the oval lawn. Three shrubs in big stone pots on one side. Three on the other. A folding wooden lounger.

She enjoyed making love, but she enjoyed this too. The way she could think here, without the rest of her life rushing in and crowding her.

Jean rarely spoke about her parents. People simply didn't understand. They were teenagers before it dawned on them that Auntie Mary from next door was their father's girlfriend. Everyone pictured some kind of steamy soap opera. But there was no intrigue, no blazing rows. Her father worked in the same bank for forty years and made wooden birdhouses in the cellar. And whatever her mother felt about their bizarre domestic arrangement she never spoke about it, even after Jean's father died.

Her guess was that she never spoke about it when he was alive either. It happened. Appearances were kept up. End of story.

Jean felt ashamed. As any sane person would. If you kept quiet about it you felt like a liar. If you told the story you felt like something from a circus.

No wonder the children all headed off so fast in such different directions. Eileen to her religion. Douglas to his articulated lorries. And Jean to George.

They met at Betty's wedding.

There was something formal about him, almost military. Handsome in a way that young men no longer were these days.

Everyone was being rather silly (Betty's brother, the one who died in that horrible factory accident, had made a hat out of a napkin and was singing "I've got a lovely bunch of coconuts" to much general hilarity). Jean could see that George was finding it all rather tiresome. She wanted to tell him that she was finding it all rather tiresome, too, but he didn't look like someone you could talk to, like that, out of the blue.

Ten minutes later he was at her side, offering to get her another drink, and she made a fool of herself by asking for a lemonade, to show that she was sober and sensible, then asking for wine because she didn't want to seem childish, then changing her mind a second time because he really was very attractive and she was getting a bit flustered.

He invited her out for dinner the following week and she didn't want to go. She knew what would happen. He was honest and utterly dependable and she was going to fall in love with him, and when he found out about her family he was going to disappear in a cloud of smoke. Like Roger Hamilton. Like Pat Lloyd.

Then he told her about his father drinking himself into a stupor and sleeping facedown on the lawn. And his mother crying in the bathroom. And his uncle going mad and ending up in some dreadful hospital. At which point she just took hold of his face and kissed him, which was something she'd never done to a man before.

And it wasn't that he'd changed over the years. He was still honest. He was still dependable. But the world had changed. And so had she.

If anything it was those French cassettes (were they a present from Katie? she really couldn't remember). They were going to the Dordogne, and she had time on her hands.

A few months later she was standing in a shop in Bergerac buying bread and cheese and these little spinach tarts and the woman was apologizing for the weather and Jean found herself striking up an actual conversation while George sat on a bench across the street counting his mosquito bites. And nothing happened there and then, but when she got home it seemed a bit cold, a bit small, a bit English.

Through the wall she heard the faint sound of the shower door popping open.

That it should be David, of all people, amazed her still. She'd cooked him spaghetti Bolognese on one occasion. She'd made small talk about the new conservatory and come away feeling dull but thankfully invisible. He wore linen jackets and roll-neck sweaters in peach and sky blue and smoked little cigars. He'd lived in Stockholm for three years and when he and Mina separated amicably it only increased the sense that he was a little too modern for Peterborough.

He retired early, George lost touch with him and he didn't cross her mind until she looked up from her till in Ottakar's one day and saw him holding a copy of *The Naked Chef* and a tin of Maisie Mouse pencils.

They had a coffee across the street and when she talked about going to Paris with Ursula he didn't mock her, like Bob Green used to do. Or wonder how two middle-aged ladies could survive a long weekend in a foreign city without being mugged or strangled or sold into the white slave trade, like George had done.

And it wasn't that she was physically attracted to him (he was shorter than her and there was quite a lot of black hair protruding from his cuffs). But she never met men over fifty who were still interested in the world around them, in new people, new books, new countries.

It was like talking to a female friend. Except that he was a man. And they'd only known each other for about fifteen minutes. Which was very disconcerting.

The following week they were standing on

a footbridge over the dual carriageway and that feeling welled up inside her. The one she got by the sea sometimes. Ships disembarking, gulls squabbling over the wake, those mournful horns. The realization that you could sail off into the blue and start again in a new place.

He took her hand and held it, and she was disappointed. She'd found a soul mate and he was about to wreck it all with a clumsy pass. But he squeezed it and let go and said, "Come on. You'll be late home," and she wanted to take his hand back.

Later she was scared. Of saying yes. Of saying no. Of saying yes then realizing she should have said no. Of saying no then realizing she should have said yes. Of being naked in front of another man when her body sometimes made her feel like weeping.

So she told George. About meeting David in the shop and the coffee across the road. But not about the hands and the footbridge. She wanted him to be cross. She wanted him to make her life simple again. But he didn't. She dropped David's name into the conversation a couple more times and got no reaction. George's lack of concern began to seem like encouragement.

David had had other affairs. She knew. Even before he said. The way he cupped his hand round the back of her neck that first time. She was relieved. She didn't want to do this with someone sailing into uncharted waters, especially after Gloria's horror story about finding that man from Derby parked outside her house one morning.

And Jean was right. He was very hairy indeed. Like a monkey, almost. Which made it better somehow. Because it showed that it wasn't really about the sex. Though, during the last few months she had grown rather fond of that silky feel under her fingers when she stroked his back.

The bathroom door clicked open and she closed her eyes. David walked across the rug and slipped his arms around her. She could smell coal tar soap and clean skin. She could feel his breath on the back of her neck.

He said, "I seem to have found a beautiful woman in my bedroom."

She laughed at the childishness of it. She was very far from being a beautiful woman. But it was good, pretending. Almost better than the real thing. Like being a kid again. Getting this close to another human being. Climbing trees and drinking bathwater. Knowing how everything felt and tasted.

He turned her round and kissed her.

He wanted to make her feel good. She

couldn't remember the last time someone had done that.

He closed the curtains and led her over to the bed and laid her down and kissed her again and pushed the dressing gown off her shoulders and she was melting into that dark behind her eyelids, the way butter melted in a hot pan, the way you melted back into sleep after waking up at night, just letting it take you.

She put her hands around his neck and felt the muscles under the skin and those tiny hairs where the barber had run the razor close. And his own hands were slowly moving down her body and she could see the two of them from the far side of the room, doing this thing you only ever saw beautiful people doing in films. And maybe she did believe it now, that she was beautiful, that they were both beautiful.

Her body felt as if it were swaying back and forth with the movement of his fingers, a fairground ride that was taking her higher and faster with every swing so that she was weightless at each end, so high she could see the pleasure gardens and the ferries in the bay and the green hills across the water.

He said, "God, I love you," and she loved him back, for doing this, for understanding a part of her that she never knew existed.

But she couldn't say it. Not now. She couldn't say anything. She just squeezed his shoulder, meaning, *Keep going.*

She put her hand around his penis and moved it back and forth and it no longer seemed strange, not even a part of his body, more a part of hers, the sensations flowing in one unbroken circle. And she could hear herself panting now, like a dog, but she didn't care.

And she realized that it was going to happen and she heard herself saying, "Yes, yes, yes," and even hearing the sound of her own voice didn't break the spell. And it swept over her like surf sweeping over sand then falling back and sweeping up over the sand again and falling back.

Images went off in her head like little fireworks. The smell of coconut. Brass firedogs. The starched bolster in her parents' bed. A hot cone of grass clippings. She was breaking up into a thousand tiny pieces, like snow, or bonfire sparks, tumbling high in the air, then starting to fall, so slowly it hardly seemed like falling at all.

She held his wrist to stop his hand and lay there with her eyes closed, dizzy and out of breath.

She was crying.

It was like finding your body again after

fifty years and realizing you were old friends and suddenly understanding why you'd felt so alone all this time.

She opened her eyes. David was looking down at her and she knew that she didn't need to explain anything.

He waited for a couple of minutes. "And now," he said, "I think it's my turn."

He got to his knees and moved between her legs. He opened her gently with his fingers and pushed himself inside. And this time she watched him as he rolled forward onto his arms until she was full of him.

Sometimes she enjoyed the fact that he was doing this to her. Sometimes she enjoyed the fact that she was doing this to him. Today the distinction didn't seem to exist.

He began to move faster and his eyes narrowed with pleasure and finally closed. So she closed her own eyes and held on to his arms and let herself be rocked back and forth, and finally he reached a climax and held himself inside her and did that little animal shiver. And when he opened his eyes he was breathing heavily and smiling.

She smiled back at him.

Katie was right. You spent your life giving everything to other people, so they could drift away, to school, to college, to the office, to Hornsey, to Ealing. So little of the love came back.

She had earned this. She deserved to feel like someone in a film.

He lowered himself gently to her side and pulled her head onto his shoulder so that she could see tiny beads of sweat in a line down the center of his chest and hear his heart beating.

She closed her eyes again, and in the darkness she could feel the whole world revolving.

15

"Lord, let me know mine end, and the number of my days: that I may be certified how long I have to live."

Bob lay just below the altar steps in a polished black coffin which looked like a grand piano from this angle.

"For a man walketh in a vain shadow, and disquieteth himself in vain."

There were occasions when George envied these people (the forty-eight hours between trying on the trousers in Allders and visiting Dr. Barghoutian, for example). Not these people specifically, but the regulars, the ones you saw up at the front during carol services.

But you either had faith or you didn't. No reentry, no refunds. Like when his father told him how magicians sawed ladies in half. You couldn't give the knowledge back however much you wanted to.

He looked round at the stained-glass lambs and the scale model of the crucified Christ and thought how ridiculous it all was, this desert religion transported whole-sale to the English shires. Bank managers and PE teachers listening to stories about zithers and smiting and barley bread as if it were the most natural thing in the world.

"O spare me a little, that I may recover my strength: before I go hence and be no more seen."

The vicar made his way to the pulpit and delivered his eulogy. "A businessman, a sportsman, a family man. 'Work hard, play hard.' That was his motto." He clearly knew nothing about Bob.

On the other hand if you never set foot in a church when you were alive you could hardly expect them to pull out all the stops when you were dead. And no one wanted the truth ("He was a man incapable of see-ing a large-breasted woman without making some infantile remark. In later years his breath was not good").

"Robert and Susan would have been married for forty years this coming September. They were childhood sweethearts who met when they were both pupils at St. Botolph's secondary school . . ."

He remembered his own thirtieth wedding anniversary. Bob staggering across the lawn, slapping a drunken arm around his shoulder and saying, "The funny thing is, if you'd killed her you'd have been out by now."

"Behold I shew you a mystery: We shall not all sleep, but we shall all be changed in a moment, in the twinkling of an eye . . ."

The lesson ended and Bob was carried from the church. George and Jean moved outside with the rest of the congregation and reassembled around the grave in a muggy, gun-gray light that promised a storm before teatime. Susan stood on the far side of the hole looking puffy and broken, with her two sons on either side of her. Jack had his arm around his mother but was not tall enough to carry the gesture off with aplomb. Ben looked strangely bored.

"Man that is born of a woman hath but a short time to live, and is full of misery."

Bob was lowered into the ground on four

sturdy hessian straps. Susan, Jack and Ben each threw a white rose onto the coffin and the peace was shattered by some buffoon driving past the churchyard with his car stereo turned up.

". . . our Lord Jesus Christ; who shall change our vile body that it may be like unto his glorious body . . ."

He looked at the pallbearers and realized he'd never seen one with a beard. He wondered if it was a rule, like pilots, so they got an airtight seal when the oxygen masks came down. Something about hygiene, perhaps.

And when their time came? Did working with all those corpses make them sanguine? Of course, they only saw people afterward. Becoming a corpse, that was the hard bit. Tim's sister worked in a hospice for fifteen years and still went to sleep in the garage with the engine running when they found that growth in her brain.

The vicar asked them to say the Lord's Prayer together. George said the passages he agreed with out loud ("Give us this day our daily bread . . . lead us not into temptation") and mumbled through the references to God.

"The grace of our Lord Jesus Christ, and the love of God, and the fellowship of the holy Ghost, be with us all evermore. Amen . . . And now, ladies and gentlemen." A perky, scout-group tone entered the vicar's voice. "I would like, on behalf of Susan and the rest of the Green family, to invite you to share some food and drink in the village hall which you will find across the road directly beside the car park."

Jean shivered theatrically. "I do hate these things."

They moved with the tide of darkly suited people, chatting quietly now, down the curved gravel path, through the lych-gate and across the road.

Jean touched his elbow and said, "I'll catch you up in a few minutes."

He turned to ask her where she was going but she was already retracing her steps in the direction of the church.

He turned back again and saw David Symmonds walking toward him, smiling, his hand extended.

"George."

"David."

David had left Shepherds four or five years ago. Jean had bumped into him on a couple of occasions but George had hardly seen him. It was not active dislike. Indeed, if everyone in the office had been like David the place would have run a great deal more smoothly. No jockeying for position. No passing the buck. Bright chap, too. Brains behind the whole sustainable forest stuff which got them Cornwall and Essex.

He dressed a little too well. That was probably the best way of putting it. Expensive aftershave. Opera cassettes in the car.

When he announced that he was retiring early everyone backed off. Sick animal in the herd. Everyone feeling a little insulted. As if he'd been doing it as a hobby, this thing to which they had devoted their lives. And no real plans, either. Photography. Holidays in France. Gold C gliding badge.

It all seemed rather different now that George had gone down the same route himself, and when he recalled John McLintock saying that David was never really "one of us" he could hear the sour grapes.

"Good to see you." David squeezed George's hand. "Even if the circumstances aren't the cheeriest."

"Susan didn't seem good."

"Oh, I think Susan will be all right."

Today, for example, David was wearing a black suit and a gray roll-neck sweater. Other people might think it disrespectful, but George could see now that it was simply a different way of doing things. No longer being part of the crowd.

"Keeping busy?" asked George.

David laughed. "I thought the point of retiring was that we no longer had to be busy."

George laughed. "I guess so."

"Well, I suppose we'd better do our duty." David turned toward the door of the village hall.

George rarely felt the desire to prolong a conversation with anyone, but David, he realized, was in the same boat as himself, and it was good to be chatting with someone in the same boat. Better certainly than eating sausage rolls and talking about death.

"Got through the World's Hundred Best Novels?"

"You have a frighteningly good memory." David laughed again. "Gave up at Proust. Too much like hard work. Doing Dickens instead. Seven down, eight to go."

George talked about the studio. David talked about his recent walking holiday in the Pyrenees ("Three thousand meters above sea level and there's butterflies everywhere"). They congratulated themselves on leaving Shepherds before Jim Bowman subcontracted the maintenance and that girl from Stevenage lost her foot.

"Come on," said David, ushering George toward the double doors. "We're going to be in trouble if we're found enjoying ourselves out here."

There were footsteps on the gravel and George turned to see Jean approaching.

"Forgot my handbag."

George said, "I bumped into David."

Jean seemed a little flustered. "David. Hello."

"Jean," said David, holding out his hand. "How nice to see you."

"I was thinking," said George, "it would be a nice idea to invite David round for dinner sometime."

Jean and David looked a little startled and he realized that clapping his hands together and broaching the idea so gleefully was perhaps inappropriate on such a solemn occasion.

"Oh," said David, "I don't want Jean slaving over a hot stove on my account."

"I'm sure Jean would enjoy some relief from my company." George put his hands into his trouser pockets. "And if you're willing to take your life in your hands I can run up a passable risotto myself."

"Well . . ."

"How about the weekend after next? Saturday night?"

Jean threw George a glance which made him wonder briefly whether there was some important fact about David which he had overlooked in his enthusiasm, that he was vegetarian, for example, or had not flushed the toilet on a previous visit.

But she took a deep breath and smiled and said, "OK."

"I'm not sure I'm free on Saturday," said David. "It's a lovely idea . . ."

"Sunday, then," said George.

David pursed his lips and nodded. "Sunday it is, then."

"Good. I'll look forward to it." George held open the double doors. "Let's mingle."

16

Katie dropped Jacob off with Max and left the two of them playing swordfights with wooden spoons in June's kitchen.

Then she and Ray headed into town and had a minor disagreement at the printers. Ray thought the number of gold twirls on an invitation was a measure of how much you loved someone, which was odd for a man who thought colored socks were for girls. Whereas the ones Katie preferred looked like invitations to accounting seminars apparently.

Ray held up his favorite design and Katie

said it looked like an invite to Prince Charming's coming-out party. At which point the man behind the counter said, "Well, I don't want to be around when you two choose the menu."

Things went more smoothly at the jeweler's. Ray liked the idea of them both having the same ring and there was no way he was wearing anything more than a plain gold band. The jeweler asked if they wanted inscriptions and Katie was temporarily flummoxed. Did wedding rings have inscriptions?

"On the inside, usually," said the man. "The date of the wedding. Or perhaps some kind of endearment." He was clearly a man who ironed his underwear.

"Or a return address," said Katie. "Like on a dog."

Ray laughed, because the man looked uncomfortable and Ray didn't like men who ironed their underwear. "We'll take two."

They had lunch in Covent Garden and drew up guest lists over pizza.

Ray's was short. He didn't really do friends. He'd talk to strangers on the bus and go for a pint with pretty much anyone. But he never hung on to people for the long haul. When he and Diana split up, he moved out of the flat, said goodbye to the mutual friends and applied for a new job in London. He hadn't seen his best man in three years. An old rugby friend, apparently, which didn't put her mind at ease.

"Got pulled over by police on the M5 once," said Ray. "Wing walking on a Volvo roof rack."

"Wing walking?"

"It's OK," said Ray. "He's a dentist now." Which was worrying in a different way.

Her own list was more complex, on account of far too many friends, all of whom had some inviolable claim to an invite (Mona was there when Jacob was born; Sandra put them up for a month when Graham left; Jenny had MS which meant you always felt crap if you didn't invite her to things even though, in truth, she was bloody hard work . . .). Accommodating them all would need an aircraft hangar, and every time she added a name or crossed it out she pictured the coven getting together and comparing notes.

"Overshoot," said Ray, "like airlines. Assume 15 percent won't turn up. Hold a few seats back."

"Fifteen percent?" asked Katie. "Is that, like, the standard drop-out rate for weddings?"

"No," said Ray. "I just like to sound as if I

know what I'm talking about."

She gripped a little roll of flesh just above his belt. "At least there's one person in your life who can spot when you're talking bollocks."

Ray stole an olive from her pizza. "That's a compliment, right?"

They discussed stag and hen nights. Last time round he'd been thrown naked into the Leeds and Liverpool Canal, she'd been groped by a fireman in a posing pouch, and they'd both been sick in the toilet of an Indian restaurant. They decided to go out for a candlelit meal. Just the two of them.

It was getting late and their best man and woman were arriving for supper at eight. So they headed home, scooping up Jacob on the way. He had a cut on his forehead where Max had hit him with a garlic press. But Jacob had ripped Max's tarantula T-shirt. They were clearly still friends so Katie decided not to probe.

Back at the ranch she arranged the chicken breasts in a baking tray and poured the sauce over them and wondered whether Sarah had been a wise choice. To be scrupulously honest she'd been picked as an act of retaliation. A gobby solicitor who could give rugby players a run for their money.

It was beginning to dawn on Katie that

retaliation might not be the best motive for selecting a best woman.

But when Ed arrived he seemed nervous mostly. A large, ruddy-cheeked man, more farmer than dentist. He'd filled out since posing for the team photo in Ray's office and it was difficult to imagine him getting onto the roof of a stationary Volvo let alone a moving one.

He was ill at ease with Jacob, which made Katie feel rather superior. Then he said his wife had been through four cycles of IVF. So Katie felt crap instead.

When Sarah turned up she just rubbed her hands and said, "Right, then. This is my competition," and Katie knocked back a glass of wine straight off, just in case.

The wine was a wise move.

Ed was charming and rather old-fashioned. This did not endear him to Sarah. She told him about the dentist who'd stitched her gum to his assistant's rubber glove. He told her about the solicitor who had poisoned his aunt's dog. The chicken was not good. Ed and Sarah disagreed about Gypsies. Specifically whether or not to round them up and put them in camps. Sarah wanted Ed put in a camp. Ed, who saw women's opinions as largely decorative, decided that Sarah was a "foxy lady."

Ray tried to move the subject onto safer ground by reminiscing about their rugby days, and the two of them began a string of supposedly hilarious stories, all of which involved heavy drinking, minor vandalism and the removal of someone's trousers.

Katie drank another two glasses of wine.

Ed said he was going to begin his speech by saying, "Ladies and gentlemen, this job is rather like being asked to have sex with the Queen. It's an honor, obviously, but not a task one looks forward to with relish."

Ray found this very funny indeed. Katie wondered whether she should be marrying someone else, and Sarah, who never liked men hogging the limelight, told them how she got so drunk at Katrina's wedding that she passed out and wet herself in the foyer of a hotel in Derby.

An hour later, Katie and Ray lay next to each other in bed watching the ceiling spin slowly, listening to Ed wrestle incompetently with the sofa bed on the far side of the wall.

Ray took hold of her hand. "Sorry about that."

"About what?"

"Downstairs."

"I thought you were enjoying yourself," said Katie.

"I was. Sort of."

Neither of them said anything.

"I think he was a bit nervous," said Ray. "I think we were all a bit nervous. Well, apart from Sarah. I don't reckon she gets nervous."

There was a little yelp from next door as Ed trapped some part of himself in the mechanism.

"I'll have a word with Ed," said Ray. "About the speech."

"I'll have a word with Sarah," said Katie.

17

It blew up on Saturday morning.

Tony woke early and headed to the kitchen to make breakfast. When Jamie ambled down twenty minutes later Tony was sitting at the table emanating bad vibes.

Jamie had clearly done something wrong. "What's up?"

Tony chewed his cheek and drummed the table with a teaspoon. "This wedding," said Tony.

"Look," said Jamie, "I don't particularly want to go myself." He glanced at the clock. Tony had to leave in twenty minutes. Jamie realized that he should have stayed in bed.

"But you're going to go," said Tony.

"I don't really have much choice."

"So, why don't you want me to come with you?"

"Because you'll have a shit time," said Jamie, "and I'll have a shit time. And it doesn't matter that I'm having a shit time because they're my family, for better or worse. So every now and then I have to grit my teeth and put up with having a shit time for the greater good. But I'd rather not be responsible for you having a shit time on top of everything else."

"It's only a fucking wedding," said Tony. "It's not transatlantic yachting. How shit can it be?"

"It's not just a fucking wedding," said Jamie. "It's my sister marrying the wrong person. For the second time in her life. Except this time we know it in advance. It's hardly a cause for celebration."

"I don't give a fuck who she's marrying," said Tony.

"Well, I do," said Jamie.

"Who she's marrying is not the point," said Tony.

Jamie called Tony an unsympathetic shit. Tony called Jamie a self-centered cunt. Jamie refused to discuss the subject any further. Tony stormed out.

Jamie smoked three cigarettes and fried

himself two slices of eggy bread and realized he wasn't going to get anything constructive done so he might as well drive up to Peterborough and hear the wedding story firsthand from Mum and Dad.

18

George was fitting the window frames. There were six courses above the sill on either side. Enough brickwork to hold them firm. He spread the mortar and slotted the first one into place.

In truth it wasn't just the flying. Holidays themselves were not much further up George's list of favorite occupations. Visiting amphitheaters, walking the Pembrokeshire coast path, learning to ski. He could see the rationale behind these activities. One grim fortnight in Sicily had been made almost worthwhile by the mosaics at Piazza Armerina. What he failed to comprehend was packing oneself off to a foreign country to lounge by pools and eat plain food and cheap wine made somehow glorious by a view of a fountain and a waiter with a poor command of English.

They knew what they were doing in the Middle Ages. Holy days. Pilgrimages. Canterbury and Santiago de Compostela. Twenty hard miles a day, simple inns and something to aim for.

Norway might have been OK. Mountains, tundra, rugged shorelines. But it had to be Rhodes or Corsica. And in summer to boot, so that freckled Englishmen had to sit under awnings reading last week's *Sunday Times* while the sweat ran down their backs.

Now that he thought about it, he had been suffering from heat stroke during the visit to Piazza Armerina and most of what he recalled about the mosaics was from the stack of postcards he'd bought in the shop before retiring to the hire car with a bottle of water and a pack of ibuprofen.

The human mind was not designed for sunbathing and light novels. Not on consecutive days at any rate. The human mind was designed for doing stuff. Making spears, hunting antelope . . .

The Dordogne in 1984 was the nadir. Diarrhea, moths like flying hamsters, the blowtorch heat. Awake at three in the morning on a damp and lumpy mattress. Then the storm. Like someone hammering sheets of tin. Lightning so bright it came through the pillow. In the morning sixty, seventy dead frogs turning slowly in the pool. And at the far end something larger and furrier, a cat perhaps, or the Franzettis' dog, which Katie was poking with a snorkel.

He needed a drink. He walked back across the lawn and was removing his dirty boots when he saw Jamie in the kitchen, dumping his bag and putting the kettle on.

He stopped and watched, the way he might stop and watch if there was a deer in the garden, which there was occasionally.

Jamie was a bit of a secretive creature himself. Not that he hid things. But he was reserved. Rather old-fashioned now that George came to think about it. Different clothes and hairstyle and you could see him lighting a cigarette in a Berlin alleyway, or obscured by steam on a station platform.

Unlike Katie, who didn't know the meaning of the word *reserved.* The only person he knew who could bring up the subject of menstruation over lunch. And you still knew she was hiding things, things that were going to be dropped on you at random intervals. Like the wedding. Next week she would doubtless announce that she was pregnant.

Dear God. The wedding. Jamie must have come about the wedding.

He could do it. If Jamie wanted a double bed he would say the spare room was being used by someone else, and book him into an upmarket bed-and-breakfast somewhere. Just so long as George didn't have to use the word *boyfriend.*

He came round from his reverie and realized that Jamie was waving from inside the kitchen and looking a little troubled by George's lack of response.

He waved back, removed his other boot and went inside.

"What brings you to this neck of the woods?"

"Oh, just popping in," said Jamie.

"Your mother didn't mention anything."

"I didn't ring."

"Never mind. I'm sure she can stretch lunch to three."

"It's OK. I wasn't planning on staying. Tea?" asked Jamie.

"Thank you." George got the digestives out while Jamie put a bag into a second mug.

"So. This wedding," said Jamie.

"What about it?" asked George, trying to sound as if the subject had not yet occurred to him.

"What do you think?"

"I think . . ." George sat down and adjusted the chair so that it was precisely the right distance from the table. "I think you should bring someone."

There. That sounded pretty neutral as far as he could tell.

"No, Dad," said Jamie, wearily. "I mean Katie and Ray. What do you think about them getting married?"

It was true. There really was no limit to the ways in which you could say the wrong thing to your children. You offered an olive branch and it was the wrong olive branch at the wrong time.

"Well?" Jamie asked again.

"To be honest, I'm trying to maintain a Buddhist detachment about the whole thing to stop it taking ten years off my life."

"But she's serious, yeh?"

"Your sister is serious about everything. Whether she'll be serious about it in a fortnight's time is anyone's guess."

"But what did she say?"

"Just that they were getting married. Your mother can fill you in on the emotional side of things. I'm afraid I was stuck talking to Ray."

Jamie put a mug of tea down in front of George and raised his eyebrows. "Bet that was a white-knuckle thrill ride."

And there it was, that little door, opening briefly.

They had never done the father-son stuff. A couple of Saturday afternoons at Silverstone racetrack. Putting up the garden shed together. That was about it.

On the other hand, he saw friends doing the father-son stuff and as far as he could see it amounted to little more than sitting in adjacent seats at rugby matches and sharing vulgar jokes. Mothers and daughters, that made sense. Dresses. Gossip. All in all, not doing the father-son stuff probably counted as a lucky escape.

Yet there were moments like this when he saw how alike he and Jamie were.

"Ray is, I confess, rather hard work," said George. "In my long and sorry experience," he dunked a biscuit, "trying to change your sister's mind is a pointless exercise. I guess the game plan is to treat her like an adult. Keep a stiff upper lip. Be nice to Ray. If it all goes pear-shaped in two years' time, well, we've had some practice in that department. The last thing I want to do is to let your sister know that we disapprove, then have Ray as a disgruntled son-in-law for the next thirty years."

Jamie drank his tea. "I'm just . . ."

"What?"

"Nothing. You're probably right. We should let her get on with it."

Jean appeared in the doorway bearing a basket of dirty clothes. "Hello, Jamie. This

101

is a nice surprise."

"Hi, Mum."

"Well, here's your second opinion," said George.

Jean put the basket on the washing machine. "About what?"

"Jamie was wondering whether we should save Katie from a reckless and inadvisable marriage."

"Dad . . ." said Jamie tetchily.

And this was where Jamie and George parted company. Jamie couldn't really do jokes, not at his own expense. He was, to be honest, a little delicate.

"George." Jean glared at him accusingly. "What have you been saying?"

George refused to rise to the bait.

"I'm just worried about Katie," said Jamie.

"We're all worried about Katie," said Jean, starting to fill the washing machine. "Ray wouldn't be my first choice, either. But there you go. Your sister's a woman who knows her own mind."

Jamie stood up. "I'd better be going."

Jean stopped filling the washing machine. "You've only just got here."

"I know. I should have phoned, really. I just wanted to know what Katie had said. I'd better be heading off."

And he was gone.

Jean turned to George. "Why do you always have to rub him up the wrong way?"

George bit his tongue. Again.

"Jamie?" Jean headed into the hallway.

George recalled only too well how much he had hated his own father. A friendly ogre who found coins in your ear and made origami squirrels and who shrank slowly over the years into an angry, drunken little man who thought praising children made them weak and never admitted that his own brother was schizophrenic, and who kept on shrinking so that by the time George and Judy and Brian were old enough to hold him to account he had performed the most impressive trick of all by turning into a self-pitying arthritic figure too insubstantial to be the butt of anyone's anger.

Perhaps the best you could hope for was not to do the same thing to your own children.

Jamie was a good lad. Not the most robust of chaps. But they got on well enough.

Jean returned to the kitchen. "He's gone. What was that all about?"

"Lord alone knows." George stood up and dropped his empty mug into the sink. "The mystery of one's children is never-ending."

19

Jamie pulled into a layby at the edge of the village.

I think you should bring someone.

Christ. You avoided the subject for twenty years then it flashed past at eighty and vanished in a cloud of exhaust.

Had he been wrong about his father all along? Was it possible that he could've come out at sixteen and got no shit whatsoever? *Totally understand. Chap at school. Keen on other chaps. Ended up playing cricket for Leicestershire.*

Jamie was angry. Though it was hard to put a finger on precisely who he was angry with. Or why.

It was the same feeling he got every time he visited Peterborough. Every time he saw photographs of himself as a child. Every time he smelt plasticine or tasted fish fingers. He was nine again. Or twelve. Or fifteen. And it wasn't about his feelings for Ivan Dunne. Or his lack of feelings for *Charlie's Angels.* It was the sickening realization that he'd landed on the wrong planet. Or in the wrong family. Or in the wrong body. The realization that he had no choice but to bide his time until he could get away and build a little world of his own in which he felt safe.

It was Katie who pulled him through. Telling him to ignore Greg Pattershall's gang. Saying graffiti only counted if it was spelt correctly. And she was right. They really did end up leading shitty little lives injecting heroin on some estate in Walton.

He was probably the only boy at school who'd learnt self-defense from his sister. He'd tried it once, on Mark Rice, who slumped into a bush and bled horribly, scaring Jamie so much he never hit anyone again.

Now he'd lost his sister. And no one understood. Not even Katie.

He wanted to sit in her kitchen and pull faces for Jacob and drink tea and eat too much Marks and Spencer date-and-walnut cake and . . . not even talk. Not even need to talk.

Fuck it. If he said the word *home* he was going to cry.

Maybe if he'd been better at staying in touch. Maybe if he'd eaten a little more date-and-walnut cake. If he'd invited her and Jacob over more often. If he'd lent her money . . .

This was pointless.

He turned the ignition on, pulled out of

the layby and was nearly killed by a green Transit van.

20

Rain was coursing down the living-room window. Jean had gone into town an hour ago and George was about to head down the garden when a mass of black cloud hoved into view from the direction of Stamford and turned the lawn into a pond.

No matter. He would do some drawing.

It was not part of the plan. The plan was to finish the studio, then resurrect his dormant artistic skills. But there was no harm getting in a little practice beforehand.

He dug around in Jamie's bedroom cupboard and unearthed a pad of watercolor paper from beneath the broken exercise bike. He found two serviceable pencils in the kitchen drawer and sharpened them in a rudimentary fashion with the steak knife.

He made a mug of tea, settled himself down at the dining table and wondered, instantly, why he had put this off for so long. The scent of shaved wood, the beaten-bronze texture of the cream paper. He remembered sitting in the corner of his bedroom at seven or eight with a pad on his knee, drawing convoluted Gothic castles with secret passages and mechanisms for pouring boiling oil over invaders. He could see the vines on the wallpaper and remember the beating he got for coloring them in with a ballpoint pen. He could feel the little patch of corduroy on his green trousers which he'd rubbed smooth and which his fingers still hunted for in stressful meetings twenty, thirty years later.

He began by drawing great black loops on the first sheet. "Loosening up the hands," Mr. Gledhill had called it.

How often did he feel it now, this gorgeous, furtive seclusion? In the bath sometimes, maybe. Though Jean failed to understand his need for periodic isolation and regularly dragged him back to earth mid-soak by hammering on the locked door in search of bleach or dental floss.

He began to draw the rubber plant.

Odd to think that this was once what he wanted to do with his life. Not rubber plants, as such. But art in general. Townscapes. Bowls of fruit. Naked women. Those big white studios with the skylights and the stools. Laughable now, of course. Though at the time it possessed all the power of a world to which his father had no key.

It was not a very good drawing of a rubber plant. It was, in truth, a child's drawing of a rubber plant. Something about the almost-but-not-quite parallel lines of the slightly tapering stalks had foxed him.

He turned over another sheet and began sketching the television.

His father was right, of course. Painting was not a sensible profession. Not if you wanted a decent salary and a trouble-free marriage. Even the successful ones, the ones you read about in the weekend papers, drank like fish and were involved in the most unseemly kind of relationships.

Drawing the television posed precisely the opposite problem. The lines were all straight. Draw any curve and you could probably find it somewhere on a rubber plant. Draw any straight line and . . . to be frank, several of his lines would have been more at home in the drawing of the rubber plant. Was it acceptable to use a ruler? Well, Mr. Gledhill was long dead. Perhaps if he ruled the lines faintly then drew over them to add character.

He could use the edge of the *Radio Times.*

His mother thought he was Rembrandt and regularly gave him cheap sketchpads which she had bought with the housekeeping, on condition that he did not tell his father. George had drawn him once, when he was asleep in an armchair after Sunday lunch. He had woken up unexpectedly, grabbed the piece of paper, examined it, torn it into pieces and thrown it on the fire.

At least he and Brian had escaped. But poor Judy. Their father dies and six months later she marries another bad-tempered, small-minded alcoholic.

Who would have to be invited to the wedding. He had forgotten that. Oh well. With any luck, the infamous Kenneth would pass rapidly into a coma, as he did the first time round, and they could dump him in the box room with a bucket.

The knobs on the television were wrong. It had been a mistake to attempt the knurling on the sides. Too many lines in too small a space. The entire cabinet, in fact, had a slightly drunken feel to it, stemming, possibly, from his poor memory of the rules of perspective and the flexibility of the *Radio Times.*

At which point a lesser man might have allowed negative thoughts to enter his head, given that he was spending eight thousand pounds constructing a building in which he planned to draw and paint objects far more complex than either rubber plants or televisions. But that was the point. To educate himself. To keep his mind alive. And the

Gold C gliding badge was really not his thing.

He looked up and gazed through the window onto the garden. The bubble popped and he realized that, in his absence, the rain had ceased, the sun had come out and the world had been washed clean.

He removed his drawing from the pad, tore it carefully into small pieces and pushed them to the bottom of the kitchen bin. He stacked the pad and pencils out of sight on top of the dresser, put on his boots and headed outside.

21

Jean met Ursula in the coffee shop in Marks and Spencer.

Ursula snapped the little biscuit over her cappuccino to stop the crumbs falling on the table. "I'm really not meant to know about this."

"I know," said Jean, "but you do know about it. And I need some advice."

She didn't really need advice. Not from Ursula. Ursula only did *Yes* and *No* (she'd gone round the Picasso Museum saying exactly that, "Yes . . . No . . . No . . . Yes," as if she was deciding which ones to get for the living room). But Jean had to talk to someone.

"Go on, then," said Ursula, eating half her biscuit.

"David is coming to supper. George invited him. We bumped into him at Bob Green's funeral. David couldn't really refuse."

"Well . . ." Ursula spread her hands on the table, as if she was flattening a big map.

And this was what Jean liked about Ursula. Nothing fazed her. She'd smoked a marijuana cigarette with her daughter ("I felt seasick, then threw up"). And, in actual fact, a man did try to mug them in Paris. Ursula shooed him away as if he were a bad dog, and he retreated at speed. Though, when Jean thought about it later, it was possible that he was simply begging or asking for directions.

"I don't really see the problem," said Ursula.

"Oh, come on," said Jean.

"You're not planning to be lovey-dovey with each other, are you?" Ursula ate the second half of her biscuit. "Obviously you'll feel uncomfortable. But, frankly, if you can't live with a bit of discomfort you really shouldn't embark on that kind of adventure."

Ursula was right. But Jean returned to the car feeling troubled. Of course the dinner would be fine. They'd survived far more uncomfortable dinners. That dreadful evening with the Fergusons, for example, when she found George in the toilet listening to cricket on the radio.

What Jean didn't like was the way everything was becoming looser and messier, and moving slowly beyond her control.

She pulled up round the corner from David's house knowing that she had to apologize to him for George's invitation, or tell him off for accepting it, or do some third thing she couldn't quite put her finger on.

But David had just been phoning his daughter.

His grandson was going into hospital for an operation. David wanted to go up to Manchester to help out. But Mina had got in first. So the kindest thing he could do was to keep his distance. Which Mina would doubtless chalk up as further proof of his failure as a father.

And Jean realized that everybody had a messy life. Except Ursula, maybe. And George. And if you were going to have any kind of adventure it was going to be uncomfortable now and then.

So she put her arms around David and

they held each other, and she realized that this was the third thing she couldn't quite put her finger on. This was the thing which made it all right.

22

"The Derby Hotel story," said Katie. "It's not actually true, is it?"

"Of course not," said Sarah. "Though I was so sick it came out of my nose. Which I seriously do not recommend."

"Ray's not usually like that," said Katie.

"Glad to hear it."

"Come on." Katie was a little peeved that Sarah wasn't showing the requisite sisterly support. "You're not usually like that either . . . Hang on a second." Katie got up and went over to the toy box to resolve a dispute between Jacob and another child over a one-legged Action Man.

She came back and sat down again.

"Sorry," said Sarah. "That was out of order." She licked her teaspoon. "And this is probably out of order, too. But, sod it, I'm going to ask anyway . . . This is the real thing, right? Not just a rebound relationship?"

"Jesus, Sarah, you're meant to be my best

woman, not my mum."

"So your mum doesn't like him," said Sarah.

"Nope."

"Well, he's not the consultant pediatrician with the Daimler."

"Oh, I think they gave up on that long ago," said Katie.

Sarah tried to balance her teaspoon on the rim of her mug.

"He's a good person," said Katie. "Jacob loves him. And I love him." That was the wrong way round, somehow. But changing it would have made her seem defensive. "He's also made Ed promise to show him the speech beforehand."

"I'm glad," said Sarah.

"About Ray? Or Ed?" asked Katie.

"About Ray," said Sarah, "and you."

She put her teaspoon down and they waited for the atmosphere to warm up again.

"Incidentally," said Sarah. "How's your little brother doing these days? I haven't seen him in yonks."

"Fine. Bought himself a place in Hornsey. Haven't seen him much myself to be honest. Proper boyfriend, too. I mean, like, an actual pleasant well-adjusted human being.

Of course, you'll meet them at the wedding."

They sat for a few moments watching Jacob direct some kind of aerial combat between the disabled Action Man and an octopus made of blue felt.

"I'm doing the right thing," said Katie.

"Good," said Sarah.

23

Jean came back at four. Her extended lunch with Ursula had worked its usual magic. The Jamie debacle was forgotten and George was grateful for a supper of Irish stew over which they were able to commiserate amiably with each other about the forthcoming union.

"Does anyone like their children's spouses?" He ran a triangle of crust around the bowl to mop up the remaining liquid.

"Jane Riley's husband seemed nice."

Jane Riley? George was repeatedly amazed by the ability of women to remember people. They walked into a crowded room and drank it down. Names. Faces. Children. Jobs.

"John and Marilyn's party," said Jean. "The tall chap who'd lost his finger in some kind of machine."

"Oh yes." It came fuzzily back. Perhaps it was the retrieval system men were missing. "The accountant."

"Surveyor."

After doing the washing up he retired to the living room with *Sharpe's Enemy* and read the last twenty pages ("Two bodies marked this winter. The one whose hair had been spread on the snows of the Gateway of God, and now this one. Obadiah Hakeswill, being lifted into his coffin, dead . . ."). He was tempted to start another of his still-unread Christmas presents. But you had to let the atmosphere of one novel seep away before launching into the next, so he turned the television on and found himself midway through a medical documentary about the last year in the life of a man dying from some kind of abdominal cancer.

Jean made some caustic comment about his ghoulish taste and retired elsewhere to write letters.

He might have chosen a different program if one were available. But a documentary left you edified at least. And anything was better than some tawdry melodrama in a hair salon.

On-screen the chap pottered round his garden, smoked cigarettes and spent a great deal of time under a tartan rug on the sofa wired up to various tubes. If anything, it was slightly tedious. A rather reassuring message if one thought about it.

The chap went outside and had some trouble bending down to feed his chickens.

Jean was squeamish, that was the truth of the matter. *How We Die* might not be everyone's choice of bedtime reading. But Jean read books by people who had been kidnapped in Beirut or survived for eight weeks on a life raft. And whilst everyone died sooner or later very few people needed to know how to repel sharks.

Most men of George's age thought they were going to live forever. The way Bob had driven, it was clear that he had had no concept of what might happen in five seconds' time, let alone five years.

The chap on television was taken to the seaside. He sat on the shingle in a deck chair until he got too cold and had to return to the camper van.

Obviously it would be nice to go quietly in one's sleep. But going quietly in one's sleep was an idea cooked up by parents to make the deaths of grandparents and hamsters less traumatic. And doubtless some people did go quietly in their sleep but most did so only after many wounding rounds with the Grim Reaper.

His own preferred exits were rapid and decisive. Others might want time to bury the hatchet with estranged children and tell their wives where the stopcock was. Personally, he wanted the lights to go out with no warning and the minimum attendant mess. Dying was bad enough without having to make it easier for everyone else.

He popped to the kitchen during the ad break and returned with a cup of coffee to find the chap entering his last couple of weeks, marooned almost permanently on his sofa and weeping a little in the small hours. And if George had turned the television off at this point the evening might have continued in a pleasantly uneventful manner.

But he did not turn the television off, and when the man's cat climbed onto the tartan rug in his lap to be stroked someone unscrewed a panel in the side of George's head, reached in and tore out a handful of very important wiring.

He felt violently ill. Sweat was pouring from beneath his hair and from the backs of his hands.

He was going to die.

Maybe not this month. Maybe not this year. But somehow, at some time, in a manner and at a speed very much not of his choosing.

The floor seemed to have vanished to reveal a vast open shaft beneath the living room.

With blinding clarity he realized that everyone was frolicking in a summer meadow surrounded by a dark and impenetrable forest, waiting for that grim day on which they were dragged into the dark beyond the trees and individually butchered.

How in God's name had he not noticed this before? And how did others not notice? Why did one not find them curled on the pavement howling? How did they saunter through their days unaware of this indigestible fact? And how, once the truth dawned, was it possible to forget?

Unaccountably he was now on all fours between the armchair and the television, rocking back and forth, attempting to comfort himself by making the sound of a cow.

He considered grasping the nettle and lifting his shirt and undoing his trousers to examine the lesion. A part of his mind knew that it would be reassuringly unchanged. Another part of his mind knew with equal certainty that it would be broiling like a fist of live bait. And a third part of his mind knew that the precise nature of what he would find was irrelevant to this new problem which was bigger and considerably less soluble than the health of his skin.

He was not used to having his mind occupied by three entirely separate voices. There was so much pressure inside his head it seemed possible that his eyes might burst.

He tried moving back to the armchair, for propriety's sake if nothing else, but he couldn't do it, as if the terrifying thoughts now haunting him were borne on some ferocious wind which was partly blocked by the furniture.

He continued to rock back and forth and resigned himself to keeping the mooing at as low a volume as possible.

24

Jamie parked round the corner from Katie's house and composed himself.

You never did escape, of course.

School might have been shit, but at least it was simple. If you could remember your nine times table, steer clear of Greg Pattershall and draw cartoons of Mrs. Cox with fangs and bat wings you pretty much had it sorted.

None of which got you very far at thirty-three.

What they failed to teach you at school was that the whole business of being human just got messier and more complicated as you got older.

You could tell the truth, be polite, take everyone's feelings into consideration and still have to deal with other people's shit. At nine or ninety.

He met Daniel at college. And at first it was a relief to find someone who wasn't shagging everything in sight now they were away from home. Then, when the thrill of having a steady boyfriend faded, he realized he was living with a bird-watching Black Sabbath fan and the horrifying thought occurred to him that he might be cut from the same cloth, that even being a sexual pariah in the eyes of the good burghers of Peterborough had failed to make him interesting or cool.

He'd tried celibacy. The only problem was the lack of sex. After a couple of months you'd settle for anything and find yourself being sucked off behind a large shrub at the top of the heath, which was fine until you came, and the fairy dust evaporated and you realized Prince Charming had a lisp and a weird mole on his ear. And there were

Sunday evenings when reading a book was like pulling teeth, so you ate a tin of sweetened condensed milk with a spoon in front of *French and Saunders* and something toxic seeped under the sash windows and you began to wonder what in God's name the point of it all was.

He didn't want much. Companionship. Shared interests. A bit of space.

The problem was that no one else knew what they wanted.

He'd managed three half-decent relationships since Daniel. But something always changed after six months, after a year. They wanted more. Or less. Nicholas thought they should spice up their love life by sleeping with other people. Steven thought he should move in. With his cats. And Olly slid into a deep depression after his father died so that Jamie turned from a partner into some kind of social worker.

Fast-forward six years and he and Shona were in the pub after work when she said that she was going to try and fix him up with a cute builder who was decorating the Prince's Avenue flats. But she was drunk and Jamie couldn't imagine how Shona, of all people, had correctly ascertained the sexual orientation of a working-class person. So he forgot about the conversation completely until they were over in Muswell Hill, and Jamie was doing a walk-through, zapping the interior measurements and having a vague sexual fantasy about the guy painting the kitchen when Shona came in and said, "Tony, this is Jamie. Jamie, this is Tony," and Tony turned round and smiled and Jamie realized that Shona was, in truth, a wiser old bird than he'd given her credit for.

She slipped away and he and Tony talked about property development and cycling and Tunisia, with a glancing reference to the ponds on the heath to make absolutely sure they were singing from the same hymn sheet and Tony pulled a printed business card from his back pocket and said, "If you ever need anything . . ." which Jamie did, very much.

He waited a couple of nights so as not to seem desperate, then met him for a drink in Highgate. Tony told a story about bathing naked with friends off Studland and how they had to empty wastebins and turn the black bags into rudimentary kilts to hitch back to Poole after their clothes were nicked. And Jamie explained how he reread *The Lord of the Rings* every year. But it felt right. The difference. Like two interlocking pieces of jigsaw.

After an Indian meal they went back to Jamie's flat and Tony did at least two things to him on the sofa that no one had ever done to him before then came back and did them again the following evening, and suddenly life became very good indeed.

It made him uncomfortable, being dragged along to Chelsea matches. It made him uncomfortable, ringing in sick so they could fly to Edinburgh for a long weekend. But Jamie needed someone who made him uncomfortable. Because getting too comfortable was the thin end of a wedge whose thick end involved him turning into his father.

And, of course, if a banister broke or the kitchen needed a new coat of paint, well, that made up for the Clash at high volume and work boots in the sink.

They had arguments. You couldn't spend a day in Tony's company without an argument. But Tony thought they were all part of the fun of human relationships. Tony also liked sex as a way of making up afterward. In fact, Jamie sometimes wondered whether Tony only started arguments so they could make up afterward. But the sex was too good to complain.

And now they were at one another's throats over a wedding. A wedding that had bugger all to do with Tony and, to be honest, not a lot to do with Jamie.

There was a crick in his neck.

He lifted his head and realized that he'd been leaning his forehead on the steering wheel for the last five minutes.

He got out of the car. Tony was right. He couldn't make Katie change her mind. It was guilt, really. Not having been there to listen.

There was no use worrying about that now. He had to make amends. Then he could stop feeling guilty.

Fuck. He should have bought cake.

It didn't matter. Cake wasn't really the point.

Half past two. They'd have the rest of the afternoon before Ray got home. Tea. Chat. Piggybacks and airplanes for Jacob. If they were lucky he'd take a nap and they could have a decent talk.

He walked up the path and rang the bell.

The door opened and he found the hallway blocked by Ray wearing paint-spattered overalls and holding some kind of electric drill.

"So, that's two of us taking the day off," said Ray. "Gas leak at the office." He held up the drill and pressed the button so that it whizzed a bit. "You heard the news, then."

"I did." Jamie nodded. "Congratulations."
Congratulations?

Ray extended a beefy paw and Jamie found his own hand sucked into its gravitational field.

"That's a relief," said Ray. "Thought you might've come to punch my lights out."

Jamie managed a laugh. "It wouldn't be much of a fight, would it."

"No." Ray's laughter was louder and more relaxed. "You coming in?"

"Sure. Is Katie around?"

"Sainsbury's. With Jacob. I'm fixing stuff. Should be back in half an hour."

Before Jamie could think of an appointment he might have been en route to Ray closed the door behind him. "Have a cup of coffee while I stick the door back on this cupboard."

"I'd prefer tea, if that's OK," said Jamie. The word *tea* did not sound manly.

"I reckon we can do tea."

Jamie sat himself down at the kitchen table feeling not unlike he had felt in the back of that Cessna before the ill-fated parachute jump.

"Glad you came." Ray put the drill down and washed his hands. "Something I wanted to ask you."

A horrifying image came to mind of Ray

126

patiently soaking up the hate waves over the past eight months, waiting for the moment when he and Jamie were finally alone together.

He put the kettle on, leant against the sink, pushed his hands deep into his trouser pockets and stared at the floor. "Do you reckon I should marry Katie?"

Jamie wasn't sure he'd heard this correctly. And there were certain questions you just didn't answer in case you'd got the wrong end of a very big stick (Neil Turley in the showers after football that summer, for example).

"You know her better than me." Ray had the look on his face that Katie had at eight when she was trying to bend spoons with mind power. "Do you . . . ? I mean, this is going to sound bloody stupid, but do you think she actually loves me?"

This question Jamie heard with horrible clarity. He was now sitting at the door of the Cessna with four thousand feet of nothing between his feet and Hertfordshire. In five seconds he'd be dropping like a stone, passing out and filling his helmet with sick.

Ray looked up. There was a silence in the kitchen like the silence in an isolated barn in a horror film.

Deep breath. Tell the truth. Be polite. Take

Ray's feelings into consideration. Deal with the shit. "I don't know. I really don't. Katie and I haven't talked that much over the last year. I've been busy, she's been spending time with you . . ." He trailed off.

Ray seemed to have shrunk to the size of an entirely normal human being. "She gets so bloody angry."

Jamie badly wanted the tea, if only for something to hold.

"I mean, I get angry," said Ray. He put tea bags into two mugs and poured the water. "Tell me about it. But Katie . . ."

"I know," said Jamie.

Was Ray listening? It was hard to tell. Perhaps he just needed someone to aim the words at.

"It's like this black cloud," said Ray.

How did Ray do it? One moment he was dominating a room the way a lorry would. Next minute he was down a hole and asking you for help. Why couldn't he suffer in a way they could all enjoy from a safe distance?

"It's not you," said Jamie.

Ray looked up. "Really?"

"Well, maybe it is you." Jamie paused. "But she gets angry with us, too."

"Right." Ray bent down and slid Rawlplugs into four holes he'd drilled inside the cupboard. "Right." He stood and removed the tea bags. The atmosphere slackened a little and Jamie began looking forward to a conversation about football or loft insulation. But when Ray placed the tea in front of Jamie he said, "So, what about you and Tony?"

"What do you mean?"

"I mean, what about you and Tony?"

"I'm not sure I understand," said Jamie.

"You love him, right?"

Jesus H. Christ. If Ray made a habit of asking questions like this, no wonder Katie got angry.

Ray slid some more Rawlplugs into the door of the cupboard. "I mean, Katie said you were lonely. Then you met this chap and . . . you know . . . Bingo."

Was it humanly possible to feel more ill at ease than he did at this moment? His hands were shaking and there were ripples in the tea like in *Jurassic Park* when the T. rex was approaching.

"Katie says he's a decent bloke."

"Why are we talking about me and Tony?"

"You have arguments, right?" said Ray.

"Ray, it's none of your business whether we have arguments or not."

Dear God. He was telling Ray to back off. Jamie never told people to back off. He felt like he did when Robbie North threw that can of petrol onto the bonfire, knowing that a bad thing was about to happen very soon.

"Sorry." Ray held up his hands. "This gay stuff's all a bit foreign to me."

"It's got absolutely nothing to do with . . . Jeez." Jamie put his tea down in case he spilled it. He felt a little dizzy. He took a deep breath and spoke slowly. "Yes. Tony and I have arguments. Yes, I love Tony. And . . ."

I love Tony.

He'd said he loved Tony. He'd said it to Ray. He hadn't even said it to himself.

Did he love Tony?

Christ alive.

Ray said, "Look —"

"No. Wait." Jamie put his head in his hands.

It was the life/school/other-people thing all over again. You turned up at your sister's house with the best of intentions, you found yourself talking to someone who had failed to grasp the most basic rules of human conversation and suddenly there was a motorway pileup in your head.

He steeled himself. "Perhaps we should just talk about football."

"Football?" asked Ray.

"Man stuff." The bizarre idea came to him

that they could be friends. Maybe not friends. But people who could rub along together. Christmas in the trenches and all that.

"Are you taking the piss?" asked Ray.

Jamie breathed deeply. "Katie's lovely. But she's hard work. You couldn't give her a biscuit against her will. If she's marrying you it's because she wants to marry you."

The drill slid off the counter and hit the stone floor tiles and it sounded like a mortar shell going off.

25

Something had happened to George.

It started that evening when she came back into the living room to find him scrabbling about under the armchair looking for the TV remote. He got to his feet and asked what she'd been up to.

"Writing a letter."

"Who to?"

"Anna. In Melbourne."

"So what have you been telling her?" asked George.

"About the wedding. About your studio. About the extension the Khans have added to her old house."

George didn't talk about her family, or the books she was reading, or whether they should get a new sofa. But for the rest of the evening he wanted to know what she thought about all these things. When he finally fell asleep it was probably due to exhaustion. He hadn't sustained a conversation this long in twenty years.

The following day continued in much the same fashion. When he wasn't working at the bottom of the garden or listening to Tony Bennett at double the usual volume he was following her from room to room.

When she asked if he was OK he insisted that it was good to talk and that they didn't do it enough. He was right, of course. And perhaps she should have been a little more appreciative of the attention. But it was scary.

Dear God, there were times when she'd prayed for him to open up a little. But not overnight. Not like he'd suffered a blow to the head.

There was a practical problem, too. Seeing David when George had no interest in what she was doing was one thing. Seeing David when George was following her every move was another.

Except that he wasn't very good at it. The listening, the taking an interest. He reminded her of Jamie at four. *Froggy wants to talk to you on the phone . . . Get on the sofa train, it's about to start!* Anything to hold her attention.

Just before they climbed into bed he'd wandered out of the bathroom holding a soiled Q-tip to ask whether she thought it was normal to have that much wax in one's ear.

David could do it. The listening, the taking an interest.

The following afternoon they were sitting in his living room with the French windows open. He was talking about stamps.

"Jersey World War Two occupation issues. The 1888 dull green Zululand one shilling. Perforates. Imperforates. Inverted watermarks . . . Lord knows what I thought I was going to achieve. Easier than growing up, I guess. I've still got them somewhere."

Most men wanted to tell you what they knew. The route to Wisbech. How to get a log fire going. David made her feel she was the one who knew things.

He lit a cigar and they sat quietly watching the sparrows on the bird table and the mackerel sky moving slowly from right to left behind the poplars. And it felt good. Because he could do silence, too. And in her experience there were very few men who could do silence.

She left late and found herself in a traffic jam by the roadworks outside B & Q. She was worrying about what to say to George to explain her lateness when it occurred to her that he knew about David. That his attentiveness was a way of making amends, or competing, or making her feel guilty.

But when she manhandled the bags into the kitchen he was sitting at the table with two mugs of hot coffee, waving a folded newspaper.

"You were talking about the Underwood boys. Well, apparently, these scientists in California have been studying identical twins . . ."

The shop was unusually quiet the following week. As a result her paranoia began to grow. And because Ursula was in Dublin there was no one she could discuss her fears with.

Mornings at St. John's were her only respite, sitting in the Jungle Corner with Megan and Callum and Sunil reading *Winnie the Witch* and *Mr. Gumpy's Outing*. Especially Callum, who couldn't sit still and look in the same direction for five seconds (sadly, she wasn't allowed to bribe him with biscuits like she did with Jacob). But as soon as she walked out of the main doors into the car park it began nagging at her all over again.

On Thursday George announced that he'd booked the marquee firm and arranged a meeting with two caterers. This from a man who forgot his children's birthdays. She was so surprised she didn't even complain about the lack of consultation.

Later that evening a sinister voice in her head began to ask whether he was making her dispensable. Ready for when she moved out. Or when he told her to go.

Yet when the day of the dinner with David rolled around he was unexpectedly cheerful. He spent the day shopping and making risotto in the time-honored male way, removing all the utensils from the drawers and laying them out like surgical instruments, then decanting all the ingredients into small bowls to maximize the washing up.

She still couldn't shake the idea that he was planning some kind of showdown, and as the tension rose during the afternoon she found herself toying with the idea of faking some kind of illness. When the doorbell finally rang just after half past seven she ran down the landing, trying to get to the door first and tripped on the loose carpet, twisting her ankle.

By the time she reached the bottom of the stairs, George was standing in the hallway wiping his hands on his stripy apron, and David was handing him a bottle of wine and a bunch of flowers.

David noticed her hobbling a little. "Are you OK?" Instinctively he moved to comfort her, then caught himself and stepped back.

Jean put her hand on George's arm and bent down to rub her ankle. It didn't hurt a great deal, but she wanted to avoid David's eye, and the fear that he might have given something away in that fraction of a second made her feel light-headed.

"Is it bad?" asked George. Thankfully he seemed to have noticed nothing.

"Not too bad," said Jean.

"You should sit down and put your foot up," said David. "To prevent it swelling." He took the flowers and wine back so that George could help her.

"I'm still in the middle of cooking," said George. "Why don't I sit you two down with a glass of wine in the living room?"

"No," said Jean, a little too firmly. She paused to calm herself. "We'll come into the kitchen with you."

George installed them at the table, pulled out a third chair for Jean's ankle, which she didn't really need, filled two wineglasses and returned to grating Parmesan.

It was always going to be a strange occasion, whoever their guest was. George didn't like other people in his kennel. So she assumed the conversation would be stilted. Whenever she dragged him along to parties she would invariably find him standing disconsolately in a circle of men, as they talked about rugby and tax returns, wearing a pained expression on his face, as if he was suffering from a headache. She hoped, at least, that David would be able to fill any silences.

But to her surprise, it was George who did most of the talking. He seemed genuinely excited to have company. The two men congratulated themselves about the decline in Shepherds' fortunes since their departure. They talked about trekking holidays in France. David talked about his gliding. George talked about his fear of flying. David suggested that learning to glide might cure the problem. George said that David clearly underestimated his fear of flying. David confessed to a snake phobia. George asked him to imagine an anaconda in his lap for a couple of hours. David laughed and said George had a point.

Jean's fear ebbed away and was replaced by something odder but equally uncomfortable. It was ridiculous but she didn't want them to be getting on this well. George was warmer and funnier than he was when they were alone together. And David seemed more ordinary.

Was this how they'd been at work? And if so, why had George not mentioned David once since leaving the company? She began to feel rather guilty for having painted David such a bleak picture of her home life.

By the time they decamped to the dining room George and David seemed to have more in common with one another than she had with either of them. It was like being back at school again. Watching your best friend striking up a relationship with another child and being left out in the cold.

She kept muscling into the conversation, trying to claw back some of that attention. But she kept getting it wrong. Sounding far too interested in *Great Expectations* when she'd only seen the TV series. Being too rude about George's previous culinary disasters when the risotto was actually very good. It was tiring. And in the end it seemed easier to take a backseat, leave them to do the talking and give her opinion when asked.

Only at one point did George seem lost for words. David was talking about Martin Donnelly's wife having to go into hospital for tests. She turned round and saw George sitting with his head between his knees. Her first thought was that he'd poisoned everyone with his cooking and was about to vomit. But he sat back, wincing and rubbing his leg, apologized for the interruption, then headed off to do a circuit of the kitchen to ease a muscle spasm.

By the end of the meal he'd drunk an entire bottle of red wine and turned into something of a comic.

"At the risk of boring Jean with an old story, a couple of weeks later we got our photos back. Except they weren't our photos. They were photos of some young man and his girlfriend. In the altogether. Jamie suggested we write 'Do you want an enlargement?' on the back before we returned them."

Over coffee David talked about Mina and the children, and as they stood on the steps watching him drive away on a little cloud of pink smoke, George said, "You wouldn't ever leave me, would you?"

"Of course not," said Jean.

She expected him to put an arm round her, at the very least. But he just clapped his hands together, said, "Right. Washing up," and headed back inside as if this were simply the next part of the fun.

26

Katie had had a shitty week.

The festival programs arrived on Monday and Patsy, who still couldn't spell *program,* shocked everyone by knowing a fact, that the photo of Terry Jones on page seven was actually a photo of Terry Gilliam. Aidan bawled Katie out because admitting he'd cocked up wasn't one of the skills he'd learnt on his MBA. She resigned. He refused to accept her resignation. And Patsy cried because people were shouting.

Katie left early to pick up Jacob from nursery and Jackie said he'd bitten two other children. She took him to one side and gave him a lecture about being like the meanie crocodile in *A Kiss Like This.* But Jacob wasn't doing recriminations that day. So she cut her losses and drove him home where she withheld his yogurt until they'd had a conversation about biting, which generated the same kind of frustration Dr. Benson probably felt when they were doing Kant at university.

"It was my tractor," said Jacob.

"Actually it's everyone's tractor," said Katie.

"I was playing with it."

"And Ben shouldn't have grabbed it from you. But that doesn't give you the right to bite him."

"I was playing with it."

"If you're playing with something and someone tries to grab it you have to shout and tell Jackie or Bella or Susie."

"You said it's wrong to shout."

"It's OK to shout if you're really, really cross. But you're not allowed to bite. Or to hit someone. Because you don't want other people to bite you or hit you, do you?"

"Ben bites people," said Jacob.

"But you don't want to be like Ben."

"Can I have my yogurt now?"

"Not until you understand that biting people is a bad thing to do."

"I understand," said Jacob.

"Saying you understand is not the same thing as understanding."

"But he tried to grab my tractor."

Ray came in at this point and made the technically correct suggestion that it was unhelpful to hug Jacob while she was telling him off, and she was able to demonstrate immediately a situation where you were allowed to shout at someone if you were really, really cross.

Ray remained infuriatingly calm until Jacob told him not to make Mummy angry because "You're not my real Daddy," at which point he walked into the kitchen and snapped the breadboard into two pieces.

Jacob fixed her with a thirty-five-year-old stare and said, tartly, "I'm going to eat my yogurt now," then went off to consume it in front of *Thomas the Tank Engine.*

The following morning she canceled her dentist's appointment and spent her day off taking Jacob into the office where he acted like a demented chimp while she and Patsy inserted five thousand erratum slips. By lunchtime he'd taken the chain off Aidan's bike, emptied a card index file and spilled hot chocolate into his shoes.

Come Friday, for the first time in two years she was genuinely relieved when Graham arrived to take him off her hands for forty-eight hours.

Ray headed out to play five-a-side football on Saturday morning and she made the mistake of attempting to clean the house. She was manhandling the sofa to get at the fluff and slime and toy parts underneath when something tore in her lower back. Suddenly she was in a great deal of pain and walking like the butler in a vampire movie.

Ray microwaved some supper and they attempted an orthopedic, low-impact shag but the ibuprofen seemed to have rendered her numb in all the unhelpful places.

On Sunday she gave in and retired to the sofa, keeping the crap mother guilt at bay with Cary Grant videos.

At six Graham turned up with Jacob.

Ray was in the shower so she let them in herself and tottered back to the chair in the kitchen.

Graham asked what was wrong but Jacob was too busy telling her what a wonderful time they'd had at the Natural History Museum.

"And there were . . . there were skellingtons of elephants and rhinoceroses and . . . and . . . the dinosaurs were ghost dinosaurs."

"They were repainting one of the rooms," said Graham. "Everything was under dust sheets."

"And Daddy said I could stay up late. And we had . . . we had . . . we had eggy. And toast. And I helped. And I gotted a chocolate stegosaurus. From the museum. And there was a dead squirrel. In Daddy's . . . Daddy's garden. It had worms. In its eyes."

Katie held her arms out. "Are you going to give your mummy a big hug?"

But Jacob was in full flow. "And . . . and . . . and we went on a double-decker bus and I keeped the tickets."

Graham crouched down. "Hang on a tick, little man, I think your mummy's hurt herself." He put a finger to Jacob's lips and turned to Katie. "Are you OK?"

"Wrecked my back. Moving the sofa."

Graham gave Jacob a serious look. "You be good to your mummy, all right? Don't go giving her the runaround. Promise?"

Jacob looked at Katie. "Is your back not comfy?"

"Not very. But a hug from my monkey boy would make it feel a lot better."

Jacob didn't move.

Graham got to his feet. "Well, it's getting late."

Jacob began to wail, "I don't want Daddy to go."

Graham ruffled his hair. "Sorry, Buster. Can't be helped, I'm afraid."

"Come on, Jacob." Katie held her arms out again. "Let me give you a cuddle."

But Jacob was working himself up into a state of truly operatic despair, punching the air and kicking out at the nearest chair. "Not go. Not go."

Graham tried to hold him, if only to stop him hurting himself. "Hey, hey, hey . . ." Normally he would have left. They'd learnt the hard way. But normally she could have scooped Jacob into her arms and hung on to him while Graham beat a retreat.

Jacob stamped his feet. "Nobody . . . Nobody listens . . . I want . . . I hate . . ."

After three or four minutes Ray appeared in the doorway with a towel round his waist. She was past caring what he might say and how Graham might react. He walked over to Jacob, hoisted him over his shoulder and disappeared.

There wasn't time to react. They just stared at the empty door and listened to the screaming getting fainter as Ray and Jacob made their way upstairs.

Graham got to his feet. She thought for a moment that he was going to make some caustic comment and she wasn't sure she could handle that. But he said, "I'll make some tea," and it was the kindest thing he'd said to her in a long time.

"Thanks."

He put the kettle on. "You're giving me a weird look."

"The shirt. It's the one I bought you for Christmas."

"Yeh. Shit. Sorry. I didn't mean to . . ."

"No. I wasn't trying to . . ." She was crying.

"Are you all right?" He reached out to touch her but stopped himself.

"I'm fine. Sorry."

"Are things going OK?" asked Graham.

"We're getting married." She was crying properly now. "Oh crap. I shouldn't be . . ."

He gave her a tissue. "That's great news."

"I know." She blew her nose messily. "And you? What about you?"

"Oh, nothing much."

"Tell me," said Katie.

"I was seeing someone from work." He took away her soggy tissue and gave her a fresh one. "It didn't work out. I mean, she was great, but . . . She wore this swimming cap in the bath to keep her hair dry."

He took out some Fig Rolls and they talked about the safe stuff. Ray putting his foot in it with Jamie. Graham's gran modeling for a knitwear catalog.

After ten minutes he made his excuses. She was sad. It surprised her and he paused just long enough to suggest that he felt the same. There was a brief moment during which one of them might have said something inappropriate. He cut it short.

"You look after yourself, OK?" He kissed her gently on the top of the head and left.

She sat quietly for a few more minutes. Jacob had stopped crying. She realized she hadn't felt the pain while she and Graham had been talking. It was back with a vengeance now. She swigged two more ibuprofen with a glass of water then shuffled upstairs. They were in Jacob's room. She stopped outside and glanced round the door.

Jacob was lying on the bed, facedown, looking at the wall. Ray was sitting next to him, patting his bottom and singing "Ten Green Bottles" very quietly and completely out of tune.

Katie was crying again. And she didn't want Jacob to see. Or Ray for that matter. So she turned and silently walked back down to the kitchen.

27

Above all it seemed so profoundly unjust.

George was not naïve. Bad things happened to good people. He knew that. And vice versa. But when the Benns were burgled by their daughter's boyfriend, or when Brian's first wife had to have her breast implants taken out, you couldn't help thinking that some kind of rudimentary justice was being done.

He knew men who had kept mistresses their entire married lives. He knew men who had gone bankrupt and registered the same company under a different name the following month. He knew a man who had broken his son's leg with a spade. Why were they not going through this?

He had spent thirty years making and installing playground equipment. Good playground equipment. Not as cheap as Wicksteed or Abbey Leisure, but better value.

He had made mistakes. He should have sacked Alex Bamford when he found him half conscious on the floor of the office washroom. And he should have asked for written evidence of Jane Fuller's back problems and not waited until she appeared in the local paper doing that fun run.

He had made seventeen people redundant, but they got a decent settlement and as good a reference as he could write without perjuring himself. It was not heart surgery, but neither was it weapons manufacture. In a modest way he had increased the happiness of a small part of the human population.

And now this had been dumped on his plate.

Still, there was no point in complaining. He had spent his life solving problems. Now he had to solve another one.

His mind was malfunctioning. He had to bring it under control. He had done it before. He had shared a house with his daughter for eighteen years without coming to blows, for starters. When his mother died he went back into the office the following morning to make sure the Glasgow deal did not fall through.

He needed a strategy, just as he would if Jean had booked a holiday for two in Australia.

He found himself a sheet of stiff, cream writing paper, drew up a list of rules, then hid it in the fireproof cash box at the back of the wardrobe with his birth certificate and the house deeds:

1. Keep busy.
2. Take long walks.
3. Sleep well.
4. Shower and change in the dark.
5. Drink red wine.
6. Think of something else.
7. Talk.

As for keeping busy, the wedding was a godsend. Last time round he had left the organization to Jean. Now that he had time to spare he could keep himself occupied and earn brownie points into the bargain.

Walking was a genuine delight. Especially the footpaths round Nassington and Fotheringay. It kept him fit and helped him sleep. True, there were difficult moments. One afternoon on the dam at the eastern end of Rutland Water, he heard an industrial siren go off, and images of refinery disasters and nuclear attack made him feel suddenly very far from civilization. But he was able to stride back to the car singing loudly to himself, then crank up *Ella Live at Montreux* to cheer himself on the journey home.

Turning the lights off to shower and change was plain common sense. And with the exception of the evening when Jean had marched into the bathroom, flicked on the light and screamed when she found him toweling himself in the dark, it was easy enough to do.

The red wine doubtless ran contrary to all medical advice but two or three glasses of that Ridgemont Cabernet did wonders for his mental equilibrium.

Thinking of something else was the most difficult task on the list. He would be cutting his toenails, or oiling a pair of shears, and it would loom from the undertow like a dark silhouette in a shark movie. When he was in town it was possible to distract himself by glancing sideways at an attractive young lady and imagining her naked. But he encountered few attractive young ladies in the course of his average day. If he had been more brazen and lived alone he might have purchased pornographic magazines. But he was not brazen and Jean was a scrupulous cleaner of nooks. So he settled for the crossword.

It was talking, however, which was the revelation. Little did he know that by sorting out the inside of his head he would add new life to his marriage. Not that it was dull or loveless. Far from it. They got on with one another a good deal better than many couples of their acquaintance who put up with a life of low-level sniping and bad-tempered silences simply because it was easier than separating. He and Jean bickered rarely, thanks largely to his own powers of self-restraint. But they did have silences.

So it was a pleasant surprise to find that he could say what was on his mind and have Jean respond with often interesting comments. Indeed there were evenings when this kind of conversation gave him such profound relief that he felt as if he were falling in love with her all over again.

A couple of weeks after embarking on his self-imposed regime George got a phone call from Brian.

"Gail's mother's here for a fortnight. So I thought I'd head down to the cottage. Make sure the builders have done their job. Wondered if you fancied joining me. It'll be a bit primitive. Camp beds, sleeping bags. But you're a hardy chap."

Ordinarily he would not have wanted to spend more than a couple of hours in his brother's company. But there was something boyish and excited in his voice. He sounded like a nine-year-old eager to show off his new tree house. And the thought of a long train journey, windy walks along the Helford and pints around the fire in the local pub was rather appealing.

He could take a sketchbook. And that big Peter Ackroyd Jean had given him for Christmas.

"I'll come."

28

Jamie vacuumed the carpets and cleaned the bathroom. He thought briefly about washing the cushion covers but, frankly, Tony wouldn't notice if they were covered in mud.

The following afternoon he cut short the visit to the Creighton Avenue flats, rang the office to say he could be contacted on his mobile, then went home via Tesco's.

Salmon, then strawberries. Enough to show he'd made an effort but not enough to make him feel too fat for sex. He put a bottle of Pouilly-Fumé in the fridge and a vase of tulips on the dining table.

He felt stupid. He was getting worked up about losing Katie, and doing nothing to hang on to the most important person in his life.

He and Tony should be living together. He should be coming home to lit windows and the sound of unfamiliar music. He should be lying in bed on Saturday mornings, smelling bacon and hearing the clink of crockery through the wall.

He was going to take Tony to the wedding. All that bollocks about provincial bigotry. It was himself he was scared of. Getting old. Making choices. Being committed.

It would be ghastly. Of course it would be ghastly. But it didn't matter what the neighbors thought. It didn't matter if Mum fussed over Tony like a lost son. It didn't matter if his father tied himself in knots over bedroom arrangements. It didn't matter if Tony insisted on a slow snog to Lionel Richie's "Three Times a Lady."

He wanted to share his life with Tony. The good stuff and the crap stuff.

He took a deep breath and felt, for several seconds, as if he was standing not on the pine floor of his kitchen but on some deserted Scottish headland, the surf thundering and the wind in his hair. Noble. Taller.

He went upstairs and showered and felt the remains of something dirty being rinsed away and sent spinning down the plughole.

He was having a shirt-selection crisis when the doorbell rang. He plumped for the faded orange denim and went downstairs.

When he opened the door his first thought was that Tony had received some bad news. About his father, perhaps.

"What's the matter?"

Tony took a deep breath.

"Hey. Come inside," said Jamie.

Tony didn't move. "We need to talk."

"Come inside and talk."

Tony didn't want to come inside. He suggested they walk to the park at the end of the road. Jamie grabbed his keys.

It happened next to the little red bin for dog shit.

Tony said, "It's over."

"What?"

"Us. It's over."

"But —"

"You don't really want to be with me," said Tony.

"I do," said Jamie.

"OK. Maybe you want to be with me. But you don't want to be with me enough. This stupid wedding. It's made me realize . . . Jesus, Jamie. Am I just not good enough for your parents? Or am I not good enough for you?"

"I love you." Why was this happening now? It was so unfair, so idiotic.

Tony looked at him. "You don't know what love is."

"I do." He sounded like Jacob.

Tony's expression didn't change. "Loving someone means taking the risk that they might fuck up your nicely ordered little life. And you don't want to fuck up your nicely ordered little life, do you?"

"Have you met someone else?"

"You're not listening to a word I'm saying."

He should have explained. The salmon. The vacuuming. The words were there in his head. He just couldn't get them out. He hurt too much. And there was something sickly and comforting about the thought of going back to the house alone, smashing the tulips from the table, then retiring to the sofa to drink the bottle of wine on his own.

"I'm sorry, Jamie. I really am. You're a

nice guy." Tony put his hands into his pockets to show that there would be no final embrace. "I hope you find someone who makes you feel that way."

He turned and walked off.

Jamie stood in the park for several minutes, then went back to the flat, smashed the tulips from the table, uncorked the wine, took it to the sofa and wept.

29

Ray turned to Katie in bed and said, "Are you sure you want to marry me?"

"Of course I want to marry you."

"You'd tell me if you changed your mind, yeh?"

"Jeez, Ray," said Katie. "What's all this about?"

"You wouldn't go through with it just because we'd told everyone?"

"Ray —"

"Do you love me?" he asked.

"Why are you talking like this all of a sudden?"

"Do you love me like you loved Graham?"

"No, actually, I don't," said Katie.

For a second she could see real pain on his face. "I was infatuated with Graham. I thought he was God's gift. I couldn't see straight. And when I found out what he was really like . . ." She put her hand on the side of Ray's face. "I know you. I know all the things that are wonderful about you. I know all your faults. And I still want to marry you."

"So, what are my faults?"

This wasn't her job. He was the one who was meant to do the consoling. "Come here." She pulled his head onto her chest.

"I love you so much." He sounded tiny.

"Don't worry. I'm not going to ditch you at the altar."

"I'm sorry. I'm being stupid."

"It's wedding nerves." She ran her hand over the little hairs on his upper arm. "You remember Emily?"

"Yeh?"

"Threw up in the vestry."

"Shit."

"They had to send her up the aisle with this massive bouquet to hide the stain. Barry's dad assumed the smell was Roddy. You know, after their stag night."

They fell asleep and were woken at four by Jacob crying, "Mummy, Mummy, Mummy . . ."

Ray started to get out of bed but she insisted on going.

When she got to his room Jacob was still half asleep, trying to curl away from a big orange diarrhea stain in the center of the bed.

"Come here, little squirrel." She lifted him to his feet and his sleepy head flopped against her shoulder.

"It's all . . . all sort of . . . It's wet."

"I know. I know." She carefully peeled off his pajama trousers, rolling them up so that the mess was on the inside then throwing them into the hallway. "Let's clean you up, Baby Biscuits." She grabbed a nappy bag and a fresh nappy and pack of wet wipes from the drawer and gently cleaned his bottom.

She put the fresh nappy on, extracted a fresh pair of pajama trousers from the basket and guided his clumsy feet into the legs. "There. That feels better, doesn't it."

She flicked the Winnie the Pooh duvet over to check that it was clean, then bundled it onto the carpet. "You lie down for a second while I sort the bed out."

Jacob cried as she lowered him to the floor. "Don't want to . . . let me . . ." But when she laid his head on the duvet, his thumb slipped into his mouth and his eyes closed again.

She tied the nappy bag and threw it into

the bin. She stripped the bed, threw the dirty sheets into the hallway and turned the mattress over. She grabbed a new set of sheets from the cupboard and pressed them to her face. God, it was lovely, the furriness of thick, worn cotton and the scent of washing powder. She made the bed, tucking the edges in tight so that it was smooth and flat.

She plumped the pillow, bent over and hoisted Jacob up.

"My tummy hurts."

She held him on her lap. "We'll get you some Calpol in a minute."

"Pink medicine," said Jacob.

She wrapped her arms around him. She didn't get enough of this. Not when he was conscious. Thirty seconds at most. Then it was helicopters and bouncy-bouncy on the sofa. True, it made her proud, seeing him in a circle listening to Bella read a book at nursery, or watching him talk to other children in the playground. But she missed the way he was once a part of her body, the way she could make everything better just by folding herself around him. Even now she could picture him leaving home, the distance opening up already, her baby becoming his own little person.

"I miss my daddy."

"He's asleep upstairs."

"My real daddy," said Jacob.

She put her hand around his head and kissed his hair. "I miss him too, sometimes."

"But he's not coming back."

"No. He's not coming back."

Jacob was crying quietly.

"But I'll never leave you. You know that, don't you." She wiped the snot from his nose with the arm of her T-shirt and rocked him.

She looked up at the Bob the Builder height chart and the sailing boat mobile turning silently in the half dark. Somewhere under the floor a water pipe clanked.

Jacob stopped crying. "Can I have a polar bear drink tomorrow?"

She pushed the hair out of his eyes. "I'm not sure whether you'll be fit for nursery tomorrow." His eyes moistened. "But if you are, we'll get a polar bear drink on the way home, OK?"

"All right."

"But if you have a polar bear drink, you won't be able to have any pudding for supper. Is that a deal?"

"That's a deal."

"Now, let's get you some Calpol."

She laid him down on the clean sheets and got the bottle and the syringe from the bathroom.

"Open wide."

He was almost asleep now. She squirted the medicine into his mouth, wiped a dribble from his chin with the tip of her finger and licked it clean.

She kissed his cheek. "I have to go back to bed now, little boy."

But he didn't want to let go of her hand. And she didn't want him to let go. She sat watching him sleep for a few minutes, then lay down beside him.

This made up for everything, the tiredness, the tantrums, the fact that she hadn't read a novel in six months. This was how Ray made her feel.

This was how Ray was meant to make her feel.

She stroked Jacob's head. He was a million miles away, dreaming of raspberry ice cream and earth-moving machinery and the Cretaceous period.

The next thing she knew it was morning and Jacob was running in and out of the room in his Spider-Man outfit.

"Come on, love." Ray pushed the hair away from her face. "There's a fry-up waiting for you downstairs."

After nursery she and Jacob got home late on account of having stopped to get the polar bear drink, and Ray was already back from the office.

"Graham rang," he said.

"What about?"

"Didn't tell me."

"Anything important?" asked Katie.

"Didn't ask. Said he'd try again later."

One mysterious call from Graham a day was pretty much Ray's limit. So, after putting Jacob to bed, she used the phone in the bedroom.

"It's Katie."

"Hey, you rang back."

"So, what's the big secret?"

"No big secret, I'm just worried about you. Which didn't seem the kind of message to leave with Ray."

"I'm sorry. I wasn't in terribly good shape when you turned up the other evening, what with my back and everything."

"Are you talking to anyone?" asked Graham.

"You mean, like, professionally?"

"No, I mean just talking."

"Of course I'm talking," said Katie.

"You know what I mean."

"Graham. Look —"

"If you want me to butt out," said Graham, "I'll butt out. And I don't want to cast any aspersions on Ray. I really don't. I just wondered whether you wanted to meet up

162

for a coffee and a chat. We're still friends, right? OK, maybe we're not friends. But you seemed like you might need to get stuff off your chest. And I don't necessarily mean bad stuff." He paused. "Also, I really enjoyed talking to you the other night."

God knows what had happened to him. She hadn't heard him sounding this solicitous in years. If it was jealousy it didn't sound like jealousy. Perhaps the woman with the swimming cap had broken his heart.

She stopped herself. It was an unkind thought. People changed. He was being kind. And he was right. She wasn't talking enough.

"I'm finishing early on Wednesday. I could see you for an hour before I pick Jacob up."

"Brilliant."

30

Toothbrush. Flannel. Shaver. Woolly jumper.

George started packing a suitcase, then decided that it was not quite outward bound enough. He dug Jamie's old rucksack out of the roof space. It was a little scuffed, but rucksacks were meant to be scuffed.

Three pairs of underpants. Two vests. The Ackroyd. Gardening trousers.

This was his kind of holiday.

They had tried it once. Snowdonia in 1980. A desperate attempt on his part to remain earthbound after the horrors of the flight to Lyon the previous year. And perhaps if he had had stouter children or a wife less addicted to her creature comforts it might have worked. There was nothing wrong with rain. It was part and parcel of getting back in touch with nature. And it had let up most evenings so that they could sit on camping mats outside the tents cooking supper on the Primus stove. But any suggestion of his that they go to Skye or the Alps in subsequent years had been met with the rejoinder, "Why don't we go camping in North Wales?" and gales of unsympathetic laughter.

Jean dropped him off in the town center just after nine and he went straight into Ottakar's where he purchased the Ordnance Survey Landranger map number 204, *Truro, Falmouth and Surrounding Area.* He then popped into Smiths and bought himself a selection of pencils (2B, 4B and 6B), a sketchpad and a good rubber. He was going to get a pencil sharpener when he remembered that the outdoor shop was only a couple of streets away. He went in and treated himself to a Swiss Army knife. He could sharpen his pencils with that, and be prepared to whittle sticks and remove stones from horses' hooves should the need arise.

He arrived at the station with fifteen minutes to spare, picked up his ticket and sat on the platform.

An hour to Kings Cross. Hammersmith and City line to Paddington. Four and a half hours to Truro. Twenty minutes to Falmouth. Then a taxi. Assuming the seat booking worked between Paddington and Truro and he didn't find himself squatting on the rucksack outside the toilet, he could get a couple of hundred pages read.

Shortly before the train arrived he remembered that he had not packed his steroid cream.

Not that it mattered. It was a treatment for eczema. Eczema was a trivial thing. He could be covered in the stuff and it wouldn't be a problem.

The phrase "covered in the stuff" and the attendant image were not ones he should have allowed to enter his head.

He looked up at the monitor to see how long it was before his train arrived but saw, instead, a disfigured tramp sitting on the adjacent bench. The near side of his face was composed entirely of scab, as if some-one had recently worked it over with a broken bottle, or as if some kind of growth was eating its way through the side of his head.

He tried to look away. He could not. It was like vertigo. The way the drop seemed to be calling you.

Think of something else.

He twisted his head downward and forced himself to concentrate on five gray ovals of chewing gum pressed into the tarmac be-tween his toes.

"I took a trip on a train and I thought about you." He sung the words quietly under his breath. "I passed a shadowy lane and I thought about you."

The disfigured tramp got to his feet.

Dear God in heaven, he was coming this way.

George kept his head down. "Two or three cars parked under the stars, a winding stream, moon shining down . . ."

The tramp walked past George and zig-zagged slowly down the platform.

He was very drunk. Drunk enough to zigzag onto the line. Too drunk to climb back off the line. George looked up. The train was arriving in one minute. He pic-tured the tramp keeling over the concrete lip, the squeal of brakes, the wet thump and the body being shunted up the rails, the wheels slicing it like ham.

He had to stop the tramp. But stopping the tramp would involve touching the tramp, and George did not want to touch the tramp. The wound. The smell.

No. He did not have to stop the tramp. There were other people on the platform. There were railway employees. The tramp was their responsibility.

If he moved round the station building to the other platform he would not have to see the tramp dying. But if he moved to the other platform he might miss the train. On the other hand, if the tramp died under the train it would be delayed. George would then miss the connection to Truro and have to sit next to the toilet for four and a half hours.

Dr. Barghoutian had misdiagnosed Katie's appendicitis. Said it was stomachache. Three hours later they were whisked through casualty and Katie was on an operating table.

How on earth had George forgotten?

Dr. Barghoutian was a moron.

He was massaging an inappropriate chemical cream into a cancer. A steroid cream. Steroids made tissue grow faster and stronger. He was massaging a cream which made tissue grow faster and stronger directly into a tumor.

The growth on the tramp's face. George was going to look like that. All over.

The train pulled in.

He picked up his rucksack and launched himself at the open door of the nearest carriage. If he could only get the journey started quickly enough he might be able to leave the rogue thoughts on the platform.

He slumped into a seat. His heart was beating the way it would have beaten if he had run all the way from home. He was finding it very difficult to sit still. There was a woman in a mauve raincoat sitting opposite him. He was beyond caring what she thought.

The train began to move.

He looked out of the window and imagined himself flying a small aircraft parallel to the train, like he did when he was a boy, pulling back on the joystick to clear fences and bridges, swinging the plane left and right to swerve round sheds and telegraph poles.

The train picked up speed. Over the river. Over the A605.

He felt sick.

He was in the upturned cabin of a sinking

ship as it filled with water. The darkness was total. The door was now somewhere below him. It didn't matter where. It led only to other places in which to die.

He was kicking madly, trying to keep his head in the shrinking pyramid of stale air where the two walls met the ceiling.

His mouth was going under.

There was oily water in his windpipe.

He put his head between his legs.

He was going to throw up.

He sat back.

His body went cold and the blood drained from his head.

He put his head between his legs again.

He felt as if he were in a sauna.

He sat up and opened the little window.

The woman in the mauve raincoat glared.

The scab would strangle him with evil slowness, a malign, crusted appendage feeding off his own body.

"I peeked through the crack, looked at the track, the one going back . . ."

Camp beds? Walks along the Helford? Pints round the fire with Brian? What in heaven's name had he been thinking? It would be a living hell.

He got out at Huntingdon, staggered to the nearest bench, sat down and reconstructed that morning's *Telegraph* crossword in his head. Genuflect. Tankards. Horse brass . . .

It was ebbing a little.

He was dying of cancer. It was a horrible thought. But if he could just store it over there, in the Thoughts About Dying Of Cancer box, he might be OK.

Gazelle. Miser. Paw-paw . . .

He had to catch the next train home. Chat to Jean. Have a cup of tea. Put some music on. Loud. His own house. His own garden. Everything exactly where it was meant to be. No Brian. No tramps.

There was a monitor to his right. He got gingerly to his feet and moved round to the front so that he could read it.

Platform 2. Twelve minutes.

He began walking toward the stairs.

He would be home in an hour.

31

Jean dropped George off, got into the driving seat and drove back to the village.

She hadn't spent four days alone in her entire life. Yesterday she'd been looking forward to it. But now that it was happening she was frightened.

She found herself calculating the precise

number of hours she would be spending alone between working in Ottakar's and going to St. John's.

On Sunday she would spend the evening with David. But Sunday evening suddenly seemed a long way away.

It was at this point that she parked in front of the house, looked up and saw David himself standing on the path talking to Mrs. Walker from next door.

What in heaven's name was he doing? Mrs. Walker noticed when they started ordering orange juice from the milkman. God knows what the woman was thinking now.

She got out of the car.

"Ah, Jean. I'm in luck after all." David smiled at her. "I didn't know whether I'd catch George. I forgot my reading glasses when I came round for dinner."

Reading glasses? God, the man could lie for England. Jean wasn't sure whether to be impressed or terrified. She looked at Mrs. Walker. The woman seemed smitten, if anything.

"Mr. Symmonds and I were having a chat," she said. "He told me George makes a very good risotto. I thought he was pulling my leg."

"Strange but true," Jean said. "George

does cook. About once every five years." She turned to David. "He will be disappointed. I've just dropped him in town. He's visiting his brother. In Cornwall."

"That is a shame," said David.

He seemed so relaxed that Jean began to wonder whether he really had forgotten a pair of reading glasses. "Well, you'd better come inside, I guess."

He turned to Mrs. Walker. "Good to meet you."

"You, too."

They went inside.

"Sorry," said David, "I got here a little early."

"Early?"

"I thought you'd be back from the station. Bumping into the nosy neighbor wasn't part of the plan." He took his jacket off and hung it over a chair.

"The plan? David, this is our home. You can't just turn up here when you like."

"Listen." He took her hand and led her toward the kitchen table. "I've got something I want to talk to you about." He sat her down, took his reading glasses out of his jacket pocket and placed them on the table. "To wave at your neighbor when I leave."

"You've done this before."

"This?" He didn't smile. "This is something I have never done before."

She felt suddenly very uncomfortable. She was itching to make tea, wash up, anything. But he'd taken her right hand and placed his other hand over it, as if he were picking up a tiny animal and didn't want it to escape.

"I need to say something. I need to say it face-to-face. And I need to say it when you have time to think about it." He paused. "I'm an old man —"

"You're not old."

"Please, Jean, I've been practicing this for several weeks. Just let me get it out in one go without making a fool of myself."

She'd never seen him looking nervous before. "Sorry."

"When you get to my age you don't get second chances. OK, maybe you do get second chances. Maybe this is my second chance. But . . ." He looked down at their hands. "I love you. I want to live with you. You make me very happy. And I know it's selfish. But I want more. I want to go to bed with you at night and I want to wake up with you in the morning. Please, let me finish. This is easy for me. I live on my own. I don't have to take other people into consideration. I can do what I want. But it's different for you. I know. I respect George. I like George. But I've heard you talk about him and I've seen the two of you together and . . . You're probably going to say no. And if you did I'd understand. But if I never asked I'd regret it for the rest of my life."

She was shaking.

"Please. Just think about it. If you said yes I would do everything in my power to make it as painless and easy as possible for you . . . But if it's impossible, I'll pretend that this conversation never happened. The last thing I want to do is to frighten you away." He looked up and met her eyes again. "Tell me I haven't just messed everything up."

She put her hand on top of his hand, so that their four hands made a little stack on the table. "You know . . ."

"What?" He looked genuinely troubled.

"That is the kindest thing anyone has ever said to me."

He breathed out. "You don't have to give me an answer now."

"I'm not going to."

"Just think about it."

"I'm going to have trouble thinking about anything else." She laughed a little. "You're smiling. You haven't smiled since you came through the door."

"Relief." He squeezed her hand.

She pushed the chair back, walked round the table, sat on his lap and kissed him.

32

Katie and Graham didn't talk about Ray. They didn't even talk about the wedding. They talked about *Bridget Jones* and the petrol tanker hanging off the Westway on the TV news that morning and the truly bizarre hair of the woman in the far corner of the café.

It was exactly what Katie needed. Like putting on an old jumper. The good fit. The comforting smell.

She'd just asked the waitress for the bill, however, when she looked up and saw Ray coming into the café and walking toward them. For half a second she wondered whether there had been some kind of emergency. Then she saw the look on his face and she was livid.

Ray stopped beside the table and looked down at Graham.

"What's this about?" Katie asked.

Ray said nothing.

Graham calmly put seven pound coins on the little stainless steel dish and slid his arms into his jacket. "I'd better be going."

He stood up. "Thanks for the chat."

"I'm really sorry about this." She turned to Ray. "For God's sake, Ray. Grow up."

For one horrible moment she thought Ray was going to hit Graham. But he didn't. He just watched as Graham walked slowly to the door.

"Well, that was charming, Ray. Just charming. How old are you?"

Ray stared at her.

"Are you going to say anything, or are you just going to stand there with that moronic look on your face?"

Ray turned and walked out of the café.

The waitress returned to pick up the little stainless steel dish and Ray appeared on the pavement outside the window. He lifted a wastebin over his head, roared like a deranged vagrant then hurled it down the pavement.

33

By the time George got home he was feeling a good deal calmer.

The car was parked outside. Consequently he was surprised and a little disappointed to find the house empty. On the other hand, being in his own hallway was a comfort. The pig-shaped notepad on the phone table. The faint scent of toast. That piney stuff Jean used to clean the carpets. He put his rucksack down and walked into the kitchen.

He was putting the kettle on when he noticed that one of the chairs was lying on the floor. He bent down and set it back on its feet.

He found himself thinking briefly of ghost ships, everything precisely as it was when disaster struck, half-eaten meals, unfinished diary entries.

Then he stopped himself. It was just a chair. He filled the kettle, plugged it in, placed his hands flat on the Formica work surface, exhaled slowly and let the crazy thoughts slip away.

And this was when he heard the noise, from somewhere above his head, like someone moving heavy furniture. He assumed it was Jean at first. But it was a sound he had never heard in the house before, a rhythmic bumping, almost mechanical.

He very nearly called out. Then he decided not to. He wanted to know what was happening before he announced his presence. He might need the element of surprise.

He walked into the hallway and began climbing the stairs. When he reached the top he realized that the noise was coming from one of the bedrooms.

He walked down the landing. The door of Katie's old room was closed, but his and Jean's door was standing slightly ajar. This was where the noise was coming from.

Glancing down he saw the four large marble eggs in the fruit bowl on the chest. He took the black one and cradled it in his hand. It wasn't much of a weapon but it was extremely dense and he felt safer holding it. He tossed it a couple of times, letting it fall heavily back into the palm of his hand.

It was highly possible that he was about to confront a drug addict rifling through their drawers. He should have been scared, but the morning's activities seemed to have emptied that particular tank.

He stepped up to the door and pushed it gently open.

Two people were having sexual intercourse on the bed.

He had never seen two people having sexual intercourse before, not in real life. It did not look attractive. His first impulse was to step swiftly away to save embarrassment. Then he remembered that it was his room. And his bed.

He was about to ask the two of them loudly what in God's name they thought they were playing at when he noticed that they were old people. Then the woman made the noise he had heard from downstairs. And it wasn't just a woman. It was Jean.

The man was raping her.

He raised the fist containing the marble egg and stepped forward again, but she said, "Yes, yes, yes, yes," and he could see now that the naked man between her legs was David Symmonds.

Without warning the house tilted to one side. He stepped backward and put his hand on the door frame to prevent himself falling over.

Time passed. Precisely how much time passed it was difficult to say. Something between five seconds and two minutes.

He did not feel very well.

He pulled the door back to its original position and steadied himself on the banisters. He silently repositioned the marble egg in the bowl and waited for the house to return to its normal angle, like a big ship in a long swell.

When it had done so he made his way down the stairs, picked up his rucksack, stepped through the front door and pulled it shut behind him.

There was a sound in his head like the sound he might have heard if he were lying on a railway line and an express train were passing over him.

He began walking. Walking was good. Walking cleared the head.

A blue station wagon drove past.

This time it was the pavement which was tilting to one side. He came to a halt, bent over and was sick at the foot of a lamppost.

Maintaining his position to avoid messing his trousers, he fished an elderly tissue from his pocket and wiped his mouth. It seemed wrong, somehow, to dump the tissue in the street and he was about to put it back in his pocket when the weight of his rucksack shifted unexpectedly, he put his hand out to grab the lamppost, missed and rolled into a hedge.

He was buying a cottage pie and a fruit salad in Knutsford Services on the M6 when he was woken by the sound of a dog barking and opened his eyes to find himself staring at a large area of overcast sky fringed by leaves and twigs.

He gazed at the overcast sky for a while.

There was a strong smell of vomit.

It became slowly clear that he was lying in a hedge. There was a rucksack on his back. He remembered now. He had been sick in the street and his wife was having sexual intercourse with another man a couple of hundred yards away.

He did not want to be seen lying in a hedge.

It took him several seconds to remember precisely how one commanded one's limbs. When he did, he removed a branch from his hair, slipped his arms free of the rucksack and got gingerly to his feet.

A woman was standing on the far side of the street watching him with mild interest, as if he were an animal in a safari park. He counted to five, took a deep breath and hoisted the rucksack onto his shoulders.

He took a tentative step.

He took another, slightly less tentative step.

He could do it.

He began walking toward the main road.

34

Katie was going to have to apologize on Monday.

She was standing in the middle of Toddler One with Jacob swinging on her scarf while Ellen tried to tell her about World Awareness Day the following week. But there was so much Ray-related crap in Katie's head that she wasn't taking anything in. And the picture that kept coming to mind was one from that zombie film, Ellen's head being hacked off with a plank and the blood squirting out of her severed neck.

When they got onto the bus she tried to put Ray out of her head by asking Jacob what he'd been doing at nursery. But he was too tired to talk. He stuck a thumb into his mouth and slid a hand inside her jacket to massage the fleecy lining.

The bus driver was trying to break some kind of land speed record. It was raining and she could smell the sweat of the woman sitting to her right.

She wanted to break something. Or hurt someone.

She put her arm round Jacob and tried to absorb some of his calm.

Jesus, she could have taken Graham to the nearest hotel and shagged the living daylights out of him, for all the shit she was getting.

The bus stopped. Violently.

They got off. As they did so Katie told the bus driver he was a nobhead. Unfortunately Jacob was picking up an interesting piece of mud at the time so Katie tripped over him, which diminished the effect somewhat.

When they opened the front door Ray was already there. She could tell. The hall lights were off but there was something sullen and crackly in the air, like going into a cave and knowing the ogre was round the corner chewing on a shinbone.

They went into the kitchen. Ray was sitting at the table.

Jacob said, "We went on the bus. Mummy said a rude word. To the driver."

Ray didn't reply.

She bent down and spoke to Jacob. "You go upstairs and play for a bit, OK? Ray and I need to talk."

"I want to play down here."

"You can come down and play in a little while," said Katie. "Why don't you get your Playmobil truck out, eh?" She needed him to be helpful in the next five seconds or a gasket was going to pop.

"Don't want to," said Jacob. "It's boring."

"I'm serious. You go upstairs now. I'll be up soon. Here, let me take your coat off."

"Want my coat on. Want a monster drink."

"For Christ's sake, Jacob," yelled Katie. "Get upstairs. Now."

For a moment she thought Ray was going to do his famous manly diplomatic routine and persuade Jacob to go quietly upstairs by using mind power and she was going to go apoplectic at the sheer bloody hypocrisy of it all. But Jacob just stamped his feet and said, "I hate you," and huffed off with the hood of his coat still up, like a very angry gnome.

She turned to Ray, "We were having a cup of coffee together. He's the father of my child. I wanted a chat. And if you think I'm going to marry anyone who treats me the way you treated me today then you've got another think coming."

Ray stared at her without saying a word. Then he stood up, walked sullenly into the hallway, picked up his jacket and slammed the front door behind him.

Jesus.

She went into the kitchen, gripped the edge of the sink and hung on to it very tightly for about five minutes so she didn't scare Jacob by screaming or smashing something.

She took a swig of milk from the fridge and walked upstairs. Jacob was sitting on the side of his bed, still in his coat, hood up, looking tense, the way he did after parental arguments, waiting for that taxi to the orphanage.

She sat on the bed and pulled him onto her lap. "I'm sorry I got angry." She felt him soften as his little arms reached around her. "You get angry sometimes, don't you?"

"Yes," he said, "I get angry with you."

"But I still love you."

"I love you, too, Mummy."

They held each other for a few seconds.

"Where did Daddy Ray go?" asked Jacob.

"He went out. He doesn't like arguments very much."

"I don't like arguments."

"I know," said Katie.

She slid the hood from his head, brushed a few flakes of cradle cap from his hair, then kissed him.

"I love you, little squirrel. I love you more than anything in the whole wide world."

He squiddled free. "I want to play with my truck."

35

George took a bus into Peterborough and checked into the Cathedral Hotel.

He had never liked expensive hotels. On account of the tipping, mostly. Who did you tip, on what occasions, and how much? Rich people either knew instinctively or didn't give a damn if they offended the lower orders. Ordinary people like George got it wrong and doubtless ended up with spit in their scrambled eggs.

This time, however, he felt none of that

niggling anxiety. He was in shock. There was going to be unpleasantness later. He was in no doubt about that. But, for the moment, it was rather comforting to be in shock.

"Your credit card, sir."

George took his card back and slid it into his wallet.

"And your room key." The receptionist turned to a hovering porter. "John, can you show Mr. Hall to his room?"

"I think I can find my own way," said George.

"Third floor. Turn left."

Upstairs, he emptied his rucksack onto the bed. He hung the shirts, sweaters and trousers in the wardrobe and folded his underwear in the drawer below. He unpacked the smaller items and arranged them neatly on the table.

He relieved himself, washed his hands, dried them on a ridiculously fluffy towel then rehung it squarely on the heated rail.

He was coping really very well in the circumstances.

He removed a plastic tumbler from its sanitary covering and filled it with whiskey from a small bottle in the minibar. He removed a bag of KP peanuts and consumed both standing at the window looking across the jumbled gray roofscape.

It could not be simpler. A few days in a hotel. Then he would arrange to rent somewhere. A flat in the city, perhaps, or a small village property.

He finished the whiskey and put a further six peanuts into his mouth.

After that his life would be his own. He would be able to decide what to do, who to see, how to spend his time.

Looked at objectively, one could see it as a positive thing.

He crimped the top of the half-eaten peanuts and laid them on the table, then rinsed the tumbler, dried it using one of the complimentary tissues and replaced it beside the sink.

Twelve fifty-two.

A spot of lunch and then a constitutional.

36

When David had gone Jean wandered down to the kitchen in her dressing gown.

Everything glowed a little. The flowers in the wallpaper. The clouds piled in the sky at the end of the garden like snowdrifts.

She made a coffee and a ham sandwich

187

and took a couple of paracetamol for her knee.

And the glow began to fade a little.

Upstairs, when David was holding her, it seemed possible. Putting all of this behind her. Starting a new life. But now that he was gone it seemed preposterous. A wicked idea. Something people did on television.

She looked at the wall clock. She looked at the bills in the toast rack and the cheese plate with the ivy pattern.

She suddenly saw her whole life laid out, like pictures in a photo album. Her and George standing outside the church in Daventry, the wind blowing the leaves off the trees like orange confetti, the real celebration only starting when they left their families behind the following morning and drove to Devon in George's bottle-green Austin.

Stuck in hospital for a month after Katie was born. George coming in every day with fish-and-chips. Jamie on his red tricycle. The house in Clarendon Lane. Ice on the windows that first winter and frozen flannels you had to crack. It all seemed so solid, so normal, so good.

You looked at someone's life like that and you never saw what was missing.

She washed up her sandwich plate and

stacked it in the rack. The house seemed suddenly rather drab. The scale round the base of the taps. The cracks in the soap. The sad cactus.

Perhaps she wanted too much. Perhaps everyone wanted too much these days. The washer-dryer. The bikini figure. The feelings you had when you were twenty-one.

She headed upstairs and, as she changed into her clothes, she could feel herself slipping back into her old self.

I want to go to bed with you at night and I want to wake up with you in the morning.

David didn't understand. You could say no. But you couldn't have that kind of conversation and pretend it never happened.

She missed George.

37

George read the Peter Ackroyd book over a long lunch in a crowded and slightly substandard pizzeria on Westgate.

He had always thought of solitary diners as sad. But now that he was the solitary diner, he felt rather superior. On account of the book, mostly. Learning something while everyone else was wasting time. Like working at night.

After lunch he took a walk. The city center was not the best place for sauntering and it seemed a little absurd to hail a taxi in order to be dropped off in the middle of nowhere, so he began walking through Eastfield toward the ring road.

He would have to collect the car sometime. At night perhaps, to minimize the chance of bumping into Jean. But was it his car? The last thing he wanted was an unseemly argument. Or worse, to be accused of theft. Perhaps, all in all, it might be better to buy a new car.

He was walking in the wrong direction. He should have walked west. But walking west would have taken him toward Jean. And he did not want to be taken toward Jean, however picturesque the countryside in her vicinity.

He crossed the ring road, skirted the industrial estates and found himself striding, at last, between green fields.

For a while he felt invigorated by the cold air and the open sky and it seemed that he was getting all the benefits of a stout walk along the Helford, but without Brian's company and six hours on a train.

Then an elderly factory loomed into view on his left-hand side. Rusted chimneys. Box ducts. Stained hoppers. It was not a thing of beauty. Nor was the broken fridge dumped in the layby up ahead.

The grayness of the sky and the unrelenting flatness of the surrounding fields began to weigh on him.

He wanted to be working on the studio.

He realized that he would no longer be able to work on the studio.

He would have to embark on some other project. A smaller project. A cheaper project. Gliding came to mind unbidden and had to be rapidly chased away.

Chess. Jogging. Swimming. Charity work.

He could still draw, of course. And drawing could be done anywhere with little expense.

It occurred to him that Jean might want to leave the house. To live somewhere else. With David. In which case he would still be able to work on the studio.

And this was the cheering thought which enabled him to turn round and begin walking energetically back into town.

By the time he reached the center it was growing dark. But it did not yet seem late enough for him to return to the hotel and take dinner in the restaurant. Luckily, he was passing a cinema and realized that he had not watched a film on the big screen for a good many years.

Training Day seemed to be a sleazy police thriller. *Spy Kids* was clearly for younger viewers and *A Beautiful Mind,* he recalled, was about someone going insane and was therefore probably best avoided.

He bought a ticket for *Lord of the Rings: The Fellowship of the Ring.* The reviews had been favorable and he remembered enjoying the book at some time in the dim and distant past. He had his ticket clipped and found himself a seat in the center of the auditorium.

A teenage girl sitting with a group of other teenagers in the row in front turned to see who had sat behind them. George glanced around and realized that he was a solitary and somewhat elderly man sitting in a cinema full of young people. It was not quite the same as lingering near a playground, but it made him feel uncomfortable.

He got up, made his way back to the aisle and found a seat in the center of the front row where the picture would be larger and clearer and no one could accuse him of anything untoward.

The film was rather good.

Some forty minutes in, however, the camera lingered on the face of Christopher

Lee who was playing the evil Saruman and George noticed a small area of darkness on his cheek. He might have thought nothing of it except that he remembered reading a newspaper article about Christopher Lee having died recently. What had he died of? George couldn't remember. It was unlikely to have been skin cancer. But it could have been. And if it was skin cancer then he was watching Christopher Lee dying in front of his eyes.

Or perhaps it was Anthony Quinn he was thinking about.

He racked his brain, trying to recall the obituaries he had been reading over the past few months. Auberon Waugh, Donald Bradman, Dame Ninette de Valois, Robert Ludlum, Harry Secombe, Perry Como . . . He could see them, lined up like the warring minions in the film itself, the disposable foot soldiers in some vast war between elemental forces utterly beyond their control, every one of them being pushed unstoppably toward the edge of a mighty ravine in a cruel cosmic game of shove ha'penny, wave after wave disappearing over the edge and falling screaming into the abyss.

When he looked at the screen again he found himself watching close-up after close-up of grotesquely magnified faces, every one of them bearing some peculiar growth or region of abnormal pigmentation, each one of them a melanoma in the making.

He did not feel well.

Then the Orcs reappeared, and he could see them now for what they were, subhuman creatures from whose heads the skin had been peeled back so that they no longer had lips or nostrils, their faces composed entirely of raw, live meat. And whether it was because their appearance seemed like the effect of some malignant skin disease, or whether it was because they were skinless and therefore immune from skin cancer, or whether this made them unnaturally prone to it and, like albino children in the Sahara, they were dying of cancer from the moment they entered the world, he did not know, but it was more than he could stomach.

No longer caring what the other members of the audience thought of him, he stood up and steered a zigzag path back up the sloping aisle to the doorway, burst into the shockingly bright and empty foyer, staggered through the big swinging doors and found himself in the relative darkness of the street.

38

Jean was settling down with a glass of wine to watch the evening news when Brian called to say that George hadn't arrived. They agreed that he was probably sitting in a siding near Exeter cursing Virgin Trains. Jean put the phone down and forgot the conversation.

She dug a turkey burger out of the freezer, put the steamer on to boil and began peeling carrots.

She ate supper watching some romantic nonsense with Tom Hanks. The credits were rolling when Brian rang again to say that George had still not arrived. He said he would ring back in an hour if he hadn't heard anything.

The house seemed suddenly very empty indeed.

She opened another bottle of wine and drank a glass rather too quickly.

She was being silly. Accidents didn't happen to people like George. And if they did (like when he got that piece of glass in his eye in Norwich) he rang home immediately. If he ended up in hospital there would be a sheet of paper in his jacket pocket with Brian's phone number on it with directions to the cottage and very possibly a hand-drawn map.

Why was she even thinking about such things? Too many years spent worrying about teenage children going to parties and taking drugs. Too many years spent remembering birthdays and unplugging hot curling tongs left on bedroom carpets.

She poured another glass of wine and tried to watch more television, but she couldn't sit still. She washed up. Then she emptied the fridge. She cleaned the gunk from the little drainage outlet at the back, washed the racks in hot, soapy water, swabbed the sides down and dried them with the tea towel.

She tied the top of the rubbish bag and took it into the garden. Standing beside the bin she heard the *whack-whack-whack* of a police helicopter. She looked up and saw the black silhouette sitting at the top of a long cone of searchlight in the dirty orange sky above the town center. And she couldn't suppress the stupid idea that they were looking for George.

She went inside and locked the door and realized that if she heard nothing in the next hour she was going to have to ring the police.

39

Jamie staggered through the next few days like a zombie and lost a mansion in Dartmouth Park to John D. Wood by having self-pitying daydreams about Tony instead of sucking up to the elderly owners.

On the third day he made himself a laughingstock in the office by doing some lazy cutting and pasting and advertising a third-floor studio flat with a swimming pool on Primelocation.com.

At which point he decided to pull himself up by his bootstraps. He found a Clash CD in the glove compartment of the car, put it on loud and made a mental list of all the things about Tony which drove him up the wall (smoking in bed, lack of culinary skills, unashamed farting, the spoon-tapping thing, the ability to talk for half an hour about the complexities of installing a Velux window . . .).

Back at home, he ritually broke the CD in half and threw it in the bin.

If Tony wanted to come back he could make the first move. Jamie wasn't going to crawl. He was going to be single. And he was going to enjoy it.

40

The atmosphere in the town center was becoming noticeably more rowdy as young people began gathering for a night of heavy drinking. So George made his way down Bridge Street to the river for some peace and quiet and an explanation for the hovering helicopter.

When he reached the quayside he realized that whatever was happening was both more serious and more interesting than he had imagined. An ambulance was parked on the road and a police car was pulled up behind, its blue light revolving in the cold air.

Ordinarily he would have walked away, not wanting to be thought ghoulish. But nothing was ordinary today.

The helicopter was so low that he could feel the noise as a vibration in his head and shoulders. He stood by the little chain-link fence next to the Chinese restaurant, warming his hands in his trouser pockets. A searchlight from the base of the helicopter was moving in zigzags over the surface of the water.

Someone had fallen into the river.

A gust of wind blew a brief crackle of walkie-talkie noise toward him then whisked it away again.

In its own macabre way it was rather wonderful. Like a film. The way life rarely was. The little yellow oblong of the ambulance window, the sliding clouds, the water choppy under the downdraft from the helicopter, everything brighter and more intense than usual.

Farther down the river two paramedics in fluorescent yellow jackets were walking methodically down the towpath, shining torches into the water and poking submerged objects with a long pole. Looking for a body, presumably.

A siren whooped and was immediately turned off. A car door slammed.

He glanced down at the water in front of him.

He had never really looked at the river this closely before. Not at night. Not when the level was up. He had always assumed that he would have no problems if he fell into any water. He was a decent swimmer. Forty lengths every morning whenever they stayed in a hotel with a pool. And when John Zinewski's Fireball capsized he had been scared, briefly, but it had never occurred to him that he might drown.

This was different. It did not even look like water. It was moving too swiftly, coiling and eddying and rolling over on itself like a large animal. Upstream of the bridge it was heaped in front of the stanchions like lava negotiating a rock. Below the stanchions it vanished into a black sinkhole.

He could suddenly see how heavy water really was when it was moving en masse, like tar or treacle. It would drag you down or grind you against a concrete wall and there would be nothing you could do about it, however good a swimmer you were.

Someone had fallen in the river. He realized suddenly what this meant.

He imagined the first shock of the violent cold, then the desperate scrabble for a handhold on the bank, the stones greasy with moss, fingernails breaking, clothes becoming rapidly waterlogged.

But maybe this was what they had wanted. Maybe they had thrown themselves in. Maybe they had made no attempt to climb out, and the only struggle was the struggle to let go, to silence that hunger for light and life.

He pictured them trying to swim down into the dark. He recalled the passage on drowning in *How We Die.* He saw them trying to breathe water, their windpipe closing in spasm to protect the soft tissue of the lungs. With their windpipe closed they would have been unable to breathe. And the longer they spent not breathing the weaker they would become. They would start to swallow water and air. The water and the air would be churned into a foam and the whole grisly process would take on an unstoppable momentum. The foam would make them gag (these details had stuck really quite vividly in his memory). They would vomit. The vomit would fill their mouth and in that terminal gasp when the lack of oxygen in their bloodstream finally relaxed the spasm in their windpipe, they would have no option but to swallow it down, water, air, foam, vomit, the lot.

He had been at the riverside for five minutes. He had seen the helicopter ten minutes ago. God knows how long it had taken for the alarm to be raised, or the helicopter to arrive. Whoever it was they were almost certainly dead by now.

He felt some of the same horror he had felt on the train, but it did not overwhelm him this time. Indeed, it was balanced by a kind of solace. He could imagine doing this. The drama of it. The way you could imagine dying peacefully if only the right piece of music was playing. Like that Barber *Adagio* they always seemed to be playing on Classic FM when he was in the car.

It seemed so violent, suicide. But here, now, up close, it seemed different, more a case of doing violence to the body that kept you shackled to an unlivable life. Cutting it loose and being free.

He looked down again. Six inches beyond his toes the water heaved and slithered, now blue, now black in the revolving light from the police car.

41

Jean rang Jamie and got no answer. She rang Katie, but Katie was clearly busy and Jean didn't want to be told that she was being paranoid, so she hung up before they had an argument.

She rang the hospital. She rang Virgin. She rang Wessex Trains and GNER. She rang the police and was told to ring back in the morning if he was still missing.

She had brought this on herself. By thinking of leaving him.

She tried to sleep, but every time she began to drift off she imagined a knock at the door and a young policeman standing on the step looking serious, and she felt sick and giddy and terrified, as if someone were about to hack off one of her limbs.

She finally got to sleep at five in the morning.

42

George was not in the mood for sitting in a restaurant. So he went into a newsagent's and bought himself a tired sandwich, an orange and a slightly spotty banana.

He returned to his hotel room, made an instant coffee and ate his snack supper. Having done this, he realized that he had nothing left to do, and it was only a matter of time before his mind slipped its anchor and began to drift.

He opened the minibar and was about to remove a can of Carlsberg when he stopped. If he woke in the small hours and had to hold the forces of darkness at bay he was going to need his wits about him. He swapped the Carlsberg for a Mars bar and found the Eurosport channel on the television.

Five young men appeared, standing on a mountainous outcrop wearing helmets and rucksacks in the obligatory Day-Glo colors now worn by young people in the great outdoors.

George was working out how to increase

the volume using the remote control when one of the young men turned unexpectedly, ran toward the precipice in the background and launched himself into the void.

George lunged at the television in an attempt to grab the man.

The shot altered and George saw the man plunging down a vast rock face. One, two, three seconds. Then his parachute opened.

George's heart was still hammering. He changed channel.

On channel 45 a scientist received an electric shock, his hair stood on end and his skeleton became briefly visible. On 46 a group of pneumatically breasted women in bikinis gyrated to pop music. On 47 the camera panned over the aftermath of a terrorist outrage in a country with an incomprehensible language. On 48 there was an advert for cheap jewelry. On 49 there was a program about elephants. On 50 there was something in black-and-white with aliens.

If there were only four channels he might have been forced to watch one of them, but the sheer number was addictive and he went round the clock several times, pausing for a few seconds over each image until he became a little nauseous.

He opened the Ackroyd, but reading seemed an onerous task at this point in the evening, so he went next door and began running a bath.

He was getting undressed when he remembered that there were parts of his body he did not want to see. He turned the bathroom lights off and stripped to his vest and underpants, intending to remove these just prior to climbing into the bath.

But as he was sitting on the edge of the bed removing his socks he saw, on his left bicep, a constellation of tiny red dots. Six or seven, maybe. He rubbed at them, thinking they might be some kind of stain or clothing fluff, but they were neither. Nor were they tiny scabs. And rubbing did not remove them.

As the floor gave way over a wide, yawning shaft in the now-familiar manner he briefly consoled himself with the thought that he would not be thinking about Jean and David for a while.

The cancer was spreading. Either that or some new variety of cancer had taken root now that the first had weakened his immune system.

He had no idea how long the spots had been there. He had no memory of having ever examined his biceps in detail before. There was a voice in his head telling him that they had probably been there for years.

There was another voice in his head saying that this meant they were symptoms of a process which had already done its deadly work below the surface.

The crouching was making him uncomfortably aware of the sandwich, the banana, the orange and, in particular, the Mars bar. He did not want to throw up again, and in a hotel to boot. So, keeping his eyes closed, he forced himself to his feet and strode back and forth between the window and the door, hoping to repeat the calming effect of the afternoon's walk. By the time he had done this two hundred times the rhythm was going some way to alleviating the panic.

This, however, was the point at which he heard water lapping on a tiled floor. It took him several seconds to work out what might be making the sound of water lapping on a tile floor. When he did so he opened his eyes and sprinted toward the bathroom, tripping on the corner of the bed and smacking his head against the door frame.

He got to his feet and stumbled into the darkness of the bathroom, slowing down to prevent himself slipping again on the flooded floor. He turned the taps off, threw all the available towels onto the ground, gently removed the plug then knelt beside the toilet to get his breath back.

The pain in his head was considerable, but it brought some relief, being a more everyday kind of pain that peaked and ebbed in a predictable fashion.

He put his hand to his forehead. It was warm and wet. He really did not want to open his eyes to find out whether this was due to blood or bathwater.

He flipped the door closed behind him with his foot so that the darkness thickened.

Fuzzy pink lights hovered on the back of his eyelids like a distant goblin village.

He did not need this. Not today, of all days.

When he had got his breath back he clambered slowly to his feet and made his way into the bedroom, keeping his eyes tightly closed. He turned the lights off and put his clothes back on. Opening his eyes, he removed a selection of cans, bottles and snacks from the minibar and returned to the chair in front of the television. He opened a can of Carlsberg, found the music video channel and waited for more pneumatically breasted, gyrating women in the hope that they might stimulate a sexual fantasy gripping enough for him to forget where he was, and who he was, and what had happened to him over the last twelve hours.

He ate a Snickers.

He felt like a small child after a long, long day. He wanted someone bigger and stronger to carry him to a warm bed where he could fall into a deep sleep and be transported swiftly to the beginning of a new morning in which everything would be good and clean and simple again.

The woman singing on the television looked about twelve years old. She had no breasts to speak of and was wearing jeans and a torn T-shirt. There would have been something unsavory about watching her if she did not seem so terribly angry bouncing up to the camera every few bars to shout into the lens. She reminded George of a younger Katie in one of her more volatile moods.

The music was raucous and tuneless, but as the drink began to do its work, he realized how young people, possibly drunk themselves, or under the influence of mind-altering drugs, could find it entertaining. The driving rhythm, the simple melody. Like watching a lightning storm from the safety of one's living room. The idea that there was something even more violent happening outside one's head.

The young woman was followed by two black men chanting over an insistent disco beat. They were wearing baggy trousers and baseball caps and using some kind of impenetrable ghetto slang. On the surface they seemed a lot less angry than the young woman in the previous video, but they gave the very definite impression that, unlike the angry young woman, they would not think twice about burgling your house.

They had three female backing singers who were wearing very little clothing indeed.

He opened a small bottle of vodka.

By midnight he had drunk himself into a stupor and was wondering why he had not done so earlier. He felt very relaxed and kept forgetting where he was. Which was good.

He went to the bathroom, relieved himself, staggered back to the bedroom and collapsed onto the eiderdown. His brain felt emptier than it had done at any time in the past few months. The thought occurred to him that he could become an alcoholic. And at this precise moment it seemed a not unreasonable solution to his problems.

Then he passed into unconsciousness.

In the middle of the night he found himself making a final descent into an airport. Heathrow, possibly. Or Charles de Gaulle. He was in a plane which also happened to be a helicopter and the woman sitting next to him was carrying a lapdog, which didn't happen on real planes.

He felt oddly serene. Indeed, the plane, or helicopter, felt like the arms of that bigger, stronger person he had previously imagined carrying him to bed.

He looked out of the window into the darkness. The view was breathtakingly beautiful, the traffic far below pulsing like lava in the cracks of a great black stone.

There was music playing, either in his head or on the complimentary headphones, something lush and orchestral and infinitely calming. And the check pattern on the woven cover of the seat in front of him was rippling slightly, like little waves bouncing off a harbor wall and intersecting with themselves to create a shimmering grid of wet sunlight.

Then the plane, or helicopter, hit something.

There was an almighty bang and everything moved several yards sideways. This was followed by a second of stunned silence. Then the plane veered downward to the right and people were screaming and the air was suddenly full of food and hand luggage and the little dog was airborne, like a balloon on the end of its lead.

George tried desperately to unclip his seat belt but his fingers were mitteny and numb and refused to obey his commands and he was looking through the tiny Plexiglas porthole at burning aviation fuel and thick black smoke pouring from the underside of the right-hand wing.

Suddenly the roof of the plane was ripped back like the lid of a sardine tin and a monstrous wind began cartwheeling small children and cabin crew out into the dark.

A drinks trolley danced down the aisle and tore the head off a man sitting to George's left.

Then he wasn't in the plane anymore. He was sledging down Lunn Hill with Brian. He was helping Jean extract the heel of her shoe from a grating in Florence. He was standing up in Mrs. Amery's class trying to spell *parallel* over and over again with everyone laughing at him.

Then he was back inside the plane, and simultaneously standing in his own back garden in the middle of the night, looking up at the bedroom and wondering what was causing that odd grunting noise coming from inside, when the exterior of the house was lit up by a fierce orange light, and he turned and saw it coming in, like a tidal wave of wreckage, but airborne, lit by the gasoline meteor at its center.

The ground shook. A shopfront was spattered with gallons of hot black plastic. A reclining seat bounced down a residential street on a peacock's tail of white sparks. A human hand fell onto a roundabout in a children's playground.

The nose cone plowed into a multistory car park and George woke to find himself in sodden clothing on a large bed in a room he did not recognize with the taste of sick in his mouth, a pain like a metal spike driven into the side of his head and the knowledge that the dream had not ended, that he was still out there, falling through the night, desperate for that final impact which would put the lights out for good.

43

Jean was woken at nine by the phone ringing. She leapt out of bed, ran into the hallway and picked it up.

"Jean. It's me." It was David.

"I'm sorry, I thought it was . . ."

"Are you all right?" asked David.

So she told him about George.

"I shouldn't worry," said David. "He's managed a business. If he needs help he knows how to get it. If he hasn't got in touch it's because he doesn't want to worry you. There's bound to be some perfectly rational explanation."

She realized that she should have rung David last night.

"Besides," he said, "you're on your own in the house. After Mina and I separated I didn't sleep properly for a month. Look. Why don't you stay here on Sunday night? Let me look after you."

"Thank you. I'd like that very much."

"You don't need to thank me," said David. "For anything."

44

When Jamie got home from work the following day, his singleness seemed finally like an opportunity rather than a challenge. He put some U2 on, turned up the volume, made a mug of sobering tea and ironed his trousers.

Trousers done, he went into the bathroom and showered, pausing after washing his hair for a quick wank, picturing a tall Canadian guy with veiny biceps and tiny hairs tapering to a blond V in the small of his back who wandered into the ski-lodge bathroom, dropped his fluffy white towel, stepped into the cubicle, bent down, took Jamie's cock into his mouth and slipped a finger up his arse.

Falling asleep half an hour or so later, after reading an article about epilepsy in *The Observer,* he felt as if he were embarking on a new life.

45

Katie didn't know quite what she felt.

Ray hadn't come back. He was walking the streets, or sleeping on someone's sofa. He was going to pitch up in the morning with a bunch of flowers or a box of shitty chocolates from a petrol station and she was going to have to give in because he looked all tortured. And she couldn't find the words to say how much this was going to piss her off.

On the other hand she and Jacob did have the house to themselves.

They watched *Ivor the Engine* and read *Winnie the Witch* and found the flip cartoon Jamie had made on the corner of Jacob's drawing pad, of a dog wagging its tail and doing a poo and the poo getting up and turning into a little man and running away.

Jacob insisted they make one of their own and she managed to draw a little flip cartoon of a poorly structured dog in a high wind, three frames of which Jacob then colored in.

At bath time he kept his eyes closed for six whole seconds while she rinsed the shampoo from his hair, and they had a discussion about how big a skyscraper was, and the fact that it could still fit into the world even if the skyscraper was ten times as big because the world was truly massive and it wasn't just the earth, it was the moon and the sun and the planets and the whole of space.

They had filled pasta and pesto for tea and Jacob said, "Are we still going to Barcelona?"

And Katie said, "Of course," and it was only later, after Jacob had gone to bed, that she began to wonder. Was it true, what she'd said to Ray? Would she refuse to marry someone who treated her like that?

She'd lose the house. Jacob would lose another father. They'd have to move into some shabby little flat. Beans on white bread. Cutting work every time Jacob was ill. Arguing with Aidan to hang on to a job she hated. No car. No holidays.

But if she went ahead? Would they bicker

like her parents and drift apart? Would she end up having some halfhearted little affair with the first bloke who made an offer?

And it wasn't so much the thought of living like that which depressed her. A few years of single-parenting in London and you could put up with pretty much anything. It was the compromise which hurt, the prospect of chucking away all the principles she once had. Still had. The thought of listening to Mum's smug lecturettes about young women wanting it all, and no longer being able to answer back.

It was going to have to be a bloody big box of chocolates.

46

The hangover put George's other problems out of his mind almost as effectively as the alcohol itself had done.

He had occasionally drunk to excess in his early twenties, but he could remember nothing quite like this. There seemed to be grains of genuine sand between his eyeballs and the surrounding socket. He took two ibuprofen, threw up and realized that he would have to wait for the pain to recede of its own accord.

He would have preferred not to shower, but he had wet himself while sleeping. He had also cut his head on the door frame and when he caught sight of his face in the mirror he looked not unlike the tramp he had seen on the station platform the day before.

He closed the curtains, turned the knob to hot, shut his eyes, removed his clothing, maneuvered himself into the jet of water, massaged some shampoo gingerly into his scalp then turned slowly like a kebab to rinse himself.

Only when he got out of the shower did he remember the sodden state of the towels. He fumbled his way blindly to the bedroom, extracted his own from the rucksack, dried himself gently then carefully inserted his body into a clean set of clothes.

A part of him wanted to sit on the edge of the bed for a couple of hours without moving. But he needed fresh air, and he needed to get away from this mess.

He put the wet towels into the bath and swilled his mouth with a pea of toothpaste and a little cold water.

He packed the rucksack, then discovered that bending over was beyond him and was forced to lie on the carpet to tie his laces.

He considered remaking the bed, but hiding the stains seemed worse than leaving them visible. He did, however, take a moist lump of toilet paper to the blood on the wall outside the bathroom.

He would never be able to come to this hotel again.

He put on his jacket, checked that he hadn't lost his wallet, then sat for a few minutes gathering his strength before hoisting his rucksack onto his back. It seemed to contain actual bricks and halfway to the lift he had to lean against the wall of the corridor and wait for the blood to return to his head.

In the foyer he was hailed by the man behind the desk with a cheery "Morning, Mr. Hall." He kept walking. They had his credit card details. He did not want to tell them what he had done to the room, or avoid telling them what he had done to the room. He did not want to stand in front of the desk swaying a little with a mysterious head wound.

A porter opened the door, he stepped into the noise and glare of the morning and began walking.

The air seemed to be filled with smells designed specifically to test his stomach to its very limit: car fumes, cooked breakfasts, cigarette smoke, bleach . . . He breathed through his mouth.

He was going home. He needed to talk to someone. And Jean was the only person he could talk to. As for the scene in the bedroom, they could deal with that later.

Indeed, at this point in time, dealing with the scene in the bedroom seemed less of a problem than taking a bus. The five-minute walk to the station felt like crossing the Alps and when his bus arrived he was packed into a confined space with thirty unwashed people and shaken vigorously for twenty-five minutes.

Having disembarked in the village he sat for a few minutes on the bench by the bus stop to gather his wits and let the grinding throb in his head die down a little.

What was he going to say? Under normal circumstances he would never have confessed to Jean that he was going insane. But under normal circumstances he would not be going insane. Hopefully his bedraggled state would engender sympathy without his having to explain too much.

He got to his feet, lifted his rucksack, took a deep breath and walked toward the house.

When he stepped through the front door she was standing in the kitchen.

"George."

He deposited his rucksack by the stairs and waited for her to come into the hall.

He spoke very quietly in order to keep the pain to a minimum. "I think I may be going mad."

"Where have you been?" Jean said this quite loudly. Or maybe it just sounded loud. "We've been worried sick."

"I stayed in a hotel," said George.

"A hotel?" said Jean. "But you look as if —"

"I was feeling . . . Well, as I was saying I think I might be —"

"What's that on your head?" asked Jean.

"Where?"

"There."

"Oh, that."

"Yes, that," said Jean.

"I fell over and hit a door frame," explained George.

"A door frame?"

"In the hotel."

Jean asked whether he had been drinking.

"Yes. But not when I banged my head. I'm sorry. Could you talk a little more quietly?"

"Why on earth were you staying in a hotel?" said Jean.

It was not meant to be happening like this. He was the one who was graciously putting certain matters to one side. He was the one who deserved the benefit of the doubt.

His head hurt so much.

"Why didn't you go to Cornwall?" said Jean. "Brian was ringing, wondering what had happened."

"I need to sit down." He made his way to the kitchen and found a chair which screeched horribly on the tiles. He sat and cradled his forehead.

Jean followed him. "Why didn't you call me, George?"

"You were . . ." He nearly said it. Out of spite, mostly. Luckily he did not have the words. The sexual act was like going to the lavatory. It was not something one talked about, least of all in one's own kitchen at nine-thirty in the morning.

And as he struggled and failed to find the words, the image came to mind again, that man's scrotum, her sagging thighs, his buttocks, the warm air, the grunting. And he felt something like a blow to his belly, a deep, deep wrongness, partly fear, partly disgust, partly something way beyond either of these things, as disturbing as the sensation he might have felt if he looked out of the window and saw that the house was surrounded by ocean.

He did not want to find the words. If he described it to another human being he would never be free of the picture. And with this realization came a kind of release.

There was no need to describe it to another human being. He could forget about it. He could put it to the back of his mind. If it lay undisturbed for long enough it would fade and lose its power.

"George, what were you doing in a hotel?"

She was angry with him. She had been angry with him before. This was his old life. It felt comforting. It was something he could deal with.

"I'm frightened of dying." There. He had said it.

"That's absurd."

"I know it's absurd, but it's true." He felt a glow of a kind he never expected to feel, this morning of all mornings. He was talking to Jean more frankly than he had ever done.

"Why?" she asked. "You're not dying." She paused. "Are you?"

She was scared. Well, perhaps it was good for her to feel a little scared. He began to untuck his shirt, just as he had done in Dr. Barghoutian's consulting room.

"George . . . ?" She steadied herself with a hand on the back of the chair.

He lifted his vest and lowered the waistband of his trousers.

"What's that?" she asked.

"Eczema."

"I don't understand, George."

"I think it's cancer."

"But it's not cancer."

"Dr. Barghoutian said it was eczema."

"So why are you worried about it?"

"And there are these tiny red spots on my arm."

The phone rang. Neither of them moved for a couple of seconds. Then Jean shot across the room at a surprising speed, saying, "Don't worry. I'll get it," though George had shown no intention of moving anywhere.

She picked the phone up. "Hello . . . Yes. Hello . . . I can't talk right now . . . No, nothing's the matter . . . He's here now . . . Yes. I'll call you later." She put the phone down. "That was . . . Jamie. I rang him last night. When I was wondering where you were."

"Have you got any of those codeine tablets left?" George asked.

"I think so."

"I have a very bad hangover."

"George?"

"What?" he asked.

"Do you think it might be a good idea if you went to bed? See if you feel any better in a couple of hours."

223

"Yes. Yes, that might be a very good idea."

"Let's get you upstairs," said Jean.

"And the codeine. I think I really do need the codeine."

"I'll dig some out."

"And maybe not the bed. Maybe I'll just lie on the sofa."

47

Ray didn't turn up the following morning. Or the following evening. Katie was too cross to ring the office. Ray was the one who needed to make a peace offering.

But when he didn't turn up the day after that she gave in and called, if only to put her mind at rest. He was in a meeting. She called an hour later. He was out of the office. She was asked if she wanted to leave a message but the things she wanted to say weren't things she wanted to share with a secretary. She rang a third time, he was away from his desk and she began to wonder whether he'd left instructions that he didn't want to talk to her. She didn't ring again.

Besides, she was enjoying having the house to herself and she was in no mood to give it up before she had to.

On Thursday evening she and Jacob laid

out the Brio train set on the living-room carpet. The bridge, the tunnel, the freight crane, the chunky track with its interlocking jigsaw ends. Jacob arranged a crocodile of trucks behind Thomas then crashed them into a landslide of Lego. Katie arranged the trees and the station and made a mountain backdrop from Jacob's duvet.

She'd wanted a girl. It seemed ridiculous now. The idea that it mattered. Besides, she couldn't quite picture herself kneeling on the carpet mustering enthusiasm for Barbie's visit to the hair salon.

"Bash-crash. It chops the driver's . . . it chops . . . it chops the driver's arm off," said Jacob. "Nee-naw, nee-naw, nee-naw . . ."

She knew nothing about petrol engines or outer space (Jacob wanted to be a racing driver when he grew up, preferably on Pluto), but in twelve years' time she preferred the prospect of body odor and Death Metal to shopping expeditions and eating disorders.

After Jacob had gone to bed she made herself a gin and tonic and sort of looked at the latest Margaret Atwood without actually reading it.

They took up so much space. That was the problem with men. It wasn't just the leg sprawl and the clumping down stairs. It was the constant demand for attention. Sit in a room with another woman and you could think. Men had that little flashing light on top of their heads. *Hello. It's me. I'm still here.*

What if Ray never came back?

She seemed to be standing to one side, watching her life pan out. As if it was happening to someone else.

Perhaps it was age. At twenty life was like wrestling an octopus. Every moment mattered. At thirty it was a walk in the country. Most of the time your mind was somewhere else. By the time you got to seventy it was probably like watching snooker on the telly.

Friday came and went with no sign of Ray.

Jacob said he wanted to go and see Granny, and it seemed as good a plan as any. She could put her feet up while Mum did a bit of child care. Dad and Jacob could do some man stuff at the aerodrome. Mum would ask about Ray but in Katie's experience she never liked to spend long on the subject.

She rang home and Mum seemed unnaturally excited by the prospect. "Besides, we've got to make some decisions about the menu and the seating plan. We've only got six weeks to go."

Katie's heart sank.

At least Jacob would be happy.

48

Jean rang Brian. She said George hadn't been feeling well and had come home. He asked whether it was serious. She said she thought not. And he was so relieved he didn't ask any questions, for which she was very grateful indeed.

He'd been fast asleep on the sofa for the last five hours.

Was it serious? She had absolutely no idea what to think.

He'd turned up at nine thirty that morning with a gash on his head looking like he'd slept in a ditch.

She assumed something terrible had happened to him. But the only explanation he offered was that he'd stayed in a hotel. She asked why he hadn't rung to stop her worrying but he wouldn't answer. He'd obviously been drinking. She could smell the alcohol on him. She got quite cross at this point.

Then he said that he was dying and she realized he wasn't well.

He explained that he had cancer. Except

it wasn't cancer. It was eczema. He insisted on showing her a rash on his hip. She actually started to wonder whether he was going mad.

She wanted to ring the doctor, but he was adamant that she do nothing of the kind. He explained that he had already been to the doctor. There was nothing more the doctor could say.

She rang Ottakar's and the school office and said she'd be off work for a few days.

She rang David from the phone upstairs. He listened to the whole story and said, "Maybe it's not so strange. Don't you think about dying sometimes? Those nights when you wake up at three and can't get back to sleep? And retiring does funny things to you. All that time on your hands . . ."

George began to stir round about teatime. She made him some cocoa and some toast and he seemed a little more human. She tried to get him to talk, but he made no more sense than he'd done first thing that morning. She could see that he found it painful discussing the subject so after a while she let it drop.

She told him to stay where he was and got him his favorite books and music. He seemed tired, mostly. An hour or so later she made their supper and brought it through so they could eat it together on the coffee table in front of the television. He ate everything and asked for another codeine and they watched a David Attenborough program about monkeys.

Her panic began to recede.

It was like turning the clock back thirty years. Jamie with his glandular fever. Katie with her broken ankle. Tomato soup and toast soldiers. Watching *Crown Court* together. *Doctor Dolittle* and *The Swiss Family Robinson.*

The next day George announced that he was going to retire to the bedroom. He took the television upstairs and installed himself in bed, and to tell the truth Jean was a bit sad.

She popped in every half an hour or so to check that he was OK, but he seemed quite self-sufficient. Which was one of the things that she'd always admired about him. He never moaned about being ill. Never thought he should be the center of attention. Just retreated to his basket, like a poorly dog, and curled up until he was ready to chase sticks again.

By the evening he told her that he would be fine on his own so she went into town the following morning and sold books for four hours and met Ursula for lunch. She started telling her what was happening, then realized that she couldn't really explain without talking about the cancer and the eczema and the fear of dying and the alcohol and cut on the head, and she didn't want to make him seem crazy, so she said he'd canceled the Cornwall trip on account of a nasty tummy bug, and Ursula told her all about the joys of staying in Dublin with your daughter and her four children while her builder husband was ripping out the bathroom.

49

Obviously, it was a surprise to find that one was insane. But what surprised George most was how painful it was.

It had never occurred to him before. His uncle, those unwashed people who shouted at buses, Alex Bamford that Christmas . . . *Crazy* was the word he had always used. As in *crazy paving,* or *crazy golf.* Everything jumbled and out of order and rather amusing.

It seemed less amusing now. Indeed, when he thought about his uncle stuck in St. Edward's for ten years without a visit from his family, or that disheveled man who tap-danced for small change in Church Street, he could feel the corners of his eyes pricking.

If he were given the choice he would rather someone had broken his leg. You did not have to explain what was wrong with a broken leg. Nor were you expected to mend it by force of will.

The terror came and went in waves. When a wave washed over him he felt much as he did several years ago when he watched a small boy run into the road outside Jacksons, narrowly missing the hood of a braking car.

Between the waves he gathered his strength for the next one and tried desperately not to think about it in case this brought it on more quickly.

What he felt mostly was a relentless, grinding dread which rumbled and thundered and made the world dark, like those spaceships in science-fiction films whose battle-scorched fuselages slid onto the screen and kept on sliding onto the screen because they were, in fact, several thousand times larger than you expected when all you could see was the nose cone.

The idea of genuinely having cancer was beginning to seem almost a relief, the idea of going into hospital, having tubes put into his arm, being told what to do by doctors and nurses, no longer having to grapple with the problem of getting through the next five minutes.

He had given up trying to talk to Jean. She tried hard, but he seemed unable to make her understand.

It was not her fault. If someone had come to him with similar problems a year ago, he would have reacted in the same way.

Part of the problem was that Jean did not get depressed. She worried. She got angry. She got sad. And she felt all of these things more strongly than he ever did (when he cleared out the cellar, for example, and put that old birdhouse on the bonfire she actually punched him). But they always blew over in a day or two.

She kept him company, however, cooked his meals and washed his clothes and he was very thankful for all of these things.

He was also thankful for the codeine. The box was nearly full. Once he had shaken off the horror of waking up he could fix his mind on those two tablets at lunchtime knowing they would wrap him in a soft haze till he could open a bottle of wine at supper.

He had tried to spend that first night on the sofa, but it was uncomfortable and Jean was of the opinion that crazy behavior encouraged crazy ideas. So he relocated upstairs. In the event it was not as bad as he had expected, being in the bed where he had seen that thing happening. When one thought about it, bad things had happened pretty much everywhere: murders, rapes, fatal accidents. He knew, for example, that an elderly lady had burnt to death in the Farmers' house in 1952, but it was not something you could sense when you went round there for drinks.

He soon realized that being upstairs had its benefits. One did not have to answer the door if one was in bed, there were no unexpected visitors and one could close the curtains without starting an argument. So he moved the television and the video player into the bedroom and battened down the hatches.

After a few days he girded his loins and ventured to the shop to rent some videos.

And if he woke at night and the Orcs with the boiled, skinless faces were waiting in their silent hundreds in the moonlit gardens he found that he could gain some temporary respite by going into the bathroom, wedging himself between the toilet and the bath and singing very quietly to himself the songs he remembered singing when he was a small child.

50

Katie and Jacob staggered in through the door and dumped their bags.

Mum kissed them both and said, "Your father's in bed. Bit under the weather."

"What's wrong?"

"I'm not sure, to be honest. I think it might be all in the mind." She winced slightly when she said the words "all in the mind," as if she had just opened a tub of something that had gone off.

"So, he's not actually ill?" asked Katie.

"He has eczema."

"Can I watch my *Bob the Builder* video?" asked Jacob.

"I'm sorry but Grandpa's got the video player upstairs," said Mum.

"You don't have to go to bed because you've got eczema," said Katie. She had that feeling she often got with her parents, that something was being kept from her, a feeling which only got more sinister as they aged.

"Can I watch my video with Grandpa?" asked Jacob, tugging at Katie's trousers.

"Let me finish talking to Granny," said Katie.

"He says he's worried about dying," said Mum, in a stage whisper.

"But I want to watch it now," said Jacob.

"Two minutes," said Katie.

"You know what he's like," said Mum. "I have no idea what is going through that head of his."

"Is Grandpa dying?" asked Jacob.

"Grandpa's absolutely fine," said Mum.

"Except he's not," replied Katie.

"I want a biscuit," said Jacob.

"Well, it just so happens that I bought some Jaffa Cakes this morning," said Mum to Jacob. "Isn't that a coincidence."

"Mum, you're not listening to me," said Katie.

"Can I have two?" said Jacob.

"You're very cheeky this morning," said Mum.

"Please can I have two biscuits?" said Jacob turning to Katie.

"Mum . . ." Katie caught herself. She didn't want a row before she'd got her coat off. She wasn't even sure precisely what she was angry about. "Look. You take Jacob off to the kitchen. Give him a biscuit. One biscuit. I'll go up and talk to Dad."

"OK," said Mum in a cheery sing-song.

"Do you want some orange juicy with that biscuit?"

"We went on a train," said Jacob.

"Did you, now?" said Mum. "What kind of train was it?"

"It was a monster train."

"Now that sounds like a very interesting kind of train. Do you mean it looked like a monster, or do you mean there were monsters on it?"

The two of them disappeared into the kitchen and Katie began walking upstairs.

It felt wrong, going to Dad's bedside. Dad didn't do illness. His own or other people's. He did soldiering on and taking one's mind off things. Dad having a breakdown was in the same category as Dad taking up hairdressing.

She knocked and went in.

He was lying in the center of the bed with the duvet pulled to his chin, like a frightened old lady in a fairy tale. He turned the television off almost immediately, but from what she could see he appeared to be watching . . . Was it really *Lethal Weapon?*

"Hullo, young lady." He seemed smaller than she remembered. The pajamas didn't help.

"Mum said you weren't feeling very well." She couldn't work out where to put herself.

Sitting on the bed was too intimate, standing was too medical and using the armchair would mean touching his discarded vest.

"Not very. No."

They were silent for a few moments, both of them staring into the slatey green oblong of the TV screen with its skewed little bar of reflected window.

"Do you want to talk about it?" She couldn't believe she was saying these words to Dad.

"Not really."

She had never heard him sound so straightforward. She got the eerie sense that they were doing actual communication for the first time. It was like finding a new door in the living-room wall. It was not entirely pleasant.

"I'm afraid your mother doesn't really understand," said Dad.

Katie had no idea what to say.

"Not really her kind of thing."

Christ. Parents were meant to sort this stuff out for themselves.

She didn't want this on her plate. Not now. But he needed someone to talk to, and Mum was clearly not keen on the job. "What isn't her kind of thing?"

He took a long, quiet breath. "I'm frightened." He stared at the television.

"What of?"

"Of dying . . . I'm frightened of dying."

"Is there something you're not telling Mum?" She could see a stack of videos beside the bed. *Volcano, Independence Day, Godzilla, Conspiracy Theory* . . .

"I think . . ." He paused and pursed his lips. "I think I have cancer."

She felt giddy and a little faint. "Do you?"

"Dr. Barghoutian says it's eczema."

"And you don't believe him."

"No," he said. "Yes." He thought hard. "No. Not really."

"Perhaps you should ask to see a specialist."

Dad frowned. "I couldn't do that."

She nearly said, *Let me have a look,* but the idea was gross in too many ways. "Is this really about cancer? Or is it about something else?"

Dad scrubbed ineffectually at a little jam stain on the duvet. "I think I might be going insane."

Downstairs Jacob was squealing as Mum chased him round the kitchen.

"Perhaps you should talk to someone."

"Your mother thinks I'm being silly. Which I am of course."

"Some kind of counselor," said Katie.

Dad looked blank.

"I'm sure Dr. Barghoutian could refer you."

Dad continued to look blank. She pictured him sitting in a little room with a box of tissues on the table and some bushy-tailed young man in a cardigan and she could see his point. But she didn't want to be the only person on the receiving end of this. "You need help."

There was a bang from the kitchen. Then a wail. Dad didn't react to either noise.

Katie said, "I've got to go."

He didn't react to this either. He said very quietly, "I've wasted my life."

She said, "You haven't wasted your life," in a voice she normally reserved for Jacob.

"Your mother doesn't love me. I spent thirty years doing a job that meant nothing to me. And now . . ." He was crying. "It hurts so much."

"Dad, please."

"There are these little red spots on my arm," said Dad.

"What?"

"I can't even bring myself to look at them."

"Dad, listen." She put her hands to the side of her head to help her concentrate. "You're anxious. You're depressed. You're . . . whatever. It's got nothing to do with

Mum. It's got nothing to do with your job. It's happening inside your head."

"I'm sorry," said Dad. "I shouldn't have said anything."

"Christ, Dad. You've got a nice house. You've got money. You've got a car. You've got someone to look after you . . ." She was angry. It was the anger she'd been saving for Ray. But she couldn't really do anything about it, not now the lid was off. "You haven't wasted your life. That's bollocks."

She hadn't said *bollocks* to Dad for ten years. She needed to get out of the room before things really started to go downhill.

"Sometimes I can't breathe." He made no attempt to wipe the tears from his face. "I start sweating, and I know something dreadful is about to happen, but I have no idea what it is."

Then she remembered. That lunchtime. Him running out and sitting on the patio.

Downstairs Jacob had stopped wailing.

"It's called a panic attack," she said. "Everyone has them. OK, maybe not everyone. But lots of people. You're not strange. Or special. Or different." She was slightly alarmed by the tone of her own voice. "There are drugs. There are ways of sorting these things out. You have to go and see someone. This is not just about you. You have to do something. You have to stop being selfish."

She seemed to have veered off course somewhere in the middle there.

He said, "Maybe you're right."

"There's no maybe about it." She waited for her pulse to slow a little. "I'll talk to Mum. I'll get her to sort something out."

"Right."

It was the patio all over again. It frightened her, the way he soaked it all up and didn't answer back. It made her think of those old men shuffling round hospitals with five o'clock shadow and bags of urine on wheelie stands. She said, "I'm going downstairs now."

"OK."

For a brief moment she thought about hugging him. But they'd done enough new things for one morning. "Can I get you a coffee?"

"It's all right. I've got a flask up here."

She said, "Don't do anything I wouldn't do," in a wholly inappropriate comedy Scots accent, out of relief mostly. Then she closed the door behind her.

When she reached the kitchen, Jacob was sitting on Mum's knee, being fed chocolate ice cream from the tub. As an anesthetic, no doubt. On top of the chocolate biscuit, presumably.

Mum looked up and said, in a jaunty voice, "So, how did your father seem to you?"

The ability of old people to utterly fail to communicate with one another never failed to astonish her. "He needs to see someone."

"Try telling that to him."

"I did," said Katie.

"I got a bump," said Jacob.

She bent down and cuddled him. There was ice cream in his eyebrows.

"Well, as you doubtless found out," said Mum, "trying to get your father to do anything is pointless."

Jacob wriggled free and began trawling through his Batman rucksack.

"Don't talk about it," said Katie, "just do it. Talk to Dr. Barghoutian. Drive Dad to the surgery. Get Dr. Barghoutian to come here. Whatever."

She could see Mum bridling. She could also see Jacob marching toward the hallway with *A Christmas to Remember* in his sticky paws. "Where are you going, monkey nuts?"

"I'm going to watch *Bob the Builder* with Grandpa."

"I'm not sure that's a good idea."

Jacob looked crestfallen.

Perhaps she should let him go. Dad was

depressed. He wasn't eating lightbulbs. The distraction might even be welcome. "Go on then. But be nice to him. He's feeling very tired."

"OK," said Jacob.

"And Jacob?"

"What?"

"Don't ask him if he's dying."

"Why not?" asked Jacob.

"It's rude."

"OK." Jacob toddled off.

She waited, then turned to Mum. "I'm serious. About Dad." She waited for her to say *Look here, young lady . . .* but she didn't. "He's suffering from depression."

"I realized that," said Mum, tartly.

"I'm just saying . . ." Katie paused and lowered her voice. She needed to win this argument. "Please. Take him to the doctor. Or get the doctor to come here. Or go to the surgery yourself. This is not going to go away on its own. We've got the wedding coming up and . . ."

Mum sighed and shook her head. "You're right. We don't want him making a fool of himself in front of everyone, do we."

51

Mel Gibson was hanging from a chain in a rudimentary shower and an Oriental man was torturing him with a pair of jump leads.

George was so engrossed that when he heard a knock on the door his first thought was that Katie had arranged an immediate visit from Dr. Barghoutian.

When the door opened, however, it was Jacob.

"I want to watch my video," said Jacob.

George fumbled for the remote. "And what's your video?"

Mel Gibson screamed, then vanished.

"Bob the Builder," said Jacob.

"Right." George suddenly remembered the last time Jacob had joined him in this room. "Is your daddy with you?"

"Which daddy?" asked Jacob.

George felt a little dizzy. "Is Graham here?" It seemed to be a day on which anything was possible.

"No. And Daddy Ray isn't here. He went . . . He went away and he didn't come back."

"Right," said George. He wondered what Jacob meant. It was probably best not to ask. "This video . . ."

"Can I watch it?"

"Yes. You can watch it," said George.

Jacob ejected *Lethal Weapon,* inserted *Bob the Builder* and rewound it with the casual skill of a technician at mission control.

Which was how young people took over the world. All that fiddling with new technology. You woke up one day and realized your own skills were laughable. Woodwork. Mental arithmetic.

Jacob fast-forwarded through the adverts, stopped the tape and climbed onto the bed next to George. He smelt better this time, biscuity and sweet.

It occurred to George that Jacob wasn't going to talk about panic attacks, or suggest counseling. And this was a reassuring thought.

Did they ever go insane, children? Properly insane, not just handicapped like the Henderson girl? He was unsure. Perhaps there was not enough brain to malfunction till they reached university.

Jacob was looking at him. "You have to press PLAY."

"Sorry." George pressed PLAY.

Cheery music began and the titles came up over a starlit model snowscape. Two plastic reindeer trotted off into the pine trees and a toy man roared into the shot on his motorized skidoo.

The motorized skidoo had a face.

Jacob stuck his thumb in his mouth and held on to George's index finger with his free hand.

Tom, the aforesaid toy man, went into his polar field station and picked up the ringing phone. The screen split to show his brother, Bob, at the other end of the line, calling from a builder's yard in England.

A steamroller, a digger and a crane were standing outside the office.

The steamroller, the digger and the crane had faces, too.

George cast his mind back to Dick Barton and the Goons, to Lord Snooty and Biffo the Bear. Over the intervening years everything seemed to have got louder and brighter and faster and simpler. In another fifty years children would have the attention spans of sparrows and no imagination whatsoever.

Bob was dancing round the builder's yard, singing, "Tom's coming for Christmas! Tom's coming for Christmas . . . !"

Maybe George was fooling himself. Maybe old people always fooled themselves, pretending that the world was going to hell in a handcart because it was easier than admitting they were being left behind, that the future was pulling away from the beach, and they were standing on their little island bidding it good riddance, knowing in their hearts that there was nothing left for them to do but sit around on the shingle waiting for the big diseases to come out of the undergrowth.

George concentrated on the screen.

Lethal Weapon was rather trite, too, when one thought about it.

Bob was helping prepare the town square for the annual Christmas Eve concert by Lenny and the Lasers.

Jacob hotched a little closer and took hold of George's hand.

While Bob worked round the clock to make the concert go smoothly, Tom stopped to rescue a reindeer from a crevasse en route to the ferry and missed the boat. The Christmas reunion was off.

Bob was very sad.

Unaccountably, George was rather sad, too. Especially during the childhood flashback in which Tom got a toy elephant for Christmas and broke it and wept, and Bob mended it for him.

A little while later Lenny (of the Lasers) heard about Bob's plight and flew to the North Pole in his private jet to bring Tom back in time for Christmas Eve, and when

Tom and Bob were reunited at the concert there were actual tears running down George's face.

"Are you sad, Grandpa?" asked Jacob.

"Yes," said George. "Yes, I am."

"Is that because you're dying?" asked Jacob.

"Yes," said George. "Yes, it is." He put his arm round Jacob and pulled him close.

After a couple of minutes Jacob squeezed free.

"I need a poo." He got off the bed and left the room.

The tape ended and the screen was filled with white noise.

52

Katie pulled up a chair.

"We're going to hire the long marquee." Mum put her glasses on and opened the catalog. "It'll fit. Just. But the pegs will have to go in the flower border. Now . . ." She extracted an A4 sheet showing the floor plan of the tent. "For the top table we can go round or oblong. It's eight per table and a maximum of twelve tables which makes —"

"Ninety-six," said Katie.

"— including the top table. Did you bring

your list of guests?"

Katie hadn't.

"Honestly, Katie, I can't do this all by myself."

"It's been a little hectic recently."

She should have told Mum about Ray. But she couldn't stand the idea of Mum being smug about it. Handling Dad was difficult enough. And by the time they were discussing rich chocolate mousse versus tiramisu it was too late.

She wrote a guest list off the top of her head. If she missed an aunt, Ray could bloody well explain himself. Assuming the wedding happened. Oh well, she'd deal with that eventuality another time.

"I told you Jamie might be bringing someone, didn't I," said Mum.

"His name's Tony, Mum."

"Sorry. I was just . . . You know, I didn't want to jump to any conclusions."

"They've been together for longer than me and Ray."

"And you've met him," said Mum.

"You mean, will Dad be able to cope?"

"I mean, is he nice?"

"I've only met him once."

"And . . . ?" asked Mum.

"Well, if the leather shorts and the blond fun wig are anything to go by . . ."

"You are teasing me, aren't you."

"I am."

Mum looked suddenly serious. "I just want you to be happy. Both of you. You're still my children."

Katie took Mum's hand. "Jamie is sensible. He'll probably choose a better man than either of us."

Mum looked even more serious and Katie wondered whether she'd overstepped the mark a little.

"You are happy with Ray, aren't you?" asked Mum.

"Yes, Mum, I'm happy with Ray."

"Good." Her mother readjusted her glasses. "Now. Flowers."

After an hour or so, they heard footsteps and Katie turned round to see Jacob grinning in the doorway, his trousers and nappy dragging from one leg.

"I did a poo. I did it . . . I did it in the toilet. All on my own."

Katie scanned the perfect beige carpet for brown chunks. "Well done you." She got up and walked over. "But you really should have given me a shout first."

"Grandpa said he didn't want to wipe my bottom."

After she'd put Jacob to bed Katie came downstairs to find Mum pouring two glasses of wine and saying, "There's something I need to talk to you about."

Katie took the wine, hoped it was something trivial and the pair of them went through to the living room.

"I know you've got a lot to think about at the moment and I know I shouldn't be saying this to you." Mum sat down and took an uncharacteristically large gulp of wine. "But you're the only person who really understands."

"OK . . ." said Katie, gingerly.

"Over the last six months . . ." Mum put her hands together as if she was about to pray. "Over the last six months I've been seeing someone."

Mum said the phrase "seeing someone" very carefully, as if it were French.

"I know," said Katie, who really, really, really did not want to be talking about this.

"No, I don't think you do," said Mum, "I mean . . . I've been seeing another man." She paused and said, "A man who is not your father," just to make it absolutely clear.

"I know," Katie said again. "It's David Symmonds, isn't it. The chap who used to work with Dad."

"How on earth did you . . . ?" Mum gripped the arm of the sofa.

It was briefly rather fun, having Mum on

the back foot. And then it wasn't, because her mother looked terrified.

"Well . . ." Katie cast her mind back. "You said you'd met him in the shop. He's separated from his wife. He's an attractive man. For his age. You said you'd met him again. You started buying expensive clothes. And you were . . . you were holding yourself in a different way. It seemed pretty clear to me that you were . . ." She let the sentence dangle.

Mum was still gripping the arm of the sofa. "Do you think your father knows?"

"Has he said anything?"

"No."

"Then I think you're safe," said Katie.

"But if you noticed . . ."

"Girl radar," said Katie.

Girl radar? It sounded wrong as soon as it came out of her mouth. But Mum was relaxing visibly.

"It's OK, Mum," said Katie, "I'm not going to give you a hard time."

Was it OK? Katie wasn't sure. It looked a bit different now it was out in the open. So long as Mum didn't want sex tips.

"Except it's not OK," said Mum, plowing doggedly on.

For a short, fuddled moment Katie wondered if Mum was pregnant. "Why not?"

She examined the varnish on her nails. "David has asked me to leave your father."

"Ah." Katie stared into the wobbly orange light coming from the fake coal fire and remembered Jamie, years ago, taking it apart to examine the little metal propellers turned by the hot air coming off the bulbs.

"Actually," said Mum, "that's unfair to David. He said he wants me to come and live with him. But he understands that I might not want to. That it might not be possible."

Now Katie was on the back foot.

"He doesn't want to rush me. And he's happy for things to stay as they are. He just wants . . . He wants to spend more time with me. And I want to spend more time with him. But it's very, very difficult. As you can imagine."

God, he smoked those weird ladies' cigars, didn't he. "What about Dad?"

"Well, yes, there is that, too," said Mum.

"He's in the middle of having a nervous breakdown."

"He's certainly not very well."

"He can't leave the bedroom."

"Actually, he does come down occasionally," said Mum. "To make tea and go to the video shop."

Katie said, quietly but firmly, "You can't

leave Dad. Not at the moment. Not while he's like this."

Katie had never stood up for Dad before. She felt oddly noble and grown up, putting her prejudices to one side.

"I'm not planning to leave your father," said Mum. "I just wanted . . . I just wanted to tell you." She leaned over and took Katie's hand for a few moments. "Thank you. I feel better for having got it off my chest."

They sat in silence. The orange light flickered under the plastic coals and Katie heard a distant burst of Hollywood gunfire from upstairs.

Mum eased herself off the sofa. "I'd better go and see if he needs anything."

Katie sat for several minutes, staring at the foxhunting print on the far wall. The storm over the hill. The lopsided farm dog. The fallen rider who, she could see now, was about to be crushed by the hooves of the horses jumping the hedge behind him.

She'd seen it every day for eighteen years and never really looked at it.

She poured herself another glass of wine.

The frightening thing was how alike they were. She and Mum. Putting the thing with David to one side for the moment. Putting the thing with Ray to one side for the moment.

Mum was in love.

She replayed the words in her head and knew that she should feel moved. But what did she feel? Only sadness for that fallen rider whose approaching death she'd never seen before.

She was crying.

God, she missed Ray.

53

The following weekend Jamie went to Bristol to stay with Geoff and Andrew. Something else he was able to do now he was single again. He and Geoff had seen each other pretty much every month since college. Then Jamie made the mistake of bringing Tony along.

God, the last visit would be burnt into his memory forever. Andrew talking about imaginary numbers and Tony assuming it was some kind of intellectual one-upmanship. Despite Andrew being an actual maths lecturer. Tony getting his own back with the KY toothpaste story and some rather theatrical belching. So that Jamie had to send flowers and a long letter when they got back to London.

Geoff had put on a bit of weight since their last meeting, and he'd gone back to wearing glasses. He looked like the wise owl in a children's story. He had a new job, too, doing the finances for a software firm that did something utterly incomprehensible. He and Andrew had moved into a rather grand house in Clifton and adopted a Highland terrier called Jock who clambered into Jamie's lap as they sat in the garden drinking tea and smoking cigarettes.

Then Andrew arrived, and Jamie was shocked. The age difference had never seemed relevant. Andrew had always been the leaner, fitter man. But he looked old now. It wasn't just the stick. You could break an ankle at eighteen. It was the way he moved. As if he expected to fall.

He shook Jamie's hand. "Sorry I'm late. Got held up in some stupid committee. You're looking well."

"Thank you," said Jamie, wanting to return the compliment but not being able to.

Jamie and Geoff cycled to a postcard pub in the country while Andrew and Jock took the car.

It seemed sad, at first, the way Geoff's life was being narrowed by Andrew's illness.

But Geoff seemed as devoted as he'd ever been, and eager to do anything to help Andrew. And this made Jamie sad in a different way.

He simply didn't understand. Because he could suddenly see Tony's point. Andrew was a generous man. But he didn't do small talk and he didn't ask questions. When the conversation moved out of his sphere he switched off and waited for it to move back.

Andrew retired to bed early and Jamie and Geoff sat in the garden finishing off a bottle of wine.

Jamie talked about Katie and Ray and tried to explain why the relationship made him uneasy. The way Ray cramped her style. The gulf between them. And only when he was doing this did he realize how much of what he was saying applied to Geoff and Andrew. He tried to change the subject.

Geoff could read him like a book. Perhaps every conversation came round to this subject eventually. "Andrew and I have a very nice life together. We love one another. We look after one another. We don't have as much sex as we once did. To be honest, we don't really have sex at all. But, without putting too fine a point on it, there are ways of dealing with that."

"Does Andrew know?"

Geoff didn't answer the question. "I'll be there for him. Always. Until the end. That's the thing he knows."

An hour later Jamie lay on the pull-out bed, looking at the roll of carpet and the defunct skiing machine and the cello case and felt that rootless ache he always felt in business hotels and spare rooms, the smallness of your life when you took the props away.

It disturbed him, Geoff and Andrew. And he wasn't sure why. Was it Geoff having sex with other men and Andrew knowing and not knowing? Was it the thought of Geoff watching his lover growing old? Was it because Jamie wanted the unconditional love they had? Or because that unconditional love seemed so unattractive?

The following week he spent three days running the interviews for the new secretary and sorting out all the attendant paperwork. He went to Johnny's leaving do. He saw *A Beautiful Mind* with Charlie. He went swimming for the first time in two months. He ate a takeaway Chinese in the bath with *The Dark Side of the Moon* cranked up to nine downstairs. He read *The Farewell Symphony* and the fact that he finished it in three days almost made up for how fantastically depressing it was.

He needed someone.

Not for sex. Not yet. That came a couple of weeks later, in his experience. You started finding ugly guys attractive. Then you started finding straight guys attractive. Then you had to do something about it pretty quickly because by the time you started thinking you'd settle for sex with one of your female friends you were heading for a whole barrel-load of trouble.

He needed . . . The word *companion* always made him think of elderly play-wrights in silk smoking jackets holed up in Italian coastal towns with their handsome secretaries. Like Geoff, but with more glamour.

He wanted . . . There was that feeling when you held someone, or when someone held you. The way your body relaxed. Like having a dog on your lap.

He needed to be close to someone. Wasn't that what everyone wanted?

He was getting a bit old for the outdoor stuff and clubs always seemed to him like stag nights, with the hormones flowing in the opposite direction. Men doing what they'd done since they came down from the trees, gathering in herds to get drunk and talk bollocks, anything to avoid the nightmares of being serious or having nothing to do.

Besides, Jamie's track record was not good. Simon the Catholic priest. Garry and his Nazi memorabilia. Christ, you'd think people would either confess these things up front or avoid mentioning them at all, instead of announcing them over breakfast.

Halfway round Tesco he put a tin of sweetened condensed milk into his basket but came to his senses at the checkout and quietly slid it to the side of the conveyor belt when no one was watching.

Back at home he was lying on the sofa toggling idly between *Antiques Roadshow* and something about the Great Wall of China when he realized that he could ring Ryan.

He went to get his address book.

54

At four o'clock the following day Katie made the mistake of saying to Jacob, "Well, buddy, half an hour and we'll head back to London."

Cue tears and high-volume wailing.

"I hate you."

"Jacob . . ."

She tried talking him down but he was winding up for a big one. So she put him in the living room and closed the door and said he could come out when he'd calmed down.

Mum caved almost immediately and went in, saying, "Don't be mean to him." Two minutes later he was eating Maltesers in the kitchen.

What was it with grandparents? Thirty years ago it was smacking and bed with no tea. Now it was second helpings of pudding and toys on the dining table.

She packed the car and said goodbye to Dad. When she told him Mum was going to the doctor he looked petrified but she'd run out of sympathy several hours back. She kissed him on the forehead and closed the bedroom door quietly behind her.

She manhandled a thrashing Jacob into the car and *Hey presto,* as soon as he knew resistance was futile he slumped backward, silent and exhausted.

Two and a half hours later they pulled up outside the house. The hall light was on and the curtains were closed. Ray was there. Or had been.

Jacob was in a coma, so she lifted him out of his seat and carried him to the front door. The hallway was silent. She hefted him

261

upstairs and laid him down on his bed. Maybe he'd sleep through. If Ray was lurking she didn't want an argument while ministering to a waking child. She slipped his shoes and trousers off and put the duvet over him.

She heard a noise and went back downstairs.

Ray appeared in the hallway carrying the blue holdall and Jacob's Spider-Man rucksack from the car. He paused, briefly, looked up, said, "Sorry," then took everything through to the kitchen.

He meant it. She could see. There was something broken about him. She realized how rarely she ever heard someone say sorry and mean it.

She followed him and sat down on the opposite side of the table.

"I shouldn't have done that." He was nudging a ballpoint pen round in little circles with his finger. "Running off. It was stupid. You should be able to go out for coffee with who you like. It's none of my business."

"It is your business," said Katie. "And I would have told you —"

"But I would have been jealous. I know. Look . . . I'm not blaming you for anything . . ."

Her anger had vanished. She realized that he was more honest and more self-aware than any member of her own family. How had she not seen this before?

She touched his hand. He didn't respond.

"You said you couldn't marry someone who treated you like that."

"I was angry," said Katie.

"Yeh, but you were right," said Ray. "You can't marry someone who treats you like that."

"Ray —"

"Listen. I've been doing a lot of thinking over the last few days." He paused, briefly. "You shouldn't be marrying me."

She tried to interrupt but he held up his hand.

"I'm not the right person for you. Your parents don't like me. Your brother doesn't like me —"

"They don't know you." Those three days alone in the house she'd been glad of the space and the quiet. Now she could see him walking out for a second time and it terrified her. "Anyway, it's got nothing to do with them."

He narrowed his eyes a little while she was talking, letting it wash over him like the pain from a headache. "I'm not as clever as you. I'm not good with people. We don't like the same music. We don't like the same books. We don't like the same films."

It was true. But it was all wrong.

"You get angry and I don't know what to say. And, sure, we get along OK. And I like looking after Jacob. But . . . I don't know . . . In a year's time, in two years' time, in three years' time —"

"Ray, this is ridiculous."

"Is it?"

"Yes," she said.

He looked directly at her. "You don't really love me, do you?"

Katie said nothing.

He carried on looking at her. "Go on, say it. Say, 'I love you.' "

She couldn't do it.

"You see, I love you. And that's the problem."

The central heating clicked on.

Ray got to his feet. "I need to go to bed."

"It's only eight o'clock."

"I haven't slept for the past few days. Not properly . . . Sorry."

He went upstairs.

She looked around the room. For the first time since she and Jacob had moved in she could see it for what it was. Someone else's kitchen with a few of their belongings pasted onto it. The microwave. The enamel bread bin. Jacob's alphabet train.

Ray was right. She couldn't say it. She hadn't said it for a long time now.

Except that it was wrong, putting it like that.

There was an answer, somewhere. An answer to everything Ray had said which didn't make her feel selfish and stupid and mean-spirited. It was out there. If only she could see it.

She took hold of the ballpoint pen Ray had been playing with and lined it up with the grain of the tabletop. Maybe if she could place it with absolute accuracy her life wouldn't fall apart.

She had to do something. But what? Unpack the bags? Eat supper? It all seemed suddenly pointless.

She went to the sideboard. Three plane tickets for Barcelona were sitting in the toast rack. She opened the drawer and took out the invitations and the envelopes, the guest list and the list of presents. She took out the photocopied maps and hotel recommendations and the books of stamps. She carried it all to the table. She wrote names at the top of all the invitations and put them into the envelopes with the folded sheets of A4. She sealed them and stamped them and arranged them in three neat white pagodas.

When they were done she grabbed the house keys and took the envelopes to the end of the road and posted them, not knowing whether she was trying to make everything come out right by positive thinking, or whether she was punishing herself for not loving Ray enough.

55

Jean booked an appointment and drove George to the surgery after school.

It was not something she was looking forward to. But Katie was right. It was best to take the bull by the horns.

In the event he proved surprisingly malleable.

She put him through his paces in the car. He was to tell Dr. Barghoutian the truth. None of this nonsense about sunstroke or coming over light-headed. He was not to leave until Dr. Barghoutian had promised to do something. And he was to tell her afterward exactly what Dr. Barghoutian had said.

She reminded him that Katie's wedding was coming up and that if he wasn't there to give his daughter away and make a speech then he was going to have some explaining to do.

He seemed to enjoy the bullying in some perverse way and promised to do everything she asked.

They sat next to one another in the waiting room. She tried to chat. About the Indian architect who had moved in across the road. About cutting the wisteria down before it got under the roof. But he was more interested in an elderly copy of *OK* magazine.

When his name was called she patted him gently on the leg to wish him luck. He made his way across the room, stooping a little and keeping his eyes fixed firmly on the carpet.

She tried a bit of her P. D. James but couldn't get into it. She'd never liked doctors' waiting rooms. Everyone always looked so shabby. As if they hadn't been taking enough care of themselves, which they probably hadn't. Hospitals weren't so bad. So long as they were clean. White paint and clean lines. People being properly ill.

She couldn't leave George. What she felt was irrelevant. She had to think about George. She had to think about Katie. She had to think about Jamie.

Yet when she imagined not leaving him, when she imagined saying no to David, it was like a light at the end of a dark tunnel going out.

She picked up George's *OK* magazine and read about the Queen Mother's hundredth birthday.

Ten minutes later George emerged.

"Well?" she asked.

"Can we go to the car?"

They went to the car.

Dr. Barghoutian had given him a prescription for antidepressants and booked him in to see the clinical psychologist the following week. Whatever the two of them had talked about it had clearly exhausted him. She decided not to pry.

They went to the chemist's. He didn't want to go inside, mumbling something she couldn't quite catch about "books on diseases," so she went in herself and picked up some brussels and carrots from the grocer's next door while they were doing the prescription.

He opened the bag as they were driving home and spent a great deal of time examining the bottle. Whether he was horrified or relieved she couldn't tell. Back in the kitchen she took charge of it, watched him swallow the first pill with a glass of water, then put the remainder in the cupboard above the toaster.

He said, "Thank you," and retreated to the bedroom.

She hung up the washing, made a coffee, filled in the check and the order form for the marquee people, then said she had to pop out to talk to the florist.

She drove over to David's house and tried to explain how impossible the decision was. He apologized for having made the offer at such a difficult time. She told him not to apologize. He told her that nothing had changed, and that he would wait for as long as she needed.

He put his arms round her and they held one another and it was like coming home after a long and difficult journey and she realized that this was something she could never give up.

56

Jamie was drinking a cappuccino on Greek Street waiting for Ryan.

He wasn't being entirely honorable, Ryan being Tony's ex. He knew that. But Ryan had agreed to come, so Ryan wasn't being entirely honorable, either.

Fuck it. What was honor anyway? The only person he knew with real integrity was Maggie and she had spent her life since college picking up nasty diseases in flyblown corners of West Africa. Didn't even own furniture.

Besides, Tony had dumped him. If something happened with Ryan, what was wrong with that?

Fifteen minutes late.

Jamie got himself a second coffee and reopened Daniel Dennett's *Consciousness Explained* which he'd bought in one of his periodic fits of self-improvement (the exercise ball, that stupid opera CD . . .). At home he was reading *Pet Sematary,* but reading that in public was like leaving the house in your underwear.

This does not mean that the brain never uses "buffer memories" to cushion the interface between the brain's internal processes and the asynchronous outside world. The "echoic memory" with which we preserve stimulus patterns briefly while the brain begins to process them is an obvious example (Sperling, 1960; Neisser, 1967; see also Newell, Rosenbloom, and Laird, 1989, p. 1067).

There was a review on the back from *The New York Review of Books* which described it as "clear and funny."

On the other hand, he didn't want to look like someone who was having difficulty reading *Consciousness Explained.* So he let his eyes drift over the pages, turning them every couple of minutes.

He thought about the new Web site and wondered whether the background music had been a mistake. He remembered last year's trip to Edinburgh. That purr of tires on the cobbles outside the hotel. He wondered why no one used them these days. Ambulances and wheelchairs, probably. He imagined Ryan placing his hand very briefly on his thigh and saying, "I'm so glad you got in touch."

Twenty-five minutes late. Jamie was beginning to feel obtrusive.

He gathered his belongings and bought a *Telegraph* from the newsagent on the corner. He bought a pint of lager in the pub over the road, then found an empty table on the pavement from which he could keep an eye on the café.

Three minutes later a man wearing leather trousers and a white T-shirt slid onto the bench on the other side of the table. He put a motorcycle helmet down on the table, mimed a little gun with his right hand, pointed the barrel at Jamie's head, cocked his thumb, made a clicking noise and said, "Estate agent."

Jamie was a little disturbed by this.

"Lowe and Carter," said the man.

"Er, yeh," said Jamie.

"Courier. We're in the building across the street. Pick up stuff from your place every now and then. You've got a desk in the far corner by the big window." He held out his hand to be shaken. "Mike."

Jamie shook it. "Jamie."

Mike picked up *Consciousness Explained,* which Jamie had left on the table where it could give a general impression without needing to be physically read. There was a thick Celtic band tattooed around Mike's upper right arm. He examined the book briefly then put it down. "A masterful tapestry of deep insight."

Jamie wondered whether the man was psychiatrically ill.

Mike laughed quietly. "Read it off the back cover."

Jamie turned the book over to verify this.

Mike sipped his drink. "I like courtroom dramas myself."

For a second Jamie wondered whether Mike meant he liked doing things that resulted in him going to court.

"John Grisham, that kind of stuff," said Mike.

Jamie relaxed a little. "Having a bit of trouble with the book myself, to be honest."

"Been stood up?" Mike asked.

"No."

"I saw you sitting across the road."

"Well . . . Yeh."

"Boyfriend?" asked Mike.

"Ex-boyfriend's ex-boyfriend."

"Messy."

"You're probably right," agreed Jamie.

Glancing over Mike's shoulder, he saw Ryan standing outside the café, looking up and down the street. He seemed balder than Jamie remembered. He was wearing a beige raincoat and carrying a little blue rucksack.

Jamie turned away.

"Tell me a secret," said Mike. "Something you've never told anyone."

"When I was six my friend, Matthew, bet me I wouldn't pee in this flowerpot in my sister's bedroom."

"And you peed in the flowerpot."

"I peed in the flowerpot." Out of the corner of his eye Jamie saw Ryan shake his head and begin walking off toward Soho Square. "I guess it's not a secret, technically, because she found out. I mean, it smelt really bad after a few days." Ryan was gone. Jamie relaxed a little. "I had this little plastic guitar I'd got on holiday in Portugal. She burnt it. In the garden. But it burnt, like, amazingly well. I mean, Portugal probably didn't do Trading Standards in 1980. I remember this scream and the sound of strings snapping. She's still got this scar on her arm."

His parents would look at Mike and assume he stole cars. The razor cut, the five earrings. But this . . . this thing passing between them, this nameless charge you could feel in the air . . . it made everything else seem shallow and stupid.

Mike held his eye and said, "You hungry?" and seemed to mean at least three things.

They went to a little Thai restaurant on Greek Street.

"I used to do tiling. Upmarket stuff. Fired Earth. Marble. Slate. Kitchens. Fireplaces. The bike's for money. Get me through the Alexander Technique and massage courses. Then I'm going freelance. Make some money so I can move back up north so I can afford a place with a consulting room."

A fine drizzle was falling in the street. Jamie was three pints down and the lights reflecting off the wet vehicles were tiny stars.

"Actually," said Jamie, "the thing I like

best about Amsterdam . . . well, the whole of Holland, actually, is . . . there are these amazing modern buildings everywhere. Over here people just build the cheapest thing possible."

Jamie was a bit vague about Alexander Technique. He couldn't really imagine Mike doing any kind of therapy. Too much swagger. But every so often Mike would touch Jamie's hand with a couple of fingers or look at him and smile and say nothing and there was a softness there which seemed sexier for being so well hidden the rest of the time.

Nice arms, too. Little ridges of flesh over the veins, without being wiry. And strong hands.

The massage. He could imagine that.

Mike suggested they go to a club. But Jamie didn't want to share him. He looked at the salt cellar and steeled himself and asked if Mike wanted to come back to his place and felt, as he always did, that little lurch, half thrill, half panic. Like the parachute jump. But better.

"Is this, like, an estate agent's dream pad? Steel balcony? Island kitchen with granite work surface? Arne Jacobsen chairs?"

"Victorian terrace with a white sofa and a Habitat coffee table," said Jamie. "And how do you know about Arne Jacobsen chairs?"

"I've been in some very nice houses in my time, thank you very much."

"Business or pleasure?" asked Jamie.

"A little bit of both."

"So, was that a yes, or are you keeping me in suspense?"

"Let's catch a tube," said Mike.

They watched their reflections in the black glass opposite as the carriage rumbled through Tufnell Park and Archway, their legs touching and the electricity flowing back and forth, other passengers getting on and off oblivious, Jamie aching to be held, yet wanting the journey to last for hours in case what came later didn't match up to what he was picturing in his head.

Two Mormons got onto the train and sat in the two seats facing them. Black suits. Sensible haircuts. The little plastic name badges.

Mike leant close to Jamie's ear and said, "I want to fuck your mouth."

They were still laughing when they stumbled through the front door of the flat.

Mike pushed Jamie against the wall and kissed him. Jamie could feel Mike's cock hard inside his jeans. He slid his hands inside Mike's T-shirt and saw, through the living-room door, a tiny red light blinking.

"Hang on."

"What?"

"Answerphone."

Mike laughed. "Thirty seconds. Then I'm coming to get you."

"There's some beer in the fridge," said Jamie. "Vodka and other stuff's in the cupboard by the window."

Mike detached himself. "Fancy a spliff?"

"Sure."

Jamie went into the living room and pressed the button.

"Jamie. Hi. It's Katie." She was drunk. Or did she just sound drunk because Jamie was drunk? "Shit. You're not in, are you. Shit."

She wasn't drunk. She was crying. Bloody hell.

"Anyway . . . today's exciting news is that the wedding's off. Because Ray doesn't think we should get married."

Was this good or bad? It was like seeing the adjacent train start to move. It made him feel a little wobbly.

"Oh, and we went home for the weekend and Dad's in bed because he's having a nervous breakdown. I mean a real one, like, with panic attacks and nightmares about dying and everything. And Mum's thinking of leaving him for that bloke from the office."

Jamie's first thought was that Katie herself

was having some kind of breakdown.

"So, I thought I'd better ring you because the way things have been going over the last few days you've probably been involved in some truly hideous road accident and the reason you're not answering your phone is because you're in hospital, or dead, or you've left the country or something . . . Give me a ring, OK?"

Beep.

Jamie sat for a moment, letting it sink in, or drift away, or whatever it was going to do. Then he stood up and made his way to the kitchen.

Mike was lighting a joint from the gas stove. He stood up, took a drag and held the smoke down with the obligatory startled expression. He looked a bit like Jamie felt.

Mike breathed out. "Want some?"

There was going to be some ghastly scene, wasn't there. You drag someone halfway up the Northern Line for sex which doesn't happen and suddenly you've got a disappointed and muscular stranger in the house who no longer has any reasons to be nice to you.

He wondered if Mike had ever stolen a car.

"What's up?" asked Mike.

"Family trouble."

"Big?"

"Yup," said Jamie.

"Death?" Mike took a saucer off the draining board and laid the joint on the rim.

"No." Jamie sat down. "Not unless my sister kills her fiancé. Or my father kills himself. Or my father kills my mother's lover."

Mike leaned down and took hold of Jamie's arm. Jamie was right. They were surprisingly strong hands.

Mike eased Jamie to his feet. "In my professional opinion . . . you need something to take your mind off things." Mike pulled him close. His cock was still hard.

For a brief second Jamie imagined Katie's drunken prophecy coming true. An unseemly struggle. Jamie slipping and cracking his skull on the corner of the kitchen table.

He pulled away. "Hang on. This is not a good time."

Mike put a hand around the back of Jamie's neck. "Trust me. It'll be good for you."

Jamie pushed back against Mike's hand but it didn't give.

Then Mike's eyes did the soft thing. "What are you going to do if I go away? Sit here and worry? It's too late to ring anyone. Come on. A couple of minutes and you won't be thinking about anything outside this room. I guarantee it."

And again it was like the parachute jump. But even more so. The fog of alcohol cleared briefly and it occurred to Jamie that this was why Tony had left. Because Jamie always wanted to be in control. Because he was frightened of anything different or improper. And as the fog closed over again it seemed to Jamie that he had to have sex with this man to prove to Tony that he could change.

He let Mike pull him close.

They kissed again.

He put his hands around Mike's back.

It was good to be held.

He could feel something thawing and cracking, something which had imprisoned him for far too long. Mike was right. He could let go, leave other people to sort out their own problems. For once in his life he could live in the moment.

Mike slid his hand down to Jamie's crotch and Jamie felt his cock stiffen. Mike popped open the button and pushed down the top of his boxer shorts and wrapped Jamie's cock in his hand.

"Feeling better?" asked Mike.

"Uh-huh."

With his free hand, Mike offered Jamie

the joint. They took a drag each and Mike put it back down on the saucer.

"Suck me," said Mike.

And it was at this point that Mike's eyes did something entirely different. He let go of Jamie's cock and seemed to be staring at an object several miles behind Jamie's head.

"Shit," said Mike.

"What?" asked Jamie.

"My eyes."

"What's wrong with your eyes?"

"I can't . . ." Mike shook his head. He was starting to sweat, little beads of perspiration standing out on his forehead, on his arms. "Shit. I can't see anything properly."

"What do you mean?"

"I mean I can't see anything properly." Mike staggered sideways and slumped onto a chair.

Katie was right. It was just going to happen a different way. It was Mike who was going to have the seizure. An ambulance would come. He wouldn't have a clue about Mike's name or address . . .

Christ. The joint. Was it OK to bury a joint in the garden while someone was having a seizure? What if Mike choked on his tongue while Jamie was outside?

Mike doubled over. "I've gone blind. Jesus. My stomach."

His *stomach?*

"Those bloody prawns."

"What?" asked Jamie, who was beginning to wonder, for the second time that evening, whether Mike had some kind of mental problem.

"It's OK," said Mike. "It's happened before."

"What has?"

"Get me a bowl."

Jamie's brain was so full he took a couple of seconds working out what kind of bowl Mike meant. By the time he'd worked it out, Mike had vomited onto the floor in front of his chair.

"Oh crap," said Mike.

Jamie saw himself, standing in his own kitchen looking down at a big omelet of sick with his penis sticking over the waistband of his boxer shorts, and he suddenly felt very bad for having left the café before Ryan arrived, even if Ryan had a horrible rucksack and thinning hair, and he knew that this was his punishment. And being uptight and controlling was bad, obviously it was bad, but it was also good, too, because if he'd been a little more uptight and controlling this wouldn't have happened.

He tucked himself back in.

"I'm really sorry," said Mike.

Jamie opened the drawer and handed him the tea towel with the London bus pattern that he'd never liked much.

Mike wiped his face. "I need to go to the toilet."

"Top of the stairs," said Jamie.

"Where are the stairs?" asked Mike.

Dear God, the man was unable to see.

Jamie helped Mike up the stairs then returned to the kitchen so that he didn't have to smell or hear what was about to happen in the bathroom.

He wanted Mike out of the house. But he also needed to be a better person. And being a better person meant not wanting Mike out of the house. Being a better person meant looking after Mike. Because when shit happened to nice people they could say that it was an accident, or bad luck, or just the way the world worked. But when shit happened to horrible people they knew it was their fault and that made the shit so much worse.

He put on the washing-up gloves from under the sink. He got two Tesco bags from the cupboard and put one of them inside the other. He got the cake slice from the thingumajig drawer and knelt down and began scraping the sick off the floor and dolloping it into the bags. It was not a pleasant task (there would doubtless be worse upstairs). But it was good having an unpleasant task to do.

Penitence. That was the word he was looking for.

Oh Jesus. Sick was going down the cracks between the boards.

He wiped the floor with a couple of squares of kitchen roll and threw them into the Tesco bags. He filled a jug with soapy water, scrubbed the cracks with the vegetable brush, then threw the vegetable brush into the Tesco bags.

There was a bad noise from the toilet.

He poured some bleach onto the floor, rubbed it over the whole area with a cloth wipe, then disposed of it in the bags along with the vegetable brush. He wiped the cake slice with a second cloth wipe and thought, briefly, about leaving it overnight in a solution of bleach, but realized he would probably never use it again and threw it into the Tesco bags along with everything else. He tied the handle of the inner bag, then the handle of the outer bag. He then put them into a third bag in case of leakage, tied the handle of the third bag, carried it down the hallway, opened the front door and threw it into the bin.

There was another bad noise from the toilet.

He loved Tony. It was suddenly and painfully clear. Their stupid arguments. Over the wedding. Over the binoculars. Over the ketchup. They meant nothing.

He was going round to Tony's flat. Right after he'd sorted all this out. No matter what the time was. Say sorry. Tell him everything.

They were going to the wedding together. No. Better than that. He'd take Tony up to Peterborough next weekend.

Except that Dad was having some kind of breakdown. He ought to make a few inquiries about that first.

Whatever. He'd take Tony up to Peterborough as soon as possible.

He went up to the bathroom and knocked quietly.

"You OK?"

"Not terribly," said Mike.

Even through the door the smell was not good. He asked Mike if he needed any help with some trepidation, and heard Mike say "No" with considerable relief.

"Imodium," said Jamie. "I've got some Imodium in the bedroom."

Mike said nothing.

Several minutes later Jamie was sitting at

the kitchen table with a selection of over-the-counter pharmaceuticals spread out in front of him, like a native trader waiting for the men from the big boat.

Imodium. Antacid tablets. Paracetamol. Ibuprofen. Aspirin. Antihistamines. (Were antihistamines intended for that kind of allergic reaction? He wasn't sure.)

He put the kettle on and checked that he had all the requisite teas and coffees to hand. There was a good half liter of semi-skimmed in the fridge. There was no drinking chocolate but there was an unopened tin of cocoa from an abortive baking project.

He was fully equipped.

After ten or so minutes he heard the *kersnick* of the bathroom door being unlocked, then Mike's feet on the stairs. He was clearly descending with some care.

A hand appeared on the door frame and Mike maneuvered himself into view. He did not look healthy.

Jamie was about to ask what he could offer in terms of medication and hot drinks when Mike said, "I'm so sorry," and headed down the hall toward the front door.

By the time Jamie had got to his feet Mike had closed the front door behind him. Jamie paused. Being good meant looking after people. It didn't mean keeping them prisoner. And obviously Mike could see now. Or he wouldn't have left.

Would he?

Jamie went to the window and lifted the edge of the curtain to glance up and down the street. It was empty. He was fairly certain that blind people didn't move at that kind of speed.

He went upstairs. The bathroom was spotless.

He was still too drunk to drive. He grabbed his keys and jacket and went out the front door, locking it behind him.

He could have rung for a taxi but he didn't want to wait. It would take half an hour to walk to Tony's flat, but he needed the fresh air. And if he woke Tony up, well, this was more important than sleep.

He set off down Wood Vale Gardens and over Park Road in front of the hospital. The rain had stopped and most house lights were off by now. The streets were full of a dirty orange glow and the shadows under cars were thick and black.

Tony was right. He'd been selfish. You had to make compromises if you wanted to share your life with another person.

He crossed Priory Road.

He'd ring Katie tomorrow. She was probably getting everything out of proportion.

Which was understandable if she and Ray were having a rough patch. His father going crazy? His mother leaving? He didn't know which was harder to imagine.

A drunken cyclist zigzagged past.

His father worrying too much and his mother saying she couldn't take much more. That he could imagine. That was pretty much situation normal.

It would be all right. It would have to be all right. He was going to that wedding with Tony come hell or high water.

He was walking down Allison Road when a small dog came out of an alleyway. No, not a dog. A fox. That weightless trot. That bushy tail.

A car engine started up and the fox slid into an alleyway.

He reached Vale Road at half past midnight.

His mood had lifted during the walk. He thought about trying to look sad, then realized it was a stupid idea. He didn't want Tony back because he'd had a horrible evening. It was the horrible evening which made him realize that he wanted Tony back. Forever. And that was a happy thought.

He rang the bell and waited for thirty seconds.

He rang the bell again.

Another thirty seconds passed before he heard footsteps. Tony opened the door wearing his boxer shorts and nothing else. There was a steely expression in his eyes. "Jamie . . . ?"

"I'm sorry," said Jamie.

"It's OK. What's happened?"

"No. I mean sorry for everything. Everything else."

"Meaning?"

Jamie gathered himself. He should have planned this a little more carefully. "For making you leave. For . . . Tony, look, I've had a shitty evening and it's made me realize lots of things —"

"Jamie, it's the middle of the bloody night. I've got work in the morning. What is this about?"

Deep breath. "I miss you," said Jamie. "And I want you back."

"You're pissed, aren't you."

"No. Well, I was. But I'm not now . . . Listen, Tony. I'm serious."

Tony's expression didn't change. "I'm going back to bed. It's probably a good idea if you went back to bed as well."

"You've got someone in there with you, haven't you." Jamie was starting to cry. "That's why you don't want me to come in."

"Grow up, Jamie."

"Fuck."

Tony started to close the door.

Jamie had assumed Tony would let him in at the very least. So they could talk. It was the same selfishness all over again. Thinking everyone would fall in with his plan. Jamie could see it now. But it was too difficult to say this in half a second.

"Wait." He stepped onto the threshold to prevent Tony closing the door.

Tony recoiled slightly. "Christ. You smell of vomit."

"I know," said Jamie, "but it's not my vomit."

Tony placed the flat of his hand on Jamie's chest and pushed him back down onto the step. "Good night, Jamie."

The door closed.

Jamie stood on the step for a few minutes. He wanted to lie down on the little patch of concrete by the dustbins and sleep there till morning so Tony came out and saw him and felt sorry for him. But he could see straight-away that this was as stupid and self-indulgent and childish as the rest of his stupid, self-indulgent, childish plan.

He sat on the curb and wept.

57

Jean was going to have to arrange the wedding herself. She was clearly not going to get much help from the rest of the family.

Honestly. She loved her daughter. But for all Katie's talk about women being as good as men, she could be heroically disorganized sometimes.

"Laid-back" was the term Katie used.

Coming home from university with all her clothes in black rubbish bags and leaving them in the open garage so the binmen took them away. Spilling that paint over the cat. Losing her passport in Malta.

Poor George. She did give him the runaround. It was like two creatures from different planets.

Twelve years arguing over toothpaste. George assuming she did it deliberately to wind him up. Spitting it into the sink and refusing to rinse it away so it hardened into lumps. Katie unable to believe that anyone in their right mind could get worked up about something so trivial.

She still did it, actually. She'd done it this morning. Jean had cleaned it up. Just like old times.

Actually, Jean was secretly rather proud of

the way Katie refused to take orders from anyone. Of course there were times when she worried. That Katie would never get a decent job. Or fall pregnant by accident. Or never find a husband. Or get into some kind of trouble (she'd been cautioned once for being rude to a policewoman).

But Jean liked the fact that she'd brought such a free spirit into the world. She would look at her daughter sometimes and see little gestures or expressions that she recognized as her own, and wonder whether she might have been more like Katie had she been born thirty years later.

How ironic that Jamie should turn out to be gay. Now, if he were getting married he would have his guest list and invitations printed several years in advance.

Never mind.

The first time round arranging a wedding seemed like planning the D-Day landings. But after working in the bookshop and helping out at the school, she realized it was no more difficult than buying a house or booking a holiday, just a string of small tasks, all of which had to be done by a certain time. You wrote a list of things to do. You did them. You ticked them off.

She arranged the flowers. She booked the disco Claudia had used for Chloë's wedding. She finalized the menu with the caterers. She booked the photographer.

It was going to be perfect. For her sake if no one else's. It was going to run like clockwork and everyone was going to have a good time. She was going to put her feet up at the end of the day and feel a sense of achievement.

She wrote Katie a letter detailing all the things she still needed to do (taped music for the register office, Ray's suit, present for the best man, rings . . .). It would drive Katie up the wall, but judging by her daughter's performance at the weekend it seemed entirely possible that Katie might actually forget she was getting married.

She ordered the place cards. She bought herself a new dress and took George's suit for dry cleaning. She ordered a cake. She booked three cars to bring the immediate families back to the village. She put names on their invitations and addressed the envelopes.

She briefly considered crossing David off the list. George had insisted on inviting him after their dinner. Something about boosting their numbers to avoid being "swamped by Ray's clan." But she didn't want George asking uncomfortable questions. So she sent him an invitation. It didn't mean he had to come.

58

It had been almost enjoyable, seeing Dr. Barghoutian.

Obviously, his benchmark for what was and was not enjoyable had been lowered considerably over the last few weeks. Nevertheless, talking about his problems to someone who was being paid to listen was oddly soothing. More soothing than watching *Volcano* or *The Peacemaker,* during which he could always hear a kind of churning bass note of fear, like someone doing building work across the street.

Strange to discover that describing his fears out loud was less frightening than trying not to think about them. Something about seeing your enemy out in the open.

The pills were less good. He had trouble sleeping that first night and noticeably more trouble the second night. He wept a great deal and had to fight back the urge to go on long walks in the early hours of the morning.

He was taking a couple of codeine at breakfast now, then drinking a large whiskey mid-morning, brushing his teeth vigorously afterward so as not to arouse Jean's suspicions.

The idea of going into a psychiatric hospital was beginning to seem more and more attractive. But how did one get into a psychiatric hospital? What if you drove your car into a neighbor's garden? What if you set light to your bed? What if you lay down in the middle of the road?

Did it count if one did that kind of thing deliberately? Or was pretending to be insane itself a symptom of insanity?

And what if the bed was more flammable than expected?

One could perhaps pour water over a large circle of carpet around the bed to act as some kind of barrier.

The third night was pretty much unbearable.

Nevertheless, he doggedly continued to take the pills. Dr. Barghoutian had said that there might be side effects and, on the whole, George preferred treatments which involved pain. After falling off the stepladder he had gone to see a chiropractor who did little more than clap her hands at the back of his head. After several more weeks of discomfort he went to an osteopath who gripped him firmly from behind and hoisted him violently making his vertebrae crack. Within a couple of days he was walking normally again.

Nevertheless he was grateful when his appointment with the clinical psychologist rolled round on day six of the medication.

He had never met a clinical psychologist, professionally or otherwise. In his mind they were not that far removed from people who read tarot cards. It was entirely possible that he would be asked about seeing his mother naked and being bullied at school (he wondered what had happened to the infamous Gladwell twins). Or was that psychotherapy? He was a little unclear about these distinctions.

In the event, his meeting with Ms. Endicott entailed none of the touchy-feely nonsense he was expecting. In fact he could not remember the last time he had had such an engaging conversation.

They talked about his job. They talked about his retirement. They talked about his plans for the future. They talked about Jean and Jamie and Katie. They talked about the forthcoming wedding.

She asked about the panic attacks, when they occurred, what they felt like, how long they lasted. She asked if he had considered suicide. She asked precisely what frightened him and was endlessly patient while he struggled to put into words things which were difficult to put into words (the Orcs, for example, or the way the floor seemed to give way). And if he was embarrassed by some of these things, her attention was earnest and unwavering.

She asked about the lesion and said Dr. Barghoutian could refer George to a dermatologist if that might help. He said, "No," and explained that he knew, in his heart of hearts, that it was only eczema.

She asked whether he had any friends with whom he had discussed these things. He explained that one did not discuss these things with friends. He certainly would not want any of his friends bringing similar problems to him. It was unseemly. She nodded in agreement.

He left the surgery with no tasks to perform and no exercises to do, only the promise of a second appointment in a week's time. Standing in the car park he remembered that he had failed to mention the side effects of the medication. Then it dawned on him that he was not the person who had got on the bus that morning. He was stronger, more stable, less frightened. He could cope with the side effects of a few pills.

Later that afternoon he was lying in bed watching some golf championship on BBC2. The game had never really appealed to him. But there was something reassuring about the sensible jumpers and all that greenery stretching into the distance.

It seemed unjust that all his efforts at sorting out the mental aspects of the problem had done nothing to sort out the physical aspect of the problem.

It occurred to him that if the lesion were on a toe or a finger he could have it removed and simply be done with it. Then he would have to do nothing except take the tablets and return to the surgery each week till everything returned to normal.

A plan was forming in his head.

The plan, it seemed to him, was rather a good plan.

59

Katie posted the invitations, left a message for Jamie, then sat back down at the table.

She wanted to break something. But she wasn't allowed to break things. Not after the roasting she'd given Jacob for kicking the video player.

She picked up the big knife and stabbed

the breadboard seven times. When she stabbed it for the eighth time the blade broke and she cut the edge of her hand on the snapped-off end sticking up from the breadboard. There was blood everywhere.

She wrapped her hand in a kitchen towel, got out the first-aid tin, stuck a couple of large plasters over the cut, then cleaned up and threw the broken knife away.

She was obviously not going to get any sleep. The bed meant lying next to Ray. And the sofa meant admitting defeat.

Did she love Ray?

Did she *not* love him?

She hadn't eaten since four. She put the kettle on. She took down a packet of Maryland Chocolate Chip Cookies, ate six standing up, felt slightly sick and put the remainder back into the cupboard.

How could Ray sleep at times like this?

Had she ever loved him? Or was it just gratitude? Because he got on so well with Jacob. Because he had money. Because he could fix every machine under the sun. Because he needed her.

But, shit, those were real things. Even the money. Christ, you could love someone who was poor and incompetent and share a life that staggered from one disaster to the next. But that wasn't love, that was masochism.

Like Trish. Go down that road and you ended up living in a shed in Snowdonia while Mr. Vibrational Healing carved dragons out of logs.

She didn't give a damn about the books and the films. She didn't care what her family thought.

So why did she find it so hard to say she loved him?

Maybe because he'd marched into that café like Clint Eastwood and hurled a wastebin down the street.

In fact, now that she came to think about it, he had a bloody nerve. He disappeared for three days. Didn't even let her know he was alive. Then he pitched up, said sorry a few times, told her the wedding was off and expected her to say that she loved him.

Three days. Jesus.

You wanted to be a father, you had to show a damn sight more responsibility than that.

Maybe they shouldn't get married. Maybe it was a ridiculous idea, but if he was going to try and blame it on her . . .

God. That felt better. That felt a lot better.

She put down her mug and marched upstairs to wake him up and read him the riot act.

60

George decided to do it on Wednesday.

Jean was taking a long-planned trip to see her sister. She had made vague noises about canceling if George needed company but he was insistent that she should go.

When she finally rang from Northampton to say that she had arrived safely and to check that George was OK, he gathered the equipment. He would not have a great deal of energy or time once he had begun, so everything had to be in place.

He washed two codeine down with a large tumbler of whiskey. He stacked three elderly blue towels in the bathroom. He put the cordless phone on the kitchen table, filled the tray of the washing machine with powder and left the door open.

He took an empty, two-liter ice-cream carton from the back of the larder, made sure the lid fitted, then carried it upstairs with a couple of bin liners. He laid the bin liners on the floor and balanced the ice-cream tub on the bath taps. He opened the first-aid kit and placed it on the bathroom shelf.

The whiskey and codeine were beginning to take effect.

He went back downstairs, got the scissors out of the drawer and sharpened them with the little gray whetstone they used for the carving knife. For good measure he sharpened the carving knife too, and took both implements upstairs, laying them on the end of the bath opposite the taps.

He was scared, naturally. But the chemicals were beginning to dull the fear, and the knowledge that his problems would soon be over spurred him on.

He closed the curtains in the bathroom and the doors in the hallway. He turned off all the lights and waited for his eyes to become accustomed to the darkness. He removed his clothes, folded them and left them in a neat pile at the head of the stairs.

He was going into the bathroom when he realized that he did not want to be found unconscious on the floor of his own bathroom wearing no clothes. He put his underpants back on.

He turned the shower to warm, pointed the spray at the far wall and slid the plastic shuttering across.

The bath mat was thick and furry. Could it be washed? He was not entirely sure. He moved it to the far side of the room for safety's sake.

He placed his foot onto the base of the

bath to test the temperature of the water. Perfect. He stepped in.

This was it. Once he had started there would be no turning back.

He made a final check that everything was in place. The scissors, the ice-cream tub, the bin liners . . .

The first part, he knew, would be the hardest. But it would not last for long. He took a deep breath.

He picked up the scissors in his right hand, then ran the fingers of his left hand over his hip, looking for the lesion. He gripped the flesh around it, and the queasy prickle that spread from his fingers and up his arm (much as if he were picking up a spider or dog mess) only confirmed the necessity of what he was doing.

He pulled the lesion away from his body.

He glanced down, then looked away.

His flesh was stretched into a white peak, like hot cheese on a pizza.

He opened the jaws of the scissors.

Take a deep breath, then blow out as the pain comes. That was what the osteopath had said.

He pressed the blades of the sharpened scissors around the stretched skin and squeezed hard.

He did not need to remember to breathe

out. It happened entirely of its own accord.

The pain was so far beyond any pain he had felt before that it was like a jet aircraft coming in to land a couple of feet above his head.

He looked down again. He had not expected such a large volume of blood. It looked like something from a film. It was thicker and darker than he would have predicted, oily almost, and surprisingly warm.

The other thing he noticed when he looked down was that he had failed to sever completely the flesh around the lesion. On the contrary, it was flapping from his hip like a small and very raw steak.

He took hold of it again, reopened the scissors and attempted to make a second incision. But the blood made gripping difficult and the fat seemed tougher this time.

He leant over, put the scissors on the end of the bath and picked up the carving knife.

When he stood upright, however, a swarm of tiny white lights drifted across his field of vision and his body seemed farther away than it was meant to be. He put his hand out to steady himself on the tiled wall. Unfortunately, it was still wrapped around the carving knife. He let go of the carving knife and pressed his hand against the wall. The knife fell into the bath and came to land with its point embedded in the top of George's foot.

At this moment the entire room began to rotate. The ceiling swung into view, he got a vivid close-up of that little avocado-green magnet contraption which held the soap, then the hot tap struck him in the back of the head.

He lay on his side staring down the length of the bath. It looked as if someone had killed a pig in it.

The lesion was still attached to his body.

Holy mother of God. The traumatized cancer cells were doubtless flowing through the isthmus of flesh between flap and hip, setting up little colonies in his lungs, his bone marrow, his brain . . .

He knew, now, that he did not have the strength to remove it.

He had to get to hospital. They would cut it off for him. Perhaps they would cut it off for him in the ambulance if he explained the situation carefully enough.

He got very slowly onto his hands and knees.

His endorphins were not working terribly well.

He was going to have to negotiate the stairs.

Damn.

He should have done the whole thing in the kitchen. He could have stood in that old plastic bath the kids used in summer. Or was that one of the items he removed from the back of the garage in 1985?

Very possibly.

He leant over the side of the bath and grabbed one of the towels.

He paused. Did he really want to press towel fluff into an open wound?

He got carefully to his feet. The little white lights came and went again.

He glanced down. It was difficult to make out what was what in the general area of the wound, and looking at it made him feel a little sick. He turned his head away and rested his eyes briefly on the spattered tiling.

Breathe in. Hold. Breathe out. Three. Two. One.

He glanced down again. He picked up the severed flap by its outer side and pressed it back into place. It did not fit very well. Indeed, the moment he let go it slid out of the wound and swung unpleasantly on its damp red hinge.

Something was actually pulsing in the

wound. It was not a reassuring sight.

He took hold of the flesh again, held it in place, then pressed the towel on top of it.

He waited for a minute then got to his feet.

If he rang an ambulance straightaway they might come too soon. He would do a little tidying first, then ring.

First of all he had to clean the shower.

When he reached up to take hold of the showerhead, however, it seemed higher than he remembered and his torso was not keen on being stretched.

He would leave it and invent some story for Jean when she got back from Sainsbury's.

Was she at Sainsbury's? It was all a little hazy.

He decided to put his clothes on instead.

This, too, he realized, was not going to be easy. He was wearing a pair of blood-soaked underpants. There were clean pairs of underpants in the chest of drawers in the bedroom, but they were on the far side of ten yards of cream carpet, and there was a considerable volume of blood running down his leg.

He could have planned this better.

He pressed the towel a little more firmly against the wound and wiped the blood from the floor by standing on top of the other two towels and shuffling slowly around the bathroom for a couple of minutes. He tried to bend down to pick up the two towels prior to tossing them into the bathtub, but his body was no keener on being bent than it was on being stretched.

He decided to cut his losses. He staggered into the bedroom and dialed 999.

When he looked back to the doorway, however, he saw that he had left footprints on the cream carpet. Jean was going to be very unhappy.

"Police, fire or ambulance?"

"Police," said George, not thinking. "No. Wait. Ambulance."

"Just connecting you . . ."

"You're through to the ambulance service. Can I take your number, caller?"

What was his phone number? It seemed to have slipped his mind. He used it so rarely.

"Hello, caller?" asked the woman on the other end of the line.

"I'm sorry," said George. "I can't remember the number."

"That's OK. Go ahead."

"Right, yes. I seem to have cut myself. With a large chisel. There is quite a lot of blood."

Katie's number, for example. He could remember that with no trouble whatsoever. Or could he? To be honest, that number seemed to have slipped his mind as well.

The woman on the other end of the line said, "Can you tell me your address?"

This, too, took some effort to recall.

After putting the phone down he realized, of course, that he had forgotten to find the chisel before getting into the bath. Jean was going to be cross enough already. If she discovered that he had made the mess while cutting the cancer off with her special scissors she would be incandescent.

The chisel, however, was in the cellar, and the cellar was a long way away.

He wondered whether he had remembered to put the phone down.

Then he wondered whether he had got around to remembering his address before putting the phone down. Assuming he had indeed put the phone down.

They could trace calls.

At least they could in films.

But in films you could make someone pass out by squeezing their shoulder.

He caught sight of himself in the hall mirror and wondered why a crazy, old, naked, bleeding man was standing next to their phone table.

309

The cellar steps were really very difficult.

Before he and Jean got much older it might be an idea to put in a new staircase with a shallower rake. A handrail might not go amiss, either.

Crossing the cellar he put his foot on something which felt very like one of those small Lego bricks Jacob sometimes left lying around the house, the ones with the single nobble. He stumbled and dropped the towel. He picked the towel up again. It was covered in sawdust and a variety of dead insects. He wondered why he was holding a towel. He put it on the lid of the freezer. For some reason the towel appeared to be soaked in blood. He would have to tell someone about that.

The chisel.

He reached into the little green basket and retrieved it from beneath the claw hammer and the retractable tape measure.

He turned to leave, his knees buckled softly beneath him and he rolled sideways into the paddling pool which they kept semi-inflated to prevent mold forming on the inner surfaces.

He was looking at a picture of a fish from very close up. There was a spout of water coming from the top of the fish's head, which suggested that it was a whale. But it was also red, which suggested that it might be another kind of fish altogether.

He could smell rubber and hear the splash of water and see little scallop shapes of sun sparkle dancing in front of him, and that rather attractive young woman from the hotel in Portugal in her lime-green bikini.

If his memory served him correctly, that was the place where they served the poisonous dessert in the scooped-out pineapples.

He seemed to be in a great deal of pain, though it was hard to say precisely why.

He was also very tired.

He would sleep for a while.

Yes, that seemed like a good idea.

61

Katie was going to save her marriage.

She rang the office at eight. She was planning to leave a message and was caught on the hop when Aidan answered the phone (if he didn't sound so bloody perky she might have suspected him of sleeping in the office; she couldn't imagine him doing extra work if other people weren't watching).

"Let me guess," said Aidan, wearily. "You're sick."

It would have been simpler to say yes, but

it was a day for being honest. And, in any case, she'd never liked agreeing with Aidan. About anything. "I'm fine, actually. But I need the day off."

"No can do."

There was a gurgling noise in the background. Was it possible that he was urinating while talking on the cordless phone? "You can live without me for a day."

"The Henley had the fire officer round. Their license for the ballroom has been revoked. So, we have some work to do."

"Aidan?" she said, in that growly snap you used to make bad children stop what they were doing right now.

"What?" he said, in that slightly quivery voice bad children used when you did the growly snap.

"I'm staying at home. I'll explain later. I'll find you a new venue tomorrow."

Aidan reasserted himself. "Katie, if you're not here by ten o'clock —"

She put the phone down. It was entirely possible that she no longer had a job. It didn't seem terribly important.

Ray turned up just after nine, having dropped Jacob at nursery. He rang the office and talked to a few people to make sure everything didn't crash and burn in his absence. Then he said, "What now?"

Katie threw him his coat. "We take a tube into London. You get to choose what we do this morning. I get to choose what we do this afternoon."

"OK," said Ray.

They were going to start all over again. But this time she wouldn't be single and desperate. She'd find out whether she liked him instead of just needing him.

They could deal with his anger-management issues later. Besides, if the wedding was off, it was someone else's job.

Ray wanted to go on the Millennium Wheel. They bought a pair of advance tickets then ate ice creams sitting on a bench watching a big tide heading for the North Sea.

"Remember wafers?" said Katie. "You'd get this little brick of ice cream sandwiched between these crisscross-patterned biscuits. Maybe you can still get them . . ."

Ray wasn't really listening. "It's like being on holiday."

"Good," said Katie.

"Only problem with holidays," said Ray, "you have to go home afterward."

"Apparently, going on holiday is the fourth most stressful thing you can do," said Katie. "After death of a spouse and changing your job. And moving house. If I remember correctly."

"Fourth?" Ray said, staring at the water. "What about if your kid dies?"

"OK. Maybe not the fourth."

"Wife dies. Kid with disability," said Ray.

"Terminal disease," said Katie. "Loss of limb. Car crash."

"House burning down," said Ray.

"Declaration of war," said Katie.

"Seeing a dog run over."

"Seeing a person run over."

"Actually running a person over," said Ray.

"Actually running a dog over."

"Running an entire family over."

They were laughing again.

Ray was disappointed by the wheel. Too well engineered, he said. He wanted the wind in his hair and a rusty handrail and the faint possibility that the whole structure might collapse.

Katie was thinking she should have included a height rule in her plan for the day. She felt ill. Marble Arch, Battersea Power Station, the Gherkin tower, some green hills over there which looked like they were in bloody Nepal. She stared down at the blond wood of the central oval bench and tried to imagine she was in a sauna.

Ray said, "When we were kids we had

these cousins who lived in this old farm-house. You could get out of the bedroom window and climb up onto the roof. I mean, if Mum and Dad had known they'd have gone ballistic. But I can still remember it, even now, that feeling of being above every-thing. Roofs, fields, cars . . . Like being God."

"How long have we got to go?" asked Katie.

Ray seemed amused. He glanced at his watch. "Ooh, about another fifteen min-utes."

62

Except that it wasn't a swimming pool because her lime-green bottom (her name was Marianna, he recalled) slid sideways to the right and there was this rhythmic bang-ing which was the sound of oars striking water because he was watching the Boat Race on television (on second thought it might have been Marlena), but maybe not on television because he was leaning on a sturdy granite balustrade, though he could also feel carpet pressed against the side of his face, which suggested that he might, after all, be indoors, and the commentator was saying something about the kitchen, and one way of drawing a rubber plant would be to photograph it and then project a slide onto a large piece of paper masking-taped to a wall and trace it, which some people might think of as cheating, though Rembrandt used lenses, or so they said in that article in *The Sunday Times* magazine, or perhaps it was Leonardo da Vinci, and no one accused them of cheating because it was what the picture looked like which mattered, and they were dressed in white and they were lifting him up into the air and it wasn't a circle of light, more an upright rectangle at the top of a flight of steps, though now he came to think about it he may have thrown the slide projector out in 1985 along with the plastic bath, and someone was saying "George . . . ? George . . . ? George . . . ?" and then he went into the rectangle of bright light and something was placed over his mouth and the doors closed and he was ascending now in a kind of crystal lift shaft directly above the house, and when he looked down he could see the unfinished studio and the blocked guttering above the bathroom window that he really should have got around to clearing, and a steam train on the Nene Valley Railway and the three lakes of the country park and the bedspread of fields and that little restaurant in Agrigento and the butterflies in the Pyrenees and the crisscrossing contrails of jets and the blue of the sky turning slowly to black and the hard little fires of the stars.

63

Jean had always found her sister hard work. Even before she was born-again. To be honest, it was slightly better after she was born-again. Because then there was a reason for Eileen being hard work. You knew you'd never get on because she was going to heaven and you weren't, so you could give up trying.

But, God, the woman could make you feel greedy and self-centered just by the way she wore a shapeless faun cardigan.

She was sorely tempted, over lunch, to mention David. Just so she could see her sister's face. But Eileen would probably consider it her moral duty to share the information with George.

It didn't matter now. The ordeal was over for another year.

By the time she got home she was looking forward to a conversation with George. About anything.

She was juggling her keys, however, when she realized something was wrong. She could see, through the little square of frosted glass, that the phone table was at an angle. And there was something dark lying at the foot of the stairs. The dark thing had arms. She hoped to God it was a coat.

She opened the door.

It was a coat.

Then she saw the blood. On the stairs. On the hall carpet. There was a bloody handprint on the wall beside the living-room door.

She shouted George's name, but there was no answer.

She wanted to turn and run and phone the police from a neighbor's house. Then she imagined the conversation on the phone. Not being able to say where he was, or what had happened to him. She had to be the first to see him.

She stepped inside, every tiny hair on her body standing on end. She left the door ajar. To keep that connection. To the sky. To the air. To the ordinary world.

The living room was exactly as she had left it that morning.

She went into the kitchen. There was blood all over the lino. He had been in the middle of doing some washing. The door of the machine was open and a box of detergent tablets was sitting on the work surface above it.

The cellar door was open. She walked slowly down the steps. More blood. Great smears of it all over the inside of the paddling pool, and lines of it running down the side of the freezer cabinet. But no body.

She was trying very, very hard not to think about what had happened here.

She went into the dining room. She went upstairs. She went into the bedrooms. Then she went into the bathroom.

This was where they had done it. In the shower. She saw the knife and looked away. She staggered backward and slumped onto the chair in the hallway and let the sobs take her over.

They had taken him somewhere afterward.

She had to call someone. She got to her feet and stumbled along the landing to the bedroom. She picked up the phone. It seemed suddenly unfamiliar. As if she'd never seen one before. The two pieces that came apart. The little noise it made. The buttons with black numbers on them.

She didn't want to ring the police. She didn't want to talk to strangers. Not yet.

She rang Jamie at work. He was out of the

office. She rang his home number and left a message.

She rang Katie. She wasn't in. She left a message.

She couldn't remember their mobile phone numbers.

She rang David. He said he'd be there in fifteen minutes.

It was unbearably cold in the house and she was shaking.

She went downstairs and grabbed her winter coat and sat on the garden wall.

64

Jamie stopped at an all-night petrol station on the way home from Tony's flat and bought a packet of Silk Cut, a Twix, a Cadbury's Boost and a Yorkie. By the time he fell asleep he'd eaten all the chocolate and smoked eleven of the cigarettes.

When he woke the following morning someone had folded a wire coat hanger into the space between his brain and his skull. He was late, too, and had no time for a shower. He dressed, threw back an instant coffee with two ibuprofens, then ran for the tube.

He was sitting on the tube when he remembered that he hadn't rung Katie back. When he got out at the far end he took his mobile out of his pocket but couldn't quite face it. He would ring this evening.

He got into the office and realized he should have made the call.

This couldn't go on.

It was bigger than Tony. He was at a crossroads. What he did over the next few days would set the course for the rest of his life.

He wanted people to like him. And people did like him. Or they used to. But it wasn't so easy anymore. It wasn't automatic. He was beginning to lose the benefit of every-one's doubt. His own included.

If he wasn't careful he'd turn into one of those men who cared more about furniture than human beings. He'd end up living with someone else who cared more about furni-ture than human beings and they'd lead a life which looked perfectly normal from the outside but was, in truth, a kind of living death that left your heart looking like a raisin.

Or worse, he'd lurch from one sordid liaison to the next, grow hugely fat because no one gave a shit about what he looked like, then get some hideous disease as a result of being fat and die a long, lingering death in a hospital ward full of senile old men who smelled of urine and cabbage and howled in the night.

He got stuck into typing up the particulars for Jack Riley's three new builds in West Hampstead. Doubtless including some typing error or a mislabeled photograph so that Riley could storm into the office asking for someone's arse to be kicked.

Last time round Jamie had added the phrase "property guaranteed to depreciate between signing and closing," printed the details out to amuse Shona, then had to snatch it back when he saw Riley standing in reception talking to Stuart.

Bedroom One. 4.88m (16' 0") max x 3.40m (11' 2") max. Two sliding-sash windows to front. Stripped wooden floor. Telephone point . . .

He wondered sometimes why in God's name he did this job.

He rubbed his eyes.

He had to stop moaning. He was going to be a good person. And good people didn't moan. Children were dying in Africa. Jack Riley didn't matter in the greater scheme of things. Some people didn't even have a job.

Just knuckle down.

He pasted in the photographs of the interior.

Giles was doing the pen thing over on the facing desk. Bouncing it between his thumb and forefinger then throwing it up into the air and letting it twirl an even number of times before catching it by the handle end. Like Jamie used to do with penknives. When he was nine.

And maybe if it was someone else, Josh, or Shona, or Michael, it wouldn't have mattered. But it was Giles. Who wore a cravat. And took the foil off a Penguin, folded it in half, then rewrapped the bottom of the bar in the now-double-thickness foil forming a kind of silver paper cornet to prevent his fingers getting chocolatey so that you wanted to put a bullet through his head. And he was making the noise, too, every time the pen fell back into his hand. That little *clop* noise with his tongue. Like when you were doing a horse for children. But only one *clop* at a time.

Jamie filled in a couple of Terms of Business and printed out three Property Fact Finds.

He didn't blame Tony. Christ, he'd made a total arse of himself. Tony was right to slam the door in his face.

How the hell could you ask someone to love you when you didn't even like yourself?

He typed up the accompanying letters, put

everything into envelopes and returned a string of phone calls from the previous day.

At half past twelve he went out and got a sandwich for lunch and ate it sitting in the park in the rain under Karen's umbrella, thankful for the relative peace and quiet.

His head was still aching. Back at the office he cadged two ibuprofen from Shona then spent a large part of the afternoon mesmerized by the way the clouds moved very interestingly past the little window on the stairs, wanting desperately to be on the sofa at home with a large mug of proper tea and a packet of biscuits.

Giles started doing the pen thing again at 2:39 and was still doing it at 2:47.

Did Tony have someone with him? Well, Jamie couldn't really complain. Only the poisoned prawns stopped him shagging Mike. Why the hell shouldn't Tony have someone there?

That was what it meant, didn't it. Being good. You didn't have to sink wells in Burkina Faso. You didn't have to give away your coffee table. You just had to see things from other people's point of view. Remember they were human.

Like Giles fucking Mynott didn't.

Clop. Clop. Clop.

Jamie needed a pee.

He got off his stool and turned round and bumped into Josh who was carrying a cup of startlingly hot coffee back to his desk.

Jamie heard himself saying, very loudly, "You. Total. Fucking. Moron."

The office went very quiet.

Stuart walked over. It was like watching the headmaster coming across the playground after he'd torn Sharon Parker's blazer.

"Are you all right, Jamie?"

"I'm sorry. I'm really sorry."

Stuart was doing his Mr. Spock impression, giving absolutely no indication of what he was thinking.

"My sister has just canceled her wedding," said Jamie. "My father's having a nervous breakdown and my mother's leaving him for someone else."

Stuart softened. "Perhaps you should take the rest of the afternoon off."

"Yes. Thank you. I will. Thanks. Sorry."

He sat on the tube knowing he was going to hell. The only way to reduce the hot forks when he got there was to ring Katie and Mum as soon as he got home.

An old man with a withered hand was sitting opposite him. He was wearing a yellow mac and carrying a greasy satchel of papers and looking directly at Jamie and muttering to himself. Jamie was very relieved when he got off at Swiss Cottage.

Ringing Mum was going to be tricky. Was he meant to know about her leaving Dad? Was Katie even meant to know? She could have overheard a conversation and jumped to conclusions. Which she was prone to do

He'd ring Katie first.

When he got home, however, there was a message on the machine.

He pressed PLAY and took off his jacket.

He thought, at first, that it was a prank call. Or a lunatic dialing a wrong number. A woman was hyperventilating into the phone.

Then the woman was saying his name, "Jamie . . . ? Jamie . . . ?" and he realized that it was his mother and he had to sit down very quickly on the arm of the sofa.

"Jamie . . . ? Are you there . . . ? Something dreadful has happened to your father. Jamie . . . ? Oh, damn, damn, damn, damn, damn."

The message clicked off.

Everything was very quiet and very still. Then he threw himself across the room, knocking the phone to the carpet.

His parents' number. What the fuck was their number? Jesus, he must have dialed it seven thousand times. Zero one seven three three . . . Two four two . . . ? Two two four . . . ? Two four four . . . ? Christ.

He was halfway through ringing Directory Inquiries when the number came back to him. He rang it. He counted the rings. Forty. No answer.

He rang Katie.

Answerphone.

"Katie. This is Jamie. Shit. You're not in. Bugger. Listen. I've just had this scary call from Mum. Ring me, OK? No. Don't ring me. I'm going up to Peterborough. Actually, maybe you're there already. I'll talk to you later. I'm going now."

Something dreadful? Why were old people always so fucking vague?

He ran upstairs and grabbed the car keys and ran down again and had to lean against the wall in the hallway for a few seconds to stop himself passing out, and it occurred to him that in some obscure way he had caused this, by not ringing Katie back, by standing Ryan up, by not loving Tony, by not telling Stuart the whole truth.

By the time he crossed the M25, however, he was feeling surprisingly good.

He had always rather liked emergencies. Other people's, at any rate. They put your own problems into perspective. It was like being on a ferry. You didn't have to think about what you had to do or where you had to go for the next few hours. It was all laid out for you.

Like they said. No one committed suicide in wartime.

He was going to talk to his father. Properly. About everything.

Jamie had always blamed him for their lack of communication. Always thought of his father as a dried-up old stick. It was cowardice. He could see that now. And laziness. Just wanting his own prejudices confirmed.

Baldock, Biggleswade, Sandy . . .

Another forty minutes and he'd be there.

65

Katie and Ray were standing in front of a sculpture called *Lightning with Stag in Its Glare.* Basically, a girder sticking out of the wall with this jagged black metal spike dangling from it, and some pieces of junk on the floor nearby, which were meant to represent the stag and a goat and some "primitive creatures," though they could have represented the Crucifixion or the recipe for Welsh rarebit from where Katie was standing.

The aluminum stag was originally made from an ironing board. She knew this because she'd read the little cardboard explanatory note in some detail. She'd read quite a lot of the little cardboard explanatory notes, and stared out of a lot of windows and imagined the possible private lives of many of their fellow visitors because Ray was spending a lot of time examining the art. And it was pissing her off.

She'd come here for all the wrong reasons. She'd wanted to be in her element, but she wasn't. And she'd wanted him to be out of his element, but he wasn't.

You could say what you liked about Ray but you could drop him in the middle of Turkmenistan and he'd be in the nearest village by nightfall eating horse and smoking whatever they smoked out there.

He was winning. And it wasn't a competition. It was childish to think it was a competition. But he was still winning. And she was meant to be winning.

They finally reached the café.

He was holding a cube of sugar so that the bottom corner was just touching the surface of his tea and a brown tide line was slowly making its way up the cube. He was saying, "Obviously most of it's rubbish. But . . . it's like old churches and stuff. It makes you slow down and look . . . What's up, kiddo?"

"Nothing."

She could see now. The dustbin-throwing wasn't the problem. It was the not winning.

She liked the fact that she was more intelligent than Ray. She liked the fact that she could speak French and he couldn't. She liked the fact that she had opinions about factory farming and he didn't.

But it counted for nothing. He was a better person than she was. In every way that mattered. Except the dustbin-throwing. And, in truth, she might have thrown a few dustbins in her time if she'd been a little stronger.

Ten minutes later they were sitting on the big slope looking back down into the vast space of the turbine hall.

Ray said, "I know you're trying really hard, love."

Katie said nothing.

Ray said, "You don't have to do this." He paused. "You don't have to marry me because of Jacob and the house and money and everything. I'm not going to throw you out onto the street. Whatever you want to do, I'll try and make it work."

66

Jamie was crossing the waiting room when a dapper man in his late sixties sprung off one of the orange plastic chairs and blocked Jamie's path in a slightly disturbing manner.

"Jamie?"

"Yes?"

The man was wearing a linen jacket and a charcoal roll-neck sweater. He did not look like a doctor.

"David Symmonds. I'm a friend of your mother's. I know her from the bookshop where she works. In town."

"OK."

"I drove her here," the man explained. "She rang me."

Jamie wasn't sure what he was meant to do. Thank the man? Pay him? "I think I should go and find my mother." There was something disconcertingly familiar about the man. He looked like a newsreader, or someone from a TV advert.

The man said, "Your mother got home and found that your father had been taken to hospital. We think someone broke into the house."

Jamie wasn't listening. After his panicked

331

phone calls standing in front of the locked house back at the village he wasn't in the mood for interruptions.

The man continued: "And we think your father disturbed them. But it's OK . . . Sorry. That's a ridiculous word. He's alive at any rate."

Jamie felt suddenly very weak.

"There was a great deal of blood," said the man.

"What?"

"In the kitchen. In the cellar. In the bathroom."

"What are you talking about?" asked Jamie.

The man took a step backward. "They're in cubicle 4. Look . . . it's probably best if I slipped away. Now that you're here to look after your mother." The man was clasping his hands together like a vicar. There were ironed creases down the front of his canvas trousers.

Someone had tried to murder Jamie's father.

The man continued: "Send her my very best wishes. And tell her I'm thinking of her."

"OK."

The man stood to one side and Jamie walked to cubicle 4. He paused outside the curtain and braced himself for what he was about to see.

When he pushed the curtain aside, however, his parents were laughing. Well, his mother was laughing and his father was looking amused. It was something he hadn't seen in a long time.

His father had no visible wounds and when the two of them turned to look at Jamie he got the surreal impression that he was intruding on a rare romantic moment.

"Dad?" said Jamie.

"Hello, Jamie," said his father.

"I'm sorry about the phone message," said his mother. "Your father had an accident."

"With a chisel," his father explained.

"A chisel?" asked Jamie. Was the man in the waiting room a lunatic?

His father laughed gingerly. "I'm afraid I made rather a mess at home. Trying to clean up."

"But everything's all right now," said his mother.

Jamie got the impression that he could apologize for intruding and walk away and no one would be offended or puzzled in the slightest. He asked his father how he was feeling.

"A little sore," said his father.

Jamie couldn't think of any reply to this,

so he turned to his mother and said, "There was some guy in the waiting area. Told me he drove you here."

He was going to explain about the best wishes but his mother shot to her feet with a startled look on her face and said, "Oh. Is he still there?"

"He was heading off. Now you didn't need him anymore."

"I'll see if I can catch him," she said, and disappeared toward the waiting area.

Jamie moved into the chair beside his father's bed and as he sat down he remembered who David Symmonds was. And what Katie had said in her phone message. And the image came to mind of his mother sprinting through the waiting area, out of the hospital and into the passenger seat of a little red sports car, the door slamming, the engine being gunned and the pair of them vanishing in a cloud of exhaust.

So when his father said, "Actually, it wasn't an accident," Jamie thought his father was referring to the affair and came close to saying something very stupid indeed.

"I have cancer," said his father.

"I'm sorry?" said Jamie because he really didn't believe what he'd just heard.

"Or at least I did," said his father.

"Cancer?" asked Jamie.

"Dr. Barghoutian said it was eczema," continued his father. "But I wasn't sure."

Who was Dr. Barghoutian?

"So I cut it off," said his father.

"With a chisel?" Jamie realized that Katie had been right. About everything. There was something seriously wrong with his father.

"No, with a pair of scissors." His father seemed unfazed by what he was saying. "It seemed to make sense at the time." His father paused. "In fact, to be honest, I didn't manage to cut it off completely. Much more difficult than I'd imagined. Thought for a while they were going to stitch the damn thing back on. But it's better to chuck it away and let the wound granulate from the bottom up, apparently. This nice young lady doctor explained. Indian, I think." He paused again. "Probably best not to tell your mother."

"OK," said Jamie, not entirely sure what he was agreeing to.

"So," said his father, "how are you?"

"I'm fine," said Jamie.

They sat in silence for a few moments.

Then his father said, "I've been having a spot of bother recently."

"Katie told me," said Jamie.

"It's all sorted out now, though." His

father's eyes were starting to close. "If you don't mind, I'm going to have a little nap. It's been a tiring day."

Jamie had a moment of panic when he thought his father might be dying unexpectedly in front of him. He had never seen someone dying and wasn't sure of the signs. But when he examined his father's face it looked exactly as it did when he was dozing on the sofa at home.

Within seconds his father was snoring.

Jamie took hold of his father's hand. It seemed like the right thing to do. Then it felt like rather an odd thing to do, so he let it go again.

A woman was groaning in a nearby cubicle, as if she was in labor. Though surely that would happen somewhere else, wouldn't it?

Which part of his body had his father tried to cut off?

Did it matter? There wasn't going to be an answer to that question, which made it seem normal.

Jesus. It was his father who had done this. The alphabeticizer of books and winder-up of clocks.

Perhaps it was the beginning of dementia.

Jamie hoped to God his mother hadn't done a runner. Or he and Katie might be left looking after their father as he began his slow descent toward a horrid little residential home somewhere.

It was an uncharitable thought.

He was trying very hard to give up uncharitable thoughts.

Perhaps that was what he needed. Something to come along and smash his life to pieces. Go back to the village. Look after his father. Learn to be properly human again. A sort of spiritual thing.

His mother reappeared with a swish of curtain. "Sorry about that. I just caught him as he was leaving. Someone from work. David. He gave me a lift."

"Dad's asleep," said Jamie, though that was pretty obvious from the snoring.

Were she and that man having sex? It was a day of revelations.

His mother sat down.

Jamie took a deep breath. "Dad said he had cancer."

"Oh, yes, that," said his mother.

"So he didn't have cancer?"

"Not according to Dr. Barghoutian."

"Right."

Jamie wanted to tell her about the scissors. But when he formed the sentence in his head it seemed too bizarre to say out loud. A sick daydream he would regret sharing quite so eagerly.

His mother said, "I'm sorry, I should have told you before you got here."

Once again, Jamie was not entirely sure what she was referring to.

She said, "Your father has not been terribly well recently."

"I know."

"We're hoping it will sort itself out in time," said his mother.

So she wasn't running away with the man. Not in the immediate future.

Jamie said, "God. Everything happens at once, doesn't it."

"Meaning?" His mother had a worried look on her face.

Jamie said, "What with the wedding being off and everything."

His mother's expression changed from one kind of worried to a different kind of worried and Jamie realized, instantly, that she didn't know about the wedding being off, and that he'd fucked things up, and Katie was going to kill him, and his mother wasn't going to be very chuffed either, and he really should have returned Katie's call straightaway.

"What do you mean, the wedding's off?" asked his mother.

"Well . . ." Jamie trod carefully. "She

mentioned something on the phone . . . She left a message . . . I haven't spoken to her since she left it . . . It is possible that some wires got crossed."

His mother shook her head sadly and let out a long sigh. "Well, I guess that's one less thing we have to worry about."

67

Katie and Ray came back via the nursery.

Jacob was unnaturally interested in why the two of them were picking him up together. He could sense that something wasn't right. But she successfully distracted him by saying they'd seen a grand piano hanging from the ceiling (*Concert for Anarchy,* 1990, by Rebecca Horn; Christ, she could probably get a job at the place) and Jacob and Ray were soon talking about how Australia was upside down, but only sort of, and how cavemen came after dinosaurs but before horse-drawn carriages.

When they got back home she checked the answerphone and heard a freakish voice saying that something dreadful had happened to her father. So freakish she assumed the father in question was someone else's. Then the woman said she was going to ring

Jamie, and Katie realized it was Mum and it scared the crap out of her. So she replayed the message. And it was the same second time around. And then she really started to panic.

But there was another message. From Jamie.

"I've just had this scary call from Mum. Ring me, OK? No. Don't ring me. I'm going up to Peterborough. Actually, maybe you're there already. I'll talk to you later."

Jamie didn't say what was wrong with Dad, either.

Shit.

She told Ray she was taking the car. Ray said he'd drive her to Peterborough. She said he had to stay behind to look after Jacob. Ray said they'd take Jacob with them. Katie told him not to be ridiculous. Ray said he wasn't going to let her drive while she was this upset.

Jacob heard the last part of this exchange.

Ray squatted down in front of him and said, "Grandpa's ill. So, what do you say we have an adventure and drive up and see him to make sure he's all right?"

"Will he want some chocolate?" asked Jacob.

"Possibly," said Ray.

"He can have the rest of my chocolate buttons."

"I'll get the chocolate buttons," said Ray. "You go and find your pajamas and toothbrush and some clean pants for tomorrow, all right?"

"All right." Jacob pottered off upstairs.

Dad had tried to commit suicide. She could think of no other explanation.

Ray said, "Get your stuff together. I'll do me and Jacob."

What else could have happened to him stuck in that bedroom? Pills? Razor blades? Rope? She needed to know, if only to stop the pictures in her head.

Maybe he'd wandered out of the house and been hit by a car.

It was her fault. He'd asked for help and she'd passed the buck to Mum, knowing she was totally out of her depth.

Shit, shit, shit.

She grabbed a jumper from the drawer and the little rucksack from the wardrobe.

Was he even alive?

If only she'd talked to him for a bit longer. If only she'd cut work and spent the week with her parents. If only she'd pressed Mum a little harder. Christ, she didn't even know whether he'd been to the doctor. For the last couple of days she hadn't even thought

341

about him. Not once.

It was a little easier in the car. And Ray was right. She'd have rammed someone by now. They struggled northward through the tail end of the rush hour, jam after jam, red light after red light, Ray and Jacob going through several thousand verses of "The Wheels on the Bus."

By the time they reached Peterborough Jacob was asleep.

Ray pulled up outside the house and said, "Stay there," and got out.

She wanted to protest. She wasn't a child. And it was *her* father. But she was exhausted, and glad that someone else was making the decisions.

Ray knocked on the door and waited for a long time. There was no answer. He went round the back.

At the end of the street, three kids were taking turns to ride a bike over a little ramp made of a plank and a wooden crate, like she and Juliet used to do when they were nine.

Ray was taking a very long time. She got out of the car and was halfway down the path beside the house when he reappeared.

He held up his hand. "No. Don't go back there."

"Why?"

"There's no one in."

"How do you know?" she asked.

"I broke in through a window at the back." He turned her round and marched her toward the car.

"You what?"

"We'll sort it out later on. I need to ring the hospital."

"Why can't I look inside the house?" asked Katie.

Ray took hold of both her shoulders and looked into her face. "Trust me."

He opened the driver's door, retrieved his mobile from the glove compartment and dialed.

"George Hall," said Ray. "That's right."

They waited.

"Thank you," said Ray into the phone.

"Well?" asked Katie.

"He's at the hospital," said Ray. "Get in."

"And what did they say about him?"

"They didn't."

"Why not?" asked Katie.

"I didn't ask."

"Jesus, Ray."

"They don't tell you anything if you're not family."

"I'm bloody family," said Katie.

"I'm sorry," said Ray. "But please, get into the car."

She got into the car and Ray pulled away.

"Why wouldn't you let me see in the house?" asked Katie. "What was in there?"

"There was a lot of blood," said Ray, very quietly.

68

Shortly after Jean sent Jamie off to find something to eat in the hospital canteen a doctor appeared. He was wearing a dark blue V-neck pullover and no tie, the way doctors did these days.

He said, "Mrs. Hall?"

"Yes?"

"My name is Dr. Parris."

He shook her hand. He was rather good-looking. There was something of the rugby player about him.

He said, "Could we step outside for a moment?" and he said it so politely that it never occurred to her to be worried. They stepped outside.

"So?" she asked.

He paused. "We'd like to keep your husband in overnight."

"OK." It sounded like a very sensible idea.

He said, "We'd like to make a psychiatric assessment."

She said, "Well, yes, he has been feeling rather down recently." She was impressed by the hospital's thoroughness, but puzzled as to how they knew. Perhaps Dr. Barghoutian had put something in George's medical records. Which was a bit alarming.

Dr. Parris said, "If someone's harmed themselves we like to know why. Whether they've done it before. Whether they're likely to do it again."

Jean said, "He broke his elbow a couple of years ago. Usually, he's very careful about that kind of thing." She really didn't understand what Dr. Parris was getting at. She smiled.

Dr. Parris smiled back, but it was not a proper smile. "And he broke his elbow . . . ?"

"Falling off a stepladder."

"They didn't tell you about the scissors, did they."

"What scissors?" she asked.

So he told her about the scissors.

She wanted to tell Dr. Parris that he'd mixed George up with someone else. But he knew about the blood and the bathroom and the eczema. She felt stupid for believing his ridiculous story about the chisel. And frightened for George.

He was losing his mind.

She wanted to ask Dr. Parris what exactly was wrong with George, whether it would get worse, whether it was something permanent. But these were selfish questions and she didn't want to make a fool of herself for a second time. So she thanked him for talking to her, he went away and she returned to the chair beside George's bed and waited for Dr. Parris to leave the ward and wept a little when no one was watching.

69

Jamie sat drinking coffee and eating a cheese-and-onion pasty in the Kenco Restaurant (*Chef's Specials, Midweek Carvery, International Cuisine, and much more . . . !*).

He was in major shit. Ideally he wanted to sit here until Katie arrived and she and his mother tore a few chunks off each other and came to some kind of truce before he ventured back down to casualty.

He rather liked the Kenco Restaurant. In much the same way that he rather liked motorway service stations and airport lounges. In much the same way that other people rather liked going round cathedrals or walking in the countryside.

The black plastic trays, the fake plants and

the little trellises they'd added to give it a garden-center feel . . . You could think in places like this. No one knew who you were. You weren't going to be accosted by colleagues or friends. You were on your own but you weren't alone.

At teenage parties he was always wandering into the garden, sitting on a bench in the dark, smoking Camel cigarettes, the lit windows behind him and the faint strains of "Hi, Ho, Silver Lining" thumping away, staring up at the constellations and pondering all those big questions about the existence of God and the nature of evil and the mystery of death, questions which seemed more important than anything else in the world until a few years passed and some real questions had been dumped into your lap, like how to earn a living, and why people fell in and out of love, and how long you could carry on smoking and then give up without getting lung cancer.

Maybe the answers weren't important. Maybe it was the asking which mattered. Not taking anything for granted. Maybe that's what stopped you growing old.

And maybe you could put up with anything so long as you got half an hour a day to come somewhere like this and let your mind wander.

An old man with lizardy skin and a square of gauze stuck over his Adam's apple sat down with a mug of tea at the table opposite. The fingers on the man's right hand were so yellow with nicotine they looked varnished.

Jamie glanced at his watch. He'd been away for forty minutes. He felt suddenly rather guilty.

He swigged the last of the gritty coffee, stood up and walked back down the main corridor.

70

Jean watched George sleeping.

She was thinking about the day they'd visited George's uncle in that dreadful hospital in Nottingham, just before he died. Those sad old men sitting round the television smoking and shuffling down corridors. Was that going to happen to George?

She heard footsteps, and Katie appeared from between the curtains, flushed and panting. She looked wretched.

"How's Dad?"

"Your father's OK. There's no need to worry."

"We were so scared." She was out of

breath. "What happened?"

Jean explained. About the accident with the chisel. And now that she knew it wasn't true, it sounded ridiculous and she wondered why she'd fallen for it herself. But Katie seemed too relieved to ask questions.

"Thank God for that . . . I thought . . ." Katie caught herself and lowered her voice in case George could hear what she was saying. "Let's not even talk about it." She rubbed her face.

"Talk about what?" said Jean, quietly.

"I thought he might have . . . Well, you know," whispered Katie. "He was depressed. He was worried about dying. I couldn't think of any other explanation for you being in such a state."

Suicide. That was what the doctor was talking about, wasn't it. Harming yourself.

Katie touched her shoulder and said, "Are you OK, Mum?"

"I'm fine," said Jean. "Well, to be honest, I'm not fine. It's been difficult to say the least. But I'm glad you and Jamie are here."

"Talking of which . . ."

"He's gone to the canteen," said Jean. "Your father was asleep and he hadn't eaten. So I sent him off."

"Ray said the house was a mess."

"The house," said Jean. "My God, I'd

forgotten about the house."

"Sorry."

"You'll come back with me, won't you," said Jean. "They're keeping your father in overnight."

"Of course," said Katie. "We'll do whatever's best for you."

"Thank you," said Jean.

Katie looked at George. "Well, he doesn't seem to be in pain."

"No."

"Where did he cut himself?"

"On his hip," said Jean. "I guess he must have fallen over onto the chisel when he was holding it." She leant forward and flicked the blankets back to show Katie the dressed wound, but his pajama trousers had been pushed a little too far down and you could see his pubic hair so she quickly flicked the blanket back again.

Katie picked up her father's hand and held it. "Dad?" she said. "It's Katie." Dad murmured something incomprehensible. "You're a bloody idiot. But we love you."

"So, is Jacob here?" asked Jean.

But Katie wasn't listening. She sat down on the other chair and started to cry.

"Katie?"

"I'm sorry."

Jean let her cry for a while, then said,

"Jamie told me about the wedding."

Katie looked up. "What?"

"About you wanting to call the wedding off."

Katie looked pained.

"It's OK," said Jean. "I know you're probably worried about bringing it up. What with your father's accident. And everything being arranged. But the very worst thing would be to go ahead just because you didn't want to cause a fuss."

"Right," said Katie, nodding to herself.

"The most important thing is that you're happy." She paused. "If it makes you feel any better, we've had our doubts all along."

"We?"

"Your father and I. Ray's obviously a decent man. And Jacob clearly likes him. But we've always felt that he wasn't quite right for you."

Katie said nothing for a worryingly long time.

"We love you very much," said Jean.

Katie interrupted her. "And it was Jamie who told you this."

"He said you rang him." Something was clearly going wrong, but Jean wasn't sure what.

Katie stood up. There was a steely look in her eye. She said, "I'll be back in a few minutes," and disappeared through the curtains.

She seemed very angry indeed.

Jamie was in trouble. Jean could tell that much. She sat back and closed her eyes and let out a long breath. She didn't have the energy for this. Not now.

Your children never really grew up. Thirty years on and they still behaved like five-year-olds. One minute they were your best friend. Then you said the wrong thing and they went off like firecrackers.

She leant forward and took George's hand. You could say what you liked about her husband, but at least he was predictable.

Or used to be.

She squeezed his fingers and realized she hadn't got the faintest idea what was going on in his head.

71

When Jamie entered the waiting room he saw Ray and Jacob sitting opposite one another at the far end of the green plastic seats. Ray was doing the magic trick with the coin. The one fathers had been doing all over the world since the beginning of time.

Jamie sat down in the seat next to Jacob and said, "Hello, boys."

Jacob said, "Ray can do magic."

Ray looked at Jamie and said, "So . . . ?"

For a few seconds Jamie had no idea what Ray might be talking about. Then he remembered. "Oh, yeh. Dad. Sorry. I've been in the canteen. He's fine. Well, actually he's not fine. I mean, there are other problems, but physically, he's fine. Mum rang everyone because . . ." There was no way to explain why Mum rang everyone without giving Jacob nightmares. "I'll explain later."

"Is Grandpa dead," said Jacob.

"He's very much alive," said Jamie. "So there's nothing for you to worry about."

"Good," said Ray. "Good." He breathed out, like someone acting relieved in a play.

Then Jamie remembered the wedding thing and felt uncomfortable not mentioning it. So he said, "How are you?" with a meaningful tone to indicate that this was genuine concern, not just politeness.

And Ray said, "I'm OK," with a meaningful tone to indicate that he knew exactly what Jamie was talking about.

"Do the magic," said Jacob. "Magic it. Magic it into my ear."

"OK." Ray turned to Jamie and there was the faintest hint of a smile and Jamie allowed himself to consider the possibility that Ray might be a reasonably pleasant human being.

The coin was a twenty pence piece. There was a twenty pence piece in the back pocket of Jamie's cords. He quietly fished it out and held it secretly in his right hand. "This time," said Jamie, "Ray is going to magic the coin into my hand." He held up his right fist.

Ray looked at Jamie, and clearly thought Jamie was trying to arrange some man-on-man touching if his frown was anything to go by. Then it clicked, and he smiled, a proper smile this time, and said, "Let's give it a go."

Ray put the coin theatrically between his thumb and forefinger.

"I have to do the sprinkle," said Jacob, clearly terrified that someone else might do the sprinkle first.

"Go on, then," said Ray.

Jacob sprinkled invisible magic dust over the coin.

Ray did a little flourish with his free hand, lowered it over the coin like a handkerchief, squeezed it into a fist and whipped it away. The coin had vanished.

"The hand," said Jacob. "Show me the magic hand."

Ray opened his fist slowly.

No coin.

Jacob's eyes were wide with wonder.

"And now," said Jamie, holding up his fist, *"bzzang!"*

He was just about to open his hand and reveal the coin when Ray said, "Katie . . . ?" and the look on his face was not good. And Jamie turned round and saw Katie marching toward him, and the look on her face was not good, either.

He said, "Katie. Hi," and she punched him in the side of the head so that he was knocked off his seat onto the floor and found himself looking, in close-up, at Jacob's shoes.

He heard a slightly deranged person cheering approvingly from the other side of the room, and Ray saying, "Katie . . . What the bloody hell . . . ?" and Jacob saying, "You hit Uncle Jamie," in a puzzled voice, and the sound of footsteps running.

By the time he'd levered himself into a sitting position there was a security guard approaching them saying, "Whoa, whoa, whoa, let's calm it down a bit here, people."

Katie said to Jamie, "What the fuck did you tell Mum?"

Jamie said, to the security guard, "It's OK, she's my sister."

Ray said to Jacob, "I think you and I are going to go and see Granny and Grandpa."

The security guard said, "Any more funny business and I'll have the lot of you out of here," but no one was really listening to him.

72

Five minutes later Jean heard a second set of footsteps, heavier than Katie's. She thought, at first, that it was another doctor. She braced herself.

But when the curtains opened it was Ray, with Jacob on his shoulders.

She realized, instantly, what had happened. Katie had told Ray. About her and George having doubts. About Ray not being good enough for their daughter.

Ray put Jacob down.

Jacob said, "Hello, Grandma. I had . . . I got . . . some . . . some chocolate buttons. For Grandpa."

Jean had no idea what a man like Ray might do when he was angry.

She got off her chair and said, "Ray. I'm really sorry. It's not that we don't like you. Far from it. We just . . . I'm so, so sorry."

She wanted the ground to swallow her up, but it didn't, so she ducked between the curtains and ran.

73

Katie watched Jamie get to his feet and three things then occurred to her in rapid succession.

Firstly, she was going to have to do some serious explaining to Jacob. Secondly, she'd lost her final shred of moral superiority over Ray. Thirdly, it was the first time she'd punched someone properly since that argument over the red sandals with Zoë Canter in junior school, and it felt bloody brilliant.

She sat down next to her brother. Neither of them spoke for a few moments.

"I'm sorry," she said, though she wasn't. Not really. "I've been having a crap few weeks."

"Snap," said Jamie.

"Meaning?"

"Tony chucked me."

"Shit. I'm sorry," said Katie, and over Jamie's shoulder she saw a woman who looked very like Mum running toward the main corridor of the hospital as if she was being chased by an invisible dog.

"And it wasn't a chisel," said Jamie, "he was 'cutting the cancer off,' apparently.

With scissors."

"Well, that makes a bit more sense," said Katie.

Jamie looked a little disappointed. "I thought I'd get a better reaction than that."

So Katie explained, about the visit home and the panic attacks and *Lethal Weapon.*

"Oh, I forgot," said Jamie. "He was here."

"Who?"

"Mum's fancy man."

"What do you mean, he was here?" she asked.

"He gave her a lift, apparently. He was keeping a pretty low profile. For obvious reasons. I bumped into him when I arrived."

"So, what's he like?"

Jamie shrugged.

"Would you shag him?" she asked.

Jamie raised his eyebrows and she realized that recent events were sending her a little bonkers.

"Sharing an aging bisexual lover with my own mother," said Jamie. "I think life is probably difficult enough already." He paused. "Dapper. Suntan. Roll-neck sweater. A little too much aftershave."

She leaned forward and took hold of his hands. "Are you OK?"

He laughed. "Yeh. Surprisingly enough I am."

She knew precisely what he meant. And at that moment it really was all right. The two of them sitting quietly together. The eye of the storm.

"So, are you getting married?" Jamie asked.

"God knows. Mum's over the moon. Of course. So, naturally, there's a part of me that wants to marry Ray just to piss her off." She went silent for a moment. "It should be simple, shouldn't it. I mean, you either love someone or you don't. It's not exactly quantum theory. But I haven't got a clue, Jamie. Not a clue."

A young Asian man in a dark blue suit walked in through the double doors and went up to the desk. He seemed sober but his shirt was covered in blood.

She remembered all those cartoons of boys sitting in hospital waiting rooms with pans on their heads, and wondered if it was actually possible to get a pan stuck on your head.

Cutting the cancer off with scissors. It was utterly logical when you thought about it. Rather strong treatment for eczema, though.

The Asian man fell over. Not in a slumpy way. But rigid. Like a rake, or the big hand of a very fast clock. He made a loud noise when he hit the floor. It was funny and not funny all at the same time.

He was stretchered away.

Then Ray and Jacob appeared.

Jacob said, "He was . . . There was a . . . Grandpa was snoring."

Ray said, "You haven't seen your mum, have you?"

"Why?" asked Jamie.

"She went a bit weird then legged it."

Jacob looked at Jamie. "Magic the coin."

"Later, OK?" He stood up and ruffled Jacob's hair. "I'll go and find her."

Ten minutes later they were heading back to the village.

They took Mum in their car. Katie got into the back with Jacob. Mum was clearly not too chuffed about sitting in the front with Ray but Katie was perversely entertained by the sight of the two of them trying to sustain a polite conversation.

Besides, she liked being in the back with Jacob. The children. No responsibilities. The adults sorting everything out. Like that summer in Italy when the engine of the Alfa Romeo ruptured outside Reggio Emilia and they pulled over at the side of the road and the man with the amazing mustache came and said that it was *completamente morte* or something like that and Dad actually vomited into the grass, though at the time it was just another bit of strange parental behavior and a bad smell, and she and Jamie sat on the verge playing with the binoculars and the little wooden snowflake puzzle, drinking fizzy orange without a care in the world.

74

Jamie was kneeling on the stairs with a washing-up bowl of soapy water sponging his father's blood from the carpet.

That was the problem with books and films. When the big stuff happened there was orchestral music and everyone knew where to get a tourniquet and there was never an ice-cream van going by outside. Then the big stuff happened in real life and your knees hurt and the disposable cloth wipe was disintegrating in your hands and it was obvious there was going to be some kind of permanent stain.

Jamie got back to the house first and when Katie and Ray pulled up beside him, Mum shot out of the passenger door like the car was on fire, which was a little odd. And there was this panic going on because Jacob obviously couldn't go into the house on account of the blood (Ray's description made it sound more like redecoration than spillage). But the panic was being done entirely with hand gestures so that Jacob didn't get wind of what was happening.

And Jamie could see what Katie meant about Ray being capable. Because he pulled a tent out of the boot and told Jacob the two of them were sleeping in the garden because there was a crocodile in the house and if Jacob was really lucky he wouldn't have to go inside and wash and he could wee in the flower bed.

But it wasn't a job. You didn't marry someone because they were capable. You married someone because you were in love. And there was something unsexy about being too capable. Capable was a dad thing.

Though, obviously, if Ray was their father he would have gone to the doctor. Or used the right tools and not left something semi-attached.

Jamie was still soaping the stairs when Katie materialized in front of him.

"You don't think he was going to keep it, do you?" She was waving an empty ice-cream tub.

"What's *it,* by the way?" asked Jamie.

"Left hip," said Katie, making a little scissor gesture next to the pocket of her jeans.

"How much?" asked Jamie.

"Large burger," said Katie. "Apparently. I

didn't see the actual wound. Anyway . . . that's the bathroom done. Mum's finished the kitchen. Give me that stuff and you can go out and see how Ray and Jacob are doing."

"You'd rather clean blood out of a carpet than go and talk to your fiancé."

"If you're going to be horrible you can do it yourself."

"Sorry," said Jamie. "Offer accepted."

"Besides," said Katie, "much as it pains me to say this, women are just better at cleaning."

The sky was overcast and the garden was very dark indeed. Jamie had to stand on the patio for thirty seconds before he could see anything at all.

Ray had pitched the tent as far away from Katie's family as possible. When Jamie reached it a disembodied voice said, "Hello Jamie."

Ray was sitting with his back to the house. His head was a silhouette, his expression unreadable.

"I brought you a coffee." Jamie handed it over.

"Cheers."

Ray was sitting on a camping mat. He hotched backward, offering Jamie the other end.

Jamie sat down. The mat was slightly warm. There were little breathy snores from inside the tent.

"So, what did he do to himself?" asked Ray.

"Shit," said Jamie. "Nobody's told you, have they. I'm sorry."

Jamie told the story and Ray let out a long whistle. "What a nutter."

He seemed impressed and for a couple of seconds Jamie was oddly proud of his father.

They sat in silence.

It was like the teenage-party thing. Without "Hi, Ho, Silver Lining." And Jamie wasn't alone in the garden. But it was all right. Ray had been banished in some obscure way and that made him an outsider, too. Plus Jamie couldn't see him, so he didn't take up as much space as usual.

Ray said, "I did a runner."

"Come again."

"Katie went out for a coffee with Graham. I followed them."

"Ooh, that's not good, is it."

"Wanted to kill him, to be honest," said Ray. "I threw this dustbin. Knew I'd blown it. So I bottled. Slept at the house of this bloke from work." He paused. "Of course, that was worse than following her to the caff."

Jamie didn't know what to say. Talking to Ray was hard enough in broad daylight. With no body language it was pretty much impossible.

"Actually," said Ray, "it's not really about Graham. Graham was just a . . ."

"Catalyst?" said Jamie, glad of a chance to make a contribution.

"A symptom," said Ray, politely. "Katie doesn't love me. I don't think she ever has. But she's trying really hard. Because she's frightened I'm going to chuck her out of the house."

"Uh-huh," said Jamie.

"I'm not going to chuck her out of the house."

"Thank you." It sounded weird. But correcting it would have sounded weirder.

"But you don't marry someone if you don't love them, do you," said Ray.

"No," said Jamie, though people obviously did.

They sat for a while, listening to a distant train (how strange that you only ever heard them at night). It was oddly pleasant. What with Ray being a bit crestfallen. And Jamie not being able to see him. So Jamie said, "God, the famous Graham," in a sort of speaking-out-loud way as if he was talking to a friend.

He could feel Ray flinch. Even in the dark. "You've met him," said Jamie. "You know what he's like."

"I try to keep a low profile," said Ray.

Jamie sipped his coffee. "Well, obviously he's incredibly good-looking." This was probably not the right thing to say. "But that's all he is. He's boring. And shallow. And weak. And actually not very intelligent. Except you don't really notice at first. Because he's cute, and laid-back, and confident. So you kind of assume he's got some grand plan." He glanced back toward the house and noticed a broken pane in the kitchen window which had been neatly filled with a rectangle of wood. "He works for an insurance company . . . It's not often that someone has a job that makes mine seem exciting."

Jamie was rather enjoying talking to Ray in the dark like this. The strangeness, the secretness. The way it made things easier to say. So much so that Jamie let his guard down and found himself having a brief but very specific sexual fantasy about Ray and only realized what he was doing about three seconds in, which was like treading on a slug in the kitchen at night, because it was wrong in so many ways.

Ray said, "Your mum's not too chuffed

about having me in the family, is she."

And Jamie thought, *What the hell,* and said, "Not much. But she thought the sun shone out of Graham's arse. So she's hardly the world's best judge of character." Was this wise? He could have done with seeing Ray's face at this point. "Of course when Graham walked out on Katie and Jacob she decided he was a servant of Satan."

Ray wasn't saying anything.

A light went on upstairs and his mother appeared briefly at the bedroom window and glanced down into the dark garden. She looked small and sad.

Jamie said, "You hang on in there," and realized he wanted Ray and Katie to stay together and wasn't entirely sure why. Because he needed something to go right when everything else was going wrong? Or was he starting to like the man?

"Thanks, mate," said Ray.

And Jamie paused and said, "Tony chucked me." He wasn't entirely sure why he said this either.

"And you want to get back together . . ."

Jamie tried to say yes but the thought of saying it made him feel slightly choked up and he didn't feel close enough to Ray for that. "Mmm-hmm."

"Your fault or his?"

Jamie decided to go for it. It was a kind of penance. Like diving into a cold pool. It would be character building. If he cried, sod it. He'd made a fool of himself enough times already this week. "I wanted to be with someone. And I wanted to stay single at the same time."

"So you can, like, shag other blokes?"

"No, not even that." Strangely, he didn't feel like crying. Quite the opposite, in fact. Perhaps it was the darkness, but it was easier talking about this to Ray than to anyone in his own family. Katie included. "I didn't want to compromise. I didn't want to share stuff. I didn't want to have to make sacrifices. Which is stupid. I can see that now." He paused. "You love someone, you've got to let something go."

"Spot on," said Ray.

"I fucked up," said Jamie. "And I'm not sure how to mend it."

"You hang on in there, too," said Ray.

Jamie brushed an insect off his face.

"The stupid thing . . ." said Ray.

"What's the stupid thing?" asked Jamie.

"I love her. She's bloody hard work, but I love her. And I know I'm not very bright. And I know I do some moronic things. But I care about her. I really do."

On cue, the kitchen door opened and

Katie emerged carrying a plate.

"Where are you?" She walked gingerly onto the lawn and trod on something. "Shit." She bent down to retrieve a dropped fork.

"We're here," said Jamie.

She made her way over. "There's supper inside. Why don't you two go and get something to eat and I'll sit with Jacob."

"You give me that," said Ray. "I'll stay out here."

"All right," said Katie. She sounded like she'd had enough disagreements for one day. She gave the plate to Ray. "Spaghetti Bolognese. You sure you don't want a man portion?"

"I'll be fine," said Ray.

Katie got down onto her hands and knees and put her head inside the tent. She snuggled close to Jacob and kissed his cheek. "Sleep tight, banana." Then she got up again and turned to Jamie. "Come on. We'd better go and keep Mum company."

She headed back toward the house.

Jamie got to his feet. He put his hand on Ray's shoulder and patted it gently. Ray didn't react.

He walked over the damp grass toward the lit house.

75

Katie knew there was going to be a row over supper. She could feel it in the air. If things went particularly badly they could have an argument about her own wedding, Dad's mental health and Mum's lover all at the same time.

Halfway through the spaghetti Bolognese Mum said she sincerely hoped Dad wouldn't be having any more silly accidents. There was a slightly hunted look on her face and it seemed pretty obvious to Katie that she knew the chisel story was bollocks but wanted to make sure neither of them did. There was one of those uneasy silences where you can hear everyone chewing and the scrape of cutlery and Jamie saved the situation by saying, "And if he does, let's hope he does it in the garden," which allowed them to defuse the tension with a bit of forced laughter.

They were clearing the plates when Mum dropped the big one. "So, is there going to be a wedding or not?"

Katie gritted her teeth. "I just don't know, OK?"

"Well, we're going to have to know pretty soon. I mean it's all very well us being sympathetic, but I've got to make some rather difficult phone calls and I'd rather not leave them any longer than I have to."

Katie put her hands flat on the table to calm herself. "What do you want me to say? I don't know. Things are difficult at the moment."

Jamie paused in the doorway with the plates.

"Well, do you love him or not?" asked Mum.

And that was when Katie really lost it. "What the hell do you know about love?"

Mum looked as if she'd been slapped.

Jamie said, "Hang on. Hang on. Let's not have a shouting match. Please."

"Butt out," said Katie.

Jean sat back in her chair and closed her eyes and said, "Well, if you're feeling like that then I think it's safe to assume that there's going to be no wedding."

Jamie's hands were actually shaking. He put the plates back down on the table. "Katie. Mum. Can we just leave this, OK? I think we've all been through enough already."

"What the fuck has this got to do with you?" said Katie, and she knew it was childish and spiteful but she needed sympathy, not a bloody lecture.

Then Jamie lost it, too, which she hadn't seen in a very long time.

"It's got everything to do with me. You're my sister. And you're my mother. And the two of you are screwing everything up."

"Jamie . . ." said Mum, as if he was six.

Jamie ignored her and turned to Katie. "I've spent the last twenty minutes sitting outside with Ray and he's a really nice guy and he's busting a gut to make it easy for you."

Katie said, "Well, you've changed your tune."

"Shut up and listen," said Jamie. "He's putting up with all this crap. And he's giving you a place to live for as long as you like even though you don't love him, because he cares for you and he cares for Jacob. He drives up here and sits in the garden because he's perfectly aware that Mum and Dad don't like him —"

"I never said that," countered Mum weakly.

"And I've sat with Dad today and talked to him and there is something seriously wrong with him and he didn't have an accident with a stupid fucking chisel. He was chopping himself up with a pair of scissors and you're hoping it'll all blow over. Well, it's not going to blow over. He needs someone to listen to him or he's going to stick his head in the oven and we're all going to end up feeling like shit because we pretended there was nothing wrong."

Katie was so stunned by Jamie's sudden character change that she didn't hear what he was saying. No one spoke for a couple of seconds and then Mum started to cry very quietly.

Jamie said, "I'm going to take some pudding into the garden," and walked out, leaving the plates on the table.

76

Jean went upstairs and lay down on the bed and cried until she had run out of tears.

She felt desperately lonely.

Because of Jamie, mostly. Katie she could understand. Katie was going through a difficult time. And Katie argued with everyone, about everything. But what had come over Jamie? Did he have any idea of what she had been through today?

She no longer understood the men in her family.

She sat up and blew her nose on a tissue from the box on the bedside table.

Though, to be frank, she wasn't sure that

she ever had.

She remembered Jamie at five. Going off to his room "to be private." Even now they would be talking sometimes and it was like talking to someone in Spain. You got the basics. The time of day. Directions to the beach. But there was a whole level you were missing because you didn't speak the language properly.

And it might have been all right if she could just give him a cuddle sometimes. But he wasn't the cuddling sort. No more than George was.

She walked over to the window and pulled the curtains back and looked down into the darkened garden. There was a tent somewhere in the shadows under the trees at the far end.

The idea of swapping places with Ray seemed suddenly very attractive, being down there in a sleeping bag with Jacob.

Away from the house. Away from her family. Away from everything.

77

When George came round they'd gone. Jean, Katie, Jamie, Jacob, Ray. He was rather relieved, to be honest. He was exceedingly tired, and his family could be hard work. Especially en masse.

He was beginning to think that he could do with a spot of reading, and wondering how he might be able to get his hands on a decent magazine, when the curtains were opened by a large man in a battered canvas jacket. He was entirely bald and carrying a clipboard.

"Mr. Hall?" He rotated a pair of wire-rimmed spectacles up onto his very shiny head.

"Yes."

"Joel Forman. Psychiatrist."

"I thought you chaps went home at five o'clock," said George.

"That would be lovely, wouldn't it." He flicked through some papers on the clipboard. "Sadly, people only get crazier as the day wears on, in my experience. Self-medication, usually. Though I'm sure that doesn't apply to you."

"Certainly not," said George. "Though I've been taking some antidepressants." He decided not to mention the codeine and the whiskey.

"What flavor?"

"Flavor?"

"What are they called?"

"Lustral," said George. "They make me

feel absolutely terrible, to be honest."

Dr. Forman was one of those men who did humor without smiling. He looked like a villain from a James Bond film. It was disconcerting.

"Weeping, sleeplessness and anxiety," said Dr. Forman. "Always makes me laugh when I read that under possible side effects. I'd chuck them, frankly."

"OK," said George.

"You were doing some amateur surgery, I hear."

George explained, slowly and carefully, in a measured voice with a little self-deprecating humor thrown in, how he had ended up in hospital.

"Scissors. The practical approach," said Dr. Forman. "And how are you now?"

"I feel better than I have done in quite a long time," said George.

"Good," said Dr. Forman. "But you'll still be seeing the psychologist at your GP's surgery, won't you." This was not phrased as a question.

"I will."

"Good," said Dr. Forman again, jabbing the paper on the clipboard with the end of his pen in a little rounding-off flourish. "Good."

George relaxed a little. His examination

was over, and unless he was very much mistaken, he had passed. "Only a week ago I was thinking I could do with a stay in some kind of institution. Rest from the world. That kind of thing."

Dr. Forman did not react at first and George wondered whether he had given away a piece of information which was going to change Dr. Forman's assessment. Like reversing over the examiner's foot after a driving test.

Dr. Forman put the clipboard back under his arm. "I'd stay away from psychiatric hospitals if I were you." He clicked his heels together. It was part changing of the guard, part Wizard of Oz. George wondered if Dr. Forman was himself a little unhinged. "Talk to your psychologist. Eat properly. Get to bed early. Do some regular exercise."

"Which reminds me," said George. "Do you know where I can get hold of something to read?"

"I'll see what I can do," said Dr. Forman, and before George could specify the kind of reading material he might like, the psychiatrist had shaken George's hand and vanished through the curtain.

Half an hour later a porter came to take him to a ward. George felt a little insulted by the wheelchair until he attempted to stand. It wasn't pain per se, but the sensation of something being very wrong in his abdominal region and the suspicion that if he stood up his insides might exit through the hole he had made earlier in the day. When he sat down again, sweat was pouring from his face and arms.

"You going to behave now?" said the porter.

Two nurses appeared and he was hoisted into the chair.

He was wheeled to an empty bed on an open ward. A tiny leathery Oriental man was sleeping in the bed to his left in a cat's cradle of tubes and wires. To his right a teenage boy was listening to music through headphones. His leg was in traction and he had brought most of his possessions into hospital: a stack of CDs, a camera, a bottle of HP Sauce, a small robot, some books, a large inflatable hammer . . .

George lay on the bed staring at the ceiling. He would have given anything for a cup of tea and a biscuit.

He was on the verge of catching the attention of the teenage boy to find out whether there was any conceivable overlap in their literary tastes when Dr. Forman materialized at the foot of the bed. He handed George two paperbacks and said, "Leave them with the nurses when you've finished, OK? Or I will hunt you down like a dog." He gave a brief smile then turned and walked away, exchanging a few words with one of the nurses in a language which was neither English nor any other language that George recognized.

George turned the books over. *Treason's Harbour* and *The Nutmeg of Consolation,* by Patrick O'Brian.

The aptness of the choice was almost creepy. George had read *Master and Commander* last year and had been meaning to try some of the others. He wondered whether he might have said something while unconscious.

He read eighty or so pages of *Treason's Harbour,* ate a limp institutional supper of beef stew, boiled vegetables, peaches and custard, then slipped into a dreamless sleep, interrupted only by a long and complex visit to the toilet at 3:00 a.m.

In the morning he was given a bowl of cornflakes, a mug of tea and a brief lecture about wound care. The charge nurse asked whether he possessed a ground-floor toilet and a wife who could move him around the house. He was presented with a wheelchair, told to return it when he could walk unaided, and given his demob papers.

He rang Jean and said he could come home. She seemed underwhelmed by the news, and he felt a little tetchy about this until he remembered what he had done to the carpet.

He asked if she could bring some clothes.

She said they would try to pick him up as soon as possible.

He sat back and read another seventy pages of *Treason's Harbour.*

Captain Aubrey was writing a letter home about Byrne's lucky snuffbox when George looked up and saw Ray walking down the ward. His first thought was that something dreadful had happened to the rest of his family. And, indeed, Ray's usual hail-fellow-well-met demeanor had given way to something rather dour.

"George."

"Ray."

"Is everything all right?" asked George.

Ray dumped a holdall on the bed. "Your clothes."

"I'm just surprised to see you, that's all. I mean, as opposed to Jean. Or Jamie. I don't mean to be rude. I just feel a little embarrassed that they've made you do this." He tried to sit up. It hurt. A lot.

Ray offered his hand and gently pulled George upright so that he was sitting on the side of the bed.

"Everything is all right, isn't it?" said George.

Ray let out a world-weary sigh. *"All right?"* he said. "I wouldn't go that far. *A bloody mess.* That's probably nearer the mark."

Could Ray be drunk? At ten in the morning? George could not smell any alcohol, but Ray did not seem completely in control of himself. And this was the man who was driving him home.

"You know what?" asked Ray, sitting down on the edge of the bed beside George.

"What?" said George quietly, not really wanting to know the answer.

"I think you might be the sanest member of the family," said Ray. "Apart from Jamie. He seems to have his head screwed on properly. And he's a homosexual."

The little Oriental man was staring at them. George crossed his fingers and hoped his English was not good.

"Has something happened at home?" asked George, tentatively.

"Jean and Katie were yelling at each other over the breakfast table. I suggested that everyone calm down a little and was told to *quote* fuck off *unquote.*"

"By Jean?" asked George, not quite able to believe this.

"By Katie," said Ray.

"And what was this argument about?" asked George. He was beginning to regret having passed Dr. Forman's test. A few more days in hospital seemed suddenly rather inviting.

"Katie doesn't want to get married," said Ray. "Which will probably be a relief to you."

George had no clue how to answer this. He toyed with the idea of falling off the bed so that someone else would come and rescue him, but decided against it.

"So I said I'd pick you up. Seemed a lot easier than staying at the house." Ray took a deep breath. "Sorry. Shouldn't be taking it out on you. Been a bit stressful recently."

The two of them sat side by side for a few moments, like a pair of elderly gentlemen on a park bench.

"Anyway," said Ray. "We'd better get you home, or they'll wonder where we've got to." He stood up. "You going to need any help getting into those clothes?"

For a fraction of a second George thought Ray was about to start removing his hospital pajamas and the prospect was so unnerving that George found himself emitting an audible squeak. But Ray simply pulled the curtains around George's bed and went off to fetch a nurse.

78

Katie felt wrung out.

You expected crises to resolve stuff, to put it into perspective. But they didn't. When they'd got to Peterborough she'd imagined staying for a few days, a week maybe, just her and Jacob. Keep an eye on Dad and make sure he wasn't planning to hack something else off. Give Mum a hand. Be a better daughter and atone for the guilt about disappearing last time.

But when Dad got back with Ray and told everyone they could go home, she was relieved. Another day in that house and they were going to kill each other.

The wheelchair was a shock, but Dad seemed strangely buoyant. Even Mum seemed keener on looking after him on her own than sharing the house with her children.

As they were leaving, Katie steeled herself and apologized.

Mum said, "Let's just forget about it, shall we."

And Dad overcompensated by saying, "Thank you for coming. It was lovely to see you," despite the fact that this was the first time he had actually been awake in her presence.

Which reminded Jacob that he hadn't given Grandpa his chocolate buttons. So Ray went outside and retrieved the packet from the glove compartment and Dad made a show of opening it and eating a couple and declaring that they were delicious despite the fact that the car heater seemed to have fused them into a kind of brown porridge.

They drifted to their cars and drove away and Ray and Jacob played I Spy for half an hour and Katie found that she was actually looking forward to getting back to the house she'd been so desperate to get away from only the day before.

When they arrived Ray and Jacob put the train set together on the living-room floor while she made supper. She bathed Jacob and Ray put him to bed.

Neither of them had the energy to argue and they spent the next few days playing the role of dutiful parents so as not to trouble Jacob. And she could see them turning slowly into the people they were pretending to be, the problem they were meant to solve drifting slowly into the background, the two of them turning into a team whose job it was to bring up a child and run a household despite the fact that they had nothing in common, having conversations about what was needed from Tesco and what they were going to do at the weekend, going to bed and putting out the light and rolling away from each other and trying not to dream about the lives they could have led.

79

Jean canceled work.

She really hadn't known what to expect when George came out of hospital. In the event he seemed surprisingly normal. He apologized for all the upset he had caused and said he was feeling a good deal better than he had done for some time.

She asked whether he wanted to talk about what had happened, but he told her there was no need to worry. She said he should tell her if he ever started feeling the same way again and he reassured her that he wasn't going to feel the same way again. Pretty soon it became clear that Dr. Parris had got things out of proportion and that her more paranoid imaginings had been unfounded.

He was still in a lot of pain, clearly. But he was determined not to use the wheel-chair. So she spent most of that week helping him out of bed and in and out of his salt bath and holding his hand as he made his way downstairs, then driving him back and forth to the surgery to have his dressing changed.

After three or four days he was moving around on his own, and by the beginning of the second week he was able to drive the car, so she went back into work, telling him that he could call her at any time if he needed help.

She rang the florists and the caterers and the car hire company and canceled them. The florists were downright rude, so she found herself telling the caterers and the car people that her daughter had been taken seriously ill and they were so understanding it made her feel worse than being shouted at.

She couldn't face ringing guests and telling them the wedding was off, so she decided to leave it for a few days.

And it was good. Obviously it was good. Only days ago she thought their lives were falling to pieces. And now they were getting slowly back to normal. She couldn't have asked for any more.

But she sat at the kitchen table some evenings and thought about the washing and the cooking and the cleaning and she could feel something dark and heavy weighing on her, and just getting up to put the kettle on was like wading through deep water.

She was depressed. And it was not something she was used to feeling. She worried. She coped. She got cross. But she was never down for more than a few hours at a time.

It was uncharitable, but she couldn't help wishing there was more wrong with George. That he needed her more. But in no time at all he was back out in the studio, laying bricks and sawing wood.

She felt as if she was lost at sea. George was on his island over there. And David was on another island. And Katie. And Jamie. All of them with solid ground under their feet. And she was drifting between them, the tide slowly dragging her farther and farther away.

She drove over to David's house the following week and parked round the corner. She was about to get out of the car when she realized she couldn't do it. When they'd first got together it seemed like the beginning of a new life, something different and exciting, an escape. But she could see it now

387

for what it was, an affair, like any other affair, tawdry and cheap, a selfish compensation for the mess her real life had become.

She imagined sitting in the staff room at St. John's, drinking tea and eating Garibaldi biscuits with Sally and Bea and Miss Cottingham and felt, for the first time, as if she bore some kind of stain, that they would be able to look at her and see what she had been doing.

She was being silly. She knew that. They were no different from other people. She knew, for a fact, that Bea's son was in some kind of trouble with drugs. But it seemed wrong that she should be making love with David one afternoon and teaching children to read the following morning. And if she had to make the choice between the two she would have chosen David without hesitation, but that seemed even worse.

She drove away and rang David later that evening to apologize. He was charming and sympathetic and said he understood what she must be going through. But he didn't. She could hear it in his voice.

80

George was lying on the bed with his

trousers off, having his dressing changed.

The practice nurse was rather attractive, if a little on the plump side. He had always liked women in uniforms. Samantha, that was her name. Cheerful, too, without being talkative.

In truth, he was going to miss these sessions when they came to an end in a couple of weeks' time. It was like having one's hair cut. Except that he always had his hair cut by an elderly Cypriot man and it was a lot less painful.

The nurse peeled back the large plaster over the wound. "OK, Mr. Hall. Time to grit your teeth."

George took hold of the edges of the bed.

The nurse pulled the end of the bandage. The first couple of feet of pink ribbon came away smoothly. Then it snagged. George did anagrams of the word *bandage* in his head. The nurse gave a gentle yank and the remains of the bandage lifted free of the wound making him say something he would never normally say in front of a woman. "I'm sorry about that."

"No apology needed."

The nurse held the old dressing up. It looked like a large conker that had been soaked in blood and lemon curd. She dropped it into the little swing bin by the side of the bed. "Let's get you a clean one."

George lay back and closed his eyes.

He rather liked the pain now that he had got used to it. He knew what it was going to be like and how long it was going to last. And as it ebbed away his head felt unnaturally clear for five or ten minutes, as if his brain had been hosed clean.

From a nearby room he heard someone say, "Scoliosis of the spine."

He was relieved about the wedding. It was sad for Katie. Or perhaps it was a relief for her, too. They had not been able to talk much during her visit. And to be honest they rarely talked about that kind of thing. Though Ray did seem a little strange at the hospital, which only served to confirm his uneasiness about the relationship.

Either way George was glad that the house was not going to be invaded by a marquee full of strangers. He was still feeling a little too fragile to relish the prospect of standing up and speechifying.

Jean seemed rather relieved, too.

Poor Jean. He really had put her through the wringer. She had not seemed like her usual self over the past few days. She was clearly still worried about him. Seeing that carpet every day probably did not help.

But he was out of the bedroom, they were

having conversations, and he was able to do a few chores round the house. When he was a little fitter he would take her out for dinner. He had heard good reports about that new restaurant in Oundle. Excellent fish, apparently.

"There," said Samantha, "that's you done."

"Thank you," said George.

"Come on, let's sit you up."

He would buy Jean some flowers on the way home, something he had not done in a very long time. That would cheer her up.

Then he would ring the carpet fitters.

81

Jamie was waiting for a prospective buyer in the Prince's Avenue flat, the one where he'd met Tony for the first time.

The owners were moving to Kuala Lumpur. They were tidy and childless, thank goodness. No abstract expressionistic ballpoint pen on the skirting boards, no scree of toys on the dining-room floor (Shona was showing a couple round the Finchley four-bed when the woman twisted her ankle on a Power Ranger Dino Thunder Bike). Worked in the city and hardly touched the place from what he could see. You could have licked the cooker. IKEA furniture. Bland prints in brushed steel frames. Soulless but salable.

He walked into the kitchen, touched the paintwork with the tips of his fingers and remembered watching Tony with a brush in his hand, before they'd even talked, when he was still a beautiful stranger.

Jamie could see now, with absolute clarity, what he'd done.

He'd bided his time. He'd got away. He'd built a little world in which he felt safe. And it was orbiting far out, unconnected to anyone. It was cold and it was dark and he had no idea how to make it swing back toward the sun.

There'd been a moment, in Peterborough, shortly after Katie punched him, when he realized that he needed these people. Katie, Mum, Dad, Jacob. They drove him up the wall sometimes. But they'd been with him all the way. They were a part of him.

Now he'd lost Tony and he was drifting. He needed a place he could go when he was in trouble. He needed someone he could call in the small hours.

He'd fucked it up. Those horrible scenes in the dining room. His mother saying, "You know nothing." She was right. They were strangers. He'd made them into strangers. Deliberately. What right did he have to tell them how they should run their lives? He had made damn sure they had no right to tell him how he should run his.

The bell rang.

Shit.

He took a deep breath, counted to ten, put his selling brain in and answered the door to a man with a very obvious toupee.

82

Katie had just finished the washing up.

Jacob was in bed. And Ray was sitting at the kitchen table putting new batteries into the cordless phone. She turned round and leant against the sink, drying her hands on a tea towel.

Ray clicked the back of the phone into place. "We have to do something."

She said, "I know," and it felt good, finally, to talk about the subject instead of sniping about nursery runs and the lack of tea bags.

Ray said, "I don't mind how we work this out." He tilted his chair backward and slotted the phone into its cradle. "Just so long as it doesn't involve going anywhere near your family."

For a fraction of a second she wondered whether she ought to be offended. But she couldn't because Ray was right, their behavior had been abysmal. Then it struck her as actually quite funny and she realized she was laughing. "I'm so sorry about putting you through all of that."

"It was . . . educational," said Ray.

She couldn't tell from his expression whether he was amused or not so she stopped laughing.

"Told your dad he seemed like the sanest person in the whole family." Ray stood one of the old batteries on its end. "Put the wind up him a bit." He stood the other battery on its end next to the first. "I hope he's OK."

"Fingers crossed."

"Jamie's a decent bloke," said Ray.

"Yeh."

"We had a good talk. In the garden."

"About?" asked Katie.

"Me and you. Him and Tony."

"Uh-huh." It seemed a bit risky to ask for details.

"I always thought, you know, being gay, he would be weirder."

"Probably best not to say that to Jamie."

Ray looked up at her. "I might be stupid. But I'm not that stupid."

"I'm sorry. I didn't mean —"

"Come here, you," said Ray. He pushed his chair back.

She went and sat on his lap and he put his arms round her and that was it. Like the world flipping inside out.

This was where she was meant to be.

She could feel every muscle in her body relaxing. She touched his face. "I've been so horrible to you."

"You've been appalling," said Ray. "But I still love you."

"Just hold me."

He pulled her close and she buried her face in his shoulder and cried.

"It's OK," said Ray, rubbing her back gently. "It's OK."

How had she been so blind? He'd seen her family at their worst and taken it all with good grace. Even with the wedding canceled.

But he hadn't changed. He was the same person he'd been all along. The kindest, most dependable, most honorable person in her life.

This was her family. Ray and Jacob.

She felt stupid and relieved and guilty and happy and sad and slightly wobbly on account of feeling so many things at the same time. "I love you."

"It's all right," said Ray. "You don't have to say it."

"No. I mean it. I really do."

"Let's not say anything for a bit, OK? It gets too complicated when we argue."

"I'm not arguing," said Katie.

He lifted her head and put a finger on her lips to stop her speaking and kissed her. It was the first time they had kissed properly in weeks.

He led her upstairs and they made love until Jacob had a nightmare about an angry blue dog and they had to stop rather quickly.

83

When Jamie got home from work he rang Tony. No answer. He rang Tony's mobile and left a message asking him to ring back.

He cleaned the kitchen and ate supper in front of a film about a giant alligator in a lake in Maine. Tony didn't ring back.

He rang Tony's flat early the following morning. No answer. He rang Tony's mobile at lunchtime and left another message, keeping it as simple and straightforward as possible.

He went swimming after work to stop himself waiting for the return call. He did sixty lengths and came out feeling exhausted and relaxed for five whole minutes.

He tried ringing the flat again when he got home but to no avail.

He was tempted to go round and knock on the door. But he was beginning to think Tony was avoiding him and he didn't want another scene.

It wasn't sadness. Or not like any sadness he'd felt before. It was as if someone had died. It was just a thing to be lived with in the hope that it would get slowly less painful.

He kept ringing, every morning and every night. But he no longer expected an answer. It was a ritual. Something that gave shape to the day.

He'd retreated to a small room somewhere deep inside his head, running on autopilot. Getting up. Going to work. Coming home.

He imagined stepping into the road without looking and being hit by a car and not feeling any pain, any surprise, not feeling anything really, just a kind of detached interest at what was happening to this person who wasn't really him anymore.

The following day he got a surprise phone call from Ian and agreed to go out for a drink. They'd met ten years back on a beach in Cornwall and realized they lived four streets away from each other back in London. Training to be a vet. Poor bloke came out at twenty-five, tested positive after four years of monogamy, went into a tailspin and started committing a slow expensive suicide with cigarettes, alcohol, cocaine and chaotic sex till he lost a foot in a motorbike accident, spent a month in hospital and disappeared to Australia.

Jamie had got a postcard of a wombat a few months later saying things were looking up, then nothing for two years. Now he was back.

He'd be having a crappier time than Jamie. Or he'd be bearing up stoically. Either way, a couple of hours in his company promised to make Jamie's troubles seem manageable in comparison.

Jamie arrived late and was relieved to find he'd got there first. He was in the process of buying himself a lager, however, when a lean, tanned man in a tight black T-shirt with no discernible limp said, "Jamie," and wrapped him in a bear hug.

And for fifteen or twenty minutes it all went swimmingly. It was good to hear how Ian had turned everything round. And his stories about bizarre horse diseases and big spiders were genuinely funny. Then Jamie explained about Tony, and Ian brought up the subject of Jesus, which didn't happen in bars very often. He wasn't completely whacko about it. Made it sound more like an amazing new diet. But coupled with the new body it was unnerving. And when Ian headed off for a pee, Jamie found himself staring at two men on the far side of the bar, one dressed as a devil (red velour cat-suit, horns, trident), one as an angel (wings, white vest, puffball skirt), who were doubt-less en route to a fancy dress party with the cowboy at the bar (chaps, spurs), but it made Jamie feel as if he'd taken some ill-advised drug, or that everyone else had. And he realized that he was meant to be at home here, but he wasn't.

Then Ian came back to the table and sensed Jamie's unease and changed the subject to his own rather active love life which seemed contrary to most of the teachings of Christianity insofar as Jamie understood them. Jamie was beginning to suffer that befuddled incomprehension old people felt when you told them about the Internet and he wondered whether he'd just failed to keep up with what had been hap-pening in churches recently.

He went home, after a slightly uneasy parting with Ian during which he promised to think seriously about the possibility of coming to an evangelical meeting in Kings Cross, and Ian gave him another bear hug which Jamie now realized was a Christian hug, not a real one.

Several hours later he had a dream in which he was chasing Tony through an endless series of interconnecting rooms, some from his old school, some from properties he'd sold over the past few years, and he was shouting but Tony couldn't hear him and Jamie couldn't run because of the tiny creatures on the floors, like baby birds with human faces, which mewed and squealed when he trod on them.

When he finally woke at seven he found himself going straight to the phone to ring Tony. He caught himself just in time.

He was going to sort this out. He'd go round to Tony's flat after work. Say his piece. Give him shit for not answering the phone. Find out if he'd moved. Whatever. Just put an end to all this waiting.

84

David was having a new boiler installed, so Jean was sitting with him in the garden of the Fox and Hounds. The idea made her nervous at first, but David was right. The place was empty and they were yards from the car if they needed to slip away.

She was drinking a gin and tonic, which she didn't normally do on her way home from the school. If George asked questions she could always blame Ursula. She needed some Dutch courage. Her life was an unholy mess at the moment and she had to make it simpler.

She said, "I'm not sure how long we can carry on doing this."

"You mean you want to stop?" asked David.

"Maybe. Yes." It sounded so harsh now she was saying it out loud. "Oh, I don't know. I just don't know."

"What's changed?"

"George," she said. "George being ill." Wasn't it obvious?

"And that's all?" asked David.

He seemed untroubled, and she was beginning to find his confidence annoying. How could he sail through all this? "It's not a small thing, David."

He took her hand.

She said, "It feels different now. It feels wrong."

He said, "You haven't changed. I haven't changed."

It exasperated her sometimes. The way

men could be so sure of themselves. They put words together like sheds or shelves and you could stand on them they were so solid. And those feelings which overwhelmed you in the small hours turned to smoke.

He said, "I'm not trying to bully you."

"I know." But she wasn't sure about this.

"If you were ill, if you were seriously ill, I would still love you. If I was seriously ill, I hope you'd still love me." He looked into her eyes. For the first time he looked sad and this put her at ease. "I love you, Jean. It's not just words. I mean it. I'll wait if I have to. I'll put up with things. Because that's what love means. And I know George is ill. And I know it makes your life difficult. But it's something we have to live with and sort out. And I don't know how we'll do it, but we will."

She found herself laughing.

"What's funny?"

"Me," she said. "You're absolutely right. And it's infuriating. But you're still right."

He squeezed her hand.

They sat in silence for a few moments. David fished something from his shandy and a large agricultural vehicle rumbled by on the far side of the hedge.

"I feel dreadful," she said.

"Why?" he asked.

"The wedding."

He looked relieved.

"I was so thrown by what was happening to George that I . . . Katie must be having a dreadful time. Planning to get married. Then canceling the wedding. The two of them living together. I should have been sympathetic. But we just argued."

"You had enough on your plate."

"I know, but . . ."

"At the least the wedding's off," said David.

It seemed like a callous thing to say. "But it's so sad."

"Not as sad as getting married to someone you don't love," said David.

85

They were getting married.

Katie felt excited about it in a way she hadn't before. She knew she was doing the right thing this time. They were going to be in charge. It really was going to be their wedding. And a part of her was secretly pleased that the news was going to piss people off.

She'd worried about asking Ray. Would he believe her? Would he want to take the risk of her getting cold feet a second time?

Then she thought, *Fuck it.* What else were you supposed to do when you loved someone and wanted to marry them? And if the invitations had already been sent, well, it seemed wise to pop the question pretty quickly.

So she girded her loins and asked. On bended knee. So she could make it funny if it all went horribly wrong.

He lit up. "Of course I'll marry you."

She was so surprised she found herself trying to make him change his mind. "Are you absolutely sure?"

"Hey." He took hold of her shoulders.

"What?"

"I said yes. I said I wanted to marry you."

"I know, but —"

"You know what?" asked Ray.

"What?"

"You're back again."

"Meaning?"

"The old you," he said.

"So you really do want to get married? In a fortnight?"

"Only if you promise not to ask me again."

"I promise."

They stared at each other for five seconds or so, letting it sink in. Then they jumped up and down like children.

She expected Mum to be angry. Given the hassle. But she seemed oddly resigned. Apparently, she hadn't even got around to telling the guests it was off. Maybe she suspected this was going to happen all along.

Katie said they'd arrange everything. All she needed were the phone numbers. There was nothing Mum had to do. "And Ray and I are going to pay. After all we've put you through it seems only fair."

"Well, if you insist," said Mum. "Though I'm not sure how your father is going to feel about it."

"Richer," said Katie, but Mum didn't laugh. "How is Dad, incidentally?"

"He seems fine." She didn't seem very happy about this.

"Good," said Katie. Perhaps Mum was just having a bad day. "That's really good news."

The florists were downright rude. They could still squeeze the job in but it would cost more. Katie said she'd get flowers from someone nicer and put the phone down, full of an uplifting righteous indignation she hadn't felt for a long time, and thought, *Bugger flowers.* Ray suggested they pick up a bouquet on the morning of the wedding and this struck them both as very funny.

The caterers were more understanding.

Indeed they seemed to think she'd just come out of hospital, which involved some rapid footwork on Katie's part, and when she mumbled something about tests coming back negative there was actual cheering from the other end of the line. "We'd be honored to provide the food."

The cake people weren't even aware that the wedding was off and clearly thought Katie was insane.

86

When George gave Jean the flowers she cried. It was not the reaction he was expecting. And she was not crying because the flowers were especially beautiful, that much seemed obvious (he had been forced to buy them from the little supermarket near the bus stop and even he could tell that they were not superior flowers).

She was, perhaps, still upset about his misadventure in the bath. Or about the carpet (the fitters were not coming till the following week). Or about the row she had had with Katie and Jamie. Or about the wedding being off. Or about the wedding being on again. Or about the fact that Katie and Ray were now organizing it themselves so that she no longer had a controlling stake in the event. The possibilities were numerous. And, in his experience, women could get upset about things that never even occurred to most men.

He decided not to pry.

His own feelings about the wedding were ones of weary acceptance. He would wait to see what happened and deal with it when it did. If Katie and Ray made a hash of things they were, at least, paying for it.

The idea of giving a speech was less worrisome than it had been. He was feeling stronger now and the problem did not seem as insurmountable as it had done previously.

If only he'd known that her marriage to Graham wasn't going to last, he would have kept a copy of the speech he used first time around.

He could do a little potted biography, perhaps. Illustrate how the small tearaway of thirty years ago had turned into . . . into what? "An accomplished young woman"? "An accomplished young woman and a wonderful mother"? "The woman you see before you"? None of the phrases sounded quite right.

"The best daughter in the world"? That was perhaps overstating the case a little.

"Into my very favorite daughter." That was

it. Lightly humorous. Complimentary without being sentimental.

Maybe he should run it past Jean. To be honest, tone was never his forte. Striking a serious note. Striking an ironic note. Which is why he had always ducked out of making speeches at leaving do's and Christmas parties. There were always smoother men than him eager to step into the breach.

He would leave out the first marriage and some of the more serious teenage misdemeanors. No one was going to be amused by Katie spilling coffee into a bar fire and causing an explosion that took wallpaper off. Or were they? These things were so hard to judge.

He would tell them about her plans to be a racing driver, and the morning she borrowed his car keys, loosened the hand brake of the Vauxhall Chevette and rolled into the garage door, very nearly chopping Jamie in half.

The one thing he wasn't going to do was to write the thing till a couple of days before the event. He did not want to tempt fate, and his daughter was entirely capable of canceling the wedding a second time.

Another subject he ought to avoid.

He rang the restaurant in Oundle and booked a table. Jean was still under the weather and stronger medicine than flowers was clearly called for. And the reports were correct. The fish was very good indeed. George had sea bream with spinach and pine kernels and one of those nouvelle cuisine puddles of sauce. Jean had the trout.

There was a little black cloud over her head during the main course. So when dessert came he threw caution to the wind and asked what the matter was.

She took a very long time indeed to answer. Which George could understand. He had suffered from a few mental wobbles recently which were not easily put into words.

Finally, Jean spoke. "In the hospital."

"Yes?"

"I said something to Katie."

"Yes?" George relaxed a little. It was mother-daughter stuff. High temperature, short duration.

"I was rather stupid."

"I'm sure you weren't."

"I told her I was relieved," said Jean. "That the wedding was off."

"OK."

"I said we'd had our doubts about Ray from the beginning."

"Which, of course, we had."

"She told Ray. I'm absolutely sure of it. I

could see it in his eyes."

George chewed this over for a minute or two. When men had problems they wanted someone to give them an answer, but when women had problems they wanted you to say that you understood. It was something David had told him at Shepherds, the summer when Pam's son joined that cult.

He said, "You're worried that Ray hates you."

"Hates us, actually." Jean's mood lifted visibly.

"Well, I suspect he's always known that we don't see eye to eye with him."

"That's not quite the same as having it spelled out."

"You're quite right. And now that I come to think about it, his behavior was a little strange when he came to pick me up at the hospital."

"In what way?" Jean looked nervous again.

"Well . . ." George scanned his memory of the meeting rapidly to make sure it contained nothing that might upset Jean. "He said everything was a bloody mess back at the house."

"Well, he was right there."

"He said that I was the sanest person in the family. I think it was meant to be a joke." It was obviously a better joke than

George realized because Jean started laughing quietly. "It seemed a little unkind to you, I have to say." He took hold of Jean's hand. "It's good to see you laughing. I haven't seen you laughing in a long time."

She started crying again.

"I'll tell you what I'll do." He let go of her hand. "I'll give Ray a ring. See if I can set things straight."

"Are you sure that's wise?"

"Trust me," he said.

He did not know whether it was wise. Or whether he could be trusted. To be honest, he had very little idea why he had made such a foolhardy suggestion. But there was no turning back. And if there was some small thing he could do to make Jean happier, then it was the least he could do.

87

Jamie got home from work to find a message on the answerphone from Katie saying the wedding was back on. She seemed positively jubilant. And her cheeriness made him feel more optimistic than he'd done in a while. Perhaps everyone's luck was turning.

He was tempted to ring her straight back,

but he needed to sort something else out first.

He parked just round the corner from Tony's flat and gathered his thoughts, not wanting to fuck it up this time.

Seven o'clock on a Monday evening. If Tony was going to be in at any time, he was going to be in now.

What was Jamie going to say? It seemed so obvious what he felt. But when he tried to put it into words it sounded clumsy and unconvincing and sentimental. If only you could lift a lid on the top of your head and say, "Look."

This was pointless.

He knocked on the door and wondered whether Tony had actually moved house, because the door was answered by a young woman he'd never seen before. She had long dark hair and was wearing men's pajama trousers with a pair of unlaced Doc Martens. She was holding a lit cigarette in one hand and a tattered paperback in the other.

"I'm looking for Tony."

"Ah-ha," she said. "You must be the infamous Jamie."

"I'm not sure about *infamous*."

"I was wondering when you were going to drop round."

"Do we know each other?" said Jamie, trying to make it sound literal rather than standoffish. It was starting to feel like that meeting with Ian. Not knowing what on earth was going on.

The woman juggled the paperback into her cigarette hand and held out the other to be shaken. "Becky. Tony's sister."

"Hi," said Jamie, shaking her hand. And now that he thought about it he did recognize her face from photographs and felt bad for not having taken more interest at the time.

"The one you've been avoiding," said Becky.

"Have I?" asked Jamie. Though it was less a case of avoiding. More a case of failing to make a deliberate effort. "Anyway, I thought you lived in . . ." Shit. He shouldn't have started that sentence. She let him carry on without help. "Somewhere a long way away."

"Glasgow. Then Sheffield. You coming in, or are we going to stand out here talking?"

"Is Tony in?"

"Are you only coming in if he's here?"

Jamie got the distinct sense that Tony wasn't in and that Becky was going to give him some kind of grilling, but now didn't seem like the time to be ungracious to a member of Tony's family. "I'll come in."

"Good," said Becky, closing the door behind him.

"So, is he in?"

They walked up the stairs to the flat.

"He's in Crete," said Becky. "I'm house-sitting. I'm working at the Battersea Arts Centre."

"Phew," said Jamie.

"Meaning?" asked Becky.

"Meaning I've been trying to ring him. I thought he was avoiding me."

"He is."

"Oh."

Jamie sat himself down at the kitchen table, then realized it was Becky's flat, temporarily at least, and Tony and he weren't going out anymore and he shouldn't make himself at home quite so automatically. He stood up again, Becky gave him an odd look and he sat down for a second time.

"Glass of wine?" Becky waggled a bottle at him.

"OK," said Jamie, not wanting to seem rude.

She filled a glass. "I don't answer the phone. Makes life a lot simpler."

"Right." Jamie's head was still full of all the things he was planning to say to Tony, and none of them were very appropriate now. "The Battersea Arts Centre. Is that, like paintings, exhibitions . . ."

Becky gave Jamie a withering look and poured herself another glass. "It's a theater. I work in the theater." She said the word *theater* very slowly, as if talking to a small child. "I'm a house manager."

"Right," said Jamie. His own experience of theater was limited to one forced visit to *Miss Saigon* which he had not enjoyed. It seemed best not to share this with Becky.

"You really weren't paying very much attention when Tony talked about his family, were you?"

Jamie was having trouble remembering a conversation in which Tony told him what his sister did. It was possible that Tony had never actually told him. This too seemed like something best to keep to himself. "So . . . when's Tony getting back?"

"Not entirely sure. Another couple of weeks I think. It was all rather spur of the moment."

Jamie did a quick calculation in his head. Two weeks. "Shit."

"Shit because?"

Jamie wasn't sure if Becky was prickly in general, or whether she was being specifically prickly with him. He trod carefully. "I wanted him to come to something. A wedding, actually. My sister's wedding. She's getting married."

"That is what people generally do at their weddings."

Jamie was beginning to understand why Tony hadn't made a bigger effort to introduce his sister. This woman could give Katie a run for her money. "We had an argument."

"I know."

"And it was my fault."

"So I gathered," said Becky.

"Anyway, I was thinking if I could get him to come to the wedding . . ."

"I think it was the wedding he was avoiding. By going to Crete."

"Ah."

Becky stubbed out her cigarette in the little glass ashtray in the center of the table and Jamie concentrated on the way the smoke floated up and broke into little spirals to take his mind off the uncomfortable silence.

"He loved you," said Becky. "You do know that, don't you."

"Did he?" It was a stupid thing to say. But he was too shocked to care what he sounded like.

Tony loved him. Why the fuck had Tony never said so? Jamie had always assumed Tony felt exactly the same as him, not wanting to leap in and make commitments.

Tony loved him. He loved Tony. How in God's name had he managed to screw things up quite so spectacularly?

"You didn't realize, did you," said Becky.

There was absolutely nothing Jamie could say.

"Jesus," said Becky. "Men are morons sometimes."

Jamie was about to say that if Tony had only told him, then none of this would have happened. But it didn't sound like a very grown-up response. Besides, he knew precisely why Tony had never told him. Because he'd never allowed Tony to tell him, because he didn't want Tony to tell him, because he was terrified of Tony telling him. "How can I get in touch with him?"

"God knows," said Becky. "He's staying with some friend who's got a time-share thing out there."

"Gordon."

"Sounds right. He thought the mobile would work."

"It doesn't. I tried."

"Snap," said Becky.

"I need a cigarette," said Jamie.

Becky smiled for the first time. She gave him a cigarette and lit it for him. "You are in a state, aren't you."

"Look," said Jamie. "If he rings —"

"He hasn't."

"But if he does —"

"You're serious, aren't you," said Becky.

Jamie steeled himself. "I love him. I just didn't realize until . . . Well, God, Tony chucked me. Then my sister canceled the wedding. Then my dad had some kind of nervous breakdown and ended up in hospital. And we all drove to Peterborough and everyone basically scratched each other's eyes out. And it was horrible. Really horrible. Then the wedding was back on again."

"This is going to be a really fun event, isn't it."

"And I realized Tony was the only person who —"

"Oh Jesus. Just don't cry. Please. Men crying does my head in. Have another drink." She poured the remains of the wine into his glass.

"Sorry." Jamie wiped his slightly moist eyes and swallowed the lump.

"Drop an invite round," said Becky. "Write something soppy on it. I'll stick it on top of his post pile. Or on his pillow. Whatever. If he gets back in time I'll kick his arse and make him come."

"Really?"

"Really." She lit another cigarette. "I met

his previous boyfriends. Nobheads. In my humble opinion. Obviously you and I haven't known each other long but, trust me, you seem like a major improvement."

"Ryan seemed nice." In his mind, Jamie was introducing Becky to Katie and wondering whether the two of them would become friends for life or spontaneously combust.

"Ryan. God. What an arsehole. Hated women. You know, you can't work with them because they're not tough enough and they bugger off to have children. Probably not even gay. Not properly. You know the type. Just can't stomach the idea of sex with women. Hated children, too. Which always winds me up. I mean, where do you think adults come from, for God's sake? You want bus drivers and doctors? You need children. I'm glad I'm not the poor bloody woman who spent a chunk of her life wiping his arse. Didn't like dogs, either. Or cats. Never trust a man who doesn't like animals. That's my rule. You don't fancy sharing a Tesco curry, do you?"

88

Jean rang David. The boiler was fixed and he had the house to himself again, so she dropped in on her way back from the book-shop.

She told him about the wedding and he laughed. In a kind way. "Oy oy oy. Let's hope the day itself is less eventful than the buildup."

"Are you still coming?"

"Would you like me to?"

"Yes," she said. "Yes I would." She wouldn't be able to hold him. But if Jamie and Ray had a row, or Katie changed her mind halfway through the ceremony, she wanted to be able to glance across the room and see the face of someone who under-stood what she was going through.

He gave her a hug and made her a cup of tea and sat her down in the conservatory and told her about the eccentric plumber who'd been working on the boiler ("Polish, apparently. Degree in economics. Says he walked to Britain. German monastery. Fruit picking in France. Bit of a roguish air, though. Not sure whether I entirely believed him").

And good as it was to be talking, she real-ized that she wanted to be taken to the one remaining place where she forgot, however briefly, who she was and what was happen-ing in the rest of her life. And it was a little scary, wanting something that much. But it didn't stop the wanting.

She took hold of his hand and held his eye and waited for him to realize what she was thinking without her having to say it out loud.

He smiled back and raised one eyebrow and said, "Let's go upstairs."

89

George missed his second therapy session on account of being in hospital. As a result he was rather dreading his next meeting with Ms. Endicott, much as he had once dreaded being sent to Mr. Love to explain why he had thrown Jeffrey Brown's satchel onto a roof.

But she listened respectfully to the story and asked some very specific questions about what he had hoped to achieve and what he felt at various points during the whole process, and George got the distinct impression that he could have announced that he had eaten his wife in a pie and Ms. Endicott would have asked about the kind of gravy he had served with it, and he was not sure whether this was a good thing or not.

It was beginning to annoy him. He explained that he felt a good deal better now and she asked in what precise way he felt better. He described his feelings about Katie's wedding and Ms. Endicott asked for a definition of "Buddhist detachment."

When, at the end of the session, Ms. Endicott said that she was looking forward to seeing him the following week, George made an ambiguous "Uh-huh" noise because he was not sure whether he would be coming the following week. He half expected Ms. Endicott to pounce on his deliberate ambiguity, but their forty-five minutes were up and they were now clearly allowed to behave like normal human beings again.

90

Jamie got back late from Tony's flat. Too late to ring people with children at any rate. So he decided to drive over to Katie and Ray's the following day, pick up an invitation and offer his congratulations in person.

He liked Becky. She had softened over the microwave curry, even if her opinions of estate agents hadn't. He liked most stroppy women. Growing up with Katie, no doubt. What he really couldn't stand were winsome head tilts and hair flicking and pink mohair (why they appealed to rugby players and scaffolders was a mystery he was never going to solve). He wondered briefly whether she was a lesbian. Then he remembered a story of Tony's about her and some boy breaking their parents' toilet seat during a party. Though people changed, of course.

He talked about Katie and Ray's roller-coaster relationship and managed to convince Becky that Ray was a suitable candidate for castration, then had to steer her carefully round to thinking he was an honorable kind of guy, which was considerably harder because, when he thought about it, it was very hard to put his finger on precisely what had changed.

She talked about growing up in Norwich. The five dogs. Their mum's allergy to housework. Their father's pathological devotion to steam railways. The car crash in Scotland ("We crawled out and walked away without a scratch and we turned round and the back of the car was torn off and there was, literally, half a dog on the road. Had a few nightmares about that. Still do"). The boy they fostered who had an obsession with knives. The time Tony and a friend set light to a powered model plane, launched it from the bedroom window and watched it bank slowly at the end of the garden, flaming dramatically, then turn and fly into the half-built house next door . . .

Jamie had heard most of the stories before, in one form or another. But he was listening properly this time.

"Sounds grim."

"It wasn't actually," said Becky. "It's just the way Tony tells it."

"I thought your parents chucked him out. After that thing with him and . . ."

"Carl. Carl Waller. Yeh. But Tony wanted to get chucked out."

"Really?"

"Being gay was a godsend." Becky lit a cigarette. "Meant he could be an outlaw without having to mainline heroin or steal cars."

Jamie digested this slowly. A thousand miles between them and he felt closer to Tony than he'd ever done. "But you and Tony. You were sort of estranged, too, weren't you. And now you're flat-sitting."

"We met up when I moved down to London. A few weeks back. Suddenly realized we liked each other."

Jamie found himself laughing. Out of relief, really. That Tony could make the same kind of mistakes he'd made himself.

"What's so funny?" asked Becky.

"Nothing," said Jamie. "It's just . . . It's good. It's really good."

Everyone's luck really did seem to be turning. Maybe there was something in the air.

When he reached Katie's place the following evening the door was opened by her and Ray together, which seemed symbolic, and he found himself saying, "Congratulations" with the sincerity he wasn't able to muster the first time round.

He was ushered into the kitchen, getting the tiniest grunt of greeting from Jacob who was deeply involved in a *Fireman Sam* video in the living room.

Katie seemed a little giddy. Like those people you saw interviewed on the news who'd been winched out of something ghastly by a helicopter.

Ray seemed different, too, though it was hard to tell whether this was just because Jamie felt differently about him now. Certainly he and Katie were getting on better. They were touching each other, for starters, which Jamie hadn't seen before. In fact when *Fireman Sam* finished and Jacob pottered through in search of a carton of apple juice, there was definite Oedipal tension ("Stop hugging Mummy," "I want to hug Mummy"). And the thought occurred to

Jamie that Katie and Ray had fallen in love only after going through all the crap that most people saved for the end of their relationship. Which was one way of doing things.

Jamie asked about an invitation for Tony, and Ray seemed unnaturally excited by the possibility that he might be coming.

"It's a bit of a long shot," said Jamie. "He's incommunicado in Greece. I'm just hoping he gets back in time."

"We could track him down," said Ray with a can-do gleefulness that felt not quite appropriate.

"I think we have to leave it in the lap of the gods," said Jamie.

"Your call," said Ray.

At which point Katie yelled, "Jacob," and they all turned round to see him deliberately emptying his apple juice carton onto the kitchen floor.

Ray made him apologize, then dragged him out to play in the garden, to show him that stepfathers had other uses besides monopolizing mothers.

Jamie and Katie had been chatting about the wedding for ten minutes when Katie got a phone call from home. She reappeared a few moments later looking slightly troubled.

"That was Dad."

"How is he?"

"He seemed fine. But he wanted to talk to Ray. Wouldn't tell me what it was about."

"Maybe he wants to be manly and pay for everything."

"You're probably right. Well, we'll find out when Ray rings him back."

"Not that I rate Dad's chances," said Jamie.

"So, now," said Katie, "what are you going to write to Tony?"

91

George's mistake was to stand naked in front of the mirror.

He had paid his last visit to the surgery. The wound had granulated and no longer needed daily packing. Now he simply removed the previous day's dressing after breakfast, slipped into a warm salt bath for ten minutes, got out, dried himself gently and applied a fresh dressing.

He was taking the tablets and rather looking forward to the wedding. With Katie and Ray running the show there was very little for him to do. Making a brief speech seemed a very simple contribution to the proceedings.

The mirror was foolish bravado in part, a celebration of the fact that he had put his problems behind him and was not going to let them restrict his behavior any longer.

Not that the reason mattered much now.

He got out of the bath, toweled himself dry, sucked his stomach in, pulled his shoulders back and stood to attention in front of the sink.

It was the cloud of red dots on his bicep which caught his attention first, the ones he had seen in the hotel room and managed to forget about. They seemed larger and more numerous than he remembered.

He felt sick.

The obvious thing to do was to back swiftly away from the mirror, get dressed, take a couple of codeine and open a bottle of wine. But he was unable to stop himself.

He began examining his skin in detail. On his arms. On his chest. On his stomach. Turning round and looking over his shoulder so that he could see his back.

It was not a good thing to do. It was like looking at a petri dish in a laboratory. Every square inch held some new terror. Dark brown moles, wrinkled like sultanas; freckles clumped into archipelagos of chocolate-colored islands; bland flesh-colored bumps, some slack, some full of fluid.

His skin had become a zoo of alien life forms. If he looked closely enough he would be able to see them moving and growing. He tried not to look closely.

He should have gone back to Dr. Barghoutian. Or to another, better doctor.

He had arrogantly thought he could solve his problems with long walks and crosswords. And all the time, the disease had laughed and spread and tightened its hold and given birth to other diseases.

He stopped looking into the mirror only when his vision blurred and his knees buckled, pitching him onto the bathroom floor.

At which point the picture of his own naked skin, still vivid in his mind's eye, mutated into the skin of that man's buttocks going up and down between Jean's legs in the bedroom.

He could hear them again. The animal noises. The wrinkled flesh being wobbled and swung. The things he had not seen but could imagine only too clearly. That man's organ going in and out of Jean. The sucking and the sliding. The pink folds.

In this house. In his own bed.

He could actually smell it. The toilet scent. Intimate and unwashed.

He was dying. And no one knew.

His wife was having sex with another man.

And he had to give a speech at his daughter's wedding.

He was clinging to the bottom rung of the heated towel rail, like a man trying not to be swept away by a flood.

It was like before. But worse. There was no floor beneath him. The bathroom, the house, the village, Peterborough . . . it had all peeled back and shredded and blown away, leaving nothing but infinite space, just him and a towel rail. As if he had stepped outside the spaceship and found the earth gone.

He was mad again. And there was no hope this time. He thought he had cured himself. But he had failed. There was no one else he could rely on. He was going to remain like this until he died.

Codeine. He needed the codeine. He couldn't do anything about the cancer. Or Jean. Or the wedding. The only thing he could do was to dull it all a little.

Keeping hold of the towel rail he started getting to his feet. But as he straightened himself the soft flesh of his stomach was exposed and he could feel it itching and squirming. He grabbed a towel and wrapped it round his abdomen. He transferred his hands to the rim of the bath and stood up.

He could do this. It was a simple thing. Take the pills and wait. That was all he had to do.

He opened the cabinet and took the packet down. He swigged back four tablets with water from the bath tap so as to avoid the mirror above the sink. Was four dangerous? He had no idea and did not care.

He staggered into the bedroom. He dropped the towel and somehow managed to slip into his clothes, despite his shaking hands. He climbed onto the bed and put the duvet over his head and started reciting nursery rhymes until he realized that this was where it had happened, right here, where his head was lying, and he felt like vomiting and knew he had to do something, anything, to keep himself moving and occupied until the drugs started to work.

He threw the duvet off and got to his feet and took a string of deep breaths to steady himself before heading downstairs.

Assuming Jean was busy elsewhere, he planned to grab a bottle of wine and head straight out to the studio. If the codeine did not work he would get drunk. He no longer cared what Jean thought.

But Jean was not busy elsewhere. He was halfway down the stairs when she appeared round the banisters brandishing the phone receiver saying, exasperatedly, "There you are. I've been calling you. Ray would like a chat."

George froze, like an animal spotted by a bird of prey, hoping that if he remained motionless he might blend into the background.

"Are you going to take it or not?" said Jean, waggling the phone at him.

He watched his hand rise up to take hold of the phone as he walked down the last few steps. Jean was wearing a rubber glove and holding a tea towel. She handed the phone over, shook her head and vanished back into the kitchen.

George put the phone to his ear.

The pictures in his head toggled giddily from one grotesque image to another. The tramp's face on the station platform. Jean's naked thighs. His own sick skin.

Ray said, "George. It's Ray. Katie tells me you wanted a chat."

It was like those phone calls that woke you up at night. It was hard remembering what you were meant to do.

He had absolutely no idea what he had wanted to chat to Ray about.

Was this really happening, or had he tipped over into some kind of delusional state? Was he still lying on the bed upstairs?

"George?" said Ray. "Are you there?"

He tried to say something. A small mewing noise came out of his mouth. He moved the receiver away from his head and looked at it. Ray's voice was still emerging from the little holes. George did not want this to carry on any longer.

Carefully, he put the phone back onto the receiver. He turned and walked into the kitchen. Jean was filling the washing machine and he did not have the energy for the argument that would ensue if he walked out of the door with a bottle of wine.

"That was quick," said Jean.

"Wrong number," said George.

He was halfway down the garden in his socks before he realized why Jean might not have fallen for this brilliant piece of subterfuge.

92

Jamie sat down with a mug of tea and his best pen and some writing paper he'd found in the bottom of the desk drawer. Proper paper, like the stuff he was made to use for thank-you letters when he was a kid.

He began writing.

Dear Tony,

I love you and I want you to come to the wedding.

I went up to Peterborough last week. Dad was having a nervous breakdown and ended up in hospital after chopping bits off himself with a pair of scissors (I'll explain later). When I was at the hospital I bumped into the man Mum is having an affair with (I'll explain that, too). Katie and Mum had a blazing row about the wedding. It was off. But now it's on again (I'll explain . . .

He tore off the sheet of paper, crumpled it up and began again. Tony had expended a lot of energy getting away from his own family. This wasn't the moment for Jamie to brag about the shortcomings of his own.

Dear Tony,

I love you and I want you to come to the wedding.

I went up to Peterborough last week and realized that you were my family . . .

Too mawkish.

Dear Tony,
I love you.

The wedding was off. Now it's on again.

God knows what's going to happen on the day, but I want you to be there with me

Christ. Now he was selling it as a spectator event.

Why was this so bloody difficult?

He took his tea outside and sat on the bench and lit a cigarette. There were children playing in a nearby garden. Seven, eight years old. It reminded him of being young again. Paddling pools and Olympic hurdles over bamboo canes. Bike races and jumping out of trees. A couple more years and they'd be smoking cigarettes or looking for a can of petrol. But for now it was a good noise. Like the buzz of a mower, or people playing tennis.

It was so bloody difficult because he couldn't say it to Tony's face. You said something to someone's face, saw how they reacted and adjusted the steering wheel a bit. Like selling a house ("It's a very cosmopolitan area." "We noticed that." "Sorry. Estate-agent speak. Hardwired, I'm afraid").

And Tony had changed in his absence. After everything Becky had said. When he pictured Tony now he saw someone less sorted, more vulnerable, someone more like himself.

Jamie had changed, too.

Christ, it was like chess.

No. He was being stupid.

He was trying to get Tony back. It would be good if he came to the wedding but if he missed it, so what? Sooner or later he'd come back from Greece.

Come to think of it, if the wedding was a disaster, Tony missing it might be a godsend.

Solved.

He stubbed out his cigarette and went inside.

Dear Tony,
Please come to the wedding. Talk to Becky. She knows everything.
    I love you.

Jamie

xxx

He put it into the envelope, added one of the photocopied road maps, sealed it, addressed it care of Becky, stamped it and took it to the postbox before he could change his mind.

93

In other circumstances George might have committed suicide. For two nights running he had dreamed about the drowning in Peterborough and in his dream the river called to him the way a huge feather bed might call to him, and even in the dream it was scary how much he wanted to let go and sink into the cold and the dark and have everything canceled out for good. But there were now only six days to go before the wedding and it would be ungentlemanly to do something like that to his daughter.

So, for the moment he had to find a way of getting from day to day until a time when it would be acceptable to do something drastic without it souring the celebratory atmosphere. This would doubtless be sometime after Katie and Ray had returned from their honeymoon.

He assumed, after examining himself in the mirror, that he was going to suffer some kind of organ failure. It seemed inconceivable that the human body could survive the pressure created by that kind of sustained panic without something rupturing or ceasing to function. And at first this was one more fear to add to his other fears, of the cancer, of going irreparably insane, of collapsing in front of the wedding guests. But after twenty-four hours he was willing it to happen. Stroke. Heart attack. Anything. He really did not care whether he survived or not, so long as it rendered him unconscious and absolved him of responsibility.

He could not sleep. As soon as he lay down he could feel his skin mutating beneath his clothing. He lay motionless, waiting until Jean had fallen asleep, then got out of bed, took more codeine and poured himself a whiskey. He watched the strange programs that the television pumped out in the small hours. Open-university documentaries about glaciers. Black-and-white films from the forties. Farming news. He wept and walked in circles on the living-room carpet.

The following day he went out to the studio and invented pointless tasks to tire himself out and occupy his mind (two men were fitting the new carpet in the house). Sanding window frames. Sweeping the concrete floor. Moving all the spare bricks, one by one, to the other end of the studio. Making a variety of small constructions in the style of Stonehenge.

He was having a great deal of trouble eating. A couple of mouthfuls and he felt queasy, much as he did on ferries in bad weather. He forced down a little buttered toast to reassure Jean and had to go upstairs to be sick in the toilet.

He began to lose his mind halfway through the second day. He got up from the dining table at the end of lunch, leaving his dessert untouched, saying that he had to go somewhere. He was unsure, precisely, where it was that he had to go. He remembered leaving the house by the front door. Then he remembered nothing for some considerable time. White noise filled his mind, not unlike the white noise of a television failing to tune in to a particular channel, but louder and a good deal more insistent. It was not comfortable, but it was better than leaning over the toilet bowl while the toast came back, or lying in bed feeling the lesions multiply and coalesce.

It was possible that he took a bus. Though he had no specific memory of being on a bus.

When he came round he was standing in the doctor's surgery, in front of the reception desk. A woman seated at a computer monitor was saying, "Can I help you?" Her tone of voice suggested that she had already said this several times.

She leant forward and repeated the question, but more slowly and more gently, the way you did when you realized that the person you were addressing was not a time waster but suffering from genuine mental impairment.

"I want to see Dr. Barghoutian," said George.

Yes, now that he was here, that seemed like a good idea. Perhaps that was the reason he had come.

"Do you have an appointment?"

"I don't think so," said George.

"I'm afraid Dr. Barghoutian is fully booked today. If it's urgent you could see another doctor."

"I want to see Dr. Barghoutian."

"I'm sorry. Dr. Barghoutian is seeing other patients."

George could not remember the words you used to politely disagree with someone. "I want to see Dr. Barghoutian."

"I'm really sorry, but . . ."

The trip to the surgery had clearly used up all of George's energy (perhaps he had walked). He had no idea what he was planning to say to Dr. Barghoutian, but his entire being seemed to have been focused on getting into that little room. Now that it was impossible, he simply could not conceive of what he might do instead. He felt profoundly lonely and oddly cold (his clothing was wet; perhaps it had been raining outside). He lowered himself to the floor and curled into the angle between the carpet and the wooden panel of the reception desk and cried a little.

He hugged his knees. He was not going to move again. He was going to stay here forever.

Someone placed a blanket over him. Either that or he dreamt that someone was placing a blanket over him.

He remembered reading, somewhere, that shortly before one died of exposure one felt pleasantly warm and comfortable and this was a sign that the end was near.

Except that the end was not near. And he was not going to stay in this position forever because someone was saying, "Mr. Hall . . . ? Mr. Hall . . . ?" and when he opened his eyes he found himself looking at Dr. Barghoutian who was crouching in front of him, and George had been so far away that it took him several seconds to work out where he was, and why Dr. Barghoutian should be there as well.

He was helped to his feet and ushered down the corridor and into Dr. Barghoutian's consulting room where he was eased into a chair.

He could not speak for several minutes. Dr. Barghoutian did not seem unduly concerned, simply sat back and said, "Whenever you're ready."

George summoned his energy and began to speak. On any other day he would have been disturbed by his inability to form sentences, but he was past caring. He sounded like a man crawling into an oasis in a cartoon. "Got cancer . . . Dying . . . Really frightened . . . Daughter's wedding . . ."

Dr. Barghoutian allowed him to carry on in this manner for some time. The pressure inside George's head eased a little and his grip on syntax began to return. "I want to go into hospital . . . I want to go into a psychiatric hospital . . . Please . . . I need to be looked after . . . Somewhere safe . . ."

Dr. Barghoutian let him grind to a halt. "This wedding is on Saturday, I presume."

George nodded.

Dr. Barghoutian tapped his pencil on his teeth a couple of times. "Right. Here's what we're going to do."

George felt better hearing him say the words.

"You're going to come back and see me on Monday morning."

George felt a good deal worse. "But . . ."

Dr. Barghoutian held up his pencil.

George paused.

"I will get you an appointment with a dermatologist. And if you're still feeling anxious we will see about getting you some more heavyweight psychiatric help."

George felt a little better again.

"In the meantime, I am going to write you out a prescription for some Valium, OK? Take as many as you need, though I suggest you stay off the champagne during the wedding itself. Unless you want to end up under a table."

Dr. Barghoutian wrote out the prescription. "Now, I strongly suspect that you are going to find yourself feeling a lot calmer when we next meet. If you're not, we can do something about it."

It was not the solution George had hoped for. But the idea of another meeting on Monday and the promise of more heavyweight psychiatric help was a reassurance.

He would find some way of avoiding the dermatologist.

"Now, how do you feel about getting home? Would you like the receptionist to call your wife to come and pick you up?"

The thought of Jean being telephoned to say that he had collapsed in the doctor's surgery brought him to his senses more abruptly than anything else. "No. Really. I'll be fine."

He thanked Dr. Barghoutian and stood and realized that he was, indeed, wrapped in a lightweight green blanket.

"Ten o'clock Monday morning," said Dr. Barghoutian, handing him the prescription. "I'll get the receptionist to book you in. And make sure you take this to the chemist's before you go home."

He walked out of the surgery and across the road into Boots, examining the pattern on the tiled floor to avoid eye contact with pamphlets. He did three circuits of the park, picked up his prescription, swallowed two Valium and took a taxi home.

He had wondered what he could tell Jean to explain his unplanned excursion, but when he went into the house he saw a little Spider-Man rucksack in the hallway and realized that Katie had arrived with Jacob to oversee the final arrangements, and when the three of them came in from the garden Jean seemed unfazed by his news that he had gone out for a long walk and lost track of time.

Jacob said, "Grandpa, Grandpa, come and chase me."

But George was not in the mood for chasing children. He said, "Perhaps we can play a quieter game later on," and realized that he meant it. The Valium was clearly having some effect. A fact which was confirmed when he went upstairs and fell into a deep sleep on the bed.

94

Katie was booked in to have her hair done.

Quite when this had been arranged she wasn't sure. There was nothing wrong with her hair that couldn't be sorted out by a quick trim with the bathroom scissors and a decent conditioner. Clearly she'd been running on automatic when she was time-tabling everything.

Thank God she hadn't organized bridesmaids.

She told Ray she was going to cancel the appointment, he asked why and she said she didn't fancy getting herself tarted up like something out of a bridal catalog. Ray said, "Go on. Give yourself a treat." And she thought, *Why not? New life. New hair.* And went and had most of it removed. Boyish. Ears on show for the first time in seven years.

And Ray was right. It was more than a treat. The person in the mirror was no longer simply a wife and mother. The person in the mirror was a woman in charge of her own destiny.

Mum was horrified.

It wasn't the hair specifically. It was the combination of the hair and the canceled florists and the decision not to arrive at the register office in a limousine.

"I'm just worried that —"

"That what?" asked Katie.

"I'm just worried that it won't be . . . that it won't be a proper wedding."

"Because I don't have enough hair?"

"You're being flippant."

True, but Mum was being . . . strange that there wasn't a word for it, given how often parents did it. Translating every worry into a worry about something not being done properly. Not eating properly. Not dressing properly. Not behaving properly. As if the world could be set to rights with decorum.

"Well, it's going to be a lot more proper than the last wedding."

"So you and Ray . . . ?"

"We're getting on better than we've ever done."

"That's hardly a ringing endorsement."

"We love each other."

Mum flinched slightly, then changed the subject, just like Jacob did when that word cropped up. "Your father and Ray, by the way —"

"My father and Ray by the way what?"

"They didn't have words, did they?"

"When?" asked Katie.

"The other day. On the phone." Mum seemed quite troubled by this possibility.

Katie racked her brain and came up with nothing.

"Ray rang to talk to your father. But afterward your father said it had been a wrong number. And I wondered if there'd been a misunderstanding of some kind."

A bearded man appeared at the door to ask about the positioning of guy ropes.

Katie got to her feet. "Mum, look, if it makes you feel better, why don't you ring some florists. See if anyone can do something at short notice."

"OK," said Mum.

"But not Buller's."

"OK."

"I swore at them," said Katie.

"OK."

Katie went into the garden with the bearded man. The central pole was up at the far end of the garden and sails of cream canvas were being hoisted into the air by five other men in bottle-green sweatshirts. Jacob was running in and out of the coils of

447

rope and the stacked chairs like a demented puppy, deep in some complex superhero fantasy, and Katie remembered how magical it once was to see an ordinary space transformed like this. A sofa turned upside down. A room full of balloons.

Then Jacob slipped and knocked a trestle table over and got his finger caught in the hinged legs and screamed a lot and she scooped him up and cuddled him and took him to the bedroom and dug out the Savlon and the Maisie Mouse plasters and Jacob was brave and stopped crying, and Mum came up and said she'd sorted out the flowers.

The two of them sat next to each other on the bed while Jacob transformed his red robot into a dinosaur and back into a robot again.

"So, we shall finally get to meet Jamie's boyfriend," said Mum, and the pause before she said the word *boyfriend* was so tiny it was almost imperceptible.

Katie looked down at her hands and said, "Yup," and felt very bad for Jamie.

The day was getting on. She and Jacob drove into town to pick up the cake and drop off the cassette at the register office. She'd wanted to start with a bit of "Royal Fireworks" then segue straight into "I Got

You (I Feel Good)" as soon as the knot was tied, but the woman on the phone said rather snootily that they "didn't do segueing," and Katie realized it was probably too complicated anyway. Some great-aunt would collapse and they'd be getting her into the recovery position with James Brown yelping like a randy dog. So they decided to go with that Bach double-violin piece from the compilation CD Dad gave her for Christmas.

They popped into Sandersons and Sticky Fingers to pick up the personalized tankards and the industrial-size Belgian chocolates for Ed and Sarah then drove home, nearly destroying the cake when a group of kids kicked a football in front of the car.

They sat down for supper, the four of them, Mum, Dad, her and Jacob, and it was good. No arguments. No sulks. No skirting round difficult subjects.

She put Jacob to bed, helped Mum with the washing up and the heavens opened. Mum fretted, the way parents did about bad weather. But Katie took herself up to the loft and opened the window over the garden and stood there as the marquee cracked and slapped and the wind roared like surf in the black trees.

She loved storms. Thunder, lightning,

driving rain. Something to do with that childhood dream she used to have about living in a castle.

She remembered the last wedding. Graham getting that weird allergic reaction from her shampoo the day before. Ice packs. Antihistamines. That van taking the wing off Uncle Brian's Jag. The weird woman with the mental problem who wandered into the reception singing.

She wondered what was going to go wrong this time, then realized she was being stupid. Like Mum and the rain. The fear of having nothing to complain about.

She closed the window, wiped the water off the sill with her sleeve and went downstairs to see if there was any wine left in the bottle.

95

George realized that Dr. Barghoutian was not so stupid after all.

The Valium was good. The Valium was very good indeed. He went downstairs, got himself a mug of tea and played a couple of card games with Jacob.

After Katie went into town he squeezed round the back of the marquee for a look at the studio and realized that, with the end of the garden blocked off, the studio had become a secret place of the kind that children loved and which, to be quite honest, he still rather enjoyed himself. He pulled out the folding chair and sat down for a very pleasurable ten minutes until one of the workmen slipped round the other side of the marquee and began urinating into a flower bed. George decided that coughing to make his presence known was politer than watching someone urinate in silence, so he coughed and the man apologized and vanished, but George felt that his secret space had been violated somewhat and returned to the house.

He went inside and made himself a ham-and-tomato sandwich and washed it down with milk.

The only problem with Valium was that it did not encourage rational thought. It was only after supper, when the effects of the two pills he had taken during the afternoon began to wear off, that he did the maths. There were only ten pills in the bottle to start with. If he were to carry on taking them at this rate he would run out before the wedding had begun.

It began to dawn on him that although

Dr. Barghoutian was wise, he had not been generous.

He was going to have to stop taking the pills now. And he was going to have to avoid taking any tomorrow.

The label on the little brown bottle cautioned against drinking alcohol while taking them. Bugger that. When he sat down after his speech, he was going to drain the first glass which came to hand. If he passed swiftly into a coma, that was fine by him.

The difficulty was getting to Saturday.

He could feel it coming in, even now, as he sat on the sofa with Jacques Loussier playing on the stereo and *The Daily Telegraph* folded on his lap, the way they saw that storm coming off the sea at St. Ives a few years ago, a gray wall of thickened light half a mile out, the water dark beneath it, everyone just standing and watching, not realizing how fast it was moving until it was too late, then running and yelling as the hail came up the beach horizontally like gunfire.

His body was starting to rev and churn, all the dials moving steadily toward the red. The fear was coming back. He wanted to scratch his hip. But if there was any cancer left the last thing he wanted was to disturb it.

It was very tempting to take more Valium.

God almighty. You could say all you liked about reason and logic and common sense and imagination, but when the chips were down the one skill you needed was the ability to think about absolutely nothing whatsoever.

He got up and walked into the hallway. There was some wine left from supper. He'd finish the bottle then take a couple of codeine.

When he entered the kitchen, however, the lights were off, the door to the garden was open and Katie was standing on the threshold watching the driving rain, drinking the remains of the wine straight from the bottle.

"Don't drink that," said George, rather more loudly than he intended.

"Sorry," said Katie. "I thought you were in bed. Anyway, I was planning to finish it. So you won't have to share my bacteria."

George could think of no way of saying, "Give me the bottle," without seeming deranged.

Katie drank the wine. "God, I love the rain."

George stood looking at her. She swigged more wine. After a little while she turned round and saw that he was standing looking at her. He realized that he was acting a little oddly. But he needed company.

"Scrabble," he said.

"What?" asked Katie.

"I was wondering whether you wanted a game of Scrabble." Where had that come from?

Katie wiggled her head slowly from side to side, weighing up the idea. "OK."

"Great," said George. "You go and get the box from the cupboard. I've just got to go and get some codeine. For a headache."

George was halfway up the stairs when he recalled the last game of Scrabble they had played. It had ground to a halt during a very heated debate over George's entirely legal use of the word *zho,* a cross between a cow and a yak.

Oh well, it would keep his mind occupied.

96

It was all a bit wearing.

For a third of his waking hours Jamie managed not to think about Tony at all. For another third he imagined Tony getting back in time and the two of them being reunited in various melodramatic scenes. The final third was given over to maudlin thoughts of going to Peterborough alone and getting way too much sympathy or none at all and having to remain cheerful for Katie's sake.

He was planning to head up early on Friday afternoon to miss the traffic. Thursday evening he ate a Tesco pasta bake and a fruit salad in front of a video of *The Blair Witch Project,* which was rather scarier than he'd anticipated, so that he had to pause the tape halfway through and close all the downstairs curtains and lock the front door.

He expected to have nightmares. So it came as something of a surprise to find himself having a sex dream about Tony. He wasn't complaining. It was boots-on, fresh-out-of-prison stuff. But what was slightly disturbing was that the whole thing was taking place in his parents' living room during some kind of cocktail party. Tony pushing him facedown on the sofa, shoving three fingers into his mouth and fucking him with no preliminaries whatsoever. All the details far more vivid than they were meant to be in dreams. The bend in Tony's cock, the paint stains on his fingers, the knotted vine pattern on the cushion covers pressed up against Jamie's face in extreme close-up, the chatter, the clink of wineglasses. So vivid in fact that on several occasions during the following morning he remembered what had happened and broke into a cold sweat for a fraction of a second before remembering that it wasn't real.

97

Jean didn't realize how bad it was until she went downstairs and wandered across the lawn through the drizzle in her dressing gown.

There was standing water in the marquee. Seventy people were meant to be eating in here tomorrow.

She couldn't help feeling that if she was still organizing the wedding this wouldn't have happened, though clearly she had no more control over the weather than Katie and Ray.

She felt . . . old. That was what she felt.

It wasn't just the rain. It was George, too. He'd seemed fine for a few weeks now. Then, after supper, it all slipped away. He didn't want to talk. He didn't want to help out. And she had absolutely no idea why.

She was meant to be worried, not angry. She knew that. But how could you keep on worrying when you didn't know what the problem was?

She wandered back into the kitchen and made herself some toast and coffee.

Katie and Jacob appeared half an hour later. She told Katie about the marquee and felt almost cross when Katie refused to be panicked.

Katie didn't understand. It wasn't happening in her garden. If people found themselves wading through mud they were going to blame Jean. And it was a selfish thing to think, but it was true.

She tried to put the thought from her mind. "So, little man . . ." She ruffled Jacob's hair. "What can we get you for breakfast?"

"I want some eggy," said Jacob.

"I want some eggy what?" said Katie, who was deep in the paper.

"I want some eggy, please," said Jacob.

"Scrambled, fried or boiled?" Jean asked.

"What's fried?" asked Jacob.

"He wants scrambled," said Katie absently.

"Scrambled it is." Jean kissed the top of his head. At least there was something she could do for someone.

98

Mum was right. A wedding without disasters clearly broke some unwritten rule of the universe. Like snow at Christmas. Or pain-free childbirth.

She rang the marquee people and that was fine. They'd come round with mops and heaters later on in the day.

Then Auntie Eileen and Uncle Ronnie turned up with their Labrador in tow. Because their dog sitter was in hospital. Unfortunately Jacob hated dogs. So it was shut outside to keep Jacob happy. At which point it began howling and trying to dig its way through the back door.

Then the caterers rang to say they needed to change the menu after a power failure left a freezer off overnight. Sadie rang to say she'd just got back from New Zealand and found the invitation in the post and could she come. And Brian and Gail rang to say the hotel had lost their reservation and clearly someone else had to solve this problem for them. Like the bride, for example. Or the bride's parents.

Katie gave up answering the phone and went upstairs and found Dad locked into the bathroom, possibly hiding from Eileen and Ronnie, so she went up to the top loo, peed and flushed and heard the macerator grinding away and saw the water surge to within a centimeter of the rim of the bowl. At which point some kind of death wish took her over and instead of ringing the phone number on the sticker, she thought, *I'll give it another go,* and flushed a second time with predictable results.

Two seconds later she was kneeling on the floor holding back a pond of diluted wee with a dam of cream towels saying, "Arsing, fucking, shitting," which was when Jacob appeared behind her and pointed out that she was saying rude words.

"Jacob, can you fetch Granny, and tell her to bring some bin bags?"

"It smells yucky."

"Jacob, please fetch Granny, or you will never get any pocket money, ever."

But the Labrador was back in the house and Jacob was refusing to go anywhere near the ground floor, so she went down herself, and found Mum and Dad in the hallway having some kind of altercation about Dad not pulling his weight but doing it in a fevered whisper, presumably so Eileen and Ronnie didn't hear. Katie said the loo had overflowed. Mum told Dad to sort it out. Dad declined. And Mum said something very unladylike to Dad which Katie didn't quite catch because Ray appeared at the other end of the hallway saying, "I hope you don't mind, your aunt let me in."

Mum did a horrified double take and

apologized profusely for arguing yet again in Ray's presence and asked whether she could make him a nice cup of tea and Katie reminded her that the loo was still overflowing and felt extremely pissed off that Ray had spent last night in London organizing some secret thing, and Dad slipped away while everyone's attention was diverted and Ray bounded up the stairs and Mum said she'd put the kettle on and Katie went to grab some bin bags from the kitchen for ferrying the wee-sodden towels to the washing machine and noticed en route the muddy paw prints on the dining-room carpet and tossed Ronnie a disposable cloth wipe and told him to clean up after his bloody dog, which he had to do because he was a Christian.

The macerator man said he'd be there in an hour and Eileen and Ronnie took Rover out for a long walk despite the rain and everything was fine until Katie took her dress out of the suitcase to iron it and found half a pint of coconut body wash soaked into the hem and swore so loudly Eileen and Ronnie probably heard it several fields away. So Ray held up his hands and said, "Hit me," and she did, repeatedly for some considerable time until Ray said, "OK, it's starting to hurt now."

He suggested she go into town to buy another dress and she was about to give him a hard time for thinking all female problems could be solved by shopping, when he said, calmly, "Buy a new dress. Find a café. Sit down with a book and a cup of coffee and come back in a couple of hours and I'll sort everything out here," and she kissed him and grabbed her bag and ran.

99

George had naïvely assumed that when Katie and Ray said they would arrange everything themselves this meant he would not have to do anything.

Jean did not understand that if he drove into town to get flowers he might keep going until he reached Aberdeen. She did not understand that he needed to sit somewhere quietly doing very little.

Then the toilet upstairs overflowed and everything got very hectic indeed, so he went to lie down in the bedroom. But Jean came into the bedroom to get sheets and towels for Ronnie and Eileen and she was quite rude to him. So he shut himself in the bathroom, until Jean turfed him out because people needed to use the toilet. At which point it became rapidly clear to George that these complications were only going to multiply over the coming day, and that he would very soon not be able to cope.

He had been wildly unrealistic. There was no way he could do small talk with all these people, let alone stand up in front of them and give a speech.

He did not want to embarrass Katie.

It was obvious that he could not go to her wedding.

100

Jean had been wrong about Ray.

Within an hour of his arrival everything was back on track. Katie had been sent into town. A man was coming to fix the toilet and Eileen and Ronnie had been sent to pick up the flowers with their blessed dog in tow.

And, strangely, he did seem to have control over the weather. She was making him a cup of tea just after he arrived when she looked out of the window and saw that the rain had stopped and the sun had come out. Within half an hour the men from the marquee turned up to dry the place out and he was in the garden ordering them around as if he ran the company.

True, he was a little brash sometimes. Not one of us, if you were going to put it like that. But it was beginning to dawn on her that being "one of us" was not necessarily a good thing. After all, her family were failing rather obviously to organize a wedding. Maybe a little brashness was precisely what was needed.

She began to see that Katie might be wiser than either she or George had realized.

Mid-afternoon her brother and his wife dropped in and offered to take her and George out for supper.

She explained that George was feeling a bit under the weather.

"Well, if George doesn't mind, you could come on your own," said Douglas.

She was halfway through a polite refusal when Ray said, "You go. We'll make sure someone keeps an eye on the fort."

And for the first time she was glad that Katie was marrying this man.

101

Jamie pulled into the village and felt that slight sinking in his stomach he always felt going back. The family thing. Like he was fourteen again. He parked over the road from the house, turned off the engine and gathered himself.

The secret was to remember that you were an adult now, that all of you were adults, that there was no longer any need to fight the battles you were fighting when you were fourteen.

God, he wanted Tony with him.

He glanced across at the house and saw Uncle Douglas emerging from the side gate with his wife. Mary. Or Molly. He'd better check that with someone before he put his foot in it.

He slipped down in his seat so that he couldn't be seen and waited till they'd climbed into their car.

God, he hated aunts. The lipstick. The lavender perfume. The hilarious stories about how you wet yourself during a carol service.

They drove away.

What was he going to say about Tony?

That was the problem, wasn't it. You left home. But you never did become an adult. Not really. You just fucked up in different and more complicated ways.

At this point, Katie drove up and parked beside him. They got out of their cars simultaneously.

"Hey you," said Katie. They hugged. "No Tony?"

"No Tony."

She rubbed his arms. "I'm so sorry."

"Listen, I was going to ask you about that. I mean, what have you said to Mum?"

"I haven't said anything."

"Right."

"Just tell them the truth," said Katie.

"Yeh."

Katie looked him in the eye. "They'll be fine. They have to be fine. I'm queen for the weekend. And no one is stepping out of line, all right?"

"All right," said Jamie. "Great haircut, by the way."

"Thank you."

They headed into the house.

102

Katie walked into the kitchen with Jamie and found the Blessed Saint Eileen seated at the table surrounded by a small jungle.

"We fetched your flowers," said Eileen, getting to her feet.

For a moment Katie thought it was some kind of personal gift.

"Hullo, love," said Mum, kissing Jamie.

Eileen turned to Jamie and said, "We haven't seen this young man since . . . well, I don't know how long it's been."

"A very long time," said Jamie.

"So," said Mum, looking slightly uncomfortable, "where's Tony?"

Katie realized Mum was bracing herself for the poorly timed appearance of her son's boyfriend in front of her unprepared evangelical sister. Which made her feel sorry for both Jamie and Mum. Clearly being queen for the weekend didn't give her the power to resolve everything.

"I'm afraid he's not coming," said Jamie. Katie could see him steeling himself. "We've had a few problems. To cut a long story short, he went to Crete. Which is apparently very nice this time of year."

Katie gave Jamie's back a discreet pat.

"I am sorry," said Mum and it seemed like she really did mean it.

Then Eileen said, "Who's Tony?" in a wide-eyed innocent way that sent a noticeable chill through the room.

"Anyway," said Mum, ignoring her sister completely and rubbing her hands together. "We've got lots to do."

"Tony's my boyfriend," said Jamie.

And Katie thought that if it all went wrong, if the register office burned down or she broke an ankle on the way there, it would be worth it for the expression on Eileen's face right now.

She looked as if she was receiving instructions from God on how to proceed.

It was quite hard to tell what Mum was thinking.

"We're homosexuals," said Jamie.

This, thought Katie, was over-egging the pudding a little. She pulled him toward the hallway. "Come on, you."

And a man appeared at the kitchen door saying, "I've come to mend the toilet."

103

Jamie and Katie went into the bedroom and collapsed backward onto the bed. They were laughing too much to explain the reason to Ray or Jacob. And it really was like being fourteen again. But in a good way this time.

And then Jamie needed a pee, so he walked along the landing and as he was emerging from the loo his father appeared and said, "Jamie, I need to talk to you." No greeting. No pleasantries. Just a conspiratorial whisper and a hand on Jamie's elbow.

He followed his father into his parents' bedroom and perched on the armchair.

"Jamie, look . . ."

Jamie was still fizzy from the encounter in the kitchen and there was something reassuring about his father's quiet, measured voice.

"The cancer," said his father, wincing in a slightly embarrassed way. "Come back I'm afraid."

Jamie realized that something rather serious was going on here, and sat up a little straighter. "The cancer's come back?"

"I'm frightened, Jamie. Very frightened. Of dying. Of cancer. Pretty much constantly. Not pleasant. Not pleasant at all. Can't sleep. Can't eat."

"Have you talked to Mum?"

"I've been getting on her nerves a tad," said his father. "Not able to help out much. Really do need to sit down in a quiet room. On my own."

Jamie wanted to lean across and stroke his father, the way you might stroke a worried dog. It was a peculiar urge, and probably not a wise move. He said, "Is there anything I can do to help?"

"Well, yes there is," said his father, brightening noticeably. "You see, the thing is, I really can't go to the wedding."

"What?"

"I can't go to the wedding."

468

"But you have to go to the wedding," said Jamie.

"Do I?" said his father, weakly.

"Of course you do," said Jamie. "You're the father of the bride."

His father thought about this. "You're absolutely right, of course."

There was a brief pause, then his father began to cry.

Jamie had never seen his father cry before. He'd never seen an old man of any kind cry. Except on television, during wars. It made him feel seasick and scared and sad and he had to fight back the temptation to tell his father that he didn't need to come to the wedding. Though if he did that Katie wouldn't talk to either of them for the rest of their natural lives.

Jamie got off his chair and squatted in front of his father. "Dad. Look." He rubbed his father's forearm. "We're all on your side. And we'll all be there to hold your hand. When you get inside the marquee you can knock back a few glasses of wine . . . It'll be all right. I promise."

His father nodded.

"Oh, and I'll have a word with Mum," said Jamie. "Tell her you need some peace and quiet."

He stood up. His father was in a world of

469

his own. Jamie touched his shoulder. "You OK?"

His father looked up. "Thank you."

"Give me a shout if you need anything," said Jamie.

He walked out of the room, shutting the door carefully behind him, then went to look for his mother.

He was walking down the stairs, however, when he glanced into his old room and noticed suitcases on the bed. Because he was thinking about his father's mental well-being he didn't really consider the implications of the suitcases until he met his mother in the hallway holding a stack of clean flannels.

"Mum, listen, I've just been talking to Dad and . . ."

"Yes . . . ?"

Jamie paused, working out what he wanted to say and how to phrase it. And while he was doing this another part of his brain considered the implications of the suitcases and he heard himself saying, "Those suitcases in my room . . ."

"What about them?"

"Who's staying in there?"

"Eileen and Ronnie," said his mother.

"And I'm staying . . . ?"

"We've found you a nice bed-and-breakfast in Yarwell."

It was at this point that Jamie threw an uncharacteristic wobbly. And he knew it was the wrong moment to throw a wobbly, but there was not a lot he could do about it.

104

Jean was looking for Jamie. To make up for all that hoo-ha in the kitchen. To say how sad she was that Tony wasn't coming to the wedding.

She bumped into him coming down the stairs. And clearly no one had told him about Eileen and Ronnie staying in his room.

Jean was going to explain that she'd spent a long and rather embarrassing morning in the library in town finding a special bed-and-breakfast where he and Tony would not feel out of place. She was rather proud of having done this and she'd expected Jamie to feel grateful. But he was not in the mood for feeling grateful.

"You just didn't want Tony and me sleeping in this house, did you?"

"It's not like that, Jamie."

"I'm your son, for God's sake."

"Please, Jamie, not so loud. And in any

case now that Tony's not here —"

"Yeh, that's solved all your problems, hasn't it."

A door opened somewhere nearby and the two of them went quiet.

Ray, Katie and Jacob appeared at the head of the stairs. Luckily they seemed not to have heard the argument.

"Ah, Jamie," said Ray, "just the bloke we were looking for."

"I colored in a Power Ranger," said Jacob, holding up a magazine.

"We need a favor," said Katie.

"What sort of favor?" asked Jamie, who was clearly annoyed at being interrupted in the middle of an argument.

Ray said, "Katie and I are going out for a meal, and Jean's meeting up with her brother. We wondered if you'd mind babysitting Jacob."

"Oh, I'm afraid I'm not staying here tonight," said Jamie, turning to Jean with a sarcastic smile.

"Maybe your father can look after Jacob," said Jean, trying to deflect attention away from Jamie. "I think it's about time he rolled up his sleeves and did something useful round here."

"Jesus, no," said Jamie.

"Jamie," said Jean. "Your language."

"That's naughty-naughty," said Jacob.

"I'll look after Jacob," said Jamie. "Sorry. Forget what I said about not being here. Wasn't thinking straight. Sorry. No problem. Come on, little man, let's have a look at your Power Ranger."

"It's Yellow Ranger," said Jacob.

And the two of them headed upstairs together.

"What was that all about?" asked Katie.

"Oh nothing," said Jean. "So, where are you going for supper? Or is it a big surprise?"

105

Halfway through their meal Ray started glancing at his watch.

Katie pointed out that a gentleman shouldn't really do this during a candlelit dinner with his fiancée. Ray was apologetic, but not quite apologetic enough. He clearly thought it was funny, which it wasn't, and Katie was torn between getting genuinely angry and not wanting to have a public row the night before their wedding.

A few minutes before nine o'clock, however, Ray leaned across the table and took hold of both her hands and said, "I bought

473

you a present."

And Katie said, "Uh-huh," being a bit noncommittal because of the time-checking, but also because Ray was not brilliant at presents.

Ray didn't say anything.

"So . . . ?" asked Katie.

Ray held up his finger, meaning *Wait,* or *Be quiet.* And this was odd, too.

"OK," said Katie.

Ray looked toward the window, so Katie looked toward the window, and Ray said, "Five, four, three, two, one," and absolutely nothing happened for a few seconds, and Ray said, "Shit," quietly and then fireworks erupted from the field next to the restaurant, fizzy white snakes, purple sea urchins, yellow starbursts, weeping willows of incandescent green light. And those *whumps* like someone hitting cardboard boxes with a golf club that took her straight back to bonfires and baked potatoes in silver foil and the smell of sparkler smoke.

Everyone in the restaurant was watching, and each explosion was followed by a little *ooh* or *aah* from somewhere in the room, and Katie said, "So this is . . ."

"Yup."

"Jesus, Ray, this is amazing."

"You're welcome," said Ray, who wasn't

474

watching the fireworks at all, but watching her face watching the fireworks. "It was either this or Chanel No. 5. I thought you'd prefer this."

106

Jean seldom saw Douglas and Maureen. Partly because they lived in Dundee. And partly because . . . well, to be frank, because Douglas was a bit like Ray. Only more so. He ran a haulage company for starters. One of those large men who are excessively proud of having no airs and graces.

Her opinion of people like Ray, however, had shifted over the preceding twenty-four hours, and she was rather enjoying Douglas's company tonight.

She'd already had a couple of glasses of wine when Maureen asked what was wrong with George, so she thought *To hell with it* and told them he was suffering from stress.

To which Maureen replied, "Doug went through that a couple of years ago."

Douglas finished his prawn cocktail and lit a cigarette and put his arm round Maureen and let her talk for him.

"Had a blackout driving the transit just north of Edinburgh. Came round scraping down the crash barrier on the central reservation doing seventy. Brain scans. Blood tests. Doctor said it was tension."

"So we sold one of the artics and buggered off to Portugal for three weeks," said Douglas. "Left Simon to run the office. Knowing when to let go of the reins. That's the thing."

Jean was going to say, "I didn't know." But they knew she didn't know. And they all knew why. Because she'd never been interested. And she felt bad about this. She said, "I'm really sorry. I should have asked you to stay at the house."

"With Eileen?" asked Maureen, raising her eyebrows.

"Instead," said Jean.

"I hope she's not bringing that bloody dog to the wedding," said Douglas, and they all laughed.

And Jean wondered briefly whether she could tell them about the scissors, before deciding that was taking things a bit far.

107

Jamie had never babysat before. Not properly.

He'd looked after Jacob a couple of times

when he was tiny. For an hour or two. While he was asleep, mostly. He'd even changed a nappy. It didn't actually need changing. He'd got the smells wrong and when he took it off it was empty. He just couldn't bring himself to reattach something containing urine.

But he was not going to be babysitting again. Not until Jacob was twelve at least.

This realization came to him fairly rapidly when Jacob called him into the bathroom, having finished his poo, and Jamie watched him slide off the toilet seat a little too early, dragging the final section across the seat and leaving it hanging from the rim like a wet chocolate stalactite.

Not baby poo. But actual human feces. With a hint of dog.

Jamie armed himself with a rudimentary oven glove of toilet paper and held his nose.

And obviously there were worse jobs in the world (rat catcher, astronaut . . .) but Jamie had never realized quite how far down the table parenting came.

Jacob was inordinately proud of his achievement, and the rest of the evening's activities (scrambled egg on toast, *Mr. Gumpy's Outing,* a very, very soapy bath) were punctuated by Jacob retelling his toilet adventure on at least twenty occasions.

Jamie never did get the chance to talk to his mother about his father's state of mind. And maybe it was better that way. One less person worrying. When he headed off tonight he could ask Ray to keep watch.

His father spent the rest of the evening in the bedroom.

After Jacob finally went to bed Jamie put his feet up in front of *Mission: Impossible* (there was a stockpile of action videos under the television for some unaccountable reason).

Halfway through the film Jamie paused the tape and went to pee and check up on his father. His father was not in the bedroom. Or the bathroom. His father was not in any of the rooms, upstairs or downstairs. Jamie went back and checked in cupboards and under beds, petrified that his father had done something stupid.

He was on the verge of ringing the police when he glanced into the darkened garden and saw his father standing in the center of the lawn. He opened the door and stepped outside. His father was swaying a little.

Jamie walked over and stood beside him. "How's things?"

His father looked up at the sky. "Incredible to think it's all going to end."

He'd been drinking. Jamie could smell it.

478

Wine? Whiskey? It was hard to tell.

"Music. Books. Science. Everyone talks about progress, but . . ." His father was still looking upward.

Jamie put a hand on his father's arm to prevent him toppling backward.

"A few million years and all this will be a big empty rock. No evidence we even existed. No one to even notice that there's no evidence. No one looking for evidence. Just . . . space. And some other big rocks. Whirling around."

Jamie hadn't heard someone talk like this since getting massively stoned with Scunny in college. "Perhaps we should get you back inside."

"Don't know whether it's terrifying or reassuring," said his father. "You know, everyone being forgotten. You. Me. Hitler. Mozart. Your mother." He looked down and rubbed his hands. "What's the time, by the way?"

Jamie checked his watch. "Ten twenty."

"Better head back inside."

Jamie guided his father gently toward the light of the kitchen door.

He paused on the threshold and turned to Jamie. "Thank you."

"What for?"

"For listening. Don't think I could cope

479

otherwise."

"You're welcome," said Jamie, locking the door as his father made his way toward the stairs.

When everyone returned home, Jamie took Ray aside and said his father was looking a little wobbly. He asked if Ray could keep a weather eye open overnight and not mention anything to Katie. Ray said it would be no problem.

Then he got into his car and drove to the bed-and-breakfast in Yarwell, where the locked door was answered by a large, caftaned person of indeterminate gender who was rather tetchy about Jamie not having rung to say he would be arriving so late.

108

The following morning Jean woke up, did her ablutions and pottered back to the bedroom.

George was sitting on the edge of the bed wearing the hangdog expression he'd been wearing for the last few days. She did her best to ignore him. If she said anything she was going to lose her temper.

Maybe she was insensitive, maybe she was old-fashioned, but it seemed to her that there was nothing so burdensome you couldn't put it aside for the day of your daughter's wedding.

She was stepping into her slip when he said, "I'm sorry," and she turned round and she could see that he really meant it.

"I'm so sorry, Jean."

She wasn't sure what to say. That it was all right? Because it wasn't all right. She could see that.

She sat down and took his hand and held it. Maybe that was all you could do.

She remembered the children, when they were little, teaching them to say sorry when they'd hit each other or broken something. And it was just a word to them. A way of papering over the cracks. Then you heard someone say sorry properly and you realized how powerful it was. The magic word that opened the door of the cave.

"What can I do?" she asked.

"I don't think there is anything you can do," said George.

She sat beside him on the bed and put her arms around him. He didn't move.

She said, "We'll get you through this."

Seconds later Katie was knocking on the door. "Mum . . . ? Any chance of a helping hand?"

"Give me a minute." She pulled the rest

of her clothes on and kissed George and said, "It's going to be all right. I promise."

Then she went to look after the rest of her family.

109

Jamie got out of bed and wandered into the loo.

There were knitted baby blue covers on the spare loo rolls and a set of hand-painted wall plates from the Costa Brava.

He'd woken up several times during the night, disturbed by a series of dreams in which he failed to stop grisly things happening to his father. In one of them Jamie looked down from an upstairs window to see his father, shrunk to about half his normal size and bleeding heavily, being dragged up the garden by a wolf. Consequently Jamie was rather tired and when he imagined the kind of breakfast that might be waiting for him downstairs (warm bacon with little knuckles of white gristle, stewy tea with full-fat milk . . .) it seemed more than he could bear.

He'd sleep on the sofa at his parents' house tonight. Or in the marquee.

He packed his bags, checked the coast was

clear, then tiptoed down the stairs. He was opening the door when the portly man-woman loomed out of the kitchen doorway, saying, "Would you like some breakfast?" and Jamie just ran.

110

Katie was lying in a deck chair on the roof terrace. She was looking down over Barcelona. But the terrace was the terrace outside their room in that hotel in San Gimignano. And she could see the ocean which you couldn't in San Gimignano. The air smelt of something halfway between sun lotion and really good vanilla custard. Jacob was asleep, or staying with Mum and Dad in England, or just generally absent in a way that didn't make her anxious. And actually it was a hammock not a deck chair.

Then Ray trod on the Playmobil knight and yelled, and Jacob yelled because Ray had broken the Playmobil knight and Katie was awake and she was getting married today and it was probably a moment you had to stop and savor, but savoring wasn't really possible because by the time she'd brushed her teeth and washed her face the caterers were downstairs wondering how much of the kitchen they could colonize, so she had to jump-start Mum, and then Jacob was upset because Ronnie had finished the Bran Flakes and instead of apologizing or offering to go out and get some more from the village shop he was giving Jacob a sermonette on not always being able to have what you want, though the problem had been caused by Ronnie doing precisely that. Then Ed turned up and trod in the monumental pile of crap their bloody dog had left in the middle of the path and it was clearly going to carry on in this fashion pretty much till the end of the day.

111

Jamie drove away so fast he produced a tire squeal exiting the cul-de-sac.

He carried on feeling embarrassed by his behavior till he reached the main road when he slowed down and reminded himself that it was a genuinely crap bed-and-breakfast, that the owner was rude as well as strange (female to male transsexual was Jamie's bet, but it wouldn't be a very big bet), and Jamie was only staying there because he'd been ignominiously turfed out of his own bedroom (he had forgotten to pay, hadn't he;

sod it, he'd sort that out later). So he stopped feeling ashamed and felt indignant, which was healthier.

Then he imagined telling Katie the whole story (complete with the knitted loo roll covers and tire squeals) and wondering aloud precisely which guidebooks his mother had consulted in the library, and the indignation turned into amusement, which was healthier still.

By the time he pulled up outside his parents' house he was feeling rather pleased with himself. Running away was not something he did. He tidied hotel rooms and sat through bad films and occasionally pretended to other people that Tony was just a very good friend. Which wasn't good for the soul.

He used to hate it when Tony complained in restaurants or held Jamie's hand ostentatiously in public places. But now Tony wasn't around Jamie could see how important it was. And it occurred to him that there were two parts to being a better person. One part was thinking about other people. The other part was not giving a toss about what other people thought. Sending stale naan bread back to the kitchen. Kissing with tongues on Blackfriars Bridge.

A train of thought which came to a crescendo as he entered the kitchen where, fittingly, Eileen and Ronnie were eating breakfast. At which point he felt Tony beside him, in spirit if not in body, and Jamie realized that whatever Eileen and Ronnie might think (that he needed saving, or castrating, or putting behind bars), deep down they were petrified of him. Which made him feel a bit like Batman, who looked evil, though he was actually good.

So he said, "Hullo, Eileen. Hullo, Ronnie," and gave them a broad smile. "I hope you slept well."

Then he patted them both on the shoulder and spun round, and the air in the kitchen filled with his black cloak and he swept majestically across the dining room in his matching leather boots and codpiece, through the hallway into the downstairs loo.

Which seemed to act like a short-range time machine because when he flushed the toilet and stepped back out into the hallway it was like the concourse at Euston, Eileen going one way, his sister and mother going the other, Jacob being a fighter plane, the Christian hound yowling and two startlingly redheaded women he didn't recognize standing in the kitchen doorway wearing white uniforms.

Katie said, "Hi, Jamie," and vanished.

Ray walked downstairs and came over and whispered, "Not a peep out of your dad last night."

"Thanks," said Jamie. "I'll pop up and say hello."

"How was the bed-and-breakfast?" asked Ray.

"Not good," said Jamie.

"Katie told me about your room being nicked by the happy clappers," said Ray. "I think they might have been exorcising it."

Jamie got to the landing and realized he'd been a bit distracted and hadn't responded to Ray's joke, which probably came over as rude. Never mind. His father was more important right now.

He knocked on the bedroom door.

"Come in," said his father. He sounded reassuringly buoyant.

Jamie went in and found him sitting fully dressed on the side of the bed.

"You're here," said his father. "Good." He slapped his hands onto his knees in a ready-for-action kind of way.

"How are you?" asked Jamie.

"Changed my mind," said his father.

"About what?"

"Really can't come to the wedding."

"Hang on a minute," said Jamie.

"Now, I could go to a hotel," said his

father. "But, to be honest with you, I've had my fill of hotels recently."

Jamie was not sure how to respond to this. His father looked and sounded completely sane. Except that he was clearly not.

"Obviously I can't take the car because your mother is going to need that to get to the register office. And if I simply start walking from here I'm bound to be seen by someone who recognizes me." His father slipped an Ordnance Survey map out from under the mattress. "But you have a car." He unfolded the map and pointed to Folksworth. "If you were able to drop me somewhere round about here I could walk on footpaths for ten, fifteen miles without crossing a major road."

"Right," said Jamie.

"If you could put my big waterproof and a thermos of tea in the boot, that would be helpful." His father refolded the Ordnance Survey map and slipped it back under the mattress. "Some biscuits would be good, too, if that were possible."

"Some biscuits," said Jamie.

"Something plain. Digestives. That kind of thing. Nothing too chocolatey."

"Digestives."

His father took hold of Jamie's hand and

held it. "Thank you. This makes me feel a lot better."

"Good," said Jamie.

"You'd better get downstairs and mingle," said his father. "Don't want anyone else getting wind of this, do we."

"No," said Jamie.

He stood up and went over to the door. He turned round briefly. His father was staring out of the window, rocking from one foot to the other.

Jamie went out onto the landing, closed the door behind him, ran downstairs, grabbed his mobile, shut himself in the toilet for a second time and rang the doctor's surgery. He was put through to some kind of central weekend control room. He explained that his father was losing his mind. He explained about the scissors and the wedding and the escape plan and the weeping. They said a doctor would be at the house in the next forty-five minutes.

112

Jean found Ray in the marquee where he was supervising some last-minute rearrangements to the seating plan (one of their friends had tripped and broken his front teeth on a basin that morning).

"Ray?" she asked.

"What can I do you for?"

"I'm sorry to trouble you," said Jean, "but I don't know who else I can ask."

"Go on," said Ray.

"It's George. I'm worried about him. He spoke to me about it this morning. He really didn't seem himself."

"I know," said Ray.

"You know?"

"Jamie said he was off-color yesterday. Asked me to keep an eye on him."

"He didn't say anything to me."

"Probably didn't want to worry you," said Ray. "Anyway, Jamie had a word with George this morning. Just to check."

She could feel the relief spread through her body. "That's very good of you."

"Jamie's the one you should thank."

"You're right," said Jean. "I'll do that."

She got her opportunity several minutes later when she bumped into Jamie in the hallway as he emerged from the downstairs loo.

"You're welcome," said Jamie.

He seemed rather distracted.

113

George hung on to the rim of the toilet and moaned.

Jamie had been gone for twenty minutes now. Which was more than enough time to do tea and biscuits.

It began to dawn on George that his son was not going to help him.

He was swaying back and forth like the polar bears in that zoo they went to with the children once. Amsterdam. Or Madrid, maybe.

Was he scaring people away? He had tried to talk to Jean that morning but she had run off to iron a pair of trousers, or wipe someone's bottom.

He bit his forearm hard, just above the wrist. The skin was surprisingly tough. He bit harder. His teeth went through the skin and through something else as well. He wasn't quite sure what. It made a sound like celery.

He got to his feet.

He was going to have to do this himself.

114

The ginger twins had banished them from

the kitchen so Katie and Sarah were standing in the marquee porch, Sarah turning to blow her cigarette smoke into the garden to avoid poisoning the bridal atmosphere.

A teenage boy was sweeping the dried-out floorboards. Bouquets were being stood in vases in curly cast-iron stands. A man was crouching down to check the alignment of the tables, as if he were preparing for a particularly difficult snooker shot.

"And Ray?" asked Sarah.

"He's being brilliant, actually," said Katie.

A woman was taking cutlery from a plastic crate and holding it up to the light before laying it.

"I'm sorry," said Sarah.

"What for?"

"For thinking you might be making a mistake."

"So you thought I was making a mistake?" said Katie.

"Fuck off. I feel bad enough already. You're my friend. I just wanted to make sure. Now I've made sure." Sarah paused. "He's a nice man."

"He is."

"I think even Ed might be a nice man." She turned to look across the lawn. "Well, maybe not nice nice. But all right. Better than the drunken pillock I met at your house."

Katie turned, too, and saw Ed playing airplanes with Jacob, swinging him round by his arms.

"Look," shouted Jacob. "Look."

"Ed," shouted Katie, "be careful."

Ed looked over at her and panicked slightly and loosened his grip and let go of Jacob's left hand and Jacob slid onto the wet grass in his Rupert Bear wedding trousers.

"Sorry," shouted Ed, hoisting Jacob off the ground by one wrist like a shot rabbit.

Jacob squealed and Ed attempted to stand him on his feet.

"Bloody hell," muttered Katie, walking over and wondering whether the ginger twins would allow them to use the washing machine.

At which point she glanced up and saw her father doing jumping jacks in the bathroom, which was odd.

115

Ideally, Jamie would have been sitting in the bedroom with his father. But you couldn't see the road from the bedroom. And Jamie didn't want the doctor arriving unan-nounced.

If the doctor could sort his father out, then maybe they could get through this without giving everyone else the heebie-jeebies.

So Jamie leant against the windowsill in the living room pretending to read the *Telegraph* magazine. And it was only as he was doing this that he started to wonder whether his father might end up being sectioned, which was not something he had thought about when he made the phone call.

Christ, he should have told someone else about this before deciding to solve the problem on his own.

Except you couldn't be sectioned unless you tried to kill yourself, could you. Or unless you tried to kill someone else. To be honest, Jamie's knowledge of these things came almost entirely from TV dramas.

It was entirely possible that the doctor wouldn't be able to do anything at all.

Many doctors were useless, of course. Nothing like spending three years with medical students to undermine your faith in the profession. That Markowicz guy, for example. Plaster-casted up to the neck, then choking on his own vomit.

A man got out of a blue Range Rover.

Little black bag. Shit.

Jamie leapt off the sofa, slalomed through the hallway and out of the front door to intercept him before he made a grand entrance.

"Are you the doctor?" Jamie felt like someone in a crappy film. *Fetch the hot towels!*

"Dr. Anderson." The man held out his hand. He was one of those long, stringy men who smelled of soap.

"It's my father," said Jamie.

"OK," said Dr. Anderson.

"He's having some kind of breakdown."

"Perhaps we should go and have a chat with him."

Dr. Anderson turned to walk across the road. Jamie stopped him. "Before we go in there's something I should explain. My sister's getting married today."

Dr. Anderson tapped his nose and said, "Mum's the word."

Jamie wasn't wholly reassured by this.

They went up to his parents' bedroom. Unfortunately his father wasn't in his parents' bedroom. Jamie told the doctor to sit on the bed and wait.

Jamie was checking the living room when he realized that his mother might walk into her bedroom to find a strange man sitting on her bed. He should really have locked Dr. Anderson in the downstairs loo.

His father wasn't in the house. He asked Eileen. He asked the catering women. He asked the best man, whose name he'd forgotten. He checked behind the marquee and when he emerged he realized that he had now checked everywhere, which meant his father had run away, which was really, really not good and he sprinted back across the lawn saying, "Fuck, fuck, fuck, fuck, fuck" quite loudly to himself, and bumped into Katie en route and didn't want to worry her so he laughed and said the first thing which came to mind, which happened to be, "The pigeon has flown," a line which Tony used on occasions and which Jamie had never really understood, and which Katie wouldn't understand either, but Jamie was halfway up the stairs by this time. And he burst through the bedroom door and Dr. Anderson leapt off the bed and adopted a slightly special-forces defensive posture.

"He's gone," said Jamie. "I can't find him anywhere." And then he had to sit down on the bed and put his head between his knees because he felt a bit dizzy.

"OK," said Dr. Anderson.

"He wanted me to drive him into the country," said Jamie. "So he didn't have to go to the wedding." He sat up, felt wobbly, and put his head between his knees again. Glancing sideways, he saw a sliver of pink card under the mattress. He reached over and extracted the Ordnance Survey map. His father had gone without it.

"What's that?" asked Dr. Anderson.

"This is where he wanted to go," said Jamie, unfolding the map and pointing to Folksworth. "Perhaps he took a taxi. I'm going to look for him."

Dr. Anderson removed a small card from his jacket and handed it to Jamie. "I'm not really meant to do this. But if you find him, call me, OK?"

"Thanks." Jamie slipped the card into his trouser pocket. "I'd better get going."

Halfway down the stairs they bumped into Ray.

Dr. Anderson smiled and said, "I'm the photographer."

"OK," said Ray, looking a little puzzled, possibly by the fact that Jamie and the photographer had been upstairs together.

Jamie turned to Dr. Anderson. "It's OK, he knows."

"In which case, I'm a doctor," said Dr. Anderson.

"Dad's gone missing," said Jamie. "I'm going to look for him. I'll explain later."

Then he remembered that it was Ray's wedding day, too. "I'm so sorry about this."

"I'll call you if he turns up," said Ray.

116

Jean was getting dressed and wondering where on earth George had wandered off to when there was a ring at the front door and clearly no one else was going to answer it, so she fished her good shoes out of the bottom of the wardrobe, went downstairs and opened the door.

"Alan Phillips," said the man. "Ray's father. This is my wife, Barbara. You must be Jean."

"How do you do," said Barbara.

Jean ushered them inside and took their coats.

"Very good to meet you after all this time," said Alan. "I'm sorry it's so last minute."

She'd expected a bigger man, someone with more bluster. Then she recalled Katie mentioning a chocolate factory, which seemed comical at the time, but rather appropriate now. He was the kind of man you could imagine playing with trains or growing carnations. "Have a seat."

"It's a lovely house," said Barbara, and she sounded as if she meant it, which Jean found quite touching.

There was something formal about the two of them, and this was a relief (in her darker moments she'd imagined, well . . . some things were best forgotten). On the other hand, they didn't look like the kind of people you could dump in the living room while you got on with other stuff.

Where was everyone? George, Jamie, Eileen, Ronnie. They seemed to have vanished into thin air.

"Could I get you some tea?" asked Jean. She sounded as if she was talking to Mr. Ledger who serviced the boiler. "Or coffee?" She could dig the cafetière out.

"Oh," said Barbara, "we don't want to put you to any trouble."

"It's no trouble," said Jean, though to be honest it was a little inconvenient at this point.

"In which case, two teas would be lovely," said Barbara. "Alan has half a sugar."

Jean was rescued, yet again, by Ray who came in from the car carrying a tiny yellow action figure.

"Barbara. Dad." He kissed Barbara on the cheek and shook his father's hand.

"I was just going to make your parents a

cup of tea," said Jean.

"I'll do that," said Ray.

"That's very good of you," said Jean, brightly.

Ray was about to turn and head toward the kitchen when she said, quietly, "You don't know where George is, do you? Just out of interest. Or Jamie, for that matter."

Ray paused for rather a long time, which disturbed her slightly. He was about to answer when Ed appeared from the direction of the kitchen eating a bread roll, and Ray said, "Ed."

"Mr. and Mrs. Phillips," said Ed, through the bread roll.

Alan and Barbara stood up.

"Ed Hobday," said Alan. "Goodness. I didn't recognize you."

Ed brushed the crumbs from his mouth and shook their hands. "Fatter but wiser."

"Oh no," said Barbara, "you've just filled out a bit."

Ray touched Jean's shoulder and said, quietly, "Come into the kitchen."

117

By the time George reached the edge of the village he was feeling a little calmer.

He was halfway across the field by the railway line, however, when he saw Eileen and Ronnie heading toward him. They were hoisting their dog over the stile and he was fairly sure they had not noticed him. He crept into the depression by the hawthorn so that he was out of their line of sight.

The dog was barking.

He could not retrace his steps without being seen, and a bank of brambles prevented him crossing the railway line itself. His chest tightened.

His arm was still bleeding where he had bitten it.

The barking got louder.

He lay down and rolled into the shallow drainage ditch where the grass dipped before going under the fence. His coat was green. If he lay still they might not find him.

It was snug in the ditch, and surprisingly comfortable. Interesting, too, to find himself looking at nature from so close up, something he had not done since he was a small boy. There must have been forty or fifty species of plants within his reach. And he knew the names of none. Except the nettles. Assuming they were nettles. And the cow parsley. Assuming it was cow parsley.

Six years ago Katie had given him a book token for Christmas (a lazy present, but an improvement on those ridiculous Swedish wineglasses you hung round your neck on a string). He had used it to buy the *Reader's Digest Book of British Flora and Fauna* with the intention of learning the names of trees at the very least. The only fact he could now recall from the book was that a colony of wallabies were living wild in the Cotswolds.

He realized that he did not have to walk somewhere to escape the wedding. Indeed, walking was more likely to attract attention. Better simply to lie here, or somewhere farther into the undergrowth. He could emerge at night.

Then Eileen was saying, "George?" and it occurred to him that if he did not move she might simply go away.

But she did not go away. She said his name again, then screamed when he failed to respond. "Ronnie. Come over here."

George rolled over to prove that he was still alive.

Eileen asked George what had happened. George explained that he had been out for a walk and twisted his ankle.

Ronnie helped him to his feet and George pretended to limp and it was bearable for a few minutes because although the ditch was comforting the idea of spending the next ten hours alone was not. And, to be honest, he was rather relieved to find himself in the company of other human beings.

But Eileen and Ronnie were taking him back to the house and that was not good, and as they got progressively closer he felt as if someone were lowering a black bin liner over his head.

He very nearly ran when they reached the main road. He did not care whether the dog was trained to attack. He did not care about the embarrassment of a hare-and-hounds race with Ronnie through the village (a race he would almost certainly win; there was so much adrenaline coursing through his system he could have outrun a zebra). It was simply the only option left.

Except that it was not.

There was another option, and it was so obvious that he could not believe he had forgotten it. He would take the Valium. He would take all the Valium, as soon as he returned to the house.

But what if someone had thrown the bottle away? What if someone had flushed the pills down the toilet? Or hidden them to prevent them being swallowed accidentally by a child?

He broke into a run.

"George," shouted Ronnie. "Your ankle."

He had absolutely no idea what the man

was talking about.

118

When Jean reached the kitchen Ray turned to her and said, "Got a bit of a problem."

"What sort of problem?" asked Jean.

"George," said Ray.

"Oh dear God." She had to sit down very quickly. What had George done to himself this time?

"Afraid he's gone missing," said Ray.

She was going to pass out. In front of the caterers. In front of Ray. She took a deep breath and George's head flashed past the window like some kind of supernatural apparition. She thought she might be losing her mind.

The kitchen door banged open and George burst in. She yelped but he took no notice whatsoever, just sprinted into the hallway and up the stairs.

Jean and Ray looked at each other for a few seconds.

She heard Ed saying, "That, I think, was Katie's father."

Ray said, "I'll go and see what he's up to."

She sat for a minute or two, gathering her wits. Then the door banged open a second time and it was Eileen and Ronnie and their blessed Labrador and what with thinking George might be dead then being scared out of her wits by George himself she snapped and said, "Get that bloody dog out of my kitchen," which was not diplomatic.

119

Katie did her makeup and let Sarah negotiate with Jacob.

"I'm afraid you really do have to come."

"Want to stay here," said Jacob.

"You'll be on your own," said Sarah.

"Want to stay here," said Jacob.

It wasn't a tantrum yet, just a bid for attention. But they had to stop it gaining momentum. And Sarah probably stood a better chance than Katie. Unknown quantity. Less leverage.

"Want to go home," said Jacob.

"There's going to be a party," said Sarah. "There's going to be cake. You just have to hang on for a couple of hours."

A couple of hours? Sarah wasn't very clued up about children and time measurement. Jacob was pretty much incapable of distinguishing between last week and the extinction of the dinosaurs.

"I want a biscuit."

"Jacob . . ." Sarah took his hand and stroked it. If Katie had done that he might just have bitten it. "I know you haven't got your toys and your videos and your friends. And I know everyone's busy and can't play with you at the moment . . ."

"I hate you," said Jacob.

"No you don't," said Sarah.

"Do," said Jacob.

"No you don't," said Sarah.

"Do," said Jacob.

"No you don't," said Sarah, who seemed to be reaching the end of her repertoire.

Luckily, Jacob's attention was deflected by Ray coming in and flopping onto the bed. "Jesus H. Christ."

"What's up?" asked Katie.

"I'm not sure you really want to know."

"Tell me," said Katie. "I could do with some entertainment."

"Not sure this counts as entertainment," said Ray, who sounded worryingly somber.

"Perhaps you should tell me later," said Katie. "When certain people aren't around."

Sarah got to her feet. "Right, young man. We're going to play hide-and-seek. If you can find me in ten minutes, you win twenty pence."

Jacob was out of the room almost instantly. Clearly Sarah knew more about child management than Katie had given her credit for.

"So?" asked Katie.

"I guess you're going to find out sooner or later," said Ray, sitting up.

"Find out what?"

"Your dad scarpered."

"Scarpered?" Katie stopped doing her makeup.

"Went a bit wobbly. You know, like when we were last here. Bit tense about the wedding I guess. Jamie called a doctor . . ."

"A doctor . . . ?" Katie's mind raced.

"But when he arrived your dad had vanished. So Jamie's gone to look for him."

"So where's Dad now?" Katie went a bit wobbly herself at this point.

"Oh, he's back. Says he just went for a walk and bumped into Eileen and Ronnie. Which might be true. But I was in the kitchen when he came back and he was doing about Mach 3."

"Is he OK?" asked Katie.

"Seems fine. He'd got some Valium from his GP."

"He's not about to overdose or anything . . ."

"Don't think so," said Ray. "He took a

couple. Seemed happy just holding the bottle."

"God," said Katie and took a few deep breaths, waiting for her heart to slow down. "Why didn't anyone tell me?"

"Jamie didn't want to worry you."

"I should go and talk to Dad."

"You stay here." Ray got to his feet and came over and knelt down in front of her. "Probably best to pretend you don't know anything."

Katie held Ray's hand. She didn't know whether to laugh or cry. "God. This is meant to be our wedding day."

Then Ray said something wise. Which took her by surprise. "We're just the little people on top of the cake. Weddings are about families. You and me, we've got the rest of our lives together."

And then Katie did cry a little bit.

And Ray said, "Oh shit. Jamie. He's still looking for your dad. Have you got his mobile number?"

120

When George reached the bedroom he experienced a surge of relief so deep he felt his bowels loosen a little.

Then, quite suddenly, he forgot where he had hidden the Valium and the panic rose like floodwater, thick and cold and fast, and he had to fight to keep breathing.

He knew that he knew where the bottle was. Or rather, he knew that he had known where it was ten minutes ago, because why would he forget something like that? And he knew that it was somewhere entirely logical. It was a simple matter of finding the pigeonhole in his head where he had stored the information. But the inside of his head was upside down and shaking violently and the contents of the other pigeonholes were coming out and getting in the way.

He stood facing the window, crouching a little to help himself breathe.

Under the bed . . . ? No. In the chest of drawers . . . ? No. Behind the mirror . . . ?

It was in the bathroom. He had not hidden the bottle at all. Why would he have hidden it? There was no need to hide it.

He ran into the bathroom, his bowels loosening slightly all over again. He opened the cabinet. It was on the top shelf, behind the plasters and the interdental sticks.

He twisted the top, and kept on twisting and felt the panic coming back until he realized that it was childproof and had to be pressed down. He pressed it down and twisted and very nearly dropped it when he saw Ray in the mirror, standing behind him, only feet away, actually in the bathroom, saying, "George? Are you OK? I knocked, but you didn't hear me."

George came very close to swigging the entire contents of the bottle and swallowing hard in case Ray tried to stop him.

"George?" said Ray.

"What?"

"You all right?"

"Fine. Absolutely fine," said George.

"You seemed a little worked up when you ran into the kitchen."

"Did I?" George wanted to take the pills very badly.

"And Jamie was worried about you."

George gently shook two tablets into the palm of his hand and swallowed them casually. Like people did with peanuts at parties.

"Said you'd not been feeling yourself."

"They're Valium," said George. "I got them from the doctor. They help me feel a little calmer."

"Good," said Ray. "So, you're not planning on going for another walk? Today, I mean. Before the wedding."

"No," said George, and forced a little laugh. Was this exchange meant to be amusing? He was unsure. "I'm sorry if I caused any trouble."

"No problem," said Ray.

"I'm definitely coming to the wedding," said George. He needed to go to the lavatory quite badly.

"Good," said Ray. "That's good. Well, I'd better get suited and booted."

"Thank you," said George.

Ray left and George bolted the door and dropped his trousers and sat on the toilet and emptied his bowels and swallowed the remaining six tablets, washing them down with some slightly unpleasant water from the toothbrush mug without stopping to think about the deposit in the bottom.

121

Jean apologized to Eileen for her outburst and Eileen said, "I forgive you," in a way that made Jean want to be rude all over again.

Ronnie said, "I do hope George is all right."

And Jean realized it was her fault. He'd sat on the bed looking dreadful, wanting to talk, and Katie had stuck her head round the door and she'd been swept up in all the arrangements and hadn't gone back to ask what was troubling him.

"I'll be down again in a few minutes," she said, and headed upstairs, smiling politely at Ed and Alan and Barbara as she went past the living-room door.

They hadn't got their tea, had they.

Oh well, she had more important things to do.

When she reached the bedroom George was putting his socks on. She sat down beside him. "I'm sorry, George."

"What for?"

"For rushing off this morning."

"You had things to do," said George.

"How are you feeling now?"

"A lot better," said George.

He certainly seemed all right. Perhaps Ray had got things out of proportion. "Your arm."

"Oh yes." George lifted his arm. There was a large gash on his wrist. "I must have caught it on that barbed-wire fence."

At first glance it looked like a bite. Surely the dog hadn't attacked him? "Let me sort that out before you get blood on your clothes."

She went into the bathroom and fetched the little green first-aid box and patched him up while he sat patiently on the bed.

She wished she could do more of this kind of thing. Helping in a practical way.

She stuck down a second strip of plaster to hold the little bandage in place. "There you go."

"Thank you." George put his hand in hers.

She held it. "I'm sorry I've been so useless."

"Have you?" asked George.

"I know you've not been feeling well," said Jean. "And I know . . . sometimes I don't take enough notice. And that's not right. I just . . . I find it hard."

"Well, you don't have to worry about me anymore," said George.

"What do you mean?" asked Jean.

"I mean you don't have to worry about me anymore today," said George. "I'm feeling much happier now."

"I'm glad," said Jean.

And it was true. He did seem very relaxed, more relaxed than she'd seen him looking for a while. "But if something starts to worry you, you will let me know, won't you."

"I'll be fine."

"I mean it," said Jean. "Just say the word and I'll put down whatever I'm doing. Honestly."

"Thank you," said George.

They sat for a few moments, then a phone

started ringing.

"That's not our phone, is it?" asked George.

It wasn't. "Hang on." Jean got to her feet and stepped into the corridor. The noise was coming from a mobile phone lying on the windowsill.

She picked it up and pressed the little green button and held it to her ear. "Hello?"

"Jamie?" said a man's voice. "Sorry. I think I dialed a wrong number."

"Ray?" said Jean.

"Jean?" said Ray.

"Yes," said Jean. "Is that Ray?"

"Where are you?" asked Ray.

"On the landing," said Jean, who was a little puzzled by this.

"I was trying to ring Jamie," said Ray.

"He's not here," said Jean, who always found mobile phones slightly disconcerting.

"Sorry about that," said Ray and rang off.

She glanced at her watch. Twenty minutes and they would have to leave. She'd better get George ready then round up the troops.

She put the phone back down and opened the wardrobe in the corridor to fish out her scarf and very nearly had a heart attack when she saw Sarah looking back at her from between the coats.

"Hide-and-seek," said Sarah.

122

Katie told Mum that Jamie was still looking for Dad. Mum panicked. Katie reassured her that Jamie knew where the register office was. He could be heading there at this very moment. Mum stopped panicking.

They were all standing outside the house. The air was full of aftershave and perfume and Uncle Doug's cigarette smoke and the mothbally scent of best coats. Was it sad or funny, Jamie missing the wedding? She couldn't really tell.

Sarah and Jacob were sitting next to each other on the wall. He hadn't found her hiding place, but she'd given him the twenty pence anyway. If he was any older Katie would have called it a crush.

"Dog's bottom scrapings," said Sarah.

"Poo from a horse," said Jacob, laughing like a maniac.

"Dog's bottom scrapings and a big jug of old lady's wee," said Sarah.

Katie walked over to Dad. "How're you doing?" She tried to make the question sound neutral so he didn't realize how much she knew.

He turned to her and took her hands and looked into her eyes and seemed almost tearful. He said, "My wonderful, wonderful daughter," which made her tearful, too, and they hugged briefly, which was something they hadn't done for quite a while.

Then Mum looked at her watch and officially gave up waiting for her son to arrive and the tension broke and everyone poured toward the cars.

123

Jamie should have been heading back to the house by now. But what was the point? The wedding wasn't going to happen without Dad. There was nothing to be late for.

He was standing on a muddy track in Washingley, having run like a headless chicken up and down every footpath just south of Folksworth. His trousers were covered in mud, he'd torn the sleeve of his jacket on barbed wire and he felt like shit.

He was the person his father had confided in. He was the person who had failed to stop his father doing precisely what his father had said he was going to do. He was the person who had fucked up his sister's wedding.

He now realized what a stupid idea it was looking for his father like this. His father could have set off in any direction.

He had to explain to everyone what had happened. He had to inform the police. He had to apologize. He walked back to the car, put a plastic bag on the driver's seat, got in and drove home.

He knew something was wrong as soon as he arrived. There were no cars. He parked and walked to the front door. It was locked. He rang the bell. There was no answer. He looked through the windows. The house was empty.

Maybe Ray had told them what had happened. Maybe they were all out looking for his father. Maybe they'd found him. Maybe everyone was at the hospital.

He tried not to think about these things.

He'd lost his mobile. He had to get into the house. If only to find a phone and some dry trousers. He tried the side gate. Eileen and Ronnie's dog threw itself against the far side, barking and scraping the wood with its claws. He turned the handle. It was locked.

Oh well, his trousers were already knackered . . .

He grabbed hold of the post and put his foot into one of the grooves in the stone wall and hoisted himself up. He hadn't done this kind of thing for many years and it took three attempts, but he finally got himself straddled uncomfortably over the top of the gate.

He was looking down on the other side, wondering best how to negotiate the long drop and the crazy dog when someone said, "Can I help you?"

He turned his head and found himself looking at an elderly man he vaguely recognized. The man was wearing a Shetland jumper and carrying a pair of garden shears.

"I'm fine, thanks," said Jamie, though his presence on the top of the gate was driving the dog into a frenzy.

"Is it Jamie?" asked the man with the shears.

"It is," said Jamie. His crotch was starting to hurt.

"I'm sorry," said the man, "I didn't recognize you. Haven't seen you in a long time. Not since you were a teenager. I'm Derek West, from across the road."

"Right," said Jamie. He had to go for it, despite the risk of breaking an ankle, despite the risk of squashing his aunt's dog or being eaten alive. He shifted his center of gravity a little.

"Aren't you meant to be at the wedding?" asked the man.

"Yes," said Jamie. The man was clearly an idiot.

"They left about five minutes ago."

"What?"

"They left about five minutes ago."

Jamie took a few seconds to process this information. "And they were going to the register office?"

"Where else would they be going?" asked the man.

The truth began to dawn. "With my father?"

"I presume so."

"But did you actually see him?"

"I didn't tick them off a list, as it were. No. Wait. I did see him. Because I remember him stumbling on the pavement a little. And your mother made him get into the passenger seat so she could drive. Which I did notice, because when they head off in the car together it's nearly always your father who drives. Which made me wonder whether there was something wrong with him. Is there something wrong with him?"

"Fuck," said Jamie.

Which shut Mr. West up.

He shifted his center of gravity back the other way and jumped down, ripping his jacket for a second time. He ran to the car, dropped his keys, picked up his keys, got into the car and drove away at high speed.

124

Jean felt awful.

Jamie was the final straw. Everything was out of kilter. George. Eileen and Ronnie. Alan and Barbara. It was Katie's wedding day. It was meant to feel special. It was meant to run smoothly. It was meant to be romantic.

Then something happened in the car.

There were roadworks on the dual carriageway and they had come to a halt as the traffic funneled into a single lane. George said, "I'm afraid I've not been a terribly good husband."

"Don't be ridiculous," said Jean.

George was looking straight ahead, out of the windscreen. There were drops of fine rain on the glass. "I'm a rather cold man. A rather stiff man. And I always have been. I can see that now."

She had never heard him talk this way. Was it the madness coming back? She had no idea what to think.

She put the windscreen wipers on.

"And I realize that this coldness, this stiffness has been at the root of many of my recent problems." George brushed some fluff off the door of the glove compartment.

The traffic ahead began to move again. Jean put the car into gear and pulled away.

George laid his hand over hers. This made changing gear a little difficult.

"I love you," said George.

They had not said that word to one another for a long time. There was a lump in her throat.

She glanced sideways and saw that George was looking at her and smiling.

"I've made things terribly difficult for you recently."

"There's no need to apologize," said Jean.

"But I'm going to change," said George. "I'm tired of feeling frightened. I'm tired of feeling lonely."

He put his hand on her thigh, leaned back and closed his eyes.

And she realized that her adventure was coming to an end. That she and David might never make love again. But it was all right.

Her life with George was not an exciting life. But wouldn't life with David go the same way eventually?

Perhaps the secret was to stop looking for greener grass. Perhaps the secret was to make the best of what you had. If she and

George talked a little more. If they went on a few more holidays . . .

The rain had stopped. Jean turned the wipers off and the register office came into sight on the right-hand side of the road.

She indicated and pulled into the car park.

125

George was having a very enjoyable time indeed.

They parked the car and walked toward the stone arch at the back of the register office where everyone was gathering for photographs.

"Come on, Dad." Katie took his arm and guided him down the little path.

He was Katie's father. It felt good being Katie's father.

He was giving his daughter away. And that was a good feeling, too. Because he was giving her away to a good man. *Giving her away.* What a strange phrase it was. Slightly antique. *Sharing.* That would be a better word. Though that sounded a little strange, too.

But where was Jamie?

He asked Katie.

"He's looking for you," said Katie, smiling

in a way that was rather difficult to interpret.

Why was Jamie looking for him? He was about to ask when the photographer moved Katie forward and she began talking to Ray. George made a mental note to ask her again at some later point.

The photographer looked very like Ray's best man. What was his name again? Perhaps it really was Ray's best man. Perhaps they were not having an official photographer.

"Come on, people," said the photographer. "Try not to look quite so glum."

He had a very small camera. He probably wasn't a real photographer.

Ed. That was his name.

George smiled.

Ed took four photographs then asked Katie and Ray to stand in front of the arch.

As they were moving aside, the man standing next to George introduced himself. George shook his hand. The man apologized for not having introduced himself earlier in the day. George told him not to worry. The man introduced his wife. George shook her hand, too. They seemed like very nice people.

A woman appeared from the register office. George thought, at first, that she was an air stewardess.

"If the party would like to make their way inside . . ."

George stepped aside for the ladies, then walked into the register office with the men.

It was possible that the nice couple were Ray's parents. That would explain why they were all standing together having their photographs taken. He would check with Jean when they were sitting down inside.

126

They were in the car halfway to the register office when Katie looked out of the window and saw a tramp urinating against a bus stop on Thorpe Road, which was not something you saw very often, and it seemed like a sign from God, who obviously a) had a sense of humor, and b) agreed with Ray. Expect the day to proceed with dignity and efficiency and someone was going to screw it up. Better to be together in twenty years and laugh about it, than have it run like clockwork and split up twelve months down the line.

Poor Jamie. At least he'd have a good story to tell.

Perhaps they could go round to his flat after Barcelona. Do the vows all over again. Get some confetti. Jacob would like that.

A fine drizzle began spattering the windscreen. It didn't matter. Snow, hail, driving rain. She understood now. You got married in spite of your wedding not because of it. She looked over at Ray and he broke into a smile without taking his eyes off the road.

For the next few minutes they seemed to exist in a little bubble entirely cut off from the wet world around them. Then the register office loomed into view and they pulled in through the gateway and the crowd of guests looked like exotic fish against the brickwork of the building.

They pulled into the car park and got out and the drizzle had stopped and Mum and Dad were getting out of the car next to them. And Dad was staring up into the air so intently that Katie looked up expecting to see a hot-air balloon or a flock of birds, but there was nothing up there whatsoever.

Mum cupped her hand round Dad's elbow and steered him toward the stone arch at the back of the building.

Sarah was singing "Jingle bells, Batman smells, Robin laid an egg" and swinging Jacob over a puddle. "The Batmobile lost a wheel and the Joker broke his leg."

Ray took her arm and they followed Mum and Dad and they were spotted by Uncle Douglas who was smoking downwind, and everyone broke into a loud cheer.

They reached the arch and Sandra ran up and hugged her, then Mona hugged her, and Uncle Doug held his lit cigarette out of the way and said, "You sure about this, lass?" and she was about to deliver some witty put-down (Uncle Doug was a bit of a bum-squeezer) but she could see that he meant it so she didn't.

Mona was already monopolizing Ray for a rapid grilling, having not met him yet, and the crowd parted and she saw Jenny in a wheelchair, which was a shock, and Katie bent down and hugged her and Jenny said, "Bit of relapse. Sorry," and Katie suddenly realized why she needed that second ticket and Jenny said, "This is Craig," and Katie shook hands with the young man standing behind the chair and hoped that this was an actual relationship, because that would be brilliant, although now wasn't the time for questions.

Then Ed was marshaling them for photographs, and Katie stood with Ray looking out at everyone and it was like being in front of a bar fire, all this warmth being directed their way, though Eileen and Ronnie looked a little sour, which was probably due to it not being a church and other people enjoying themselves.

Then the registrar appeared wearing a slightly frumpy navy blue suit and one of those chiffony neckties that everyone else stopped wearing at the end of the Second World War, and they were allowed inside the building which was a bit like her doctor's surgery in London. All cream paint and helpful leaflets and heavy-duty carpeting. But there was a big vase of flowers and the registrar was actually quite cheery and said, "If the bride and bridegroom would like to come with me, and the guests would like to follow my colleague . . ."

The registrar ran them quickly through the timetable for the ceremony. Then they heard the Bach double-violin piece start up and it sounded like something from a film soundtrack. Horse-drawn carriage, big house, frocks. And Katie thought, bugger segues, they should have gone for James Brown throughout. But it was too late now.

They walked round the corner to the big room at the end and waited outside while the registrar went in and said, "Could I ask you all to stand for the entrance of the bride and groom," and they went into the room where it all happened and it was very neat and very pink with velvet curtains. And Mum smiled at her. And Katie smiled back. And Dad appeared to be studying an old ticket of some kind that he'd found in his pocket.

And as they reached the front Katie saw, lying on the table, a silk cushion hemmed with fake diamonds on little tassels. For the ring, presumably.

"Please be seated," said the registrar.

Everyone sat down.

"Good afternoon, ladies and gentlemen," said the registrar. "May I begin by welcoming you all here today to the Peterborough register office, for the marriage of Katie and Ray. Today marks a new beginning in their lives together . . ."

Katie closed her eyes for Sarah's reading and sort of hummed inside her head so she didn't really have to listen ("Your friend is your needs answered. He is your field which you sow with love and reap with thanksgiving . . ."). She wondered if they could make a little wedding cake for the second ceremony in Jamie's kitchen. Date and walnut on the inside. A little sugar Batman on the top for Jacob.

"For in the dew of little things the heart finds its morning and is refreshed."

Sarah sat down and the registrar stood up and said, "It is one of my duties to inform you that this room in which we are now met has been duly sanctioned according to law for the celebration of marriages. You are here to witness the joining in marriage of Ray Peter Jonathon Phillips and Katie Margaret Hall. If any person present knows of any lawful impediment why these two people may not be joined in marriage he or she should declare it now."

And something happened in Katie's heart, and she realized it wasn't just two people being joined together, not even two families. She felt as if she were joining hands with everyone who'd done this before her, just as she'd done after giving birth to Jacob, a feeling that she finally belonged, that she was a part of the whole enterprise, a brick in that great arch which rose out of the dark behind you and swung over your head and curved into the future, and she was helping to keep it strong and solid, and helping to protect everyone beneath it.

The registrar asked her and Ray to stand and hold hands, and there were tears in her eyes, and the registrar said, "Before you are joined in matrimony here today I have to remind you both of the solemn and binding character of the vows you are about to make . . ." but Katie wasn't really listening anymore. She was up there, looking down, and the roomful of people was so tiny she could fit it into the palm of her hand.

127

Jean heard a little squeak just as Katie and Ray were beginning their vows. She turned round and saw Jamie slip into the room and stand behind that nice young lady in the wheelchair.

Now everything was perfect.

"Why I, Katie Margaret Hall," said Katie.

"May not be joined in matrimony," said the registrar.

"May not be joined in matrimony," said Katie.

"To Ray Peter Jonathon Phillips," said the registrar.

Jean turned to look at Jamie for a second time. What on earth had happened to him? He looked as if he'd been dragged through a hedge backward.

"To Ray Peter Jonathon Phillips," said Katie.

Jean's heart sank a little.

"Now the solemn moment has come," said the registrar, "for Ray and Katie to contract their marriage before you, their witnesses, families and friends."

Then Jean remembered that her heart was not allowed to sink. Not now. Jamie had been doing a good thing. And these people were good people. They would sympathize.

"So can I ask you all to stand," said the registrar, "and join together for the celebration of their marriage."

Everyone stood.

They would get home and Jamie could change into new clothes and everything would be perfect again.

"Ray," said the registrar, "will you take Katie to be your wedded wife, to share your life with her, to love, support and comfort her whatever the future may bring?"

"I will," said Ray.

"Katie," said the registrar, "will you take Ray to be your wedded husband, to share your life with him, to love, support and comfort him whatever the future may bring?"

"I will," said Katie.

From several rows back, Jean heard Douglas say, "You go, girl."

128

George looked around the room and felt oddly fond of all these people.

It was not something he was accustomed to feeling at family gatherings.

He squeezed Jean's hand. He was in love

with his wife. It made him feel warm inside.

Everything was going to be different from now on.

What, in any case, was frightening about death? It came to everyone sooner or later. It was a part of life. Like going to sleep, minus the waking up.

And there was Jamie, arriving late, as children usually did.

Jamie was a homosexual. And what was wrong with that? Nothing whatsoever. So long as one was hygienic.

And there was his husband beside him. Boyfriend. Partner. Whatever the word was. He would ask Jamie later.

No. That was the man who was operating the wheelchair for the crippled girl, wasn't it. Plump. Scruffy hair. Beard. Obviously not a homosexual now that George thought about it.

Even Douglas and Maureen were all right, really. A little vulgar. A little loud. But everyone had their faults.

And, look, there were fluorescent lights in the room, which meant that if you spread your hand out and waved it from side to side at the correct frequency you could make it look as if you had six fingers. Wasn't that strange. Like spinning a bike wheel to make it look as if it was not moving.

129

Jamie asked the woman behind the desk where the wedding was and he could see her actually scanning the desk for a weapon. He looked down and saw blood on his hands and tried to explain that his father had run away but this didn't make the woman relax. So he put on the voice he used with difficult clients and said, "My sister, Katie Hall, is getting married to Ray Phillips in this building right now and if I'm not there to witness it you will be hearing from my solicitor."

My solicitor? Who the fuck was that?

She either believed him or was too frightened to tackle him alone, because when he strode off in search of the wedding, she stayed in her chair.

He stopped by the door at the end of the corridor and opened it a crack and saw a woman vaguely like Auntie Maureen and a cleavage which definitely belonged to Uncle Brian's wife. So he slipped inside and the registrar said, " . . . constitute a formal and public pledge of your love for one another. I am now going to ask each of you in turn . . ."

His father was standing next to his mother

smiling benignly, and Jamie felt a weird combination of excitement and anticlimax having spent the journey imagining he'd be the center of attention, then finding out he wasn't, so instead of jumping up and down and telling someone about his ridiculous adventure he had to shut up and stand still.

Which was probably why he grinned and waved at Katie without thinking when he caught her eye, making her put the ring on the wrong finger, though thankfully it was funny more than anything. And when Jacob rushed forward to hug her, he couldn't resist rushing forward to hug her, and the registrar seemed a little put out by this, but quite a few other people joined in, so she had to lump it.

They poured into the car park and a friend of Katie's asked what he'd been doing to get himself in such a state and he said, "The car broke down. I had to take a short cut." They both laughed and Jamie reckoned he could probably say he'd been attacked by a leopard and everyone would take it in their stride on account of the carnival atmosphere, though his mother was quite concerned that he spruce himself up at the earliest opportunity.

"How's Dad?" he asked.

"He's in excellent form," she said, which

alarmed Jamie slightly, because he couldn't remember his mother saying something that positive about his father even when he was entirely sane.

So he accosted his father and asked how he was feeling, and his father said, "You have very strange hair," which was technically correct, but not the answer Jamie was expecting.

Jamie asked if he'd been drinking.

"Took some Valium," said his father. "From Dr. Barghoutian. Perfectly safe."

"How much?"

"How much what?" asked his father.

"How much Valium?" asked Jamie.

"Eight, ten," said his father. "Enough. Let's put it like that."

"Oh dear God," said Jamie.

"I would very much like to meet your boyfriend," said George. "How did that sound?"

"Are you planning to give a speech at the reception?"

"A speech?" said George.

"You're bleeding," said Jamie.

George held up his hand. There was blood dripping out of his sleeve. "Now that is odd."

130

George sat on the toilet seat in the upstairs bathroom while Jamie put a new dressing on his wrist and helped him into a clean white shirt.

He remembered now. Jean had put the first dressing on earlier in the day. He had cut himself on a barbed-wire fence. Though precisely how he had come into contact with a barbed-wire fence was not clear.

"So, you haven't written a speech," said Jamie.

Of course. He remembered now. It was Katie's wedding today.

"Dad?"

"What?"

"A speech," asked Jamie. "Have you written a speech?"

"What for?"

Jamie rubbed his face. "OK. Look. Katie got married this morning . . ."

George raised his eyebrows. "I'm not a total dimwit."

"They're having the reception in the garden," said Jamie. "After the meal the bride's father usually gives a short speech."

"She's getting married to Ray, isn't she," said George.

"That's right. So here's what we're going to do."

"What are we going to do?"

"I'm going to talk to Ed," said Jamie.

"Who's Ed?" asked George. The name did not ring a bell.

"Dad," said Jamie, "just listen, OK? Ed is the best man. After the meal he will announce that you're going to speak. Then you stand up and propose a toast. Then you sit down."

"OK," said George, wondering why Jamie was making quite such a song and dance about this.

"Can you do a toast?"

"That depends on whom I am meant to be toasting," said George, feeling rather smug that he had spotted the trick question.

Jamie blew out lots of air, as if he was about to lift a heavy weight. "You get up. You say, 'I would like to propose a toast to Katie and Ray. I would like to welcome . . .' No. Too complicated."

It struck George that Jamie was a little confused himself.

"You get up," said Jamie. "You say, 'To Katie and Ray.' You sit down."

"I don't make a speech," said George.

"No," said Jamie. "Just a toast. 'To Katie

and Ray.' Then you sit down again."

"Why am I not making a speech?" asked George, who was beginning to wonder why he should be following instructions from a confused person.

Jamie rubbed his face again. "Katie and Ray want to keep it short and simple."

George digested this. "All right."

"You get up," said Jamie. "You say —"

"To Katie and Ray," said George.

"You sit down."

"I sit down," said George.

"Brilliant," said Jamie.

George remained on the toilet for a few minutes after Jamie left. He felt slightly aggrieved that he was being denied the opportunity to talk at length. But when he tried to imagine what specific things he might say at length his thoughts became a little fuzzy. So perhaps it was best to follow the line of least resistance.

He got off the toilet, waited for his head to clear and made his way downstairs.

Someone handed him a glass of champagne.

Was it wise to drink champagne when he had already taken Valium? He had little experience of these things. Perhaps there was a doctor amongst the guests whom he could ask.

Gail materialized in front of him. "Brian was very sad not to have you down in Cornwall with him."

It was hard not to look at her breasts.

"He was looking forward to a bit of Boy Scouting," said Gail. "Bonfires. Sleeping bags." She shivered. "I'm going down next month. When the power shower works and the carpets are fitted."

What in the name of God was that man doing here?

On the far side of the room.

George wondered if he could be hallucinating.

"Are you all right, George?" asked Gail.

He was not hallucinating. It was definitely him. David Symmonds. The man he had seen having sexual intercourse with Jean in their bedroom. Now he was gate-crashing Katie's wedding. Did the man possess no decency whatsoever?

The world was coming back into focus. It was like that night in Glasgow. Being too drunk to talk. Then seeing the flames in the corridor and being instantly sober.

"You seem a little distracted," said Gail.

He was not going to stand for this. He moved Gail to one side and made his way through the crowd. He would tell Mr. Symmonds to leave.

Hopefully it would not be necessary to strike him.

131

Jamie tarted himself up and came downstairs, crossing his fingers and hoping that his father would remember his instructions.

He had to speak to Ed.

What should Ed say? That Katie's father was feeling a little under the weather? Perhaps he needn't say anything. *Katie's father would now like to propose a toast.* Least said soonest mended. Stick as close to the truth as you can.

He made his way through the house looking for Ed, thinking how he really, really wanted Tony to be here so he could sound off without having to think about what he was saying or who he was saying it to. And the picture of Tony inside his head was so vivid that when he stepped outside and saw Tony coming through the gate on the far side of the lawn it seemed like the most natural thing in the world.

He stopped in his tracks. Tony stopped in his tracks.

Tony was wearing his Levi's and that really nice blue floral shirt and a suede jacket

Jamie had never seen before. He was half a stone lighter and several shades browner. He looked absolutely fucking gorgeous.

And then it sank in. Tony was here. At the wedding. And the crowd seemed to part like the Red Sea and Jamie and Tony were looking at each other down a long corridor of guests. Or maybe it just felt that way.

Jamie wanted to run. But Tony was no longer his boyfriend. They hadn't spoken since that horrible nighttime meeting on the steps of Tony's flat.

Except that he was here. Which must mean . . .

Jamie was running. Or walking really fast at any rate. And even as he was doing it Jamie could see that it was a tacky soap-opera moment, but he didn't care and he could feel his heart welling up in his chest.

Then they were in each other's arms and Tony's mouth tasted of minty gum and tobacco and Jamie saw the camera spinning round them and felt the muscles of Tony's back under his hand and smelt the new body wash he'd started using and wanted him naked and it was like coming home after a thousand years and in the silence around them he heard a woman's voice saying quietly, "Now that I was not expecting."

132

Jean was standing in the hallway listening to a young man who worked for Ray. Mostly, though, she was letting her eyes drift across the growing crowd of people. Because, to be honest, he was one of those men who expected you to shut up and nod and make an appreciative noise every now and then.

And it was good letting her eyes drift across the growing crowd. She felt responsible enough to take some credit for the fact that they all seemed to be enjoying themselves (Judy was laughing; Kenneth was sober). But not so responsible that she had to imagine all possible disasters and avert them.

And there was Jamie heading toward the kitchen in a very nice dark blue suit and a white shirt (the cut on his cheek made him seem rather manly).

She could see David talking to Katie's best woman and looking a little defensive. She felt as if she were watching him from a long way away.

"Five years ago," said the man who worked with Ray, "your television signal came through the air and your phone signal came through the ground. Five years from now your TV signal's going to come through the ground and your phone signal's going to come through the air."

She made her excuses and slipped into the garden.

As she did so she saw a young man coming through the side gate carrying a dark green holdall. Suede jacket, flowery shirt. He seemed vaguely familiar.

She was wondering whether he might be a friend of Katie and Ray's when he dropped the bag and someone was hugging him and they were spinning round together and everyone was watching and she realized that it was Jamie, which meant that the man must be Tony, and they were kissing each other, in front of everyone, with their mouths open.

Her first thought was that she had to stop people seeing, by throwing something over them, like a tablecloth for example, or by shouting something loudly. But everyone had seen by now (Brian's jaw was, quite literally, hanging open) and nothing short of machine-gun fire was going to distract people's attention.

Time slowed down. The only things moving in the garden were Jamie and Tony and the ash falling off Ed's cigarette.

She had to do something. And she had to do it now.

She walked up to Jamie and Tony. They pulled apart and Tony looked at her. She felt the day teeter, like a car on the edge of a cliff.

"You must be Tony," she said.

"I am," said Tony, very deliberately keeping one arm around Jamie's waist. "You must be Jamie's mother."

"I am."

He held out his free hand. "It's good to meet you."

"It's good to meet you, too." She reached out to hug him, to show him that she really meant it, and to show everyone else that he should be made welcome. And Tony finally let go of Jamie and put his arms around her and hugged her.

He was a lot taller than he appeared from a distance so it probably looked rather comical. But she could sense the atmosphere in the garden warming and softening.

She was only planning to do it for a few seconds, but she had to keep her face pressed into Tony's shirt for quite a long time because she was crying, which caught her completely by surprise, and while she wanted everyone to know that she was welcoming Tony into her family, she didn't really want them to see her weeping helplessly in the arms of someone she'd met ten seconds ago.

Then she heard Katie shrieking delightedly, "Tony. Fucking hell. You came," which did distract people's attention.

133

George came to a halt in front of David on the far side of the dining room and stood with his legs apart and his fists clenched.

Unfortunately, David was facing in the opposite direction and did not realize that George was standing behind him. George did not want to ask him to turn round because asking for anything would suggest that David was the dominant animal. Like dogs. And George was meant to be the dominant animal.

Nor did he want to grab David by the shoulder and forcibly turn him round because that was what people did in fights in bars and he wanted the encounter to be concluded with as little fuss as possible.

So he stood, tensed, for some seconds until the woman David was talking to said, "George," and David turned round and said, "George," and smiled and juggled his little cigar into his drink hand and held the other out for George to shake.

George found himself shaking David's hand and saying, "David," which was not part of the plan at all.

"You must be very proud indeed," said David.

"That's not the point," said George.

The woman slipped away.

"No," said David. "You're right. Everyone says it. But it is rather a selfish way of looking at it. Whether Katie's happy. That's the important thing."

Christ, he was slippery. George was beginning to see how he had wormed his way into Jean's affections.

To think that he had worked with this man for fifteen years.

David raised an eyebrow. "Mind you, Sarah was telling me that Katie and Ray are paying for all this themselves." He swept an arm over the room as if he owned it. "Now that is a canny move, George."

He had to do it now. "I'm afraid —"

But David interrupted, saying, "How's the rest of life?" and George's head was starting to spin a little and David sounded so earnest and so caring that George had to fight back the urge to confess to David that he had cut himself with a pair of scissors and ended up in hospital after finding his wife having sexual intercourse with another man.

He realized that he was not going to ask David to leave. He did not have the strength. Morally or physically. If he tried to eject David he would probably cause a commotion and embarrass Katie. Maybe doing nothing was for the best. And surely today, of all days, was one during which he should put his own feelings to one side.

"George?" asked David.

"Sorry?"

"I was asking how things were going," said David.

"Fine," said George. "They're fine."

134

Katie pushed the salmon out of picking range.

She quite liked the idea of ending her wedding day not feeling bloated, and she wanted to leave a bit of space for the tiramisu.

Ray was idly fondling her leg under the table. To his left Mum and Alan were talking about hellebores and ornamental brassicas. To her right Barbara was telling Dad about the joys of caravanning. Dad looked very happy indeed, so he was presumably thinking about something else at the same time.

They were sitting about six inches higher than everyone else. It was like something off the telly. The waitresses in their white jackets. The clink of posh cutlery. The little rumble of canvas.

It was weird seeing David Symmonds seated on the far side of the marquee, chatting to Mona and dabbing the corners of his mouth with a napkin. She'd pointed him out to Ray and now she was going to ignore him, like she was ignoring the barking from Eileen and Ronnie's dog which had been relocated to a nearby garden and was mightily pissed off about the fact.

She licked her fingers and cleaned the bread crumbs from her side plate.

Tony and Jamie were still holding hands very publicly at the table. Which was sweet. Even Mum thought so. Ray's parents seemed oblivious. Maybe their eyesight wasn't up to scratch. Or maybe all men held hands in Hartlepool.

Dad touched her arm. "How's tricks?"

"Tricks is good," said Katie. "Tricks is very good."

The tiramisu arrived and it was a bit of an

anticlimax, frankly. But the chocolates that were served with the coffee were fantastic. And when Jacob came to snuggle in her lap he was more than a little disappointed to find that she'd already eaten hers (Barbara valiantly surrendered her own to keep the peace).

Then there was a loud rap on the table, the chatter subsided and Ed got to his feet. "Ladies and gentlemen, it is traditional at weddings for the best man to stand up and tell crude stories and offensive jokes and make everyone feel really uncomfortable."

"Quite right," shouted Uncle Douglas.

Nervous laughter ran round the marquee.

"But this is a modern wedding," said Ed. "So I'm going to say some nice things about Katie and some nice things about Ray. I'm going to read a few telegrams and say a few thank-yous. Then Sarah, Katie's best woman, is going to stand up and tell crude stories and offensive jokes and make everyone feel really uncomfortable."

More nervous laughter ran round the marquee.

Jacob sucked his thumb and fiddled with her wedding ring, and Ray put his arm round her and said, quietly, "I love you, wife."

135

George sipped at his dessert wine.

"Anyway, she dropped the earlobe," said Sarah. "So this policeman has to poke around in the footwell. And I don't know how many of you ever sat in that Fiat Panda, but you could lose, like, a whole dog on the floor of that car. Apple cores. Cigarette packets. Biscuit crumbs."

Judy was holding a napkin over her mouth. George was unsure whether she was trying to suppress laughter or preparing to vomit.

Katie's friend was surprisingly good at public speaking. Though George found it hard to believe the Paul Harding story. Was it really possible that a young man could climb out of Katie's bedroom window, fall from the kitchen roof and break his ankle without George knowing? Perhaps it was. So many things seemed to have been kept from him or simply escaped his notice.

He took another sip of the dessert wine.

Jamie and Tony were still holding hands. He had absolutely no idea how he was meant to react to this. Only a few months ago he would have stopped it happening to prevent other people being offended. But he was less sure of his opinions now, and less sure of his ability to stop anything happening.

His grip on the world was loosening. It belonged to the young people now. Katie, Ray, Jamie, Tony, Sarah, Ed. As it should do.

He did not mind growing old. It was foolish to mind growing old. It happened to everyone. But that did not make it painless.

He wished only that he commanded a little more respect. Perhaps it was his own fault. He recalled spending some time that morning lying in a ditch. It did not seem like a terribly dignified activity. And if one did not act with dignity, how could one command respect?

He leant over and took hold of Jacob's hand and squeezed it gently, thinking how alike they were, both of them circling in some outer orbit, thousands of miles away from the bright center where the decisions were made and the future was shaped. Though they were moving in opposite directions, of course, Jacob toward the light and himself away from it.

Jacob's hand did not respond. It remained limp and lifeless. George realized that his grandson was asleep.

He let go of Jacob's hand and emptied his wineglass.

The blunt truth was that he had failed. At pretty much everything. Marriage. Parenthood. Work.

He never did start painting again.

Then Sarah said, ". . . a few words from the father of the bride," which took him completely by surprise.

Luckily there was some introductory applause, during which he was able to gather his thoughts. As he did so he recalled the conversation he had had with Jamie before lunch.

He got to his feet and looked around at the guests. He felt rather emotional. Precisely which emotions he felt it was difficult to say. There were a number of different ones, and this in itself was confusing.

He raised a glass. "I would like to propose a toast. To my wonderful daughter, Katie. And to her fine husband, Ray."

The words, "To Katie and Ray," were echoed back at him.

He went to sit down again, then paused. It struck him that he was making a kind of farewell performance, that he would never again have sixty or seventy people hanging on his every word. And not to seize this opportunity seemed an admission of defeat.

He straightened up again.

"We spend most of our time on the planet

thinking we are going to live forever . . ."

136

Jean gripped the edge of the table.

If she'd been any nearer she could have reached across to grab George's sleeve and force him back into his seat, but Katie and Ray were in the way and everyone was watching them and she could see no way of intervening without making matters worse.

"As some of you may know, I have not been well recently . . ."

God in heaven, he was going to talk about harming himself and going to hospital and seeing a psychiatrist, wasn't he. And he was going to do it in front of pretty much every person they knew. It was going to make Jamie kissing Tony seem like very small beer indeed.

"We all look forward to retiring. Doing the garden properly. Reading those birthday and Christmas books we never got round to reading." A couple of people laughed. Jean had no idea why. "Shortly after I retired I discovered a small tumor on my hip."

Wendy Carpenter was in the middle of chemotherapy right now. And Kenneth had that lump taken out of his throat last

August. Lord alone knows what they were thinking.

"I realized that I was going to die."

Jean focused on the sugar bowl and tried to pretend she was in that nice hotel in Paris.

137

Jamie was watching his father weep in front of seventy people and experiencing something which felt very like appendicitis.

"Me. Jean. Alan. Barbara. Katie. Ray. We're all going to die." A glass rolled off a table and shattered somewhere toward the back of the marquee. "But we don't want to admit it."

Jamie glanced sideways. Tony was staring at his father. He looked as if he'd been electrocuted.

"We don't realize how important it is. This . . . this place. Trees. People. Cakes. Then it's taken away. And we realize our mistake. But it's too late."

In a nearby garden Eileen's dog barked.

138

George had lost the thread somewhat.

The dessert wine had not sharpened his mind. He had been a good deal more emotional than he had intended. He had mentioned the cancer, which was not festive. Was it possible that he had made a fool of himself?

It seemed best to round off his speech as quickly and elegantly as he could.

He turned to Katie and took her hand. Jacob was dozing on her lap, so the gesture was a little clumsier than he had planned. It would have to do.

"My lovely daughter. My lovely, lovely daughter." What was he trying to say, precisely? "You and Ray and Jacob. Never. Never take one another for granted."

That was better.

He let go of Katie's hand and glanced round the marquee for one final time before taking his seat and caught sight of David Symmonds sitting in the far corner. The man had been facing the other way during the meal. Consequently George had been spared the sight of him while he was eating.

It occurred to George not only that he might have made a fool of himself but that he might have done this while David Symmonds was watching.

"Dad?" said Katie, touching his arm.

George was frozen halfway between sitting and standing.

The man looked so self-satisfied, so healthy, so bloody dapper.

The images started to come back. The ones he had tried not to picture for so long. The man's saggy buttocks going up and down in the half-light of the bedroom. The sinews in his legs. That chickeny scrotum.

"Dad?" asked Katie.

George could bear it no longer.

139

Jean screamed. Partly because George was climbing across the table. Partly because he'd knocked a pot of coffee over and the hot, brown liquid was running toward her. She leapt backward and someone else screamed. George jumped off the table and began walking down the marquee.

She turned to Ray. "For God's sake, do something."

Ray froze for a second, then got out of his seat and headed off after George.

He was too late.

Jean saw where George was going.

140

George stopped in front of David.

It was very, very quiet in the marquee.

George took aim and swung his fist at David's head. Unfortunately David's head moved at the last minute, George missed his target and he was forced to grab hold of someone's shoulder to prevent himself falling over.

Luckily, when David stood up in order to make his escape, his feet became entangled in his chair and he fell clumsily backward, his arms circling wildly as if he was trying to backstroke out of George's reach across the tablecloth.

This gave George a second opportunity to punch him. But punching someone was considerably harder than it looked in films, and George had had very little practice in this department. Consequently his second punch hit David in the chest, which was not satisfying.

The chair was in the way. That was the problem. George kicked it to one side. He leant down, grabbed the lapels of David's jacket and head-butted him.

After this it was hard to know quite who was hitting whom. But there was a lot of blood and George was fairly sure it belonged to David, so that was good.

141

The image which stuck in Jamie's mind was that of a tiramisu and its accompanying spoon tumbling in slow motion through the air at head height. His father and David Symmonds had fallen backward onto the table. The near side had collapsed and the far side had shot up like a seesaw, firing a variety of objects into the air (one of Katie's friends was very proud of having caught a fork).

From this point on it felt more like a road accident. Everything very clear and detached and slow. No abdominal pain anymore. Just a series of tasks which had to be done to prevent further injury.

Ray bent down and began detaching Jamie's father from David Symmonds. David Symmonds's face was covered in blood. Jamie was rather impressed that a man of his father's age was capable of doing that kind of damage.

Jamie and Tony looked at one another and made one of those instant, unspoken decisions and decided to go and help. They got to their feet and jumped across the table, which would have been rather Starsky and Hutch, except that Jamie got a buttered roll stuck to his trouser leg.

They reached the far side of the marquee together. Tony knelt down next to David because he'd done a first-aid course and because David seemed to have come off worst. Jamie went to talk to his father.

Just as he arrived Ray was saying, "What in God's name did you do that for?" And his father was about to reply when Jamie's brain shifted into warp speed and it dawned on him that no one knew why his father had done it. Only him and Katie, his mother and his father. And David, obviously. And Tony, because Jamie had been filling him in on all the gossip before lunch. And the reason his mother had run out of the marquee was because she thought everyone else was going to find out. Though if Jamie acted quickly they might be able to pass the incident off as drug-induced craziness. Because after that speech it was pretty clear to everyone that his father was not in his right mind.

So when his father said, "Because —" Jamie slapped a hand across his mouth to stop him saying anything else, and he might have done it a bit too hard because the *smack* sound was quite loud and Ray and his father both looked startled, but it stopped his father talking at least.

Jamie leaned in close and whispered, "Don't say anything."

His father said, "Nnnnn."

Jamie turned to Ray and said, "Take him indoors. Upstairs. The bedroom. Just . . . just keep him there, all right?"

Ray said, "Right you are," as if Jamie had asked him to shift a sack of potatoes. He got Jamie's father to his feet and began walking him out of the marquee.

Jamie went over to Tony.

David was saying, "The man's a maniac."

Jamie said, "I'm really sorry about that." Then he turned to Tony and said, quietly, "Take him into the living room and call an ambulance."

Tony said, "I don't think he needs an ambulance."

"Or a taxi or whatever. Just get him out of the house."

"Oh, right, I see what you mean," said Tony. He put his hand under David's arm. "Come on, mate."

Jamie stood up and turned round and realized that all of this had taken only a matter of seconds and the remaining guests were sitting stock-still and completely speechless, even Uncle Douglas, which was a first. And they were clearly expecting some kind of explanation or announcement, and Jamie was the person they were expecting it from, but he had to talk to his mother first, so he said, "I'll be back in a minute," and ran out of the marquee and found her standing on the far side of the lawn being consoled by a woman he didn't recognize, while Ray and Tony ushered his father and David into the house, both of them keeping a tight hold on their charges to prevent any of the three coming into contact with one another.

His mother was crying. The woman he didn't recognize was hugging her.

Jamie said, "I need to talk to my mother on her own."

The older woman said, "I'm Ursula. I'm a good friend."

"Go back inside the marquee," said Jamie. The woman did not move. "Sorry. That sounded rude. And I didn't mean to be rude. But you really do have to go away quite quickly."

The woman backed off, saying, "OK," in that careful voice you use with psychopaths to keep them calm.

Jamie took hold of his mother's arms and

looked her in the face. "It's going to be all right."

"I can explain everything," said his mother. She was still crying.

"You don't need to," said Jamie.

"No," said his mother. "That man, the one your father hit —"

"I know," said Jamie.

His mother paused briefly and then said, "Oh my God."

Her legs went a little rubbery and Jamie had to hold her upright for a couple of seconds. "Mum . . . ?"

She steadied herself with a hand on his arm. "How did you know?"

"I'll explain later," said Jamie. "Luckily no one else knows." He couldn't remember the last time he felt this manly and competent. He had to move fast before the spell was broken. "We're going back in. I'm going to make a speech."

"A speech?" His mother looked petrified. Jamie was a little nervous himself.

"A speech about what?" asked his mother.

"About Dad," said Jamie. "Trust me."

Thankfully his mother seemed incapable of disagreeing and when he put his arm around her shoulder and steered her back across the lawn she let herself be led.

They entered the canvas doorway, the

conversation died away instantly and they moved slowly through a very pregnant silence back to their seats, their shoes clacking on the boarding beneath their feet.

Katie was holding Jacob on her lap. As Jamie and his mother reached the table, Jacob said, "Grandpa had a fight," and over his shoulder Jamie heard someone suppress a panicky giggle.

Jamie stroked Jacob gently on the head, sat his mother down and turned to face everyone. Their number seemed to have doubled magically in the last few minutes. His mind went blank and he wondered if he was about to make an idiot of himself in much the same way that his father had done.

Then his brain came back online and he realized that after what his father had done, he could pretty much string two words together and everyone was going to be mightily relieved.

He said, "Sorry about all that. It wasn't part of the plan."

No one laughed. Understandably. He had to be a bit more serious.

"My father has not been terribly well recently. As you probably gathered."

Was he going to have to mention the cancer? Yes, he was. There was no way round it.

"You'll be relieved to hear that he doesn't have cancer."

This was trickier than he had expected. The atmosphere in the marquee was tangibly funereal. He glanced down at his mother. She was staring downward and trying to squeeze her napkin into as small a ball as possible in her lap.

"But he has been very depressed. And anxious. Particularly about the wedding. Particularly about making a speech at the wedding."

He was hitting his stride now.

"He has a very nice doctor. His doctor gave him some Valium. He took rather a lot of it this morning. To help him relax. I think he probably overdid it."

Again, no one laughed, but this time there was a kind of mumbled hum which felt promising.

"Hopefully he's now upstairs in the house sleeping it off."

And this was when Jamie realized he was going to have to deal not only with his father's ill-judged speech but also with the fact that his father had head-butted his mother's lover in front of everyone. Which was going to be a good deal more difficult. He paused. For rather a long time. And the atmosphere began to cool again.

"I have absolutely no idea why my father hit David Symmonds. To be honest I'm not entirely sure whether my father knew it was David Symmonds he was hitting."

He felt like someone skiing downhill at a dangerously high speed through a forest of solid trees planted far too close to one another.

"They worked together at Shepherds some years ago. I don't know if they've seen one another since. I guess the moral is that if you don't get on with someone at work, then it's probably not a good idea to invite them to your daughter's wedding and take vast amounts of prescription drugs beforehand."

At which point, thank God, the mumbled hum turned into actual laughter. From most of his audience at any rate (Eileen and Ronnie looked as if they had been freeze-dried). And Jamie realized he was finally reaching safer ground.

He turned to Katie and saw Jacob sitting on her lap with her arms round him, burying his head against her chest. Poor guy. He was going to need a pretty heavyweight debriefing when all this was over.

"But this is Katie and Ray's special day," said Jamie, raising his voice and trying to sound upbeat.

"Hear! Hear!" shouted Uncle Douglas, raising his glass.

And it was obvious from the rather startled reaction that many of the guests had forgotten that they were at a wedding.

"Unfortunately, the groom is looking after the father of the bride at the moment . . ."

Ray appeared in the doorway of the marquee.

"I tell a lie . . ."

All eyes swiveled toward Ray who stopped in his tracks and looked a little surprised to be the center of attention.

"So, on behalf of Katie and Ray, I think we should put the events of the last ten minutes behind us and help them celebrate their wedding. Katie and Ray . . ." He grabbed a half-full glass from the table in front of him. "Here's wishing you a very happy day. And let's hope the rest of your marriage is a little less eventful."

Everyone raised their glass and there was a bout of slightly confused cheering and Jamie sat down and everyone fell silent and Sarah started clapping, then everyone else started clapping and Jamie wasn't quite sure whether it was for Katie and Ray or whether he was being congratulated for his performance, of which he was rather proud.

In fact, he was so swept up in the general

sense of relief that he was surprised when he turned to his mother and found her still weeping.

She looked over at Katie and said, "I'm so, so sorry. It's all my fault." She wiped her eyes with a napkin and got to her feet and said, "I have to go and talk to your father," and Katie said, "Are you sure . . . ?" but she was gone.

And Ray materialized beside them and said, dryly, "I am really looking forward to going to Barcelona."

And Jacob said, "Grandpa had a fight."

And Ray said, "I know. I was there."

And Katie said, "The man he hit. That was —"

"I know," said Ray. "Your father explained. In some pretty graphic detail. That's one of the reasons I'm looking forward to Barcelona. He's having a little rest, incidentally. I don't think he's planning to come downstairs in a hurry."

And Jamie suddenly realized the one blindingly obvious fact that had somehow escaped him up until now. That his father had known all along. About his mother and David Symmonds.

His head was spinning a little.

He turned to Katie. "So did Mum know that Dad knew that Mum and David Symmonds were . . . ?"

"No," said Katie, even more dryly than Ray. "Dad obviously chose our wedding day to break the happy news to her."

"Christ," said Jamie. "Why did they invite the guy?"

"That," said Katie, "is one of several questions I'm planning to ask them later on. Assuming they haven't killed each other."

"Do you think we should . . . ?" Jamie got out of his seat.

"No I don't," said Katie tartly. "They can sort this one out themselves."

Ray walked over to check that his own parents had survived the ordeal and Tony appeared carrying an open bottle of champagne and a couple of glasses. He sat himself down in Jean's empty chair and said, to Katie, "This is the first wedding I've ever been to. And I have to say, they are a lot more entertaining than I realized."

Which struck Jamie as pretty risky given Katie's state of mind. But he clearly knew the terrain, perhaps on account of having Becky as a sister, because Katie removed the champagne bottle from Tony's hand, took an almighty swig and said, "You know the best bit?"

"What?" said Tony.

"You being here."

"You are very kind," said Tony. "Though I didn't expect my entrance to be upstaged quite so dramatically."

"God," said Katie, "I am in serious need of a disco."

"A woman after my own heart," said Tony.

"And David . . . ?" said Jamie.

"Headed off to his car," said Tony. "I think he wanted to avoid a second encounter. Which was probably wise, in the circumstances."

At which point, a man carrying a large speaker bearing the words "Top Sounds" appeared like a rather overweight angel in the doorway of the marquee.

But Jamie was more worried about his father than Katie, and less keen to let his parents sort it out between themselves, so he made his excuses to Tony and slipped into the house, stopping en route to reassure several friends and relatives that his father was OK, and earnestly hoping that he was.

He knocked on his parents' bedroom door. The faint voices went quiet on the far side. He waited then knocked again.

"Who is it?" said his father.

"It's me. Jamie. I just wanted to check that you were all right." There was a brief pause. Obviously they weren't all right. It was a stupid thing to say. "It's just that people are concerned. Naturally."

"I'm afraid I made a terrible mess of everything," said his father.

It was hard to know how to respond to this through a door.

"Will you tell Katie and Ray that I'm desperately sorry for causing them such embarrassment?" said his father.

"I will," said Jamie.

There was a brief silence.

"Is David OK?" said his father.

"Yeh," said Jamie. "He's gone."

"Good," said his father.

Jamie realized that he hadn't heard his mother speak yet. And it seemed very unlikely that something awful had happened to her, but he wanted to be absolutely sure this time. "Mum?"

There was no reply.

"Mum . . . ?"

"I'm fine," said his mother. There was a note of irritation in her voice, which was strangely reassuring.

Jamie was about to say that if they needed anything . . . Then he wondered what "anything" could possibly be (wine? wedding cake?) and decided to end the conversation. "I'm going back downstairs now."

There was no reply.

So he went back downstairs and out across the lawn, reassuring more people about his father's health as he did so. The disco had begun and he slipped into the marquee and sat himself down beside Tony who was chatting about lath-and-plaster ceilings with Ed.

Ed slipped away and Jamie took a cigarette from the packet in front of Tony and lit it and Tony poured him a glass of dessert wine and the two of them watched Uncle Douglas dancing like a wounded ox, and the music was good because it filled all those little gaps during which people were tempted to wonder about the implications of what had happened earlier, though if you knew precisely what had happened earlier you did have to try not to listen to the lyrics too hard ("Groovy Kind of Love," "Congratulations," "Stand by Your Man").

For the last two weeks he'd been desperate to talk to Tony. Now, sitting next to him was enough, touching, breathing the same air. Last time they'd been together they seemed like two separate people. Somehow, in the interim they'd become a . . . what? a *couple?* The word seemed wrong now that he was finally on the receiving end.

Maybe it was good to be something you didn't know the name for.

They talked to Mona about the perils of shagging one's boss (which she had done, inadvisedly). They talked to Ray's parents who were weirdly unperturbed by the unorthodox nature of the reception (Ray's brother was in prison, apparently, which Katie had failed to mention, and Barbara's ex-husband was once discovered by the police sleeping in a skip). They talked to Craig, Jenny's gay caregiver, who was technically not meant to be talking to people on his own account while he was on duty but, sod it, Jenny was pissed and getting along famously with the spectacularly boring guy from Ray's office.

Half an hour or so later his mother came into the marquee. And it was a bit like the Queen coming into the room, everyone suddenly stopping dancing, going quiet and panicking slightly about how they were meant to behave. Except that the man from Top Sounds didn't know what had happened earlier so Kylie Minogue carried on singing "Locomotion" very loudly.

Jamie was going to jump out of his seat and run over and save her from all this unwanted attention, but Ursula (who had been doing a surprisingly athletic Locomotion with a group of Katie and Ray's friends) went over and hugged her and Jamie didn't want to trump her a second time. And within a few seconds Douglas and Maureen had joined her and his mother was soon sitting at a corner table being taken care of.

Consequently when his father entered the marquee a few minutes later he created slightly less of a stir. Again, Jamie wondered whether he should go and look after him. But his father headed straight to Katie and Ray and presumably made some kind of direct apology for his earlier behavior which must have gone down reasonably well because the encounter ended in a hug, after which his father was similarly led to a table by Ed with whom he seemed to strike up a firm intergenerational friendship (Jamie later found out that Ed had suffered a breakdown some years earlier and not left the house for several months). And it was a bit odd, his parents sitting at different tables. But it would have been odder to see them standing together, which they'd never done at any kind of gathering, so Jamie decided to postpone worrying about them till the following day.

And when Jamie and Tony stepped outside a little while later, the light was fading and someone had lit multicolored flares on bamboo canes around the lawn which was rather magical. And the day finally felt as if it had been mended as well as it could be mended.

They played hide-and-seek with Jacob and found Judy looking miserable in the kitchen because Kenneth was comatose in the downstairs loo. So they found a screwdriver and undid the lock and arranged him in the recovery position on the sofa in the living room with a blanket over him and a bucket on the carpet nearby, before dragging Judy back outside and onto the dance floor.

And then it was Jacob's bedtime, so Jamie read him *Pumpkin Soup* and *Curious George Takes a Train* and came downstairs and danced with Tony, and Lionel Richie's "Three Times a Lady" came on and Jamie laughed and Tony asked why and Jamie just pulled him close and snogged him in the middle of the dance floor for the whole three minutes and three whole minutes of Tony's cock pressed against him was more than he could actually bear and he was drunk enough by now, so he pulled Tony upstairs and told him not to make any noise or he'd kill him and they went into his old bedroom and Tony fucked him in full view of Big Giraffe and the boxed set of Doctor Dolittle.

142

Katie was relieved that Jacob was sitting in her lap when it happened.

Ray, Jamie and Tony seemed to be handling everything and all she had to do was to hug Jacob and hope that he wasn't too upset by what he was witnessing.

In the event, he seemed strangely unshocked. He'd never seen two adults fighting in real life. Apparently, Grandpa and that man were being like Power Rangers. Though Katie had trouble remembering actual blood in a Power Rangers video and Dad hadn't done a somersault or a karate kick.

If Jacob had not been sitting in her lap she had no idea what she would have done. Clearly Dad was suffering horribly, and clearly they should have taken a lot more notice of his doing a runner and taking Valium. On the other hand, you'd think you could wait till the end of lunch then take someone out into the street to thump them, instead of fucking up your daughter's wedding reception, however bad you were feeling.

And clearly Mum was horrified to find out that Dad knew about David Symmonds.

But why in God's name had she invited the guy to the wedding in the first place?

All in all, Katie was grateful she didn't have to work out what she felt about all these things while she was comforting either of her parents, or she might have gone a bit Power Ranger herself.

It was Jamie who saved the day (Man of the Match, as Ray quite rightly said). She had absolutely no idea what he was going to say when he stood up to give his speech (Jamie later confessed that he had no idea either) and she was nervous, though not as nervous as Mum who managed to actually tear her woven napkin while Jamie was talking, obviously convinced that he was about to explain to everyone precisely why Dad had done what he'd done.

But the workplace-argument story was a stroke of genius. Indeed, people were so keen on the idea that later in the evening Katie was given several entirely different explanations as to why Dad had a grudge against his former colleague. According to Mona, David had spread rumors to prevent him getting the job of managing director. According to Uncle Douglas, David was an alcoholic. Katie decided not to disagree. Doubtless by the end of the evening he would have murdered one of their factory workers and buried the body in nearby woodland.

She did sound off a bit to Ray about her parents' behavior, which was not helpful. But he just laughed at her and wrapped his arms around her and said, "Can we try and have a fun time in spite of your family?"

As a gesture of goodwill, it being their wedding, she decided to admit that he was right. Not out loud, obviously. But by not answering back.

He suggested that she get drunk instead, which turned out to be a rather good idea, because when Dad reappeared and came over to apologize she was almost past remembering what had happened earlier, let alone caring, and she was able to give him a hug, which was probably the most diplomatic of all outcomes.

Come eleven o'clock they were sitting in a little circle at the edge of the lawn. Her, Ray, Jamie, Tony, Sarah, Mona. They were talking about Ray's brother being in prison. And Jamie complained that he hadn't been told this thrilling information earlier. So Ray gave him a slightly parental look on account of this not really being a subject for amusing gossip, and told everyone about the drugs and the stolen cars and the money and the time and the heartbreak his parents had expended trying to get him back onto the straight and narrow.

Sarah said, "Bloody Nora."

And Ray said, "Eventually you realize that other people's problems are other people's problems."

Katie wrapped her arms around him drunkenly and said, "You're not just a pretty face, are you."

"Pretty?" said Tony. "I'm not sure I'd go that far. Rugged, maybe. Butch definitely."

Ray had downed enough beer by this stage to take it as a compliment.

And Katie was rather sad they weren't taking Jamie and Tony with them to Barcelona.

143

Jean paused halfway up the stairs and held on to the banisters. She felt woozy, like she did at the top of tall buildings sometimes.

Everything was suddenly very clear.

Her relationship with David was over. When George hit him, it was George she was worried about. That he had gone mad. That he was making a fool of himself in front of everyone they knew.

She didn't even know if David was still in the house.

If only she'd come to the realization yesterday, or last week, or last month. She could have told David. He wouldn't have come to the wedding and none of this would have happened.

How long had George known? Was it knowing that made him depressed? That dreadful thing he did to himself in the shower. Was it her fault?

Perhaps her marriage was over, too.

She walked along the landing and knocked on the bedroom door. There was a grunt from the far side.

"George?"

There was another grunt.

She opened the door and stepped into the room. He was lying on the bed, half asleep.

He said, "Oh, it's you," and levered himself slowly into a sitting position.

She perched on the armchair. "George, look —"

"I'm sorry," said George. He was slurring his words slightly. "That was unforgivable. What I did in the marquee. To your . . . to your friend. To David. I really shouldn't have done it."

"No," said Jean, "I'm the one who . . ." She was finding it hard to talk.

"I was frightened." George didn't seem to be listening. "Frightened of . . . To be honest, I'm not entirely sure what I was frightened of. Getting old. Dying. Dying of cancer. Dying in general. Making the speech. Things became a little hazy. I rather forgot that everyone else was there."

"How long have you known?" asked Jean.

"About what?"

"About . . ." She couldn't say it.

"Oh, I see what you mean," said George. "It doesn't really matter."

"I need to know."

George thought about this for some time. "The day I was meant to go to Cornwall." He was swaying a little.

"How?" asked Jean, puzzled.

"I came back here. And saw you. In here. On the bed. Rather burned onto my retina. As they say."

Jean felt sick.

"I really should have said something at the time. You know, got it off my chest."

"I'm sorry, George. I'm so sorry."

He put his hands on his knees to steady himself.

She said, "What's going to happen now?"

"What do you mean?"

"To us."

"I'm not entirely sure," said George. "It's not a situation I've been in very often."

Jean was not sure whether George meant

this to be funny.

They sat silently for a while.

He had seen them naked.

Making love.

Having sex.

It was like a hot coal inside her head, and it burned and scalded and there was absolutely nothing she could do about it because she couldn't tell anyone. Not Katie. Not Ursula. She was simply going to have to live with it.

Jamie knocked on the door. They had a short conversation with him and he went away again.

She felt bad for not saying thank you. She could see now how good he had been, making that speech. She would have to tell him later.

She looked at George. It was very hard to tell what he was thinking. Or whether he was thinking at all. He was still swaying slightly. He did not seem terribly well.

"Perhaps I should get you a coffee," said Jean. "Perhaps I should get us both a coffee."

"Yes, that sounds like a very good idea," said George.

She went and got two cups of coffee from a mercifully deserted kitchen.

George emptied his cup in one long gulp.

She needed to talk about David. She needed to explain that it was all over. She needed to explain why it had happened. But she was fairly sure that George didn't want to talk about the subject.

After a few minutes, he said, "The salmon was good, I thought."

"Yes," said Jean, though she had trouble remembering what the salmon was like.

"And Katie's friends seemed like a nice bunch. I suspect I've met a few of them before, but I'm not terribly good at faces."

"They did seem nice," said Jean.

"Sad to see that young lady in the wheelchair," said George. "She seemed very pretty. Dreadful shame."

"Yes," said Jean.

"Anyway," said George. He got to his feet. Jean helped him.

"Better get downstairs," said George. "Can't help. Us sitting up here. Probably creating a bit of an atmosphere."

"OK," said Jean.

"Thanks for the coffee," said George. "Feeling a bit steadier now." He paused at the door. "Why don't you go down first. I need to visit the little boys' room." And he was gone.

So Jean headed downstairs and went out to the marquee and George was right about the atmosphere because everyone seemed to have been waiting for her, which made her feel very uncomfortable. But Ursula came up and hugged her and Douglas and Maureen took her to a table and gave her a second coffee and more wine and a few minutes later George came down and sat at another table and Jean tried to concentrate on what Ursula and Douglas and Maureen were saying but it was quite hard. Because she felt as if she had just walked away from a burning building.

She watched Jamie and Tony and all she could think was how much the world had changed. Her own father had slept with the woman next door for twenty years. Now her son was dancing with another man and she was the one whose life was falling apart.

She felt like the man in that ghost story on the television, the one who didn't realize he was dead.

She went over and apologized to Katie and Ray. She thanked Jamie for his speech. She apologized to Jacob, who didn't really understand why she was apologizing. She danced with Douglas. And she managed a quiet talk with Ursula on her own.

The pain subsided as the evening wore on and the alcohol did its work and shortly after midnight, as the guests were thinning out, she realized that George had disappeared. So she said her various good nights and made her way upstairs and found George fast asleep in bed.

She tried to talk to him but he was dead to the world. She wondered whether she was allowed to sleep in the same bed. But there was nowhere else to sleep. So she undressed and put on her nightie and cleaned her teeth and slipped into bed beside him.

She stared at the ceiling and cried a little, quietly so as not to wake George.

She lost track of time. The disco stopped. The voices died away. She heard footsteps coming and going on the stairs. Then silence.

She looked at the alarm clock on the bedside table. It was half past one.

She got up, put on her slippers and dressing gown and went downstairs. The house was empty. It smelled of cigarette smoke and stale wine and beer and cooked fish. She unlocked the kitchen door and walked into the garden, thinking she would stand under the night sky and clear her head a little. But it was colder than she'd expected. It was starting to rain again and there were no stars.

She came back inside, went upstairs and

got into bed and lay there until sleep finally found her.

144

George woke from a long, deep and dreamless sleep, feeling contented and relaxed. He lay for a few moments looking up at the ceiling. There was a faint crack in the plaster round the light fitting which looked like a little map of Italy. He needed to go to the toilet. He swung his legs out of bed, put on his slippers and left the room with a spring in his step.

Halfway down the landing, however, he remembered what had happened the day before. This made him feel sick, and he was forced to hang on to the banister for a few seconds while he recovered his composure.

He went back into the bedroom to talk to Jean. But she was still deeply asleep, with her face turned to the wall, snoring quietly. He realized that it was going to be a difficult day for her and it seemed best that she did not begin it by being forcibly woken. He returned to the corridor and closed the door quietly behind him.

He could smell toast and bacon and coffee and some other less pleasant odors.

Several cigarette ends were floating in a half-full coffee cup on the windowsill. Now that he thought about it, he was a little punch-drunk. It might have been the after-effects of the Valium and the alcohol.

He had to speak to Katie.

He went to the bathroom to relieve himself, then headed downstairs.

The first person he saw through the doorway of the kitchen, however, was not Katie but Tony. This threw him somewhat. He had forgotten about Tony.

Tony was constructing a rudimentary dog sculpture from pieces of toast for Jacob's entertainment. Had he and Jamie spent the night in the house? It was not important right now, George realized that. And he was in no position to lecture anyone about morality. But his mind felt small and the question clogged it up somewhat.

When he entered the kitchen the conversation stopped and everyone turned to look at him. Katie, Ray, Jamie, Tony, Jacob. He had planned to take Katie quietly to one side. Clearly this was not going to be possible.

"Hi, Dad," said Jamie.

"George," said Ray.

They sounded rather stiff.

He girded his loins. "Katie. Ray. I want to apologize for my actions yesterday. I'm ashamed of myself and it should not have happened." No one spoke. "If there is anything that I can do to make amends . . ."

Everyone was looking at Katie. George noticed that she was holding a bread knife.

Ray said, "You're not planning to stab your father, are you?"

No one laughed.

Katie looked down at the knife. "Oh, sorry. No."

She put the knife down and there was an awkward silence.

Then Tony got out of his chair and pulled it back so that George could sit down and folded a tea towel over his arm, waiter-style, and said, "We have fresh coffee, tea, orange juice, wholemeal toast, scrambled eggs, boiled eggs . . ."

George wondered whether it was some kind of homosexual joke, but none of the others were laughing so he took the offer at face value, sat down, thanked Tony and said that he would like some black coffee and scrambled eggs if that was not too much trouble.

"I've got a dog made of toast," said Jacob.

Slowly, the conversation began again. Tony told a story about how he had fallen off his moped in Crete. Ray explained how he had organized the firework display for Katie. Jacob announced that his toast-dog was called Toasty, then bit his head off and laughed like a drain.

After twenty minutes or so the men headed off to pack bags and George found himself alone with his daughter.

Katie tapped her forehead and asked how he was doing "up there." He tapped his forehead and said he was doing rather well "up there." He explained that the events of the previous day had blown the cobwebs away. Obviously there were some problems he would still have to deal with, but the panic had subsided. He was suffering from eczema. He could see that now.

She paused and rubbed his arm and looked suddenly rather serious. George was worried that she was going to start talking about Jean and David Symmonds. He did not want to talk about Jean and David Symmonds. He would be more than happy to avoid talking about the subject for the rest of his life.

He took Katie's hand and squeezed it briefly. "Come on. You'd better get your stuff together."

"Yes," said Katie. "You're probably right."

"You go," said George. "I'll do the washing up."

Half an hour later Jean finally woke. She

seemed bruised and exhausted, like someone recovering from a hospital operation. She said very little. He asked if she was OK. She said that she was. He decided not to interrogate her any further.

Mid-morning they gathered in the front hall to say their goodbyes. Katie, Ray and Jacob were heading off to Heathrow and Jamie and Tony were driving back to London. It was a slightly somber occasion, and the house seemed unnaturally silent when they had gone.

Thankfully the caterers came to retrieve their equipment ten minutes later, followed by Mrs. Jackson and a young woman with an earring in her lip, who set about cleaning the house.

When the living room had been vacuumed, he and Jean retired to the sofa with a pot of tea and a plate of sandwiches while the kitchen was scoured. George apologized once more for his behavior, and Jean informed him that she would not be seeing David again.

George said, "Thank you." It seemed like the gracious thing to say.

Jean started to cry. George was not sure how to deal with this. He put his hand on her arm. It seemed to have no effect whatsoever, so he took it away again.

He said, "I'm not going to leave you."

Jean blew her nose on a tissue.

"And I'm not going to ask you to leave," George added, so that she knew precisely where she stood.

It was a ridiculous idea in any case. What would he do if he moved out? Or if Jean moved out? He was too old to begin a new life. They both were.

"Good," said Jean.

He offered her another sandwich.

The tent was taken down during the afternoon and George was able to do a couple of hours' work on the studio before supper. He realized that he was going to be disappointed when the building was finished. Obviously, he would then have a place in which he could draw and paint. But he would need other projects to fill his time, and if his encounter with the rubber plant was anything to go by, it would be several months before drawing and painting became wholly fulfilling.

He could start swimming at the local pool a couple of times a week. That seemed like a sensible idea. It would keep him fit and help him sleep.

Now that he came to think of it, perhaps Jean would like to join him. It might help cheer her up a little. She had always been rather fond of pools on family holidays. Obviously it had been a good few years now, and she might feel self-conscious about wearing a swimming costume in public. Women, he knew, worried about these things more than men. But he would run the idea past her and see what she thought.

Or a long weekend in Bruges. That was another possibility. He had read something about it in the newspaper recently. It was in Belgium, if his memory served him correctly, which meant that they could get there without leaving the ground.

He shivered. It was cold and getting dark. So he packed the building materials neatly away and headed back into the house. He changed into clean clothes and came back down to the kitchen.

Jean was preparing lasagna. He made himself a mug of coffee, sat at the table and began browsing through the *TV Guide.*

"Could you give me the aluminum saucepan from the drawer?" asked Jean.

George leant backward, retrieved the saucepan and handed it to her. As he did so, he caught a faint whiff of that flowery perfume Jean used. Or perhaps it was the orange shampoo from Sainsbury's. It was quite pleasant.

She thanked him and he glanced down at

the *TV Guide.* He found himself looking at a photograph of two young women who were joined at the head. It was not a pleasant picture and it did not make him feel very good. He began reading. The women were going to be featured in a documentary on Channel Four. The documentary would end with footage of an operation in which they were surgically separated. The operation was risky, apparently, and one or both of the girls might die as a result. The article did not reveal the outcome of the operation.

The kitchen floor tilted very slightly.

"What would you like with your lasagna?" asked Jean. "Peas or broccoli?"

"Sorry?" said George.

"Peas or broccoli?" asked Jean.

"Broccoli," said George. "And perhaps we should open a bottle of wine."

"Broccoli and wine it is," said Jean.

George looked down at the *TV Guide.*

It was time to stop all this nonsense.

He turned the page and stood up to find a corkscrew.

ABOUT THE AUTHOR

Mark Haddon is the author of the international bestseller *The Curious Incident of the Dog in the Night-Time,* which won the *Los Angeles Times* Book Prize for First Fiction and the Whitbread Book of the Year award. In addition to the recently published *The Talking Horse and the Sad Girl and the Villiage Under the Sea,* a collection of poetry, Haddon has also written and illustrated numerous children's books and received several awards for his television screenplays.

We hope you have enjoyed this Large Print book. Other Thorndike, Wheeler, and Chivers Press Large Print books are available at your library or directly from the publishers.

For information about current and upcoming titles, please call or write, without obligation, to:

Publisher
Thorndike Press
295 Kennedy Memorial Drive
Waterville, ME 04901
Tel. (800) 223-1244

or visit our Web site at:

www.gale.com/thorndike
www.gale.com/wheeler

OR

Chivers Large Print
published by BBC Audiobooks Ltd
St James House, The Square
Lower Bristol Road
Bath BA2 3SB
England
Tel. +44(0) 800 136919
email: bbcaudiobooks@bbc.co.uk
www.bbcaudiobooks.co.uk

All our Large Print titles are designed for easy reading, and all our books are made to last.